Estimados Carlos y
Linda:
Esperamos que disfruten
este libro tanto como
Nosotros.

Con gran afecto

Julio y Viry
11-14-08

CONTRAMAESTRE

La Demajagua, Cuba, 1895

RAUL EDUARDO CHAO

CONTRAMAESTRE

DUPONT CIRCLE EDITIONS
WASHINGTON, D.C.   LONDON   SIDNEY

DUPONT CIRCLE EDITIONS
Copyright ©2007 by Raúl Eduardo Chao

All rights reserved under International and Pan American
Copyright Conventions. Published in the United States by
DuPont Circle Editions.

www.DupontCircleEditions.com

1 3 5 7 9 10 8 6 4 2

LIBRARY OF CONGRESS CONTROL NUMBER: 2006910736

Chao, Raúl Eduardo, 1939-
Contramaestre / Raúl Chao

ISBN 978-0-9791777-0-5

Printed in the United States of America

Frontispice: The ruins of the Ingenio **La Demajagua**, property of
Carlos Manuel de Céspedes, where the first Cuban War of Independence (1868-1878)
was launched. In the 1890's *Scientific American* published this image
with the comment: *"Cuban soil is so fertile that in less than 20 years a 40 ft. tree has
grown within the spokes of one of the gear wheels of a sugar mill destroyed during a
war of 1868."* The original line drawing is in the collection of the author.

To Olga

THE CONTRAMAESTRE RIVER BANKS

The **Contramaestre River** is the most important affluent of *Rio Cauto*, which at 250 kilometers in length is the longest and mightiest river in Cuba. Contramaestre begins at the Sierra Maestra and, after going through the towns of Jiguaní and Palma Soriano, it joins the *Rio Cauto* and supplies it with more than half of its water flow. It is said that when the Spanish settlers were first exploring the *Rio Cauto* in the XVI century they baptized every affluent according to their first impressions: *Salado*, because they tasted a high salt content in its waters; *Bayamo*, honoring a *cacique* or native chieftain of the region, etc. Suddenly they found a tributary with a stronger flow than the Cauto itself. They christened it the *Contramaestre del Cauto*, which in marine jargon designates the highest deck officer under a ship's *maestre* or captain.

Preface

The Contramaestre is a river in eastern Cuba, 23 miles in length, which starts in the tall hills of Oriente province and ends up joining the Cauto River at a point called Dos Rios. The Cauto River, 160 miles long, is the strongest of all the rivers in the Antilles islands. It was at Dos Rios that José Martí, the most venerated of Cuban patriots, gave account of his life at a battle with Spanish troops on May 19, 1895, three years before the end of the Cuban War of Independence. He was 42 years old. Along the banks of Contramaestre River, a few miles upstream from Dos Rios, at a place called San Lorenzo, another Cuban patriot, Carlos Manuel de Céspedes, lost his life 21 years earlier, on February 27, 1874, when he was ambushed by a search party of the Spanish army. He was 54 years old.

But this is not the story of the Contramaestre River, nor is it a story that has anything to do with José Martí. It is rather the story of Carlos Manuel de Céspedes, the father of the Cuban nation, and a different river, the Seine, which was witness to the most important formative years of the life of this extraordinary man.

Céspedes lived in Paris, a few city blocks from the Seine, during the early years of the 1840s. There he worked as a lawyer, got to meet important political, literary and artistic men and women of universal renown and prestige and immersed himself deeply into the culture and traditions of post revolutionary France. The readings he made, the friendships he cultivated, the experiences he lived, accompanied and guided him for the rest of his life. They enriched him as a natural leader when the time came to call for the independence of Cuba from its Spanish masters. Yet many times after he left Paris he felt he was reliving the mistakes and frustrations he had observed in the French *Monarchie de Juillet*, in spite of his best intentions to avoid such human failings and pitfalls.

It has not been easy to summarize the intense experiences that the Céspedes family lived through in those short years. Carlos Manuel and María del Carmen took to French daily life with eagerness, curiosity and gusto. There was hardly an idle day in their lives once they moved to the house they leased on *rue Jacob*. By the time they left Paris they were consummate Parisians, fluent and articulate in the

French language, and they had entered into what today is called *la France profonde*. I have respected in this account all historical events that they witnessed or were a part of. With the exception of my authors' license when dealing with dialogues and inner thoughts, all facts presented here are verifiably truthful, the result of time consuming research into original documents and public records by me and by others. Any oversights or errors are my own.

I wish to acknowledge here the help of many individuals who made my work lighter and my reach much larger than I ever expected. I mention here their names without any specifics. They all well know the important role they have played in my life: my grateful thanks to Engracia and Tomás Chao, Olguita and Samuel Nodarse, Antonio María Entralgo, Juan Miyares, Ernesto Ledón, José Solá, Francisco Villaverde Lamadrid, Antonio Fernández Nuevo, Julian Bastarrica, Alfredo Joaquín Mustelier, Rafael Muñoz Candelario, Manuel Suárez Carreño, José Ramón de la Vega, Elmer Olivieri Cintrón, Eduardo Ramírez, Jaime Benítez Rexach, José Enrique Arrarás, Owen Wheeler, Manuel García Malde, Harry Szmandt, Harold Hoelscher, Sheldon Friedlander, George Owen, James Garrett, Alexander Proudfoot, Paul Hertz, W. Edwards Deming, Gerhard Löcken, Kenneth Massey, Wolfgang Mörike, Rudolph Müller, Manuel Díaz Saldaña, América Cisneros and many others too numerous to mention.

Foreword

The French Revolution and the Napoleonic Empire were long gone and the last attempt of the Bourbons to restore the dynasty had been a fiasco. People revolted on July 28, 29 and 30, 1830, in what became known as *the three glorious days*. It fell on old and spent *Marquis de Lafayette* to promote the new French sovereign at the *Hôtel de Ville*: Louis Philippe d'Orleans, son of Philippe Egalité, Louis XVI's cousin, who had voted to send him to the guillotine. He took an oath as King of the French, but not King of France. His times soon became known as the *Monarchie de Juillet*. Paris was leaving behind the last vestiges of its medieval past and France was slowly losing its grip as the center of Western Civilization. They were nevertheless extraordinary times. Victor Hugo, Honoré Balzac, Châteaubriand, George Sand, Alfred de Musset, Alexander Dumas, father and son, Flaubert, Stendhal, Lamartine, the Goncourts and Augusto Comte were best sellers in Paris at the same time. Chopin, Liszt, Berlioz, Gounod, Wagner, Schumann, Offenbach and occasionally Paganini, were all making music and competing for the same public. In politics, the men of the hour were Casimir Perrier, Jacques Laffitte, Victor Charles Duc de Broglie, François Guizot and Adolphe Thiers. The issues of the day: slavery, universal suffrage, colonialism, independence, feminism and the recovery of *La Louisiane* from the American Republic. The world of ideas was flourishing. Alex de Tocqueville had just published his *"Of Democracy in America,"* Karl Marx was writing his *"Communist Manifesto,"* and Charles Fourier was trying to popularize the utopian socialism of Henri le Duc de Saint Simon. In the midst of all this, Carlos Manuel de Céspedes y Quesada and his wife María del Carmen moved to Paris and soon welcomed as their guests four of the finest minds in Cuba, the last remaining Spanish colony in the Americas: Domingo Del Monte and his wife Rosa, Miguel Aldama, Rosa's brother, and Gertrudis Gómez de Avellaneda, a young best seller poet living in Madrid. This is the extraordinary story of the time they spent together in the City of Lights.

Maps and Figures

⚓

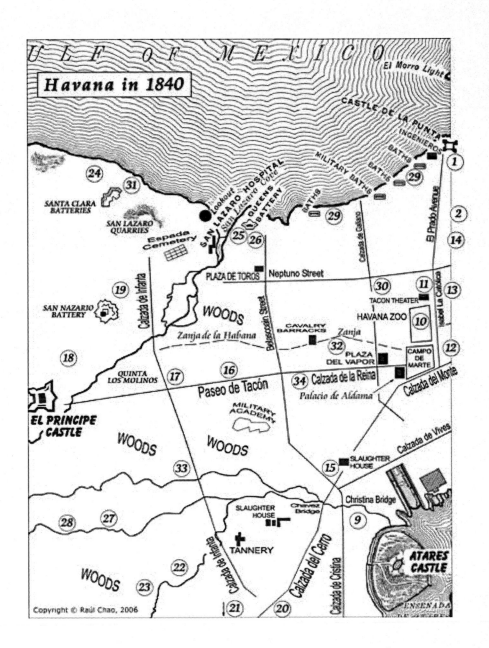

Havana in 1840

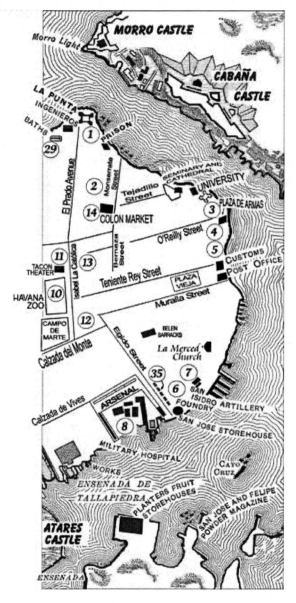

FUTURE LANDMARKS

1 Máximo Gómez Monument
2 Presidential Palace
3 National Library
4 Havana City Hall
5 Lonja del Comercio
6 José Martí's Home
7 National Archives
8 Central Railroad Station
9 Christina RR Station
10 Villanueva RR Station and later on National Capitol
11 Centro Gallego
12 Plaza de la Fraternidad
13 Havana Central Park
14 Bellas Artes Palace
15 Mercado Unico
16 Sociedad Económica de Amigos del País
17 Emergencies Hospital
18 Calixto García Hospital
19 University of Havana
20 Quinta La Purisima
21 Quinta La Covadonga
22 El Cerro Baseball Stadium
23 Asilo Santovenia
24 National Hotel
25 Maceo Park
26 Casa de Beneficencia
27 Almendares Park
28 Ermita de los Catalanes
29 Malecón Habanero
30 America Building / Theater
31 Maine Monument
32 Chinatown (Barrio Chino)
33 Las Animas Hospital
34 Iglesia de Reina
35 Remains of Old City walls

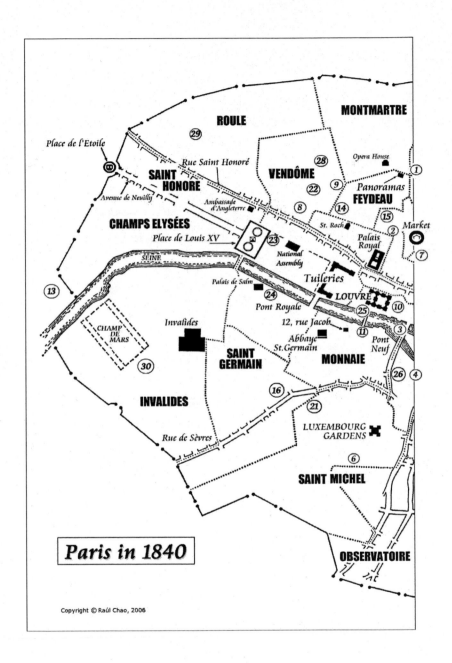

ROULE

MONTMARTRE

Place de l'Etoile

㉙

Rue Saint Honoré

SAINT HONORE

Avenue de Neuilly

VENDÔME

Opera House

㉘

㉒

⑨

Panoramas

FEYDEAU

①

CHAMPS ELYSÉES

Ambassade d'Angleterre

⑧

⑭

St. Roch

⑮

Market

Place de Louis XV

㉓

②

Palais Royal

⑦

SEINE

National Assembly

Tuileries

⑬

Palais de Salm

㉔

LOUVRE

㉕

⑩

CHAMP DE MARS

Invalides

Pont Royale

12, rue Jacob

⑪

Pont Neuf

③

⑳⑥

SAINT GERMAIN

Abbaye St.Germain

MONNAIE

㉖ ④

INVALIDES

⑯

㉑

LUXEMBOURG GARDENS

Rue de Sèvres

⑥

SAINT MICHEL

Paris in 1840

OBSERVATOIRE

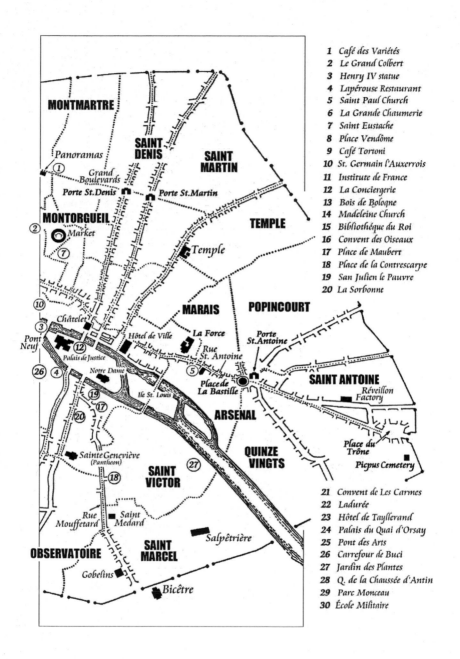

1 Café des Variétés
2 Le Grand Colbert
3 Henry IV statue
4 Lapérouse Restaurant
5 Saint Paul Church
6 La Grande Chaumerie
7 Saint Eustache
8 Place Vendôme
9 Café Tortoni
10 St. Germain l'Auxerrois
11 Institute de France
12 La Conciergerie
13 Bois de Bologne
14 Madeleine Church
15 Bibliothèque du Roi
16 Convent des Oiseaux
17 Place de Maubert
18 Place de la Contrescarpe
19 San Julien le Pauvre
20 La Sorbonne

21 Convent de Les Carmes
22 Ladurée
23 Hôtel de Tayllerand
24 Palais du Quai d'Orsay
25 Pont des Arts
26 Carrefour de Buci
27 Jardin des Plantes
28 Q. de la Chaussée d'Antin
29 Parc Monceau
30 École Militaire

THE CATHEDRAL OF HAVANA IN 1839

The **Cathedral of San Cristobal de la Havana** started as a church honoring St. Ignatius, built by the Jesuits in the XVIII century. It was converted into a parish church by Bishop Pedro Agustín Morell de Santa Cruz, who was the founder of the University of Santiago de Cuba and in 1759 the first Catholic dignitary that established his residence in Cuba. *Calle Obispo*, in Havana, owes its name to the long time residence of Morell de Santa Cruz on that street. Later on the Church of St. Ignatius was enlarged and transformed by Don José de Tres-Palacios, the first Bishop of Havana, who had it declared a Cathedral in 1789. It was finally adorned with much magnificence by Bishop Juan José Díaz Espada y Landa, his successor, who created the *Campo de Marte* in Havana and also founded the Cemetery that bore his name. Drawing by Frédéric Mialhe in *Cuba Pintoresca*, 1839-1844.

1

DOMINGO DEL MONTE leaned on the bow rail of the *Fuente Hermosa* as it was getting readied to sail from Havana towards the ports of Cádiz and Barcelona in Spain. Several seamen were on the main deck tying up ropes, sails and nettings and making last minute arrangements for the transatlantic crossing. The shipmaster was moving relentlessly from bow to stern giving orders and inspecting all preparations. On his side, repeating each of his orders in a loud voice was the boatswain, the man in charge of surveying the vessel's hull and its cargo stowage, as well as certifying the soundness of its ropes, moorings and *andaribeles* or life-lines. It was early in the morning and a crisp February wind was forcing Domingo to squint as he surveyed the magnificent harbor of Havana which he knew so well. The ship was anchored at a pier next to the custom house and the merchant's exchange, right at the point where *Teniente Rey* and *Oficios* streets meet on the inside shoreline of the harbor. From this vantage point Domingo could see some of the military installations with which the Spanish has transformed Havana into the most heavily fortified city in the new world.

Right in front of him was the fortress of *San Carlos de la Cabaña*, built after the British had agreed to exchange their recently invaded territories in Cuba for the entire peninsula of Florida, a few leagues to the north. *La Cabaña* was the largest Spanish fortification anywhere in the Americas. It had taken eleven years in construction and had seriously strained the colonial military budgets but it was considered an unassailable bastion that would protect Havana forever. Across the city he could see, facing the fortress of *El Morro* on the harbor entrance, the Castle of *La Punta*. South from where he was, the noisy and ever sullied *San Isidro* Artillery foundries stood menacingly. He could also distinguish, further away and high on a promontory at the end of a well protected cove, the *Castillo de Atarés* and the inner bay shipyards, as well as the *San Nazario* and the *Doce Apóstoles* batteries. No point on this harbor, he thought, had been left unprotected by the Spaniards, particularly after being so unashamedly surprised by the British when they seized the city in record time during the Seven Year War.

Havana in 1840 was already well established as a prosperous, sophisticated and cosmopolitan city, the third largest in the Americas, comparable only to Boston and New York. Only a few years earlier, in 1828, a neoclassical monument, the *Templete*, had been built on the southern side of the *Plaza de Armas* or central commons to commemorate the city founding three hundred years before. The origins of the name "Habana" had long been forgotten: some speculated that it was a derivative of savanna or prairie; others that it came from the Anglo-Saxon "haven." Most likely the city had been named in honor of an indigenous cacique, *Habaguanex*, who ruled western Cuba. Except that there were never any solid proofs that such a cacique existed.

The city had had its ups and downs, however. For several centuries it grew as the meeting point of the Spanish flotilla which carried the gold of the Americas towards the old country. During the reign of Philip II, on the other hand, docking taxes were so high that many ships opted to anchor at the port of Matanzas and a Sevillan functionary referred to Havana as *"a lemon not worth squeezing."* The construction of a *zanja* or canal to bring water from the Almendares River into the city, however, established Havana forever as a comfortable and reliable urban center.

The frigate *Fuente Hermosa*, in fact, had been built at the same Havana shipyards that Del Monte could see from the bow of the ship. In 1838 it had been purchased by the House of Aldama, which immediately began to use it to transport sugar, cocoanuts and pineapples from Havana to Tampa and New Orleans, and to return to port with merchandise from the looms and wood crafting factories of Alabama and the Carolinas. It was the last of the sailing merchant vessels that the Aldamas acquired. Their next acquisitions were the *Maravilla* and the *Princess Juana* in 1840, two steam powered boats that under the names of Clermont II and Northern Waters were previously owned by Fulton and Livingston's bankrupt North River Steamboat Company. The boats had been built at Brownne's Shipyard in New York City but the Aldamas had them completely refurbished before bringing them into service at their Havana docks. Their hulls were widened, two new boilers were installed and accommodations for passengers were added.

As things stood in 1839 however, the *Fuente Hermosa* was a very comfortable and safe vessel for transatlantic passage. It was just about the best of 197 ships that had been built in the Havana *astilleros* since 1740. The craftsmanship of these ships had been so masterful that when the British seized the city they appropriated 34 vessels that were never returned and served for a long time in the British navy.

From its vantage point at the *Fuente Hermosa* Del Monte took pleasure in surveying the harbor of Havana and the many vessels busily going about their errands at that early morning hour. A few *chinchorros* were bringing last minute merchandise from the Santa Catalina storehouses, on the other side of the bay. A paquebot carrying a large round sail was docking and discharging its precious cargo at the post office pier right next to the custom house. Two schooners with low hulls and two masts and spankers were patrolling the harbor and reconnoitering its shores, searching for potential contraband. Several *corbetas* and *esquifes*, a few small merchant frigates, as well as a half dozen *pataches* and *polacras*, big and small vessels of all sorts, were coming from all corners and docking everywhere at the many landing spots on the extensive and friendly shores of the Havana harbor. A busy and prosperous port, Del Monte thought. With fees for everything and a colonial government obstinately protecting this most important source of capital for the Spanish treasury.

He was interrupted by a crew officer who brought a message from Carlos Manuel de Céspedes, who had just come on board. Domingo Del Monte's visit to the *Fuente Hermosa* on that February day was to bid him and his wife a safe trip to Europe and to help them with any of the last minute bureaucratic entanglements for which the Spaniards were famous. He immediately descended to the lower deck and made his way into the passenger compartments that the Céspedes had secured for their transoceanic trip. He was somewhat heartbroken to see his friends leaving for such a long time, particularly since Rosa, his wife, had also become very close to María del Carmen, Carlos Manuel's wife. Domingo had barely time to inspect the accommodations of the Céspedes when the vessel's ship bell began to strike the familiar pattern of two pairs of rings followed by a short pause. It was an indication that all preparatory navigational activities had been finished and the starting crew was ready to man the helms, find its way out of the port, trim the sails and maintain the lookout. Domingo embraced both Carlos Manuel and María del Carmen as he wished them Godspeed.

"I will soon see you in Barcelona, or better yet, in Paris," he said with a lump in his throat. "And I promise I will bring Rosa and Miguel with me."

María del Carmen's young eyes were visibly getting teary and profoundly sad and Domingo extended his arms towards her, as he attempted to hold both of his dear friends in the same embrace. "Get a big house," he said in jest. "Count with the three of us as your guests. We are going to have the time of our lives in Paris!"

Carlos Manuel de Céspedes y López del Castillo, who many years later was called to be the first President of the Republic of Cuba in Arms, was a good friend of Domingo and had enjoyed immensely the opportunity to see him often during his just finished three years of studies at the University of Havana. Unlike Domingo, who was a first generation *criollo*, Carlos Manuel could trace his lineage in its Cuban origins back to Juan Antonio de Céspedes y Conde, who in 1630 was designated by the Spanish crown as mayor of San Salvador de Bayamo, in eastern Cuba. No other family in Cuba could boast so many blood relationships with other distinguished and well established island clans. Interspersed in the genealogical tree of the Céspedes were such last names as Anaya, Zayas-Bazán, Aguilera, Duque, Gómez-Guerra, Fleitas, Hernández-Morejón, Ramirez de Arellano, Castillo, Quesada, Orellano, Betancourt, Oñate, García-Menocal, Cancino and Bertini, to name a few. The most notable star in the family was of course Carlos Manuel, born in the seventh generation after Juan Antonio, and who came to be considered the George Washington of Cuba. All other families eventually made their own claim to fame by reference to the most notable member of the Céspedes clan.

Carlos Manuel was born in Bayamo, in eastern Cuba, on April 18, 1819. His parents were Jesús María Céspedes y Luque and Francisca de Borja López del Castillo y Ramírez de Aguilar. His siblings were Pedro, Francisco, Javier, Francisca and Manuel Hilario. After studying at the Seminary of San Carlos in Havana he graduated with a degree in Law from its rival institution, the Pontifical University of Havana in 1838. The following year he married his cousin María del Carmen, who also had Céspedes as a last name. Born of very wealthy families, and on both sides inheritors of sizable quantities of land in eastern Cuba, the couple was eager to travel abroad for their grand tour – as a couple.

No sooner were they married in Bayamo, Carlos Manuel de Céspedes and his young bride decided to undertake an extended trip to Europe. The plans and preparations were thorough, ambitious and appropriately funded. Most of all, Carlos Manuel and María del Carmen wanted to experience life in Europe. Spain was to be their first destination, but their eyes were definitely focused on Paris. They were both seriously committed to literature and music. They first met at the elegant outings that affluent families held regularly throughout the year in Bayamo. They soon discovered a common sensitivity for the beautiful while participating in the regular night *salons* at the home of Jesús María Céspedes and Francisca de Borja, Carlos' parents. Shortly thereafter, they fell in love. They were avid readers and had excellent taste in the fine arts, and that was a bond that kept them seeking each other's company for the rest of their lives.

At the time, Bayamo had a thriving cultural life which, notwithstanding Havana and Matanzas, was probably the richest in Cuba. Many fine literary figures visited regularly and held court at the *Liceo*, *la Filarmonia* and the *Sociedad Española*, where they kept its members fully informed of the most modern political thinking of the times. From a very young age Carlos Manuel became not only a regular in attendance but also its epitome of elegance, intellect and cultural passion. His fame as a young poet, literary critic, public speaker and music aficionado was only rivaled by his well deserved notoriety as the most elegant and eligible "dandy" in Bayamo and Manzanillo as well as in the sophisticated world of the provincial and colonial capitals.

On February 12, 1839, having concluded everything that required their presence in Havana, Carlos Manuel and María del Carmen, upon the recommendation and encouragement of Domingo Del Monte, booked two compartments aboard the frigate *Fuente Hermosa*. Their close friend Miguel Aldama, Domingo's brother in law, recommended the ship as one of the safest and most comfortable for the trip to peninsular Spain. Miguel had also personally chosen the *paje de nao* or dedicated officer-in-training who was to be their attendant throughout their extended journey. The ship was under the command of Señor Don Pedro de los Campos, the best and most experienced captain of the fleet owned by the House of Aldama. For the February 1839 trip, the frigate was loaded with an unknown quantity of gold and silver, as well as a cargo of "...262 precious hides that had been brought north from Buenos Ayres." The *Fuente Hermosa* was a wooden vessel capable of making a faster trip, provided the wind did not subside, than the steamships that were beginning to be used for the transatlantic route. It was said by those who favored sailing on this type of vessel that "...it was a wooden ship with iron men rather than an iron ship with wooden men."

It took them 22 days to sail from Havana to Barcelona. The Céspedes arrived with six big leather suitcases and sixteen heavy wooden trunks. Aside from their clothes they were bringing to Europe numerous books, gifts for relatives and friends, several sets of their good china, glassware and silverware, their finest linen and several containers of a certain sort of molasses the British called *treacle*, which at the time was highly valued by Europeans. They had spent most of the time onboard reading, playing chess and, for themselves and twelve other passengers on board, diddling with the guitar and singing songs together.

In 1839, the city of Barcelona was not an ideal place to settle down and study. Since the proclamation of the Cadiz Constitution in 1812 Barcelona, as most of Spain, had experienced numerous social and political upheavals. There were riots, sabotages, strikes, endless protest marches, the burning of convents, violence against civil authorities, bombardments and all other sorts of confrontations. The *Febre d'Or* (literally, gold fever) was to come forty years later, with the founding of companies such as *Transatlàntica* and *Crèdit i Docks*. Furthermore, when both the Céspedes enrolled at the University of Barcelona, the literary achievements of the *Renaixença* (cultural revival) were yet to happen.

The University of Barcelona, an outgrowth of the catholic schools and the academies founded by the Dominican friars under the support of the Kings of Aragon in the XII Century, had been formally renovated and founded anew in 1837, scarcely two years before the

Céspedes registered. They moved as soon as they arrived to a well appointed pension recommended by their uncle Francisco José de Céspedes, who had been in Barcelona during the times of Ferdinand VII and the Napoleonic Wars. It was their only address in the city: *19 Carrera de la Postaferrissa* between *Petritxol* and *Perot*, in the old city district. Both concentrated in their studies, Carlos Manuel obtaining a doctoral degree in Law and María del Carmen several diplomas in history, the humanities and art. Upon exhausting their growth possibilities in Barcelona they soon decided to move to Paris, their true anticipated intellectual frontier. While a student in Barcelona Carlos Manuel participated in the military uprising of General Juan Prim during the Carlist Wars and, earlier than they had planned and quite aside from their intentions, they had to seek refuge in Paris.

The trip to Paris, with a lot less luggage but with a greater sense of anticipation, took seven days, culminating on December 1, 1841. They had to first take a schooner to Marseille and then several carriages to Paris, with stopovers in Avignon, Saint Etienne, Nevers, Orleans and Fontainebleau. For the Céspedes the city of lights was, without doubt, an experience to behold. France, and Paris specifically, was at the crossroads of western civilization during the XVIII and most of the XIX Centuries. Paris in those days was bursting with teachers, artists, preachers, musicians, philosophers, scientists, politicians and financiers from all European countries, all of them thinking of the city as their own capital.

It was in Paris where the directions in which human intellect would move were being decided. In one swift move the authoritative role of aristocrats and the clergy had been terminated, turning Paris into the most fertile territory for independent thought and individualism in the Western world. In spite of the numerous excesses of the French Revolution scarcely 50 years before, the noble ideals of "*liberté, fraternité, equalité*" were now firmly entrenched in the minds of the bourgeoisie, which were, after all, the social class to which most intellectuals belonged. Paris, more than ever, became a paradox: the aristocrats and to a certain extent the clerics, without their rigid and rancid pretenses of superiority, had reclaimed their economic and political power. The intellectuals, however, were the ones who had enough reach to influence the political destinies of the entire continent.

Carlos Manuel and María del Carmen initially established their headquarters at an old abby turned into a hotel, across the Seine from the Louvre. It was at this simple but comfortable dwelling on the Quai Voltaire that they met two important characters who had also established residence there: Charles Baudelaire, a 1839 graduate of the *College Louis le Grand* and the future author of *Les Fleurs du Mal* (The Flowers of Evil), and Richard Wagner, a 1831 graduate of the University of Leipzig who had already composed an opera, *Der Fliegende Holländer* (The Flying Dutchman) and who was actively working on a second one: *Rienzi*. Baudelaire, at the time he met the Céspedes, was penniless, having exhausted his small inheritance with his extravagant lifestyle. Wagner, on a similar vein, had just renounced as junior director of the Opera in Riga and had fled to Paris to escape from his creditors.

It was through Baudelaire that Céspedes met a regular lunch visitor at the Hotel: Honoré de Balzac. He was the most literate of social critics of his time. He had been a notary's clerk, a journalist and a political and artistic reviewer. He was outspoken and wrote well and fast. He deplored the cultural rubble left behind by the Napoleonic era and the cynical monarchies of Louis XVIII and Charles X and severely criticized them. At the time he met Céspedes he had just published *Le Père Goriot* (Father Goriot) in which he lamented that the privileges of the *ancient régime* and the overbearing autarchy of the Church had been replaced by a novel priesthood of greed, favoritism, disdain and patronage. Céspedes found himself sharing with Balzac his empathy for those who have been pushed aside by unscrupulous power grabbers.

Carlos Manuel spent a considerable amount of his time in Paris studying and tracking the progress of French industry, as well as purchasing technologies and goods that the family required to update their investments and lifestyle in eastern Cuba. Through several *Universal Exhibitions* France had shown a steady advancement in most areas of industrial development. Steam engines were replacing human power. Looms, cotton and wool gins were making clothes affordable to the lower classes for the first time. Stained glass production was improving, as well as a better understanding of the physics of large structures. The technology of producing large panels of flat glass was exploding and Céspedes could see its potential for factories, mills, commercial buildings and even housing.

The relation between affordable technology and the development of a middle class was becoming more and more evident and Céspedes, as he was immersing himself in French life, became a champion of decent wages and prosperity as the means of social peace. He became a strong advocate of the role of government supporting and promoting small business. He was also interested in soft technology, such as furniture making and in specialties such as musical instrument making. In 1843 he sent to his brother, Francisco Javier, married to María Trinidad, one of María del Carmen sisters, a large catalog published by *Le Garde Meuble* (The Furniture Repository), a large Parisian manufacturer, showing colored plates depicting interiors and furniture with such graphic quality that the family designers back home would be able to replicate the intricate details and patterns of both furniture and upholstery.

In June of 1842, with Astolphe Louis, Marquis de Custine, whom he met through Richard Wagner, Céspedes traveled to Mainz, in Germany, for a modest Industrial Exhibition patterned after the Parisian model. A year later the Germans followed in Berlin with a 3 day industrial fair where they presented more than three thousand exhibitors. Céspedes eagerly visited Breslau, London, Austria and Holland throughout 1843. By 1844 he was so immersed in the world of Universal Expositions that he was invited to be a juror at the *1844 Exposition Nationale* in Paris.

In 1844 the French were painfully aware of the competition of other rival and mimetic expositions across most of Europe. The question came up regarding the increasing number of applicants who sold the products of others but were not true manufacturers. All jurors were well aware that the expositions were intended to promote French industrialists and not the merchants. Carlos Manuel's was the decisive vote in favor of a crystal clear manufacturing approach by all potential exhibitors. He also suggested that the merchants were given alternate venues for promotion of their wares, a proposal which the Commerce minister immediately welcomed and supported. Céspedes also insisted on not granting privileges to manufacturers of useless, eccentric or trivial products such as buffalo hide curtains or feather covered umbrellas. His position that social utility was an important criterion to justify an exhibit prevailed and, as the result, the exhibitions became more popular that ever and Paris retained its preeminent position as the Fair Capital of the World.

His friendship with the Marquis de Custine was providential for Céspedes and María del Carmen. Astolphe-Louis-Léonor, Marquis de Custine was a French aristocrat and a diplomat, with enormous contacts throughout Europe. His fortune had been made in porcelain. His father and grandfather had sympathized with the French Revolution but were both guillotined during the Terror. Among Custine's closest friends and constant companions were Balzac and François-René, Vicomte de Châteaubriand, whom Céspedes got to meet and with whom he developed a short but close relationship.

Custine fell out of favor with French society on account of a scandal in which he was involved through the intrigues of some of his enemies. Custine had been beaten and robbed and his unconscious body left in the mud on the margins of the Seine River at the level of the Canal de Saint Martin. The perpetrators spread the word that the attack had been the work of a group of homosexual soldiers whom Custine had solicited. After the incident, all social *salons* were closed to him and many of his friends began to sneer behind his back. Carlos Manuel and María del Carmen were some of the few loyal friends left. By now they had moved to *12, rue Jacob*, close to the atelier of Eugene Delacroix, a friend they had also met through Wagner. It was a dwelling attached to a garden, as María del Carmen used to say, with service rooms above the stables and the coach house. The residence itself fronted the street, which at the time was one of the most fashionable in Paris. At a fairly large *salon*, where the Céspedes received, the furniture was all carved mahogany upholstered in white and blue. At one corner, near one of the large windows facing the inside court, the Céspedes had placed a magnificent opera piano with a shiny black finish. Over a cabinet there were four large *Sèvres* flower vases and numerous frames with small paintings and sketches from Cuba and Spain. At a large curio cabinet there were several mementos from Cuba. Their Royal Doulton dishware and St. Louis stemware were elegantly stored in an antique armoire in the butler's pantry. Four large bedrooms and a pink and baby blue boudoir followed.

It was through Balzac that Céspedes got to meet and make friends with Hector Berlioz, with whom he made a very special comradeship strengthened by both men's love for literature, particularly Shakespeare, Virgil and Goethe. According to Theophile Gautier, a close family friend, Berlioz, with Victor Hugo and Eugene Delacroix were said to form the ultimate trinity of romantic art. In one way or another, with different levels of intimacy, both Carlos Manuel and María del Carmen had known all three and had the opportunity to entertain them at their new flat on *rue Jacob*. By the time Céspedes met Berlioz he had already composed (1830) his *Symphonie Fantastique* and had won the *Prix of Rome*. Berlioz was a man of strong passions, with relatively few friends, and he appreciated the warmth and casual closeness that he enjoyed visiting the Céspedes family, sometimes in the company of his sisters Anne Marguerite (who Carlos Manuel always lovingly called Nancy because she reminded him of one of María del Carmen classmates in Bayamo) and Adele. Berlioz, like Céspedes, loved Beethoven, particularly his fully instrumented symphonies. This special bond was in Berlioz's mind when he started to ask Céspedes to read some of his critical writings at the *Journal des Débats* and other Parisian newspapers before publication, a task to which Berlioz devoted many hours out of financial necessity rather than vocation.

It was also through the common friendship of Custine that young Céspedes became a frequent companion, a devoted fan and a legal advisor to Frédéric Chopin. It was actually in Barcelona, at the *Cuatro Naciones Inn* that the Céspedes had met Chopin at a reception celebrating Berlioz's premiere of *Benvenuto Cellini*. María del Carmen had the first reencounter with Chopin in Paris, upon the recommendation of Custine when she was exploring taking some piano lessons. Chopin's frail health, dignified elegance and his seemingly ever present sadness and nostalgia for his home country won María del Carmen's heart. Frédéric Chopin was a handsome man, a superb performer, particularly during improvisations, and an exquisite piano virtuoso in every sense of the word. He knew his physical limitations, particularly his multiple and unpredictable attacks of cough, which kept him home and away from his friends on many occasions. While in Paris he usually improvised at the homes of Custine, Victor Hugo or George Sand (Aurore Dudevant), with whom Chopin had an unending and perhaps unconsummated romantic affair. Less frequently, he would show up in the mornings at *12, rue Jacob*, unannounced and by himself. He would playfully assert that he felt as in his own home. He would ask for one of the great Bordeaux wines that the Céspedes always had on their cava and leisurely perform at the piano. Sometimes he fell sleep and enjoyed a nap until the early afternoon hours, at which time Carlos Manuel always accompanied him to the house he shared with Sand on *16, rue Pigalle*.

At the time the Céspedes met Chopin the genial musician was at his most productive creative period. He was giving very few public concerts, and traveling infrequently, but much of his music was being published simultaneously in Leipzig, London, Warsaw, Paris and Vienna. With his international legal expertise, Céspedes negotiated publishing rights across Europe with the houses that eventually became associated with all of Chopin's musical production: Maurice Schlesinger in Paris, J.J. Cybulski and Josef Kauffmann in Warsaw, Breitkopf & Härtel in Leipzig, Tobias Haslinger in Vienna and Wessel & Co. in London. He also litigated a case for Chopin against the London periodical *The Musical World* when it allegedly defamed Chopin as a plagiarist of Opus 41 and some mazurkas, and insulted him by saying "...*Mr. Chopin is a producer of the most preposterous and hyperbolic oddities and his works present a gaudy palette of rhetorical over-statement and excruciating cacophony...*" The paper was forced to present Chopin with a public apology and, at the suggestion of Céspedes, pay for a full gala presentation of Chopin's mazurkas at a live concert in Manchester, England, with proceeds going to a fund for renovations at *Saint Eustache Church* in Paris, which was the favorite place of worship of both María del Carmen and Carlos Manuel.

~ Ⅲ ~

HAVANA HARBOR IN 1848

A view of the entrance to the **Havana harbor** from the promontory of Belot, at the end of the harbor. On the right the town of *Regla*. On the distant right, the fortresses of *La Cabaña* and *El Morro*. Line drawing measuring 9" by 12" by A. Terington, based on a painting by D. Lancelot, shown in the 1887 book entitled *Voyages and Travels* by Leo De Colagne, New York. Original drawing in the collection of the author.

2

"If you are lucky enough to have lived in Paris as a young man,
then wherever you go for the rest of your life, it stays with you,
for Paris is a movable feast."
Ernest Hemingway

"No one can understand Paris and its history who does not understand
that its fierceness is the balance and justification of its frivolity. It is called a city
of pleasure; but it may also very specially be called a city of pain."
G. K. Chesterton

"An education isn't how much you have committed to memory, or
even how much you know. It's being able to differentiate
between what you know and what you don't.
The greatest virtues of man and woman are their curiosity."
Anatole France

AFTER THEY MOVED to *rue Jacob*, south of the beautiful building of the *Institute de France* that Mazarine had founded a hundred years earlier, the Céspedes had a longer walking trip when they visited the *Place de la Révolution*, which was already known as the *Place de la Concorde*. They both loved to walk along the Seine, on the left bank, until the *Pont de la Concorde*, and then cross it to arrive at the *Place*. Few cities in the world had such a magnificent scenario for their most important historical events.

They cherished to look at the 3000 year old, 250-ton Ramses II obelisk that the viceroy of Egypt, Mehemet Ali had donated to the people of France. "King Louis Philippe de Orleans installed this obelisk here," Carlos Manuel used to say, "in the hope that all the negatives that had occurred at the plaza would be overlooked."

"I am nevertheless humbled by these hallowed grounds where Louis XVI, King of France and Marie Antoinette, his wife were decapitated," María del Carmen would comment. "It must have been terrible. Just think, over three thousand people lost their lives here. Not only loyal citizens of the Royal family but common ordinary men and women of all social classes and occupations. Lawyers, gardeners, servants, teachers, preachers, physicians, seamstresses, furniture makers, you name it."

Céspedes, and María del Carmen to a lesser extent, were both studious observers of the French Revolution. They had read all important accounts of these events that were available at the time in the Parisian bookstores: Edmund Burke's *Reflexions on the Revolution in France*, which they found more ideological than factual; Thomas Carlyle's *The French Revolution, a History*, just out of the presses in 1837, which María del Carmen regarded as idealistic in its point of view and romantic in style but nevertheless systematic and accurate; and François Mignet's *Histoire de la Révolution Française*, which both agreed was more than anything else a political manifesto written by a fiercely liberal ideologue from his vantage point at the *Académie Française*.

Little by little and quite often with all three books in hand, María del Carmen and Carlos Manuel visited practically all venues where history had been made during those fateful days. The *Conciergerie*, where Maríe Antoinette had spent her last days. The *rue Saint Honoré*, which was the path followed by the *charrettes* (tumbrels, dumpcarts or carriages) carrying the condemned from the Ministry of Justice to the guillotine. The remains of *Temple*, at which dungeon Louis XVI and his family were kept prisoners. The *Palais de Justice* on *Place Vendôme*, where Danton pronounced those fatidic words that opened the gates to the Terror: "*the fatherland is in danger...*" The modest home of Robespierre, on an internal court at *398, rue Saint Honoré*, as well as that of Lavoisier at *47, rue Saint Honoré*. Antoine Laurent Lavoisier (1743-1794) had been undoubtedly the best scientific brain in France and possibly the most important chemist of all times. He was guillotined May 8, 1794 for his family's association with tax collectors during the *ancien régime*.

"The story goes," Carlos Manuel would comment, "that upon knowing of Lavoisier's sentence Robespierre had declared that "the Republic does not need any mavens..."

They usually went to mass at *l'Eglise de Saint Eustache*, and were thrilled to touch the very fountain were Lavoisier had been baptized, which had also seen the baptismals of Madame Pompidou, Cardinal Richelieu, Moliére, and Louis XIV.

"I love the feeling of having all these historical places at the reach of my hands," María del Carmen told her friends many times. "I love to caress with reverence a column, a chair, a book or a piece of furniture touched by one of these eminent figures."

They usually ended their explorations of Revolutionary Paris at the colonnade of the *Café de Foy*, on the patio of the *Palais-Royal*, where a normally stuttering Camille Desmoulins had delivered on July 13, 1789, a day before the fall of the Bastille, a stammer-free declamation exalting people to revolt.

"That was the day that saw the birth of the *French cocarde*, the now ubiquitous red, white and blue rosette that the French like so much to display as a symbol of their revolutionary fervor," Céspedes would comment, "although originally it was simply a green leaf from one of the chestnut trees in the central patio of the *Palais-Royal*."

Both Carlos Manuel and María del Carmen had sympathy for Desmoulins, the Abbé Sieyès, the Marquis de Lafayette, Madame Roland, the Girondines, the Chouans, the Vendées and Danton, but they abhorred Marat, Philippe Égalité, the Jacobins, the sans-culottes and Talleyrand. Robespierre, however, was an enigma. At times incorruptible, often dyspeptic, as Carlyle characterized him, they thought him both a driving force for change and a malevolent, narrow minded and stubborn dogmatist.

"A man that culminated his public career with the sublime achievement of taking Danton to the guillotine," Céspedes mentioned in a letter to Saco a few weeks before they saw each other in Paris in 1842. José Antonio Saco (1797-1879), a celebrated legal, political and diplomatic Cuban scholar, was also well versed in the history of the French Revolution. He responded: "You should have added, as the saying went at the time, that *it was the blood of Danton what choked Robespierre when he needed to defend himself.*"

"The *Place de la Revolution* has also seen disheartening times," Céspedes used to say. "It was there that the British bivouacked in 1815 after the surrender and the imprisonment of Napoleon."

"No doubt under the joyful countenance of the Duke of Wellington," María del Carmen would add.

On many a Sunday, the Céspedes would take an easy stroll from the *Place de la Revolution* to the *Palais-Royal*, which after the Revolution came to be known as the *Palais et Jardin de la Revolution*.

"This is the palace that Cardinal Richelieu –of *Les Trois Mousquetaires* fame- built for himself as the *Palais-Cardinal* in 1629 and later presented as a gift to Louis XIII," Carlos Manuel would remind his guests when he took them around Paris. "The Cardinal had a theater built into the palace and it was there that Corneille premiered *Le Cid* in 1637. Anne de Austria, in 1643, abandoned the Louvre, damp and cold as it was, for the warmth and modernity of the Cardinal's palace, and that's how it became known as the *Palais-Royal*."

"This magnificent abode," he would add, "was gifted by Louis XIV, Anne's son, to his brother Philippe d'Orleans. Philippe's son Louis Philippe turned it over to his son, the Duke of Chartres, who was first known as Louis Philippe Joseph and later as *Philippe Égalité*. He lost the palace to the Revolution after having turned it into a luxurious house of ill repute where gambling, prostitution and usury were the order of the day. The French *gendarmerie* were under strict orders of not entering the premises."

Adding more detail to the story he would continue: "After the French Revolution, during Napoleon's days of glory, Bonaparte's brother Lucien lived there. After Napoleon's fall from grace, Louis XVIII, older brother of Louis XVI, ascended to the throne and the *Palais-Royal* was returned to the Orleans family. Louis Philippe de Orleans, France's current monarch, took possession a few years ago on behalf of the family. He is the son of *Philippe Égalité*, which the family now prefers to call Philippe the Duke de Orleans. He was guillotined by the Revolution a few months after voting the death penalty for his cousin Louis XVI."

María del Carmen, a faithful reader and admirer of Victor Hugo, considered *Les Misérables* as one of her favorite novels of all times. "During the revolution of 1830," she would add, "after the barricades so vividly portrayed by Hugo went up, Charles X, the youngest of Louis XVI brothers, was deposed and that's how Louis Philippe d'Orleans became King, moved out of the *Palais-Royal* and took possession of *les Tuileries*."

"Thus ended the Bourbon dynasty that started with Henry IV (of Navarre) in 1590," Céspedes would add. "One of this days the French will proclaim a Republic and will do away forever with the crown of France."

The Céspedes, history buffs as they both were, had the habit of taking lunch on Sundays at one of the many small restaurants around the *Palais-Royal*, where they usually invited their home guests. There they delighted to listen to the stories that Carlos Manuel and María del Carmen would tell with so much enthusiam.

After Sunday lunch, the trees and statues of the gardens of *les Tuileries* were an enthralling frame for a leisurely promenade on their way back to the home on *rue Jacob*. It was María del Carmen's favorite stroll, something that in her mind made Paris a place like no other in the world. *Les Tuileries* were the first public gardens in Paris, opened to the public since the times of Louis XV. At the end of the gardens there was always an opportunity to visit *Madeleine*, the renowned *patisserie*, on the west end, near *la Concorde*.

Along the gardens, they were walking over a territory that had seen a lot of French history.

Carlos Manuel would always comment to his friends that "it was on these gardens, on August 10, 1792, that the revolutionary mobs stormed the *Palace des Tuileries* and massacred the mercenary Suisse Guard that protected the royal family. Louis XVI ran, half dressed, with his family, in the middle of the night, to seek refuge at the *Salle de Manège*, the building where the National Convention was having its meetings during the daytime."

Carlos Manuel enjoyed telling the story of young Napoleon Bonaparte on that day.

"From the 13 steps leading to the street on the north side of the gardens, young Napoleon Bonaparte, still an unknown petty officer of the National Guard, watched horrified and never forgot, how the royal family was humiliated on that day. Three days later the family would be in the *Temple* prison and their fate would be cast. I believe it was the horror of that unceremonious scene that prompted Napoleon to make a personal oath to never to allow the crowds to dominate the streets."

"It has been an important principle for both tyrants and free men ever since," would add María del Carmen. "Never allow your enemy to take control of the streets. Whoever controls the streets will end up controlling the government and the destinies of the country."

"Curiously," Céspedes used to remark, "years later in 1815, Louis XVIII, Louis XVI's brother, also broke loose and pre-empted the same rooms in the palace, in more or less the same hurry, when he found out that Napoleon had escaped from his first exile in Elba, had landed in France and was on his way to *les Tuileries.*"

Most of the Céspedes' visitors from Cuba and Spain were what the French call *amateurs de l'historie.* There was almost no limit to what they wanted to learn about French history while in France. The Céspedes were happy to oblige as their guides.

"These gardens and this building have seen an enormous share of French history," Céspedes would reiterate. "It was in June of 1794, two years after the flight of Louis XVI to the *Salle de Manège*, that the *Fête* of the Supreme Being, the pagan god of the revolution, was organized by Robespierre at the gardens of *les Tuileries*. And it was on November 9, 1799, the famous *18th of Brumaire*, that the Council of Elders was called in front of *les Tuileries* to proclaim the Consulate as the highest power in France and Napoleon as its most prominent Consul."

"Soon after he would be exalted as Emperor," he would continue, "and the terms *citoyen* and *citoyenne* were removed from the revolutionary lingo and replaced by "Sir" and "Madame" when addressing Napoleon and Josephine."

Carlos Manuel would conclude by saying that Pope Pius VII, visiting Paris with a thwarted mission to crown the Emperor, had apartments on the *Pavillion de Flore*, one of the end towers of *les Tuileries* palace, across the Seine from the Céspedes suites at the hotel on the left bank that they first occupied when they came to Paris.

"Had we been here some forty years earlier, in 1804, we could have watched the Pope sunning himself at one of *les Tuileries* palace's many terraces," María del Carmen added with a smile.

Strolling along the Seine in those days was an adventure in elegance and courtly gracefulness. West to east you would start at the *Pont d'Iena*, a magnificent structure from 1809 commemorating Napoleon's routing of the Prussian army. Its name so infuriated the heroe of Waterloo, the first Duke of Wellington, that in more than one occasion he threatened to blow the bridge at the first opportunity. Then, as you watched the Seine's graceful boats anchored on the banks or fighting the currents upstream, you could see the *Pont du Caroussel*, which had replaced in 1834 the *Pont des Saintes Pères*, built so flimsily of wood beams over a light structure of cast iron, that it proved unsuitable even for pedestrian traffic.

Continuing upstream the next bridge was the *Pont des Arts* or *Passerelle des Arts*, built of solid iron bars with a wooden deck in 1804. It was so called because it linked the Louvre, which at the time was also referred to as the *Palais des Arts*, on the right bank, with the *Institute of France* and its *Académie des Arts,* on the left bank.

It was the Céspedes' favorite bridge in Paris, romantic, seemingly frail, light and unencumbered, close to the water and with a splendid view on both sides: the *Gardens of the Tuileries* downstream and the *Île de la Cité* upstream. Many a night Carlos Manuel and María del Carmen would sit at one of the benches at the *Passerelle des Arts*, holding hands, gently sharing their dreams and promising each other eternal love and loyalty.

Then came the *Pont Neuf*. It was inaugurated by Henry IV in 1604, with two spans anchored at the center, on the western most point of the *Île de la Cité*. Whenever they showed the *Pont Neuf* to one to their visitors Carlos Manuel could not wait to tell the story of the day its first stone was placed.

"Just imagine this scenario," he would say. "It is the 31st of May of 1578 and it is raining torrentially. The placement of the first stone for this new Parisian bridge has been announced and hundreds of people have come to see the King lay the first stone. Henri III arrives at eleven in the morning with his mother, Catherine de Médicis, and his wife, Louise. Rather than being happy and behaving like the all powerful monarch of France that he is, Henri is crying. Everyone can see a handkerchief covering his eyes. He had just learned that two of his gay lovers had killed each other on a duel at the easternmost end of the Luxembourg Gardens. Catherine ends up laying the first stone all by herself and the crowd begins to call the bridge *le Pont des Pleurs*, the Bridge of Tears."

"*Pont Neuf* survived its rather inauspicious start," María del Carmen would add. "It became the first open bridge in Paris, with no shops on its surface. Along its beams and entablatures, 384 grotesque and freakish faces were carved, presumably to honor the bureaucrats at the service of his royal majesty."

The next bridge was the *Pont Saint Michel*, built of stone in 1606, with four arches and some statuary. Its shops, on the bridge since 1387, were removed by 1808, opening the view of the river for those crossing the structure. Then came the *Petit Pont*, from the *Île de la Cité* to the left bank and the *Grand Pont*, connecting the *Île de la Cité* with the right bank. It was situated at a site where there has always been a bridge crossing the Seine.

"Julius Cesar wrote about it in his *Commentaries* in about year 50 BC," Céspedes would remark.

Finally, and seldom visited by the Céspedes, there were several other bridges. A single arch structure called the *Pont au Double*, first built in 1515, twice collapsed and finally reconstructed in 1803. Its name derived from the double *dernier* (about one tenth of a pound) that was charged to crossing pedestrians. The *Pont de Saint Louis*, near Notre Dame, made of wood, which once collapsed under the weight of a procession. The old *Pont de l'Archevêché*, built in 1828 across from the Archbishop's house and finally, the *Pont Notre-Dame*, built in 1413, 200 years after the construction of the Parisian Cathedral and anchored at the *Quai des Vins*, on the noisy and bustling warehousing and commercial left bank of the River.

THE BRIDGES OF PARIS IN 1856

A drawing of the **Seine River** and several of its bridges. On the right lower corner, the back of the *façade* of the Church of St. Gervais - St. Protais, followed by the *Hôtel de Ville* and the buildings on the old *Quai de Pelletier*. On the left the *Hôtel Dieu*, the *Palais de Justice* with its dome and the *Concergierie*, with the spiral of the *Ste. Chapelle* on the back. The bridges going from the *Île de la Cité* to the right bank are, front to back: *Pont d'Arcole, Pont Notre Dame, Pont au Change* and *Pont Neuf*. In the distance the *Passarelle des Arts* and the *Pont du Carrousel*.

3

*"That men do not learn very much from the lessons of history
is the most important of all the lessons that History has to teach."*
Aldous Huxley

*"The whole history of the world is summed up in the fact that, when nations are
strong, they are not always just, and when they wish to be just,
they are no longer strong."*
Winston Churchill

*"Even tho' thrice again / The red fool-fury of the Seine /
Should pile her barricades with dead."*
Lord Tennyson

ONE FAVORITE DESTINATION of Carlos Manuel and María del Carmen during their promenades across Paris was the *Pont Neuf* and the statue of Henry IV at the *Vert Galant*. The statue had been destroyed during the riots of the French Revolution and the rioters had carted every piece of bronze –fearing it could be used for weapons manufacture against the populace– except one of the hoofs of the Kings' horse. In the best of French traditions of historical preservation the statue was recast from the original plans and the surviving hoof was placed inside the belly of the horse, hence maintaining the seniority of the artwork amongst the many other equestrian monuments in Paris.

The story of Henry IV was a favorite of Carlos Manuel, and he related it many times to visitors and friends.

"At the close of the XVI Century," he would tell, "the kingdom was devastated after many years of religious wars. Several hundred Protestants had been massacred in *Wassy* in 1572 by soldiers under the command of the Duc of Guise. Many episodes of atrocities followed, as the Catholics from the northern regions of France fought the Huguenots of the southern Loire valley, as the protestants were known. On the night of August 24, 1572, hundreds more were killed in the darkness of night, on a catholic conspiracy that got started after the bells of *Saint German l'Auxerrois* rang loud and incessantly for several hours. The signal to the friar who tolled the bells on that night came from across the street. It was the Queen herself, Catherine de Medicis, waving a handkerchief from a window at the Palace of the Louvre. The episode quickly became known as the Massacre of Saint Bartholomew."

"In central France," he would continue, "the provinces allied themselves with Henry de Navarre, a protestant; in the northern areas, the House of Lorraine allied itself with Felipe II of Spain, a devout Catholic. Paris itself remained under the control of the Duc of Guise, a devout Catholic, but Henri III, the French king in propriety, had given orders that he be assassinated. The Duc stroke first through a Catholic monk called Jacques Clement, who casually approached and knifed the unsuspected King on August 1, 1589. With the throne vacant, Henri IV lay siege to Paris but did not have enough troops to strike a decisive blow against his adversaries, now united in what became known as the Catholic League. The populace suffered the consequences of that siege: hunger and pestilence, without the possibility of a rescue operation by the Spanish armies, who were Catholic, of course."

"But the story does not end there," Carlos Manuel would conclude. "As a conciliatory gesture, Henri IV offered to convert to Catholicism if his protestant faith was unacceptable to the French. In a strategic master stroke that only a political genius could devise – Céspedes use to declare with a grave voice– the King of Navarre declared that *"Paris is well worth a Mass..."*, probably the most successful and expedient political statement of all times. On July 25, 1593, Henri IV adjured his Protestant faith and became a full fledged Catholic at a ceremony at the *Basilique Cathédrale de Saint Denis*. Since Reims was in the hands of the Spaniards and the partisans of le Duc de Guise, the bishop of Paris obliged and traveled to consecrate the new King of France at Chartres on February 27, 1594."

Carlos Manuel, already a blooming politician, admired not only the compromises that Henri de Navarre had crafted in order to become acceptable to the French, but also his magnanimity when he finally entered Paris to take possession of his throne.

"He offered the Spaniards and the League members a pardon and a safe passage out of the Paris they occupied, when it was within his power to massacre them."

"He ordered that rue Saint-Denis become a passageway with free transit for all departing Spaniards," Céspedes would go on. "Close to three thousand Spanish soldiers, plus the entire ambassadorial corps of Felipe II of Spain took advantage of the opportunity to leave Paris. A huge lesson on how to tender a silver bridge to your escaping enemies, as the Spanish saying goes."

The Céspedes used to complement the Henri IV stories by taking their guests to *Saint Denis*, the Basilica where the remains of all the Kings of France were entombed. The revolutionaries had played havoc with the extensive crypt of the Basilica, and indeed had emptied all the coffins of their remains, throwing them to the streets; but there you could see and touch, like Carlos Manuel and María del Carmen liked to do so much, every casket, every monument and every burial stone, almost all of them empty.

"An ill-omened conclusion of fifteen Centuries of French history and the best evidence of the blindness and basically anti-French nature of the French Revolution," Carlos Manuel would add.

Through the widely open and sunny hallways of the Basilica's crypt Carlos Manuel and María del Carmen would show their friends the burial remains of all the Kings and Queens of France, set up in chronological display. They would then recite the legendary names they came to know from their readings in Cuba and in Paris.

"There is no catafalque for Vercingetorix, the last Gaul ruler who lost his kingdom in the hands of Julius Cesar himself," Carlos Manuel would start. "He is presumably buried at *Alise-Sainte-Reine*, on top of the hill where he lost his last battle with the conquering Romans. But most others are here. Starting with Clovis, the first Frankish King, who vanquished Afranius Syagrius (430-487), the last Roman official in northern Gaul."

"He was followed by Theuderic, Chlodomer, Childebert, Clotaire and the rest of the Merovingians," María del Carmen would continue. "Then came the times of Charles Martel, Charlemagne, King Eudes, Lothair, Duke of Burgundy and Aquitaine and the rest of the Carolingians."

"And to culminate this illustrious parade of statesmen, heroes and cowards," Carlos Manuel would conclude, "here are also the last remains of the Capets, the most numerous and most distinguished and incestuous royal family in Europe. Its first French members were Hugo Capet, Odo and Robert I around the year 900 AC. Their kin would eventually include the House of the Valois, the Bourbons and the Orleans. It is hard to remember all the Henries, the Philippes, the Charleses, the Françoises and the Louises! Then you would come to the pitiable Louis XVI, who lost it all, the colorless Louis XVIII, the arrogant Charles X and the cynical Louis Philippe d'Orleans. They all thought they could restore the French monarchy and set the history clock backwards."

Carlos Manuel immersed himself in readings of French history as if it were his own. He would prepare tables, outlines, charts and synoptic diagrams, to keep all names straight in his memory. He could tell you who had built the *Place des Vosges* and the *San Louis Hospital* (Henri IV), or the church of *Saint Étienne du Mont* and the *Collège de France* (Francis I), and who had inherited the Kingdom of Navarre for the French crown (Louis X, son of Philip IV of France and Jeanne, Queen of Navarre). He avidly read everything that fell on his hands to understand the conditions under which France had come to its vast political and military achievements.

His first readings were done in Cuba, at the San Carlos Seminary, but when he came to Paris he found a bountiful quarry of history books in several libraries opened to scholars in and around the *Île de la Cité*. Carlos Manuel was fluent in French, German, Spanish, English and was also a noted translator of Greek and Latin Classics in his youth. He started his French readings with the genial authors and nation builders under Louis XIV, such as Molière, Racine, Boileau, La Fontaine, Lully, Rigaud, Le Brun and Le Nôtre. These were followed with the great political scientists and philosophes of the XVIII and XIX Centuries, the giants of the scientific, literary, philosophical and sociological world of the Enlightment, who had cast aside all dogmatic systems of thought, had espoused a steadfast belief in the perfectibility of men and had devoted their lives to the systematization of human knowledge.

While in Paris, the Céspedes household became a universe devoted to Diderot, D'Alambert, Voltaire, Montesquieu, Descartes, Newton, Hume, Adam Smith, Gibbon, Beccaria and Lessing, with its center of gravity on what Céspedes thought was the greatest of the social reformists of the XIX Century: Jean Jacques Rousseau, the author of *Discourse on the Moral Effects of the Arts and Sciences*.

Much as Thomas Jefferson had done half a century earlier when he began to collect books in Paris with an American national library in mind, the Céspedes began to be avid collectors of nation-building books.

"There are sources every man in political life needs to read," Céspedes would write to José Antonio Saco and Domingo Del Monte, back in Cuba. "That great collection of available political wisdom must include Montesquieu's *Spirit of the Laws*, Voltaire's *A Treatise on Tolerance* and *Candide*; Diderot's *Encyclopedia*, Hume's *An Inquiry Concerning Human Understanding*, Adam Smith's *An Inquiry into the Nature and Causes of the Wealth of Nations*, Gibbon's *The Decline and Fall of the Roman Empire*, Becaria's *On Crimes and Punishments*, and Lessing's *On the Education of the Human Race.*"

These treatises and many others, widely available in the bookstores in Paris, were among the most valuable possessions that Carlos Manuel and María del Carmen would take back to Cuba when they returned in 1844. Eventually the books were scattered throughout Puerto Príncipe, Bayamo, Manzanillo and Santiago. Céspedes, rather than engaging into speculative or abstract thinking like many of his Parisian friends, committed himself to the noble cause of bringing philosophical ideas into practice. For the rest of his existence he became an energetic and pragmatic activist for the cause of an improved Cuban society, quite often at a great personal risk and ultimately at the cost of his own life.

On his return to eastern Cuba Céspedes was planning to seek opportunities to be an impresario of modernism at every Masonic temple and tertulia where he could get invited. His creed would be at once simple and straightforward: to overcome the ignorance bred by narrow mindedness and superstition; to promote tolerance, particularly in religious issues; to bring about social peace through fair government structures that would enrich the human spirit and support equal treatment and opportunity; and, finally, to eliminate cruelty and violence from public and private life.

In order to achieve these goals, he had written to Domingo Del Monte: "Cubans could not carry the heavy baggage of a religious and political intolerant Spanish society that for many generations had endured and tolerated uncivil opportunism and corruption, and had become the antithesis of freedom and fairness."

"It is necessary to start afresh," he also wrote on an inspired letter to José Mendive in Madrid. "As a new republic we need to eliminate the social institutions and belief systems that in the past have hindered human progress. We need to create a Republic where the primary concern would be the contentment and self fulfillment of men and society."

The people he met and the stories he learned from the lips of Jacques Laffitte (1767-1844) became a mayor influence on Céspedes' thoughts and reflections during those Parisian years. Laffitte, who was already an old man at the time he met the Céspedes, had been the liberal founder and proprietor of *Banc National de France*. He had met the Céspedes through common friends in Barcelona. His house at *27, rue d'Artois* (later called *rue Laffitte*) was visited by the Céspedes quite often when they first arrived in Paris. Jacques Laffitte had been very instrumental in helping the young couple get established in Paris. He became the Céspedes banker and financial advisor, backing up not only the home they would lease at *rue Jacob* but also extending lines of credit and securing money transfers between Paris, Madrid and Havana. These transfers of currency were often required as Carlos Manuel became an important supplier of technology and goods to the Del Montes, the Aldamas, the Cisneros and the Lacrets in Puerto Principe, Bayamo and Manzanillo.

The Céspedes came to know many important political, literary and artistic personalities in Paris because of the frequency with which they visited the Laffitte household. The Laffittes, very generous and well bred people like the Céspedes, opened their entire roster of friends, business and political associates to Carlos Manuel and María del Carmen, in ways in which only parents favor their own children.

Laffitte was a staunch supporter of Louis Philippe d'Orleans, the son of the guillotined Philippe Égalité, the regicide cousin, who, as member of the National Convention in 1794, had voted to send Louis XVI to the guillotine. He was also a good friend and supporter of many veterans of the *Grande Armée de Napoleon*, as well as the protector of an old man who Carlos Manuel never got to know but for whom he had a deep admiration: the *Marquis de La Fayette*. Years later, in the mountains around Bayamo and Manzanillo, as the besieged President of the Cuban Republic in Arms, he hoped many times to have the same calculated political acumen than these French politicos, particularly when he faced his enemies within the ranks of the Cuban Legislative Assembly and his own Cabinet.

Carlos Manuel and María del Carmen had arrived in Paris in 1841 and left in 1844. These were uncertain years in France, but they were probably the most inspiring and hopeful times in the last one hundred years. The regime of the House d'Orleans tried very hard to reconcile the different sectors of French political life, particularly the ever insisting republicans, who were relentless in their campaign for a universal vote. The students organized numerous protest sessions (the so called *manifs*) at the *Place de la Madeleine* and through the *Boulevard des Capucines*. Carlos Manuel used to join these *manifs*, at least on the sidelines, just for the thrill of participating in a public expression of support for a cause that was neither agreeable nor in accord to the government wishes.

"These *manifs*," he would say, "have been my first opportunity to participate in an event where you could fully express your mind. It is a sad state of affairs in Cuba when a full-grown man has to come to

Paris to openly and safely shout to the wind his political persuasions."

He would talk to the participants, listen to their music and their *a capella* singing, pick up their pamphlets and sympathize with their causes, moving on the streets and not seeking the safety of the sidewalks. He would even entice the bystanders along the route to join in what he used to call *"these parades of sorrowful strollers."* He was pleasantly surprised to see that the government's reaction to those protest events was simply to position troops around *la Place de la Bastille* and at the *parvis* across *l'Hôtel de Ville* and *la Sorbonne*. Their mere presence was considered to be adequate to make a point and keep the order.

Barricades, as had become a tradition in French political life, were generally set up at the *quartier* of Saint Antoine, the source of the July 14 *emeutiers* that overcame the Bastille. The government invariably stood firm in its resolve not to be provoked into action and the *manifs* were always an exercise of civic expression with mutual respect, at least during those trying times of Louis Philippe d'Orleans. The *citoyens* of Paris were fundamentally tired of revolts and were wholly content with a great deal of noise but only slight vehemence. No political provocation and no violence, seemed to be the mutually agreed upon rule of engagement.

Universal suffrage, the end to slavery and the elimination of the death penalty for political crimes became the pressing agenda of the day. The Céspedes were already committed to have a role in the future of Cuba. They began to be close observers of the civilized discourse of the French as they peacefully advanced from a reluctant support of the monarchy to a staunch adherence and endorsement of the republican ideals. They knew, however, that the style of the Spaniards was different than the ways of the French and that the colonial power in Cuba would be intolerant of strife or discordance.

The broadminded and noble coexistence of monarchicals and republicans in the years where the Céspedes lived in Paris was a learned and deliberate effort from all sides to bring peace to France. A few years earlier, in 1824, Charles X, Count d'Artois and brother of Louis XVI, had been recognized as the King of France under very good auspices. The press censure that had been enforced earlier by Louis XVIII, Count de Provence, also a brother of Louis XVI, was lifted and the laws protecting free expression, movement and association were respected. Charles X, however, was mistrustful of his subjects and believed that Louis XVI had been victim of his own weaknesses. He began to foster and support numerous measures that would curtail the rights acquired during the 1789 revolution.

"Charles made a big mistake," Laffitte used to tell Carlos Manuel. "He was determined to change the laws of primogeniture, sacrilege and the compensation of émigrés. By 1830 he had set them up as likely to need reviewing. He should have known that the French people would not go for that."

"What I thought were greater errors," Céspedes would comment, "were his attempts to modify or abolish altogether the laws of freedom of the press and the electoral code. That would have completely made the French Revolution a non-event in the history of France and western civilization. And, as we well know, the French are not good at admitting fault..." he would offer with a kind smile to blunt any offense to Laffitte.

"Indeed," Céspedes would later remember in a letter to José Antonio Saco, "within a few months barricades began to be erected in Paris. From the windows the *citoyens* began to pelter the royal guards with stones. At *93, rue Richelieu*, the police commissar closed the newspaper *Les Temps*. Its director began to publish it secretly. A huge *manif* ran from the *Place de la Victoire* to the *Palais de la Bourse*. Some marchers lost their lives. The *Palais de la Bourse* was set on fire. At the *Pont des Arts* a large crowd crossed the Seine in the direction of *le Louvre*, and forcibly opened its gates. The Swiss guards opened fire and the crowd dispersed towards the gates of *Les Tuileries*. Chaos had once more dominated everyday life in Paris."

"Rioters are again controlling the streets," Carlos Manuel emphasized in his letter. "Within the last few days Charles X has hurriedly and surreptitiously taken a coach at the *Place de la Concorde*, leaving Paris forever. He had transfered a small fortune to London during his first exile at the outset of the French Revolution. He now wants to live and die peacefully abroad, as a private person, away from the uncontrolled rage of his fellow citizens. The House of Orleans is ready to step on and try to set up a constitutional monarchy. The *Marquis de Lafayette*, now an older man, has entered French history for a last time. Jacques Laffitte is also exercising his influence in French current events for what is probably his swan song."

༄ ⌘ ༄

4

"If you wou'd have guests merry with your cheer,
be so your self, or so at least appear."
Benjamin Franklin

"Important people always have copies and, as with paintings, most
people prefer the original to the copy."
Friedrich Nietzsche

"City life is thousands of people being lonesome together."
Henry David Thoreau

IN THE SPRING of 1843 the Céspedes received in Paris as house guests their dearest friends Domingo Del Monte and his wife Rosa, who were old hands in Madrid but were anxious to learn and experience the style and historical sites on the French capital; Rosa's brother Miguel Aldama, who was visiting Europe on business; and writer Gertrudis Gómez de Avellaneda, who desperately needed to get away from Madrid for a while.

Miguel de Aldama y Alfonso, who was barely 22 in 1842, had seriously compromised his personal safety in Havana. He had attended numerous meetings and had supported several clandestine activities with abolitionists and slave rebel leaders, who would later become leaders of the so called *Conspiración de la Escalera*. His father, fearing for his safety, had sent him to Europe to negotiate sugar contracts and arrange for shipments and payments against the corporate accounts at *Banco de Madrid*, at Bank of England in London and at *Rothschild Frères* in Paris. The Aldamas, with extensive sugar plantations and sugar mills in western Cuba, were themselves slave owners.

Don Domingo de Aldama, the father of Miguel, had become a multimillionaire in the boom years between 1800 and 1830, when the population in Cuba increased from barely 400,000 people to over one million. Of these, close to 200,000 were slaves imported from Africa to work on the fields, many of them via the South of the US. The crops of tobacco, vegetables, small fruits and sugar more than doubled every year for thirty straight years in the early 1800's. In the midst of this prosperity, the population of Havana boomed with fortune seekers, bureaucrats and small business entrepreneurs which arrived on every ship coming to Cuba from the old country.

Most Spaniards remained in the cities as clerks, journeymen, craftsmen, military administrators and traders, without any attachment to the countryside. Not so the Aldamas. Don Domingo, as the clan leader, invested the entire family fortune in the agricultural infrastructure needed to support the population growth. It made possible for the Aldamas, as the years passed, to bolster the most luxurious and grandiose home ever built in Havana, the *Palacio de Aldama*. Years later, in 1869, Spanish soldiers would ransack this mansion at 510 Amistad Street in the Cuban capital and the Spanish crown would confiscate all the family's extensive properties in Cuba, valued at the time at between 80 and 120 million of American dollars.

Thirty two year old Domingo Del Monte, Don Domingo de Aldama's son in law, was born in Venezuela and came to Cuba as a child. By the time he was 25 he had become an influential journalist, lawyer and literary critic. He had a hand on every cultural effort in Cuba during a good part of the XIX Century. Years later, José Martí, the Apostle of Cuban Independence, would speak of him as the "most real and legitimate Cuban of his time." He was a student of father Félix Varela, a seminal influence on Cuban pro-independence thought from his position as professor of philosophy at the San Carlos Seminary in Havana. Forced into exile by the Spanish crown, father Varela became the Vicar General of the Dioceses of New York from 1829 to 1850. He was the mentor and discoverer of José María Heredia, one of the greatest Cuban poets of his time, as well as the mentor of many illustrious pupils such as Céspedes, Luz y Caballero, Del Monte and José Antonio Saco.

Domingo Del Monte, an engaged plotter in the "*Soles y Rayos de Bolivar*" conspiracy, had married Rosa Aldama in 1834 and was the main designer of the Aldama mansion, inaugurated in Havana in 1840. Domingo was of a slight build and had a pleasant romantic physiognomy. His long hair and well kept beard made him look professorial and certainly a lot older than his years. He had strong sympathies for Cuban independence and in 1833 founded the *Academia Cubana de Literatura*, which the Spanish authorities soon found too conflictive with their colonial best interests and shut down in 1834, after many months of obstructions and harassment.

Del Monte, visiting Paris for his fifth time in 1843, made good of his multiple family contacts to expand the Céspedes circle of friends in the short eight weeks when he stayed with María del Carmen and Carlos Manuel. He was, after all, the son in law of Don Domingo, who had a very close friendship and partnership with Francisco de Arango y Parreño (1775-1837), an important Cuban jurist, economist and educator with solid business and social connections in Paris. He was also a friend of Alexander von Humboldt (1769-1859), the acclaimed Prussian naturalist and explorer, who had an extensive following in political, scientific and intellectual Parisian circles. Close friends would frequently refer to Domingo Del Monte as a consummate part time Parisian who resided regularly in Havana.

Havana, in the years between Humboldt's visit in 1796 and the visits of Avellaneda, the Aldamas and Domingo Del Monte to the Céspedes in 1843, was in a continuous turmoil of intellectual activity. When Humboldt arrived, he was taken by Arango y Pareño to meet the cream of the *criollo* aristocracy in Havana. This included the Count of O'Reilly, Mompox y Jaruco, as well as the Counts of Bayona, Peñalver and Lagunillas, and the Marquis and Marquise del Real Socorro y de Casa Calvo, all involved in numerous scholarly activities in literature, geography, anthropology and politics.

These patrician and superbly educated crowd marveled at Humboldt's forty two portable scientific instruments, which he was proud to show them in detail. Humboldt's plans included making records of zoological, geographical, meteorological, geological, anthropological, astronomical, and cartographical data from Cuba. The depth of his meticulous preparations and knowledge amazed his newly found Cuban friends. Arango y Parreño, provided him with invaluable assistance in economic analysis and statistical data on Cuba. José de la Luz y Caballero (1800-1862), a disciple of father Félix Varela and probably one of the most important American philosophers of the XIX Century, accompanied him most of the time during the months when he was exploring the island. Luz y Caballero helped him identify and catalogue what he was seeing and gathering. Humboldt was to eventually collect 60,000 plant specimens, of which 3,000 were unknown in Europe, before he set sail for Marseille and then Paris. There he wrote, years later, two important books on Cuba: *Ensayo Político sobre la Isla de Cuba*, published in 1827, and *Cuadro Estadístico de la Isla de Cuba*, published in 1831.

This most famous of European naturalists never forgot having been introduced to old Domingo de Aldama by José de la Luz y Caballero in 1796. Many years later, from 1830 to 1848, as an older man,

Humboldt was frequently employed in diplomatic missions to the court of Louis Philippe d'Orleans, with whom he always maintained the most cordial personal relations. It was in 1827, when Humboldt was 58, that Domingo Del Monte, a young man of 23 on his first trip to Paris, introduced himself to Humboldt as Don Domingo de Aldama's friend. Del Monte visited and corresponded with Humboldt regularly until the naturalist's death in 1859, at the age of 90. Von Humboldt, as a young man in his thirties, had become a very good friend of Jefferson in 1803, at the close of his trip to America to study the flora and fauna of the new continent. By then Jefferson was President of the United States and had received Humboldt with great honors in Washington, D.C.

In 1841, Domingo Del Monte became the Real Auditor of the Royal Council of Cuba. As such, he had requested a license to travel to Paris to learn and see first hand the administrative rules and methods employed by the French government in the conduct of their official chores. His credentials were impeccable and he enjoyed the trust of many official functionaries in the Cuban capital, in Madrid, in London and in Paris. He was considered a valuable resource for the Spanish crown, particularly since he spoke fluent English, French, Portuguese, Latin and German, had traveled extensively and knew well, from the inside, the worlds of the North Americans and the Europeans. In the years before 1842 he had written and published several poetry books of his own, had edited the works of several other important poets and had authored anthologies of romantic authors.

Given that his political discourse found mostly closed ears from Cubans and repeated threats of deportation from the Spaniards, he sought refuge in the letters as the means to move forward his hopes for Cuban independence. He founded and held for many years in Havana his famous *Tertulias*, regular Sunday gatherings of the *literati* with the purpose of supporting and improving each other's scholarly production through readings and critical sessions, while at the same time shaping and perfecting the message of a viable Cuban independence.

Those who knew of Del Monte's *tertulias* could not help but compare them to the celebrated *salons* that became popular in Paris towards the end of the XVIII century. Both *tertulias* and *salons* became an integral part of the Cuban and Parisian cultural scene. They were free gatherings of men and women of letters, philosophes, musicians, as well as members of the clergy and artists. They gathered regularly, perhaps for supper or a *merienda*, frequently with an improvised musical performance, but always for conversation. To be tedious or doctrinaire at a *tertulia* was unforgivable and this set them apart from the academic gatherings of formal scholarly societies. Years later Miguel Aldama, a frequent participant to his brother-in-law's *tertulias*, used to teasingly compare them to the Parisian *salons* of Madame Geoffrin, who counted every week with the presence of Diderot, Alembert, Marivaux, Turgot and, occasionally, the most priced of all preys, François Marie Arouet, aka Voltaire.

The main voices at the *tertulias* of Domingo Del Monte did not endorse violence or open rebellion. The memories of bloodshed and rebellion in Haiti, as portrayed in Victor Hugo's *Bug-Jargal* in 1826, were too ferocious and menacing for Spaniards and even for Cubans to digest. Domingo and his fellow *colloquia* participants instead opted for the promotion of institutional progressive and peaceful solutions whereby the colony will evolve into a republic, the slaves into freed salaried hands and the Spaniards living in Cuba into adopted *criollos*, with the same rights and obligations that the native Cubans had. Upon his return to Cuba after visiting the Céspedes in Paris in 1842, Del Monte became seriously engaged, as was Miguel Aldama, in the *Conspiración de la Escalera* and would be banned from Cuba, his adopted country, for the rest of his life.

An inevitable subject of Del Monte's *tertulias* was always the issue of slavery. Most Cuban landowners of the times had declared themselves as favoring annexation with the US, which still maintained slavery in the south. They feared that Spain would liberate the slaves to assuage and appease those claiming for autonomy or independence for Cuba. Back in Paris in 1849, this time with the Céspedes already back in Cuba, an exiled Domingo would write to Carlos Manuel: *"It is still hard for me to believe that someone born in Cuba, or even someone that owns land and has been in Cuba for a certain time, would rather be in the hands of those promoting slavery than free to choose his own destiny. Sooner or later the slaves will be free. The faster the forces pro independence announce the end of slavery the quicker the slaves will come to help in this crusade..."*

Gertrudis Gómez de Avellaneda (1814-1873) was 28 at the time she visited the Céspedes and coincided with Miguel Aldama and the Del Montes in Paris in the spring of 1843. She had been born in Puerto Príncipe, on eastern Cuba, the oldest daughter of a Spanish trading ship captain. She first came to Europe as a 15 year old young aspiring author who had already read Madame de Staël, Châteaubriand, Alfred de Vigny, Lamartine, Shelley, Walter Scott and Byron, as well as Boccaccio, Petrarch, Virgil and Dante. By the time she came to visit the Céspedes she had published *Sab* and *Dos Mujeres* in Madrid and was working on a play and two other novels.

As a woman in the very narrow and pompous society of early XIX Century Madrid, Gertrudis Gómez had to balance the expected dictums about femininity, which were prevalent among her socially encumbered lady friends, with her craving for freedom from any restraining gender constraints. Her first two novels were a testimony of her deeply etched beliefs about gender equality. Although later on she would be married several times, at age 28 she mistrusted matrimony. "Nothing but a doomed legalization of a foreordained tyrannical status," she would say. Hence her passionate, professed and affirmed inclinations to unconventional man-woman relationships.

Gertrudis' works were banned in Cuba as "contrary to morals and good living and full of subversive doctrines prejudicial to the lifestyle wisely defended by the Mother Church." Her personal life was indeed wild and boisterous for the times. She had a multitude of infatuations, torrid affairs, entanglements, unwanted pregnancies and distasteful and unsavory relationships, most of them ending badly. In spite of her personal unhappiness, her literary production never recoiled, hesitated or flinched, for she was dependent on her writings for her personal sustenance.

When she visited the Céspedes, her bitterness turned into an intensive inquiring exploration, feeling safe and accepted by her friends. "I wish to inundate my soul of a new vision and share the dreams and lifestyle, the history and the emotions of Paris. I hope that a Parisian experience would replenish the empty reserves of my spirit, submerged as it has been for so long in the narrow and provincial confines of La Coruña and Madrid," she wrote to the Céspedes when announcing her visit to them.

"Come whenever you wish," María del Carmen replied. "Come soon, and you would be sharing a few days, not only with us and Paris, but also with Domingo and Rosa Del Monte, and even young Miguel Aldama, her brother. We will have a delightful time. Paris is quiet and safe these days, even though we feel there are conflicts brewing under the surface. We have room for you to stay with us, as well as the Del Montes and Miguel. Come, and come soon."

Indeed she came. She was exhausted from her tiresome and endless controversial days in Madrid. Within a few days the Del Montes and Miguel Aldama also came. Domingo and Rosa came directly from Cuba, via Madrid, where they stayed only a few days and did not have the opportunity to meet Gertrudis. Miguel Aldama, young but well seasoned as a businessman, came from London, where he had closed some business that would later please his father immensely.

Strolling along the Parisian wide avenues soon became a favorite and salubrious activity for the Céspedes and their four guests. Their walks extended throughout the entire course of the boulevards, under the shade of their magnificent elm trees, trimmed into flat tops and square shapes on the pavement side and left to grow wild on the sidewalk sides. In spite of the lightness of their lofty fronds in 1843, no doubt because many branches had been cut by the populace to make barricades, the promenades were delightful and almost always in the shade, as it was appropriate in the unusual high temperatures of the spring of 1843.

"You may not want to believe it," remarked Carlos Manuel during one of these strolls through Paris, "but daily Parisian life nowadays is not very different from what it was under Louis XIV a century and a half ago. Paris has always choked inside its walls. If it were not for the *Grands Boulevards* there would not be a decent mouthful of good air to breathe these days."

Indeed, Paris had not changed much. In the early 1840's the Madeleine was just a construction site. Immediately to its east, The *Boulevard des Italiens*, then also called *Boulevard des Gands*, was the place were the rich gathered to have a good time during the daytime. At night, however, the place to be was the easternmost extreme of this magnificent concourse, the *Boulevard du Temple*. This noisy and populous thoroughfare was also called *Boulevard du Crime*, because of the many theaters showing plays where murder and intrigue figured in every plot. Louis Philippe d'Orleans, the constitutional monarch of the French people, lived at *les Tuileries*. The Louvre was already a museum, although it also housed *bona fide* artists and squatters. *La Place de la Concorde* was a huge but undefined and unpaved city square, full of garbage, muck, mud and sludge in spite of the royal efforts to boost its dignity. From there the *Champs Elysées* cut a path to the west, mostly through the countryside. It took an eager and impecunious young poet called Victor Hugo to move into what was then called the "alley of the widows." Over the Chaillot hill there was a semi assembled *Arch de Triumph* in a state of partial construction. For many years it had been a skeleton made of wood and plaster. Some people wanted to dismantle it but finally Louis Philippe ordered it finished and had it inaugurated in 1836. The Seine River was an important means of transportation of products, in an out of Paris, which were carried in barges pulled by horses moving along the banks. Paris at that time had 14 bridges, most of them requiring payment of a toll. Is spite of that, the bridges were always congested and crossing the river had become an ordeal. The three public gardens were the *Tuileries, Luxembourg* and the *Jardin des Plantes*. There were extensive private gardens, however, like *Parc Monceau*, which was owned by the Orleans family. In the center of the *Place de la Bastille* Napoleon had placed a gigantic elephant, 12 meters high, surrounded by water fountains. By 1842 it had become a refuge for truants and it was irreparably rat infested, which prompted Louis Philippe, the Citizen-King, to demolish it.

In those days Paris had a total of 12,816 oil lamposts and 1,162 gas lamps, fed from a gas factory situated on *rue Pétrelle*, north of the *Grands Boulevards*. There was, of course, a lethal rivalry between the Society of Lampost Operators, which had a contract with the City of Paris, and the gas lamp promoters, which were operatives of the gas factory of *rue Pétrelle*. Indoors, the oil lamps had become popular and by 1840 had quickly replaced candles as the means of illumination. The best oil lamps had been invented by a pharmacist on *rue de Sèvres* called M. Quinquet. His lamps, and all others using refined animal oils and fats, became known by 1815 as *quinquéts*.

Pharmacists during the first half of the XIX century had ambitions and felt responsible as the caretakers of people's health. A well read book from 1842, María del Carmen once told Carlos Manuel, stated a pharmacist's advice to one of his customers in these terms: "Take a bath only if the medical doctor orders it, but do it with care and never more than once a month. Do not stay under water for a long time. It does no good to the good reputation of a young lady to remain in the bathtub for an extended period of time." For the ladies, there were many accounts on why, when and how to bathe during any given season of the year. Yet the advice was always different for men, and evidently a double standard was followed: "A gentleman must bathe often and taking the time to enjoy it, and always in the afternoons. One should not show his face in the *Boulevards* without having first taken a good and salubrious bath."

Along the *Grands Boulevards*, on the shaded sidewalks that the Céspedes and their guests favored, several rows of chairs were usually placed by merchants or by the city. It was delicious to sit there for several hours, order a cold drink and enjoy the happy scene of people of all kinds and persuasions flowing around them. At the *Boulevard des Italiens* the sitters were mostly fashionable Parisians using the chairs for a couple of hours while their own servants waited on them. Their favorite consumption was iced drinks brought from *Tortoni's*. At the *Boulevard des Capucines* the multitude of shops and coffee houses made the strolls a bit more entertaining but also cumbersome. Men would sit there and drink a coffee or a glass of white wine, while their wives would shop in the establishments or from the street merchants. Every conceivable fashionable gadget was available, from combs to wigs, from a pair of shoes to an umbrella.

The touring merchants would announce their wares loudly, trying to suffocate the advertisement of their competitors, and Parisians took that to be amusing, convinced that life was better to live if it was noisy and fun loving. Every now and then a nanny would show up nurse-carting a small child, or a rich old lady would be cartwheeled by a humble old lady. There was never a lack of old gentlemen, former *beaus* whose time had long passed, meeting and fake-courting young girls sauntering defiantly and coquettishly down the center of the sidewalks. The gentlemen would doff their hats with a gentle motion of their hands, click their heels, and elegantly bow their frail and rather stiff bodies a few inches forward, while their bones were complaining with all sorts of cracking noises. The girls would respond with a slight reverential inclination of their torso and a flippant turn of their heads.

"You would always wonder," Carlos Manuel once said, "what would happen if a girl would ever consent to a quick tryst with one of these sapless and creaky would-be Don Juans."

"Nothing, nothing would happen," replied Gertrudis. "Nothing but a hasty retreat and a mouthful of excuses."

The great joy of the close friendship of these six people was their complete freedom to eschew the social strictures and conventions of the times and speak freely among themselves. No topic was forbidden, for ladies or gentlemen.

It was not easy to walk in the streets of Paris those days, other than in the boulevards. Too many people were hustling over sidewalks which were generally less than two feet wide. You would have to descend to the muddy and puddled pavement whenever a lady approaching you would justly claim the right of way. And you dreaded hearing at that moment a deafening *"gare,"* the roar of a cart driver going right behind and in the same direction as you. You ended up congratulating yourself if you somehow had moved instinctively at the last minute. Otherwise there would be a fateful collision, with the cart jamming your unsuspecting body into the lady that provoked the entire incident.

Over the eight weeks that their guests stayed in Paris, the Céspedes took them to the *guinguettes* on Sundays, after the traditional 11 am Mass at *Saint Eustache*. There, Carlos Manuel, María del

Carmen and Rosa would have a rather weak Parisian beer, which they drank as served, although many Frenchmen diluted them even further with water. Domingo, Miguel and Gertrudis would frequently have red wine, a *groseille* or currant juice, a lemonade or a *liqueur de cassis*, a fermented syrupy drink made from black currant. The *Grande Chaumière de Montparnasse* was the *guinguette* they frequented most often. It had been young Napoleon's favorite, south of the *Jardin de Luxembourg*. There, as in the *guinguettes* on the hill of Montmartre, onlookers watched for hours how others danced, listened to the gentle rhythms of post revolutionary Paris or joined the dancers themselves.

"This is our favorite dancing place," María del Carmen would say. "I discovered it while visiting the porcelain factory of the brothers Dagoty, on the corner of the *Boulevard* and *rue de Chevreuse*. It was a favorite of the Bonapartes and most of their dishware was molded and fired there."

"We also like to eat now and then at the *Brasserie Mayer*," added Carlos Manuel, "nearby, on the corner of *rue d'Assas* and a passage with a double line of lime trees which they are now calling *rue Vavin*. There we got to know many artists and teachers from the College of Stranislas, who was founded by Louis XVIII. I guess you know that his family name was Stanislas-Xavier Capet."

The *Grande Chaumière* was at the location of an old wind mill in the hills of Montparnasse, much like the Moulin Rouge was on the hills of Montmartre. Once the mills had become obsolete in the XVIII century, the extensive cemented flat surfaces where grains used to be spread for drying in the sun became excellent dance floors for the enjoyment of Parisians. María del Carmen and Carlos Manuel were the only ones in their sixsome who danced, sometimes often, at these habitual Sunday outings. They were both accomplished dancers from the times when they were not even engaged or in love with each other. In Paris, on a language that only the other four Cubans could understand, they romanced each other in each other's arms, much as they had done in Cuba and as tenderly as they intended to do until old age.

The pleasant sessions at the *guingette* of the *Grande Chaumière* was at times brought to a caustic and acrid end by the sudden presence of what Céspedes and others used to call "*la jeune France,*" an assortment of eccentric young men with very long hair, large beards, wearing funny looking hats and bare throats with the collars of their shirts turned inside out. They were what at the time became known as "*the radical republicans,*" generally a very caddish, unchivalrous and ungallant crowd. Their rather undefined political persuasions were even more shocking than their physical appearance. Interestingly enough they were mostly lawyers, medical students, violin and piano teachers and editors of the many small run journals that abounded in Paris. Their presence generally brought and end to the fun as couples would quit dancing and most customers would walk out. Carlos Manuel was generally infuriated by their presence.

"In the authoritarian and despotical environment of Madrid," Carlos Manuel would say, "these learned but uneducated and vulgar show offs of *"la jeune France"* would not be allowed to intrude unpleasantly at a place like the *Grande Chaumière*."

María del Carmen always tried to becalm him. "It is merely the toll to be paid in a democratic and open society," she would argue.

"This *riff-raff* of the radical republicans of *la jeune France*," Carlos Manuel would reply, "is like a gangrene on the noble soul of France. Their false intellectualism will irreparably damage the image and political progress of France. They are nothing but cultured vagrants, learned scoundrels; seeking to sap the blood of an enlightened civilization that has contributed so much to mankind. Unless France rids itself of these degenerates, they will end up fighting for do-nothing appointments in government, cowardly sitting by the sidelines when the big issues of freedom and justice are on the line. I can see them hiding under the pretense of non-violence and searching for elegant excuses for non-involvement and appeasement. They will ruin the moral fiber of France. They are the scum that every nation inevitably produces. In France, however, under their semblance of an urbane and erudite character, they have the potential of reaching the highest levels of decision making. That day, I am afraid, would mark the twilight of French civilization."

Facing such a strong and heart-felt opinion about their unwelcome visitors, the Céspedes party finished their drinks and left. Their rented coach was waiting for them under the shade of a huge cypress, by the American chapel of *Saint Luc*, at the corner of *Montparnasse* and the old *Boulevard d'Enfer*. Reflecting on the last words of Carlos Manuel, the trip home was mostly hushed and pensively silent.

REVOLUTIONARY RIOTERS DESECRATING SAINT-DENIS, 1794

Alexandre Lenoir (1761-1839) almost single-handedly saved many monuments and works of art in Paris from the fury of the revolutionary iconoclasts. Nowhere were his actions more vital than at the *Basilique de Saint-Denis*, the building honoring the dynastic patron of the Capetians in the outskirts of Paris. The necropolis underneath the church was full of ornate tombs and highly decorated Renaissance mausoleums holding the last remains of all the Kings of France since the seventh century. The building was sacked numerous times and the contents of the caskets were ruthlessly thrown away.

5

"It was not reason that besieged Troy; it was not reason that sent forth the Saracen from the desert to conquer the world; that inspired the crusades; that instituted the monastic orders. It was not reason that produced the Jesuits; above all, it was not reason that created the French Revolution. Man is only great when he acts from the passions; he is never irresistible but when he appeals to the imagination."
Benjamin Disraeli

"The instruction we find in books is like fire. We fetch it from our neighbors, kindle it at home, communicate it to others, and it becomes ours."
Voltaire

"A home without books is a body without soul."
Cicero

THE CESPEDES HAD rented their home at *12, rue Jacob* from Didier Hervi, an old bourgeois gentleman who had lived many an adventure in Paris during the French Revolution. Didier's family was in the textile business in Lyon and had been pioneers in the manufacture and dying of silk fabrics in that second most important of French cities. The Hervis had come to Paris and purchased a house on *14, rue Jacob* in 1785, scarcely four years before the advent of the revolution.

Didier's entire family perished in the guillotine during the dark days of September of 1792. During the space of four days on that felonious month, the revolutionary crowds massacred 23 priests at the prison at *l'Abbaye de Saint-Germain-des-Prés* under the directives of Billaud-Varenne, more than 300 prisoners at the fortress of *La Force* following instructions from Hebert, and 150 priests and seculars at the Convent of *Les Carmes*, under orders from Maillard, aside from other minor massacres at the prisons of *la Conciergerie, Châtelet, Salpêtrière* and *Bicêtre*.

Didier was spared because he had spent the night at a friend's house when the rioters entered their home on September 2. The home was ransacked and the entire family and servants taken to *La*

Force. After the end of the Terror the house had been returned to the Hervi family. Didier, who returned to Paris after a short exile in London, sold all of his properties in Lyon to restore the house at *14, rue Jacob* and later on purchased the home next door at number 12, which many years later he would rent to the Céspedes. At *14, rue Jacob* he started a new family with Margerithe Amélie, his first cousin, whose family had also been decimated by the revolutionaries.

Didier Hervi was a handsome man in his early seventies, twice a widower but full of energy and the natural élan which results from having survived one of the most bloodthirsty episodes in human history. He walked briskly, straight and tall like one of the many cypress trees in the garden of *les Tuileries* which had also outlived the revolution. The Céspedes loved to visit with him, living alone as he did in the endless rooms and corridors of *14, rue Jacob*. When the Del Montes, Miguel Aldama and Gertrudis came to visit, of course, their hosts were anxious to share with them Didier's many stories of revolutionary times. Many a night all six were guests of Didier next door, who received them at a well stocked library of incunabula and books from the XVI, XVII and XVIII Centuries. The conversation always gravitated towards the experiences of Didier's during the first five years of the revolution in Paris.

"In order to fully understand what happened here during the revolution," Didier recalled the day he first met the Céspedes guests, "you need to know how Paris looked during those times. This town looked in 1789 basically like it had in the XV Century. The city was surrounded by the wall of the *Fermiers Généraux*, with gates every now and then to allow for an orderly taxation of all products coming from the countryside or abroad. Inside this wall there were 3,400 hectares of city dwellings extending from Bercy to Chaillot on the right bank and from the *boulevard de Grenelle* to the *boulevard de l'Hôpital* on the left bank. Inside the confines of this wall lived 700,000 Parisians, almost a fifth of which were born in the Bourgogne, in Champagne and as far as Flanders and the *Rhénanie*. The streets were narrow, mostly paved with stones, seldom with any sidewalks and with the sewers running open down the center. The city stank of detritus and it was not possible to walk through the streets without getting covered with mud and carrying with you all these foul odors."

After a brief pause Didier continued. "The Garden of the Tuileries was not yet bordered on the north side by the *rue de Rivoli* but by the terraces of the convent of the *Feuillants*. The Tuileries and its gardens were higher than these terraces, at roughly the level where the large two ponds on the central alley are today. On both sides of this alley in fact, Robespierre had build two stone semicircular benches facing two rectangular ponds which, if I remember correctly, were the only constructions made by the revolutionaries anywhere in Paris. Other than that, a rather large building with a colonnade was built near the *Palais de la Bourse*. Everything else done during revolutionary times was meant to destroy rather than construct."

Didier went on. "The *Orangerie* and the *Jeu de Paume* did not exist at the time; the garden area near the *Place de la Revolution* looked pretty much as it does today."

He closed his eyes as if to block any distracting images while he searched his memory and continued. "The present *Place du Carrousel* was surrounded by shops and houses, which deprived the entrance to the Tuileries of a good perspective. On the right bank, further away from the river and opposite to the Louvre, you had the *Palais-Royal*, of course, and behind it the beginning of the slope leading to the hill of the windmills. The hill was already known as Montmartre, because it was the *mont* where the *martirium* of Saint Denis had taken place in the second century. The *Palais-Royal* looked very much like it does today, with two long rows of trees along *rues Montpensier* and *Beaujolais*. The Bastille was a massive compound on the east side of the city, with only one entrance on the *rue de San Antoine*, after the Churches of Saint Paul and Saint Louis. The longest street in Paris, however, was the *rue Saint Honoré*, which in places was so narrow that two *charrettes* could not cross each other."

"How about the people?" asked Gertrudis.

"I am getting to that," replied Didier. "The neighborhoods were quite selective. The nobles lived on the *faubourg Saint Germain*, along the *Marais* and the areas near the *Temple* and the *Arsenal*. The petite bourgeoisie lived in the area near *Odeon*, the *Palais-Royal* and the *Boulevard de la Bonne Nouvelle*. The working classes lived in areas where different trades concentrated. Construction workers were abundant in the neighborhood of the Church of Saint Paul, around *rue Saint Antoine*. The garment district was roughly around the *rues Saint Denis* and *Saint Martin*. *Saint Lazare* and *Montmartre* were the place chosen by high fashion manufacturers who catered to the nobility and the clergy."

"The workers of the mills and forges." he continued, "lived around Chaillot, and the *chiffonniers* or ragmen, who pushed carts all over Paris picking up old clothes and discarded goods, lived mostly on the lower levels of Montmartre. The furniture makers and the paper painters were concentrated in the faubourgs of Saint Antoine and Saint Marcel, which also attracted workers in the dying, tanning and gastronomic businesses. It was from the last two faubourgs, by the way, where almost all the rioters who took *la Bastille* came from. Those were two tough neighborhoods. In fact, three months before the rushing of *la Bastille*, a large group of rioters from the faubourgs of Saint Antoine and Saint Marcel burned down the *Ateliers Réveillon*, the best and largest manufacturer of painted papers on *rue Montreuil*. The reason they burned the factory was very simple. Their clients were the rich and the clergy and thus they were, by association, exploiters of the working classes. Those were the first revolutionaries of 1789, and to leave no doubt as to their intentions, they burned a mannequin of Monsieur Réveillon in front of the *Hôtel de Ville*. The poor man was so out of touch with the reality of his times that he took refuge in... *la Bastille*, where on July 14th he barely escaped being burned in person."

Didier continued, as the Céspedes and their friends were absorbed by these old tales and anecdotes. "People from these neighborhoods never mixed and sort of resented having strangers visiting their streets. The places to meet and mix were la *Place de Grève* in front of the *Hôtel de Ville*, and the *Palais-Royal*. There everybody came together. You could see a man handing out pamphlets, another standing on top of a chair making a speech against high prices, a third one offering his services as a *relieur* or book binder. All sorts of cracks and libertines as well as young people promenading and, here and there, a political pretender hiring followers that would applaud his diatribes."

"Go on," Domingo said after Didier took a pause. "What happened to Monsieur *Réveillon* after all?"

"Well, a regiment of French and Swiss Guards opened fire against the revolutionaries of the *Atelier Réveillon*. More than 200 people were killed, 300 were hurt. Five workers were taken to prison and tortured," added Didier. "It was much more serious than what happened at *la Bastille*, except that the building of *la Bastille* was a national symbol of the powers of the monarchy. The incident at the *Atelier Réveillon* also marked the first instance under Louis XVI in which soldiers were very reluctant and disinclined to fire against the population. It is always a deadly warning signal to governments. When your hold on the loyalties of the army is beginning to crumble... *les soldat ne veulent pas frapper le people,* the soldiers refuse to collide with the people. If you are in government and see that, run for your life," Didier said as he ended his story with the gusto and flair of a good *raconteur*.

"Those were very stressful days," interrupted Domingo. "A time of false alarms, false news, invented stories and fables and all sorts of dramatic announcements. Nobody was in charge. Initially there were no leaders. No one called for a revolution at that time. Events improvised their own momentum. None of the always smart and self assured encyclopedists ever predicted there would be a revolution within a few years. It is said that in 1789 Louis XVI asked Necker, his minister of economics, if this was a *Fronde*, which was at the time the term for a revolt. Necker replied 'No, your majesty, this is not a revolt, this is a revolution'. Governor Morris, who happened to be in Paris for business and who later would be the American ambassador to France, was also caught by surprise. He wrote in his dairy how unfortunate he was to be in Paris precisely at a time when a civil war was about to burst out."

"You are absolutely right," Didier said. "From a political standpoint Paris looked like any other city in Europe. There were no reasons to expect that a revolution would explode here, anymore than in Brussels, Vienna or Madrid. Perhaps the difference can be attributed to the University. The Latin Quarter at the time housed about 5,000 students. It is true that the glorious days of the Sorbonne were mostly gone. All Universities throughout Europe, in fact, were in frank decay. The curricula were old and obsolete. The bureaucrats were in control, establishing rules and regulations that made the conclusion of the programs of study an ordeal. In spite of that, something must have accounted for the intellectual and speaking skills of Voltaire, Robespierre, Danton and Desmoulins. The brain power that produced the encyclopedia had been nurtured in the colleges of *la Sorbonne*. Perhaps that's the reason the revolution exploded here in Paris."

Didier added, "One of my classmates at the College of Saint Louis was Lucien Curtius, who owned a Wax Museum at number 17 of the *Gallery de Montpensier* in the *Palais-Royal*. A day or two before la Bastille a group of rioters forced their way into the shop and stole two pieces of an exhibition dealing with current affairs. One was a bust of Necker, the minister, the other was an image of the Duc d'Orléans, the King's cousin and owner of the *Palais-Royal*. The rioters paraded their trophies along the boulevards and burned them in front of the *Porte de Saint Denis*. My friend Curtius was terribly scared but continued his business pretending to be a supporter of the revolution. A few months later, in 1792, he had an exhibit that included Marat in his bathtub at the time of his assassination by Charlotte Corday, a faithful representation that followed David's painting. The exhibition also included a very disturbing scene of the guillotined head of Madame du Barry on a stick. Madame was still alive and hiding at a friend's house in the *Marais*. A mob ransacked Curtius place accusing him of catering to the nobility. He found a way of safely leaving Paris and moved to London, where his daughter opened a similar business under the name of *Madame Tussaud*."

"What a dreadful story," interrupted María del Carmen. "What happened to Madame du Barry after that scare?"

"The image presented by Curtius was in very bad taste but not necessarily prophetical, because probably nothing could have saved the Countess from the scaffold. She was indeed guillotined a few months after all of Paris had seen Lucien's preview. The story was told that the Countess had commissioned a bust of hers and, in the midst of the revolution, forgot to retrieve and pay for it. When Lucien needed a female head on a pick for an exhibit, he carelessly used du Barry's in order to save time and effort. He did not realize how well known the features of Madame du Barry were. She found out in her hiding place on *rue vieille du Temple* and was, of course, both incensed and terrified."

"Who would not be?" added Gertrudis.

"If the fall of la Bastille was not a deciding point in starting the revolution but just a symbolic gesture, what happened later on that made the revolution inevitable?" asked Miguel Aldama, who until then had remained very alert and impressed bust mostly silent. "When and how did it go from a revolt of discontents and rabble rousers to a full fledged national tragedy?"

"Well, *mes amies*," answered Didier. "On July 14th nothing much happened and a lot happened. Louis XVI, so undistinguished by his rather poor political acumen, wrote on his dairy «Today is July 13th. Nothing happened. Today is July 14th. Nothing has happened today either», and so on." But in reality lots of important things were happening. On the 15th the King gave an order to redistribute to their proper quarters the troops that he had been assembling at Versailles, his residence. On July 16th, under pressure, he reappointed the popular Necker to his cabinet. Necker had been dismissed because of his insistence in cutting expenses and lowering the burden of taxes to the general population. On July 17th the King went back to Paris to receive the tricolor *cocarde* (rosette) from Bailly, the new Mayor, and from Lafayette, the new commander of the National Guard. He did not realize it but it meant he was giving his blessing to events that were under the control of others."

"What's with the *cocard*?" asked Rosa.

"Those favoring the revolution needed a way to identify themselves in front of others," answered Didier. During the days of peaceful demonstrations at the *Palais-Royal*, a young lawyer called Camille Desmoulins had stood on top of an iron grill on a popular coffee house at number 60 of the *Galerie de Montpensier*. There he made an impassionate speech which he ended with an appeal for the people to arm themselves. *"Peuple de Paris, aux armes!"* He then took a leaf from a chestnut tree and attached it to his hat. That became the symbol of support for the revolution. When on July 14th the revolutionary leaders met at the *Hôtel de Ville* and decided to raise a voluntary militia, 40,000 men strong, they chose the *cocard*, a rosette, to tie to the hat, with the traditional red and blue colors of the City of Paris and, at the suggestion of Lafayette, they added the color white to represent the King's support. Lafayette, deep down a monarchist all his life, wanted to include the King in every aspect of French life as a restraining element. In the ultimate analysis he failed and almost paid for it with his life."

"One last question," asked Rosa again. "Where were all these people living while Paris was in the throes of such dangerous times and while they themselves were making the revolution?"

"Oh, I remember very well many of their addresses. Mirabeau lived at his luxurious home the *Hôtel Radix de Sante Foy*, at numbers *1, rue de Caumartin* and number 2, *boulevard de la Madeleine*. Robespierre at number *398, rue Saint Honoré*, on a rented second floor room facing the inside patio. Desmoulins with his wife first at *1, rue de l'Odeon* and later on at number 2. The convent of the *Cordeliers* (Franciscan Friars) was at what later became the Faculty of Medicine near la *rue des Écoles*. Its members were, among others, Desmoulins, Hébert and Danton. Danton lived in front of where his statue was later placed, at the *rue Saint André des Arts*. Marat at *30, rue de Cordeliers*. The convent of the Jacobins (Dominican Friars) near *la Place Vendôme*. Its members: Robespierre, Marat, the painter David, among others."

And so on. Hervi was indefatigable in his storytelling of the French Revolution: this was, after all, the story of his own life. Many of these recollections were known by Carlos Manuel, who was a disciplined student of the French Revolution. Many others were entirely new and were added to his repertoire. Those nights spent at the Hervi's home would be unforgettable and would go by very fast. Old Didier Hervi sometimes wanted to make sure his stories were documented and trusted and would end up searching for a book in his priceless library. It included, of course, a complete set of the *Encyclopaedia* of Diderot and D'Alambert; the entire works of Voltaire and Molière; and many other valuable works, not to mention a remarkable collection of pamphlets.

"Pamphlets, my friends," he used to say, "were almost impossible to censor and were our preferred way of letting our views be known. There were more clandestine printing presses in Paris than legitimate ones. It only took a few pounds and a little work to produce two or three hundred copies of whatever subversive materials you wanted to publish. In 1791 I became, like many of my friends and cohorts, a devoted pamphleteer."

Aside from revolutionary and political materials, Hervi's library was a real depository of many important books. Carlos Manuel and María del Carmen borrowed books on history, politics and the arts quite often. Carlos Manuel would also frequently come to review and consult legal materials. The library contained also many priceless and important documents, such as a rare copy of Francisco de Florencia's *La Estrella del Norte de México*, the classical XV century book on the history of the Virgen of Guadalupe which made available to Europeans, for the first time, a translation from the náhuatl of *Nican Mopohua* ("*Aquí se narra...*"). It contained also a collection of ancient geography books, many published before the times of Louis XIV, which showed California as an island. The list of borrowed books showed the Céspedes' interests as they completed their education in Paris. Books by Richelieu, Cicero, Milton, Task, Fénelon, Horatio, Erasmus of Rotterdam, Racine, Jansénius, Aeschylus and Demosthenes. Having Hervi next door to their Paris home was a priceless opportunity for the cultivated minds of a man and a woman with a passion for learning. Throughout their lives, the Céspedes would never forget the times shared with Didier and his books.

꒰ ⛒ ꒱

6

"Good Americans when they die, go to Paris."
Oliver Wendell Holmes

"Paris is well worth a Mass."
Henri IV of France and Navarre

"In Paris they simply stared when I spoke to them in French;
I never did succeed in making those idiots understand their own language."
Mark Twain

DAILY LIFE IN Paris during the time the Céspedes and their friends explored together the city in the spring of 1843 was rather more interesting than in other cities in Europe, at least for the upper classes. In the circles where María del Carmen and Carlos Manuel moved, men's afternoons were devoted to having late breakfasts in the stylish coffee houses along the *Grands Boulevards*. A meal started with a few dozen oysters, intended to open their appetites. The opening dish was generally followed by a smallish steak, a few choice French dishes, one or two different wines, some cheese, desert and coffee. A repast like that was usually followed by some sort of physical activity, generally walking, riding, driving, gymnastics, pistol shooting, steeple chasing, fencing or pigeon hunting.

For their share of exercise the men retired to the *Bois de Bologne* or their city club. Once a week, most often, men lounged with their friends in one of several luxurious private bath houses around Paris, even if their homes were equipped with bathing conveniences. Dinner followed about eight in the evening, along the same lines as the late breakfast but more elaborate and on a larger scale. Then came the theater and the choices were plentiful: Italian opera, *Academy de Musique*, French Comedy or *Theatre Française*. After the performances a return to the coffee house or a wine lounge was always in order.

The women, on the other hand, had more interesting opportunities and initiatives to pass the time. In the mornings there were exhibitions, volunteer work on a soup kitchen or morning concerts for a play or opera rehearsal, to which a lady of good stead would always be invited. After lunch with their friends, a walk through the *Tuileries*, the *Bois de Boulogne, Luxembourg* or the *Bois de Vincennes* was almost mandatory. A carriage usually followed the ladies close by in case it became too hot or tiresome. In the afternoons, shopping with other women for a blouse, a bonnet, a visit to a modiste, a cap or lingerie entailed careful analysis and deliberation, which was carried out at a *salon* at the home of one of the friends.

At night men and women would finally get together, sometimes for the above mentioned functions, other times to either "receive," pay a visit or attend private dinners and balls. Receiving was an art and an excuse for preempting an afternoon or night on a regular basis and not having to face the question of what to do that day. A lady of status would announce to all her friends that every other Friday afternoon or Tuesday night, for instance, she would be "receiving at home." Once the custom was established it never became conflictive with someone else's date because the unwritten rules were unmistakably clear. Social position would prevail and dictate the social commitments of everyone in the group, lest the competing hostess be condemned to the most severe of social ostracisms.

Whenever visitors from out of town were received, a visit to the Cathedral of Notre Dame was always mandatory. The Cathedral was begun in 1150, under the reign of Louis VII, continued through the reign of the most famous of military wall builders, King Philippe Auguste, and finished by Saint Louis in 1257.

"The Cathedral of Notre Dame," Céspedes would explain to their friends, "was finished just in time for Saint Louis' gift to Paris of what he thought were the legitimate and authentic crown of thorns worn by Christ on His Crucifixion. It is the largest and tallest church in Paris, followed a close second by *Saint Eustache*. Its three doorways are surrounded and surmounted with statues of decapitated Christian martyrs and saints, the work of ancient master masons and sculptors, amended and updated by the revolutionaries of 1789. Above the entrances is the world-renown stained glass rosette, a most beautiful and stunning creation by the greatest of medieval craftsmen."

"The interior of Notre Dame," María del Carmen would interrupt, "shows one hundred and twenty pillars that support an equal number of majestic arches that seem to converge on a marble and porphyry main altar of exquisite beauty and richness. On the sides, hundreds of Gobelin tapestries between which you can discover, under a gloomy haze, some two dozen smaller altars and bas-reliefs fully ornamented but which appear simple in their design because of the sheer colossal magnitude of the entire nave. There resides the magnificent beauty of this church."

Other than *Saint Eustache* and the *Madeleine*, no other church in Paris could compete with *Notre Dame* except perhaps the old Church of *Sainte Geneviève*, which in 1840 was turned into the French National *Pantheon*. This immense Greek style former church was built, starting in 1764, by Louis XV, who persuaded Madame de Pompadour to finance its construction as a *Deo Gratia* for her miraculous cure from a severe illness. The architect had been Sufflot, who designed twenty two immense fluted Corinthian columns, sixty feet in height and six feet in diameter, to sustain a handsome and intricate portico. On top of it, thirty two additional columns support one of the largest domes in Paris, on top of which Sufflot placed a handsome lantern and a bronze statue, capping the total height at 282 feet. By 1842, the decision had already been made to lay to rest Frances' greatest citizens on the crypt at the *Pantheon*, starting with Voltaire and Rousseau. Only two were interred there and later removed for political reasons: Marat for having led the masses to brutality and excesses during the years preceding the Terror and Mirabeau, for allegedly having conspired with Louis XVI and the Austrians for the King's early escape from Paris.

Whenever Carlos Manuel and María del Carmen took guests on tours of Paris, a visit to the *Pantheon* had to be followed with a quick tour of the *librarie de Saint Geneviève*, almost across the street. At the time of the Céspedes' *sojourn* in Paris it contained 200,000 volumes and over 2,500 manuscripts covering all periods in the history of France. The library belonged to the *Collège Henri IV*, on nearby *rue Clovis*. Its most famous reader, during 1495 and 1500, had been Erasmus de Rotterdam (1469-1536), the famous Dutch humanist and scholar, an important figure in patristics and classical literature, who is arguably the first of *philosophes* and the founder of the liberal tradition of European culture.

Around the plaza in front of the *Pantheon*, the Céspedes guests, at the insistence of Domingo Del Monte, also visited the *Collège de Louis le Grand*, the Royal College de France at *No. 1, Place Cambrai*, as well as the quite curious XII Century tower called *La Tour Bichat*.

"This is all that remains from *La Tour de Saint-Jean-de-Latran*," Domingo observed. "It was part the Hall of the Knights *Hospitaliers*, founded in 1171, which became known later on as the *Chevaliers de Malte*. They were heirs to the Knights Templar after October 1311. During the crusades the Order of the *Hospitaliers* provided room and board and the Order of the Templars provided security to the European itinerant volunteers who were trying to recover for Christianity both Jerusalem and the sacred sites in Asia Minor."

A leisurely stroll towards the Seine on the same day they visited the *Pantheon* took the Céspedes and their guests to the *Hôtel de Cluny* and the impressive remains of the Roman *Palais des Termes*. Further down the *rue de Ciceaux* and the *rue de Canettes* they were faced with the Church of Saint Sulpice.

"This is the youngest of the Basilicas in Paris," María del Carmen would explain. "It was finished in 1777, scarcely 12 years before the revolution exploded. The interior is of Corinthian order, the statues are audacious and heroic and all decorations exceptional, particularly the seventeen figures playing musical instruments carved on the organ's surfaces. Its most interesting ornaments, however, are the two immense holy water shells at the entrance, which were presented to Francis I in 1533 by the Republic of Venice."

Carlos Manuel, never intimidated or overly impressed by fame or fortune, could not contain himself saying: "A friend of ours, a talented romantic painter by the name of Eugene Delacroix, has been asked to paint some frescos at the entrance, on the right hand side of the Church."

From Saint Sulpice the Céspedes and his guests descended on the *rue Furstenberg* and finally home through *rue Jacob*. This narrow and old street in the heart of Paris was not without its own charm and history. The Eugene Delacroix that Carlos Manuel had just referred to lived there in 1824, at a house-studio on numbers 19 and 20, as did Richard Wagner from 1841 to 1842, at number 14, the house next door to the one now occupied by the Céspedes. There Carlos Manuel and María del Carmen were frequently visited by Chopin and George Sand, even though at the time they lived quite far at *16, rue Pigalle*, on the other side of the Seine, near Montmartre. Henri-Marie Beyle (1783–1842), the French writer best know by his pseudonym, Stendhal, lived on *52, rue Jacob* from 1808 to 1820. Carlos Manuel, when showing Stendhal's house to his visitors, usually took the opportunity to mention what he liked to call *Stendhal's disease*, "a psychosomatic disorder that produces a rapid heartbeat, vertigo, lightheadedness, confusion and even hallucinations to sufferers, when they are exposed to art, particularly a large amount of art in a confined space, such as a museum." Knowing the playful sense of humor of the otherwise sober Carlos Manuel, few of his friends ever took these references to Stendhal seriously, eventhough the French writer had indeed described such a personal malady in his book *Naples and Florence: A Journey from Milan to Reggio* in 1817.

Another neighbor with a *rue Jacob* address was Jean-Auguste-Dominique Ingres (1780-1867), the French Neoclassical Painter, who lived at number 17 from 1841 to 1845. At *56, rue Jacob* was signed on September 3, 1783, in the presence of Benjamin Franklin, the peace treaty by which Louis XVI, on behalf of the French nation, recognized the independence of the United States. "All in all, not a bad place to live," Céspedes would always mention in jest.

Carlos Manuel, Domingo and Miguel met in the Céspedes' studio after they all had a brief repast in the comfortable chairs at the house's interior patio. As they shared a glass of port, they continued to casually review the many interesting personalities that had lived or frequented the *Quartier de la Monnaie*, as the neighborhood around the Céspedes home was known at the time.

Céspedes, more that Domingo or Miguel, was very interested in Franklin and Jefferson during their days in Paris. Franklin had been sent as ambassador and official diplomat to Paris by the Congress of the Thirteen Colonies at the onset of the American Independence War. His mission was to secure help from France: soldiers, weapons, ships, sailors, money. Upon his arrival he was instantly recognized as the foremost statement and philosopher living in Paris in his time. He promptly used his strategic skills to aid John Paul Jones in his pursuit and capture of British ships, as well as Baron Von Steuben, who was lending his hand in reorganizing the American army in the tragic months of the 1777 to 1878 winter at Valley Forge.

"A parade of *who was who* in Paris began to find their way to Franklin's home in Passy, just west of Paris," Carlos Manuel mentioned as they settled around the studio's large round table and began to enjoy their wine. "The Parisians embraced Franklin as the tangible incarnation and fulfillment of the enlightment philosophy: scholars, writers, painters, musicians, scientists, diplomats, all came to listen to him. Included in the admiring crowd were such prominent French public figures as Condorcet, the Duc de la Rochefoucauld, Raynal, Brissot de Warville, Danton, Mirabeau, the Abbe Sieyès and even an old and tired Voltaire. Franklin's likeness began to appear in medallions and inside the tops of pocket watches," he continued, "and even as a decoration of snuffboxes. Fashionable ladies began to wear their hair *a la Franklin*, with coiffures inspired by his ever present fur caps. During the war Franklin had his fingers and eyes in everything that was happening on the continental side and acted as mediator in many quarrels and conflicts among the

American revolutionaries. After the war, he worked frantically in winning the peace and very skillfully deflated French pretensions of leadership over the American republic."

Céspedes would remember for the rest of his life, particularly during his own ordeals with other leaders of revolutionary Cuba, how Franklin had appealed to the Continental Congress just before the declaration of independence was signed in 1776. He often quoted those words to his friends: "*Gentlemen, we must, indeed, all hang together, or most assuredly we shall all hang separately...*"

Contrary to the opinion of Miguel Aldama, who was more European than from the New World, Céspedes was a believer in America as the land of civic virtue and the cradle of a new faith of natural religion and human rights. Aldama was less enthusiastic about America's positive influence on the world and more mistrustful of the young but colossal giant that was being born north of Cuba.

Céspedes was an incessant defender of the unbound and limitless possibilities of the American experience. He reasoned with many of his friends with the type of arguments that American scholars would use many years later. "The United States Constitution of 1787," he argued, "was the trigger for the enunciation of the Rights of Man in Paris in 1789 as well as the proclamation of the French Constitution of 1791. Franklin and Jefferson were the inspiring souls and sources of both French documents."

Years later historians would identify the venue and the circumstances under which the two Americans were the source of inspiration for the French proclamations. This is the way Céspedes used to present it to his friends many years before scholars would ratify and confirm the essential facts: "It happened on the second floor of a majestic building that later became the French Mint or *Hôtel des Monnaies*, located at the point where *rue Guénégaud*, west of the Pont Neuf, meets the *Quai de Conti*. It was there that Benjamin Franklin met on numerous occasions with Honoré Gabriel Riqueti, Count of Mirabeau, to draft a document which, when approved almost without changes by the Constituent Assembly, became the first French Constitution in 1791." And right thereafter he would add: "Barely one hundred feet down the Seine, west of that location and on the same side of the river, on the palace that Cardinal Mazarine had built for the College of the Four Nations and which Napoleon turned into the *Institute de France*, also on the second floor, Thomas Jefferson met numerous times with Jean-Antoine-Nicolas de Caritat, Marquis de Condorcet, to give form to the French Declaration of the Rights of

Man and Citizen, a document fully inspired on the American Declaration of Independence and the Bill of Rights."

For Carlos Manuel, Domingo Del Monte and Miguel Aldama, Condorcet had been the indisputable leader of the Enlightment in France. Under Varela's tutelage, they had read most of his writings before visiting Paris. They also knew the works of others that had inspired Condorcet's many faceted reflections on social options and the role of technology and the social sciences on society, particularly the works of the economist Turgot and the scientist Priestley.

Jacques Turgot, Baron de l'Aulne (1727-1781), was perhaps the leading economist of 18th Century France. He had been Condorcet's long time mentor and friend, and he had appointed Condorcet as Master of the Mint in 1774. Joseph Priestley (1733-1804) first met Condorcet thought an extensive correspondence he maintained with him from London, where he had reluctantly entered into politics because of his deep concern for religious liberties. He had met Franklin during a trip of the American to London in 1766 and became his lifelong friend. Franklin was a world class scientist and showman and first knew Condorcet in 1778, when as secretary of the French Royal Academy of Sciences he invited Franklin to receive a prestigious honorary membership. It was Condorcet who delivered Franklin's eulogy on his death in 1790. Through the academy they both came to know Lavoisier, who had served in the 1770s at Turgot's Ministry of the Marine and later on in his Office of *Comptroller General de la France*. Turgot, in turn, introduced Condorcet, Franklin and Lavoisier to Adam Smith, of *Wealth of Nation's* fame.

Carlos Manuel enjoyed studying these intricate and mutually supporting public and private relationships, and these musings provided him with a valuable insight on how things were accomplished in the real life world of politics and government. These studies also educated him first hand on some of the ironies of history and politics.

"Turgot," Céspedes would tell the story, "had commissioned Lavoisier to study and prepare a report on how to humanize life at the *Châtelet*, the *Abbaye*, *l'Hôtel de la Force*, *Bicêtre*, *Salpêtrière*, the *Conciergerie* and other French prisons. Before he had time to finish it, he was accused unjustly by Marat, whom Lavoiser had vetoed for a seat at the French Royal Academy of Sciences. Lavoisier was taken to the prison at the Paris Observatory, from where he was taken to the guillotine in less than 48 hours. What was probably the last of his letters was addressed to his good friend Benjamin Franklin."

Carlos Manuel was vividly taken by all those episodes during the years when the Americans were trying to secure the support of France for its independence. As any good *raconteur* would do, he would continue his stories for all those who wanted to hear.

"Unlike Franklin," he would say, "when Jefferson arrived in Paris he was a total unknown, even though he had authored the Declaration of Independence and the Virginia Declaration of Religious Freedom. Jefferson was of course in his thirties, while Franklin was already in his seventies. It was Lafayette who introduced Jefferson to the right people. Making good use of Lafayette's endorsements, Jefferson plunged into these influential circles with an energy and exuberance that made him as personally popular and as useful to the American cause as Franklin."

"Much as Laffitte would do with Carlos Manuel de Céspedes half a Century later," interrupted Domingo Del Monte.

"Thanks for the undeserved tribute of this parallel," replied Carlos Manuel. "I would be very honored if I could approximate the personality of Jefferson from a kilometer away! But thanks anyway for your good intentions," he added lightheartedly.

"What caught the attention of most French intellectuals," Céspedes would continue, "was Jefferson's passionate refutation of George Louis LeClerc de Buffon, the great French natural historian, who had proposed that the North American soil was so impoverished compared to Europe's that its flora and fauna, including human beings, had degenerated, declined in size and showed diminished energy."

"There goes our beliefs in the sincerity and intellectual honesty of French natural historians," quipped Miguel Aldama.

"Oh, no," answered Céspedes. "This man was a genius in his time. Madame de Staël quoted many times his proverbs, such as *Genius is Having a Greater Aptitude for Patience*, or *Sharp is the Kiss of the Falcon's Beak*. He was a good friend of Voltaire and was admitted to the French Academy at age 27. He wrote *Histoire Naturelle, Générale et Particulière* in 44 volumes. It included everything known about the natural world up until his times. In the field of mathematics he wrote *Sur le Jeu de Franc-Carreau*, where he was the first to bring differential and integral calculus into probability theory. In fact, there is a classical problem in probability theory called *Buffon's Needle*, which has not been solved to date. He was a true genius."

"But apparently he was kissed on the head with the Falcon's beak," added Miguel teasingly.

"I think he wrote so much, and tried to innovate and challenge the classical knowledge in so many fields that he ended up making a lot of mistakes," replied Céspedes on a serious tone. "By the time he died in 1788, people were calling an exaggeration or a wrong conclusion in science a *buffoonery* in English, a *bouffonnerie* in French, a *bufonada* in Spanish, a *buffoneria* in Italian, and so on."

"On a more serious tone, Carlos Manuel, don't you think that this episode of Buffon's put down of the flora and the fauna of the new continent was a disguised expression of the anti North American sentiment that was brewing in France?" added Miguel.

"Oh, there is something to that, of course," replied Carlos. "Strangely enough the French have found many reasons through the years to be disdainful of the United States, quite often in ways which violate all the normal canons of logic."

"I agree. It probably goes back to the days when the French spent too many of their energies on the old continent and were very late in understanding and claiming for themselves some of the new lands on the other side of the Atlantic."

"Yes, they got there late, when the British had taken possession of the east coast of North America and the Spaniards of the South, the Center and the West of the Continent. The French went to the extreme of forming alliances with the Indians in central North America to harass and throw the Brits to the sea. It was there, while accosting the westernmost enclaves of the thirteen colonies that they first met and fought George Washington, then a young officer of the British army defending a fort in the Ohio valley. It was a logical consequence to fight him again when he became the founder of the new Republic."

"I agree. The anti United States feelings by the French started there. It soon became an obsession for the French, particularly for the *philosophes* and the politicians. That explains Buffon's blunders many years later."

"Do not forget the words of Voltaire in his *Essai sur les Mœurs* (An Essay about Customs and Morals): «*Once again America is being rediscovered and revisited with disappointment and repulsion.*» Voltaire, as most encyclopedists, including Diderot himself, made many times the point that the devastation that the conquistadores and the detestable British had made in America had rendered it a worthless land, deprived of any beauty and value. Those opinions had a great deal of impact on very learned people such as Buffon."

"For naturalists in the XVIII century, the maturity of civilizations corresponded to the age of the land they occupied. Looking at North

America as a new continent, they held the opinion that there was a psychological and intellectual immaturity in the territories they had missed to claim."

Carlos stood up, reached for several books in his library and after setting them on the table began to search for some pages he had marked as important to read.

"I have here three books that will amaze people in the future. Buffon's 1749 *Variétés dans l'Espèce Humaine*, Cornelius De Pauw's *Recherches Philosophiques sur les Américains*, published in 1768 and the Abbé Guillaume Thomas de Raynal's *Histoire Philosophique et Politique des Européens dans les Deux Indes*, published in Genève in 1781, which many people claim it was actually written by Diderot. If you want to document the origins of the anti North American feelings amongst the French intellectuals, just listen to what these learned gentlemen were saying in the second half of the XVIII century. Please notice that these men had never even visited North America."

He then began to quote from Buffon's: *"North America is a gloomy immensity, more upsetting than hostile, more distressing than frightening. In that continent, the colors die out, the contours vanish. The lines of all things get lost to the misty horizons. Ocean, earths, lagoons, all mingle and get confused. It is a diminished world, an aborted world, a shrunken universe, where the living vegetates, where the men grow pale themselves, and the species shorten their size. The species are smaller. The animals are weaker. So is man. All animals moved from the former world into the new, show, without exception, a sensitive change, of either their shape, or their instinct, or both. It could not be otherwise for men."*

"You can sense the anti North American disparagement by those few words," exclaimed Domingo.

"What did Franklin and Jefferson do when they read those opinions? They were in Paris at the time and I doubt if they remained silent," added Miguel.

"Franklin decided to take things on his own terms," replied Carlos Manuel. "He organized a large party at his mansion in Passy, and invited an equal number of Americans living in Paris and Frenchmen. The Abbé Raynal was the guest of honor. Buffon never showed up. After commenting extensively about the American "smallness" he invited everyone to stand up and be measured. He jokingly called Raynal *"a mere shrimp"* since he happened to be the smallest person in the party. Raynal refused to argue and became visibly upset. From there on, all references to size were eliminated from *L'Historie des Deux Indes*. But Raynal added a paragraph to his book that proclaimed that the land in North America was so poor that it probably will never sustain more than perhaps 10 million people altogether.

"Jefferson then took over," added Carlos Manuel. "He began to offer lectures at many *salons* and brought from America, at his own expense, a live moose from Vermont, which was a sensation in Paris; a full grown mountain lion from the Carolinas and a beautiful cougar skin from Ohio. The moose and the lion became part of the North American collection at the *Jardin des Plants* in Paris. The cougar skin went back to Virginia after the Jeffersons departed for home. The three French naturalists were thoroughly discredited by the eloquence of Thomas Jefferson and the disclosure of their absolute lack of evidence. Buffon died in 1788, without recoiling from his mistakes. Raynal fell out of favor with the revolution when he criticized the excesses of 1791 and De Pauw, who lived until 1799, changed his interests and began to write about the Greeks and the Egyptians."

"This is very French: not admitting a mistake," added Miguel.

"Years later," Carlos continued, "when the United States signed Jay's Treaty with England, a violent and dirty press campaign against the North Americans exploded in France. The French corsairs began to attack the ships from the United States all over the Atlantic and the press in North America began to refer to the situation as the "undeclared war" with the French. It was simply a continuation of the French politicians' ill will towards the United States."

"It was partly due to the refusal by Thomas Jefferson, when he became President, to allow a strong French influence in North American affairs. The French believed they were entitled to it," added Domingo.

"Of course, the worst was yet to come." replied Carlos Manuel.

"How so?" inquired Miguel.

"The worst anti United States actions in those times are associated with the sinister figure of Charles Maurice de Talleyrand Perigord, who we all know from the history of the French Revolution. He was 35 years old at the onset of the revolution and lived to be 84. In 1794 Talleyrand, afraid of the radicalization of the revolution, went into exile in America. In his frequent correspondence with Madame de Staël he mentioned not only his displeasure for not being able to participate in public affairs and on profitable business opportunities in America but also complained frequently of what he thought was the mediocrity of American life. He was desperately bored without conspiracies, spectacles, meetings and intrigue. He was also startled that the American government was closer to England than to France."

Céspedes went back to his book collection and began to quote from the correspondence of Talleyrand with Madame de Staël and with Stendhal.

"*L'Amerique est cependant tout anglaise*," he wrote to her in 1795. To Stendhal, who had also become fiercely anti American, he wrote «*Treinte-deux religions et un seul plat: rosbif-pommes de terre.*» (this is a country of thirty two religions and only one dish: steak and potatoes).

"Years later, at a meeting of the *Institute de France* on *5 Germinal*, year II, while he was back as Minister of Foreign Relations of the *Directoire*, Talleyrand wrote: "America is not the peaceful wilderness that Rousseau would have dreamed. It is full of *cabanes mal bâties, peuples de rustauds apathiques, paysans perverties et des bûcherons indolents.* (poorly built cabins inhabited by apathetic slobs, perverted peasants and sleepy lumbermen). These are poor people without desires, whose vices are aggravated by their ignorance. They do not appreciate the grandiose spectacle that surrounds them; they do not have either sensibility or good taste and are only interested in how many times a tree has to be hit with an axe before it falls," Céspedes added as he finished quoting Talleyrand.

"Somewhere I read," added Domingo, "that Talleyrand was asked by Napoleon what he thought of the Americans and Talleyrand response was: *Sire, ce sont de fiers cochons, et des cochons fiers* (My Lord, these are proud and reliable pigs)."

"Yes, I have read that too," replied Carlos Manuel.

"Stendhal has been in many ways the intellectual who has most contributed to the bad will against the Americans in France," Carlos Manuel added. "He set the pattern for many French politicians and intellectuals to follow over the years."

"Listen to Stendhal's words, and I am quoting faithfully from one of his books: *Je ne puis vivre avec des hommes incapables d'idées fines, si vertueux qu'ils soient; je préférerais cent fois les moeurs d'une cour corrompue. Washington m'eut ennuyé à la mort, et j'aime mieux me trouver dans le même salon que M. de Talleyrand. Donc, la sensation de l'estime n'est pas tout pour moi ; j'ai besoin des plaisirs donnés par une ancienne civilisation* (I can not live with men incapable of fine ideas, regardless of how virtuous they are; I do prefer a hundred times the mores of a corrupt court. The capital city of Washington bores me to death, and I'd rather be at any gathering with M. de Talleyrand. After all, a sensation of esteem is not everything for me; I need the pleasures given by an old civilization)."

"He went on," added Carlos Manuel, "The American morals are of an abominable vulgarity. Reading the best works of their most distinguished writers I can not but have a single desire: never to meet them. This is the triumph of mediocrity and egotism."

"Will this resentment ever finish?" asked Miguel.

"On the part of the French men of letters and their political leaders... I do not think so," responded Céspedes. "Their arrogance and haughtiness knows no bounds. They truly believe they are infallible and everybody else is not. They are unable to retrace their steps and acknowledge failure. They will forever persist in their errors rather than admit they were wrong. How can they live with themselves if they have to recognize that because of their revolution they practically deserted the claims they had stalked in America? How can they admit that they prioritized the rescue of a few sugar plantations in Haiti over the immense wealth they neglected to safeguard in the Louisiana? How can anyone expect them to concede that Napoleon was a cultivated dictator who made the worst land trade ever known in the history of human civilization? They have to disdain the lost lands and the vanished influence over the United States by claiming them as inferior, crude, vulgar and hollow. That would apply to anything that comes from the United States. That's the only way they can live with the reality that it was already theirs and it was all lost."

"Certain French educated classes feel very comfortable bad-mouthing America," added Domingo. "After all, in French culture what you say is as important or more important that what you do. As they continue to repeat these fallacies about the United States, the dejected fantasies become reality in their minds. Hence, they are convinced that it was not a land worth their time and trouble. No big loss for them."

"For the French, not only what they say is more important than what they do," concluded Carlos Manuel, "but the more eloquence and expressiveness they use when they say it, the more important and the more real it becomes."

"So be it with our friends the French," added Miguel.

～ ⅩⅠ ～

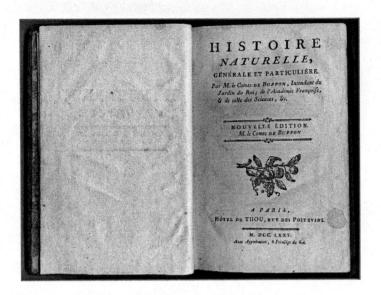

THE 1775 EDITION OF BUFFON'S *HISTOIRE NATURELLE*

George Louis Leclerc, Comte de Buffon (1707-1788) shone throughout Europe as one of its top naturalists, mathematicians, biologists, cosmologists and writers. His theories influenced two generations of scientists, Jean Baptiste Lamarck and Charles Darwin among others. He was elected to the French Academy at age 27, when he had already established a close relationship with Voltaire. He published 36 volumes of his *Histoire Naturelle* between 1749 and 1789. Eight more volumes were published by his disciples after his death. His works have never been out of print since.
Above copy from the collection of the author.

7

ON A RAINY day the Céspedes would take their guests to visit the Parisian shopping arcades or *Passages Couverts*. The idea of constructing a covered shopping gallery in Paris first occurred to Louis Philippe, Duc d'Orleans, Louis XVI cousin, who before the revolution had possession of what had been the *Palais Cardinal* and was by then the *Palais-Royal*. It can be argued that he was history's first real estate speculator and large scale property developer. After all, only the Parisian royalty and the church of France had the means to embark on large scale construction projects in the XVIII and XIX Centuries.

The rest of the Parisians were merchants, artisans, laborers, peasants, bureaucrats, teachers or intellectuals, although the term had not yet being used to designate the workers of the intellect. The Duc d'Orleans initiated the concept of building a gallery on the back gardens of his palace and had it built by 1786. The architect was Victor Louis, who designed 120 boutiques along two long identical buildings across the full length of the royal gardens. Soon other passages were built around the concept, the *Passage Feydeau* in 1791 (demolished in 1824), as well as the *Passage du Caire* in 1798, the longest ever in Paris (370 meters) and the *Passage des Panoramas* in 1799, probably still the most opulent and sumptuous during the time the Céspedes were living in Paris.

The passages were well lit and elegant places where Parisians would meet to chat and shop far from the noise, the smudge, the rubble and the detritus and hustle of city streets and the menacing speed of horse-drawn vehicles. They usually had a glass or painted ceiling, with glass paneled shops and boutiques whose fronts were separated by elegant marble columns. For the merchants they were an ideal controlled environment where their wares were protected from the environment and could be safely displayed.

Louis Sébastien Mercier, the great Parisian urbanite and anthropologist best described the benefits of the passages in these terms in 1828: *"Dans une ville de luxe et de badauderie ou il était désagréable sinon périlleux de s'aventurer dans la rue, la foule des flâneurs devait se porter vers les rares endroits qui lui offraient la possibilité de s'attarder devant les magasins sans craindre de bousculades ou d'accident..."* (In a city of luxury and curiosity where it is unpleasant if not perilous to venture in the streets, the crowd of strollers and onlookers has to behave themselves in those rare places that offer them the possibility to stay late at the stores without fearing hustles or accidents).

There were close to one hundred and fifty passages at the time the Céspedes were living in Paris. Most of them would be gone after Baron Haussmann undertook a complete redesign of the Parisian geography during the Second Empire. The passages were either destroyed to make room for great avenues, such as the *Passage du Bourg-l'Abbé*, which had to be demolished to make room for the *Boulevard Sebastopol*, or perished under the competitive impact of the *Grands Magasins*, which offered vast interior spaces and the elegant and rational display of many more goods.

The beautiful *Galerie Colbert*, a pricey passage between *rue Vivienne* and *rue Petit-Champs*, had a favorite luncheon spot for the Céspedes: *le Grand Colbert*, the most famous of watering places in Paris, where senior librarians and wealthy academics visiting the *Bibliothèque Nationale* would converge early in the afternoon.

Lunch could be followed by a visit to the *Galerie Vivienne*, whose flamboyant *décor* of Grecian motifs was ideal to browse and search for *incunabula* in its antiquarian bookstores. Three blocks west one would find the *Passage Choiseul* between the *rue des Petit-Champs* and *rue Saint Augustin*, and there one could shop for used books and fine printers and stationers along its entire two hundred meter expensively tiled length.

Of all the passages and galleries that were frequented by Carlos Manuel and María del Carmen, however, none had the allure of the *Passage des Panoramas*. It was situated between the Bourse and the *Grands Boulevards* and had been designed and built by Jean Louis Victor Grisart in 1800, at the place where the house of Montmorency-Luxembourg had been. Parisians very appropriately called it the *"el dorado"* of passages. At the *Panoramas*, five separate arcades intersected and were home to close to a hundred shops, cafés and boutiques: Galleries Feydeau, St-Marc, Des Variétés, Montmartre, and Panama.

The *Passage des Panoramas* owed it name, of course, to two enormous *Panoramas* that James Thayer, an American entrepreneur had commissioned from Pierre Prévost, an artist devoted almost exclusively to painting these oversized compositions so popular in the XIX Century. Thayer had acquired the gardens in the north side of the Hotel de Montmorency-Luxembourg, which fronted on the *Grands Boulevards*. Two towers, 56 ft in diameter and 66 ft high were built and two Panoramas painted inside them, an aerial view of Paris and a view of Toulon after the evacuation by the British in 1793. The space between the towers became the entrance to the passage. By the time the Céspedes and their guests went visiting Paris, a third tower and panorama had been built and Paris was smitten and infatuated with the whole panorama concept. They were being built everywhere.

On the eastern side of the panorama with the aerial view of Paris a medium size auditorium called the *Théatre des Variétés* had been built in 1807. Adjoining the theatre there was a *Café des Variétés*, owned by the same family that owned the *Théatre*. There, a 22 year old itinerant violinist called Jacob, recently arrived to Paris from Cologne, was allowed to play the cello for the meager coins the patrons would drop on his hat. The Céspedes were frequent visitors of the Café, which had been enlarged in 1831 and had become a favorite place to have an afternoon snack in the midst of actors, playwrights, journalists, critics and literary types. They engaged the young cellist in conversation quite often and learned that his father, Juda Eberst, was a cantor, bookbinder, music teacher and composer. The entire family had fled the Cologne area due to the Napoleonic edict requiring that Jews had to uproot themselves from their familiar places and take new, inheritable family names. They were all now in Paris, the young man having converted to Catholicism and changed his name to Jacques, after leaving behind *Offenbach am Main*, the town where they had lived for many generations.

The passages that the Céspedes so often visited in Paris were very popular throughout Europe, not only for their immense variety of goods but also for the quality and competitiveness of the prices offered. Even though England was at the peak of its industrial revolution and had become a powerhouse of looms and fabric making, Europeans and visiting Americans were convinced that the cloth manufactured in France was much more durable and fashionable and, most of all, since the workmen were paid much lower wages, you could have a superior purchase in France for a lower price.

On a letter from Domingo Del Monte to José Antonio Saco, both probably among the best dressed investors and businessmen who visited Paris often in the first half of the XIX Century, you could read: "I can freely recommend to you M. Courtois at the Montagnes Russes, number 11, *rue Neuve des Petit Champs*, facing *rue Vivienne*. You will be treated with high regard for the worth of the goods and you will be pleased with the solidity and neatness of the execution, as well as the punctuality in the delivery of all engagements..."

On another letter of Domingo, this time to Gaspar Betancourt Cisneros (1803-1866), also a fashion-conscious Cuban investor and man of the world, he stated: "The difference in prices is immense. You would be asked seven pounds and seven shillings for a good coat with the best cloth in London, but M. Courtois will only charge you one hundred Francs (four pounds) and his workmanship will probably be better..."

A letter from Cuban lyric musician Cirilo Villaverde (1812-1894), another *amateur de Paris*, to the same Gaspar Betancourt Cisneros, in 1838 stated: "French shoes spare you the torture of new shoes. They are never felt as rough and tight as a new pair of English shoes. I always visit M. Deschamps at *14, Galerie d'Orleans*, at the *Palais-Royal*. He is so popular here that his reputation has crossed the channel and he has to minister to many of his clients in London at least twice a year..."

Carlos Manuel and María del Carmen also frequented and made extensive use of the *Bibliothèque du Roi*, or Royal Library, situated within a short distance from the passages on *rue Richelieu*. What a splendid institution it was, they thought. It held nearly one million books and bound pamphlets, many of them the legacy of the difficult political times of the French Revolution, when everyone that had the means and inclination had his or her views known by putting together a few pages. The library contained eighty thousand manuscripts, some of them dating from the times of Eleanor of Aquitaine and the reigns of her sons Louis VII, King of France and Henry II,

King of England. You could also see in the library one hundred thousand medals, over a million engravings and three hundred thousand maps and charts.

The library had been founded by Saint Louis King of France, who had first collected a few books on an apartment attached to his personal chapel. It was Louis XV who formally established the library at the old residence of Cardinal Mazarine. The Cardinal was the successor of Cardinal Richelieu as Prime Minister of France. He was actually born in the Italian region of Abruzzo, then part of the Kingdom of Naples. He became immensely rich and owned the Villa Borghese in Rome by the time he governed over the French while Louis XIV was a child king. It was a great irony that the *Bibliothèque du Roi,* opened in his former residence, became the main depositary of countless abusive and satirical pamphlets called *Mazarinades*, published against him, which often invoked his Italian heritage.

There were many other shops to satisfy daily necessities in the area around the passages in Paris. María del Carmen, who had become an experienced gourmet cook in Paris visited many great kitchens which were inspired on the precepts of Jean Anthelme Brillat-Savarin (1755-1826), the renown French politician and gourmet, who is noted for his *Physiologie de Goût* (1825), a witty dissertation on the art of dining. For her own household she had trained the handmaids to serve in the style called *service á la Russe*, whereby dishes were prepared and plated into individual portions before being served to the diner and a series of dishes were served in succession. Occasionally, however, dinner at the Céspedes household would be served *à la Française*, where each course was made up of a large number of dishes served in platters or fountains from which the diners served themselves.

María del Carmen was the type of woman who could easily insert a knowledgeable analysis of French cuisine while enlivening a most intricate political, literary or philosophical conversation or polemical discussion. She would take Rosa Aldama in her shopping trips throughout Paris, but never could convince Gertrudis to come along. For the finest stationery and visiting cards needed for the Céspedes family, María del Carmen preferred to make her purchases and place her orders at *159, rue Saint Honoré*, next door to the *Eglise Réformée de l'Oratoire*, across from the Louvre. Good cutlery was purchased and conditioned at M. Renaud, at number *416, rue Saint Honoré*.

For medical supplies, general pharmacy, household chemicals and other pharmacological specialties she preferred the establishment of M. Joseau at *161, rue Montmartre*, where the service and personal attention were impeccable. She was also a good client of what she considered the best merchants for earthenware and crockery in Paris, at the establishment of Messrs. Danneville, number *16, rue d'Aguesseau,* near the *Faubourg Saint Honoré.* There were also visits, of course, to *Les Halles,* known at the time as the "stomach of Paris," the central marketplace founded by King Philippe August II when he had a shelter constructed for street food merchants and itinerant vendors who came from all over the city to sell their wares and produce around the Church of Saint Eustache.

The *rue de Richelieu,* cutting across a neighborhood where most of the Parisian passages were, ran from the *Grands Boulevards* to the Louvre. As it got close to the Seine it crossed the point where there was a gate in the Auguste Philippe barrier through which Joan of Arc once attempted to enter into Paris. It was the high society street during most of the XIX Century.

Four early American Presidents lived at *rue Richelieu* before they served in Washington: John Adams, second President of the US who in 1798 refused to pay a substantial bribe to French Minister Talleyrand, lived with his wife Abigail Adams, at number 17; Thomas Jefferson, third President of the US and main author of its Declaration of Independence, lived at number 30; James Monroe, fifth President of the US, who bought Florida from the Spaniards and who as Ambassador to France saved Thomas Paine from execution, lived at number 95; and John Quincy Adams, sixth President of the US and son of President John Adams, its first abolitionist and champion of free speech, was a resident at number 97.

In addition, the stables of Cardinal Richelieu were located at number *6, rue Richelieu;* Auguste Comte died on *rue Richelieu* at number 34; Diderot at number 39 and Molière across the street at number 40, not far from Madame de Pompadour, who expired at a rather large home at number 50. The Céspedes would also always point out to their guests that Simon Bolivar, at the time he attended the coronation of Napoleon on December 2, 1804, lived at number *55, rue Richelieu,* across the glorious and imposing building of the *Bibliothèque du Roi.*

8

"Is life so dear, or peace so sweet, as to be purchased
at the price of chains or slavery? Forbid it, Almighty God! I know not what
course others may take but as for me; give me liberty or give me death!"
Patrick Henry

"I prefer liberty with danger than peace with slavery."
Jean Jacques Rousseau

"Although volume upon volume is written to prove
slavery a very good thing, we never hear of the man who wishes
to take the good of it by being a slave himself."
Abraham Lincoln

IN THE MID 1840's, during the times the Céspedes lived in
Paris, the American term "High Life," meaning life in the upper stra-
tum of society, had not yet being coined. Whenever people wanted
to refer to someone as a seasoned person that enjoyed an interesting
and active life and had the means to sustain it, they would say: *Est-il*
du Monde? (does he/she belong to the world, or is he/she a person of
the world?). The British called it *"the ton,"* with the clear implication
that those who did not have the interest or the means did not exist at
all. And belonging *to the world* or *to the ton* meant to be seen in the
right places and in the right company.

Serious politicians and men of intellect, such as Benjamin Franklin, Condorcet, Necker and Voltaire before the revolution and Balzac,
Perrier, Laffitte, Louis Napoleon, Antonin de Noailles and others
after the revolution preferred to be seen at the *Café Procope*, where
they spent countless hours every week at meetings and scholarly
discourse. Elegant and somewhat frivolous men of fashion had as
their center of gravity the *Jockey Club*, where glamorous physical exercise prevailed over mental stress. The "men of the world" of the
Jockey Club regularly trotted their horses at the *Champs Elysées*, at the
Bois de Boulogne or on the *Boulevards*, where they congregated around
the figure of the Comte d'Artois, the future Charles X. It was the
Count, the earliest Bourbon to seek refuge in England and the last to

return to France, who introduced in Paris the English fondness for horses.

Women with social or political ambitions and ladies of fashion, on the other hand, had as the favorite place of leisure, gallantry and easy conversation, the *Café Tortoni*, at the *Boulevard des Italiens*. Tortoni had been a Neapolitan who came with a friend to Paris to supply its elegant upper classes with good *gelato*. He lost his well connected partner of an infection of the lungs and with him went all the social links the young entrepreneurs had hoped to establish in Napoleonic Paris. Tortoni persevered by himself and in a few years his café was such a success that it was difficult to get a reservation there at any time of the day.

In the mornings, for breakfast, there was never a lack of dueling survivors whose honors had just been elucidated, as well as retired army officers, who congregated in great numbers to trade personal accounts of heroism. They were served cold *pâtés*, game, fowl, fish, eggs, broiled kidneys, iced champagne, and liqueurs from every part of the globe. In the afternoons and at night, all roads leading to *Tortoni's* were choked up with carriages of the rich, the courtesans and the beautiful people of Paris, every day including Sundays. Many noble ladies, as well as young damsels, old maids, widows with matrimonial ambitions and dowagers were there regularly. Also a sizable group of old and young men, hard working or kept, athletic or unfit, who went to *Tortoni's* frequently to either feast and celebrate with their legitimate spouses or to pour out their sentimental chatter into welcoming ears. Few knew that although Tortoni succeeded in amassing a large fortune, he became morose and insane a few years after opening his Café. To the consternation of the lady who opened the Café in the mornings, breakfast one day had to be served late because, in the late hours of the night, after closing the establishment, Tortoni had hanged himself.

It was at *Tortoni's*, two days after arriving in Paris, that Gertrudis Gómez de Avellaneda was invited to have coffee with María de las Mercedes Beltrán de Santa Cruz y Montalvo, the Countess of Merlin. The Countess was eager to meet Gertrudis, whom she considered a literary genius after reading most of her yet meager but very successful works. Likewise, no writer of any transcendence visited Paris in the first half of the XIX Century without calling on the Countess of Merlin.

María de las Mercedes was a crucial figure to both the Cuban nationalistic tradition and its literature in general. During her lifetime she had authored numerous novels, travel accounts and memoirs and became, outside of Cuba, one of Cuba's most acclaimed authors. She was born into a rich and educated *criollo* family in Havana on February 5, 1789. At age 14 she traveled to Spain to complete her education, and it was there that she entered in contact with many important figures of the musical, literary and artistic worlds. There she met and married Antoine Christophe Merlin, a French Count who, when the French occupation of Spain ended in 1813, returned to Paris with his wife. There María de las Mercedes soon became one of the *belles dames* of Paris. It was not until 1840 that the Countess traveled to New York and then briefly to Havana upon the death of her husband.

Having returned to the city of her birth, María de las Mercedes wrote there *La Havanne*, an ambitious three volume summary of the socio-political situation in her native country. In 1842 she returned to Paris, where she coincided with Gertrudis Gómez de Avellaneda, who was visiting the Céspedes and was their guest at the house on *rue Jacob*. An intense friendship developed between Gertrudis and María de las Mercedes.

The Countess of Merlin already had a well earned reputation for her many literary successes: *Mis Doce Primeros Años* in 1833; *Memoires d'une Creole* in 1835; *Ocios de una Mujer de Gran Mundo*, in 1838; *L'Esclavage aux Colonies Espagnoles*, in 1840. Gertrudis, aged 28 and a well known poet on her own right, spend many hours sharing experiences and literary insights with María de las Mercedes, who was then 53. A few years after her own return to Madrid, Gertrudis contributed a biography of the Countess to the edition of María de las Mercedes' *Viaje a la Habana* published by the *Sociedad Literaria y Tipográfica* of Madrid in 1844. The Countess went on to write *Les Lionnes de Paris*, in 1845 and *Le Duc d'Athenes* in 1848, both published in Paris a few years after her death in 1852 at age 63.

Also invited for the occasion was Josefina Cipresti Polanco, a long standing and rather well dressed and coiffed resident of Paris whom the Countess had met at *Tortoni's* a few months earlier. The Countess did not know too much about Mme. Cipresti Polanco but she admired the vitality and *élan* of a woman that, not much older than herself, had a seemingly unending reservoir of energy and wisdom.

Josefina Cipresti Polanco had been born in Valencia, Estado Carabobo, Venezuela, on September 22, 1784. She was the illegitimate daughter of Don Pedro J. de Urrutia, Governor of Cumaná, Venezuela, and Georgina Cipresti y Montes, a seamstress in the small town of Cumaná, which at the time consisted of about one hundred small houses, constructed of wood and mud covered with straw. She was raised by Basilio Julián Arriaga, a foreman of the General Chartered West India Company of the United Netherlands, in the farming communities around the rivers Amacura and Maroco in northern Venezuela.

As her mother did, Josefina became a seamstress at an early age, after she immigrated to Caracas in 1797. There she soon became mistress to Roberto Antonio Dávila Uzcátegui, an auxiliary Bishop of Caracas who, for obvious reasons, could not be seen in public with her. His solution was to compel her to marry his older brother, Gaspar García Dávila Uzcátegui, a marriage of convenience that was never consummated. After years of hiding her liaison with the Bishop, Josefina started a long series of intimate affairs with several prominent nobles in the capital of Venezuela as the result of which she had a daughter in 1819, whom she baptized after her mother as Georgina Cipresti Dávila.

Josefina emigrated with her daughter to the United States in 1824, after marrying in Caracas Daniel Parkhurst Leadbetter, of Holmes County, Ohio, a Foreign Service officer assigned as Auxiliary Consul General for Venezuela who became the Representative from Ohio's 13th District between 1837 and 1841. In 1842 Josefina and Daniel moved to Paris, where he had been assigned as Commercial Attaché. Daniel died the following year, leaving Josefina, 58, and Georgina, 23, in the most abject of miseries. Fortune smiled however for mother and daughter when Josefina met an older Spanish nobleman, Ignacio Boix de la Revilla Donoso y Oliván, Count de la Paniega, 62 at the time, who was the publisher of the *Biblioteca Enciclopédica Española*. Josefina offered the wealthy Count to marry her daughter Georgina, a ravishing, seductive and well educated young woman in the prime of her life, an offer that the aging Count could not refuse.

The newlyweds and the matchmaker settled in Paris, near Napoleon's *Arch de Triomphe*, in a beautiful apartment at *85, Avenue de Neuilly* which the Count presented to his stunning wife as a wedding present. The asymmetrical couple soon made a habit of summering by the seaside in Cannes, hitting the Chamonix slopes in the winter and resting in Venice in the springtime, always in the company of the eternally vigilant Josefina. The older and mistrusting Cipresti, knowing as she well did of the many temptations of the flesh for a young woman of Georgina's enchantments, became the vigilant enforcer of her daughter's reluctant but compulsory fidelity to the Count. On their European *sejours* the family was always preceded and followed by a well staffed and befitting retinue of servants.

After the Countess, the literary genius and the courtesan had sat on the second floor of *Tortoni's*, at a table facing the Boulevard, the conversation inevitably drifted towards Cuba and its current political and human events. Gertrudis Gómez, or Tula, as she was known among her friends, had just published *Sab* in Spain, probably the first full length novel in history dealing with slavery. It was an impassioned story of a young mulatto slave who falls in love with his white owner's daughter. The novel had been very controversial in Spain, and there were rumors of condemnation by the Spanish Church, government defamation accusations by the Royal house and a threat of confiscation of all the copies for sale in the bookstores of Madrid. Aside from presenting the subhuman treatment which slaves had to bear, the novel also had a powerful message of the deplorable matrimonial and societal subservience of women in Spanish society, an additional reason for the Church to contest and oppose its publication. The countess had already read *Sab*. Josefina had not heard of Gertrudis, much less read any of her works.

Gertrudis opened the conversation. "Nowadays Havana is a city convulsed between the need for justice in the issue of slavery and its fear of economic ruin," she said. "The social mores of our times fully approve of slavery. Even among Cuban patriots known to you and I," clearly referring to María de las Mercedes, "many are either pro-slavery or totally indifferent to the cause of black men. Many own slaves themselves, if they have the means and the need. Even those who oppose the traffic of slaves do not necessarily oppose slavery itself, only the commercialization and trade in human beings."

"Naturally," added the Countess. "The Cuban economy has been booming since the first third of this Century, in good part because of its easy access to an almost unlimited supply of cheap labor. Cuban entrepreneurs are not sure the good times could be maintained if the slaves were to be freed. They fear the Spanish throne yielding to the pressures from the British since the Act of 1814. Cuban independence would signify the liberation of the slaves because the British would pressure the new Republic very hard. Of course, there is the concern that the island could fall in the hands of the powerful economic interests of Southern United States. If we become Americans, Cuba would inevitably be an enclave of pro slavers."

"On the other hand," added Gertrudis, "the Cuban *criollos* are very concerned with the results of the 1841 census in Cuba."

"Why is that so?" asked the Countess.

"The black population, slaves and free men, has finally exceeded that of whites," she explained.

"There are rumors in Europe that the British want to invade Cuba, proclaim the end of slavery, and bring Cuba into their fold as the Ethiopic-Cuban Republic," said María de las Mercedes. Both agreed this was a crazy idea, without an iota of support in the island.

"Look at the surge of annexationist ideas in Cuba after the Revolution in Haiti," said María Mercedes. "If Cuba were to fold in the arms of the United States it would be as a southern State and slavery would linger for a few more years."

"The Spanish crown has the intention of liberating all slaves if the hacendados and slave owners in Cuba were to support independence," said Tula. "I have no doubt of that. The Spaniards would rather have another Haiti on their hands than acquiesce to the desires of the *criollos* to govern themselves. But they do not believe in autonomy either. To the stubborn mother country it is all or nothing. Like a scorned woman that would rather see her lover dead than in the hands of another woman."

"Yes, the *criollos* would welcome independence with slavery. If some of them were to offer freedom to the slaves to get their support in an independence war, the vast majority of *criollos* would turn to Spain or the Americans. The hacendados are as stubborn as the Spaniards. They would rather see the island continue in the hands of Spain or to fall in the hands of the British or the Americans rather than relinquish their right to have slaves," María de las Mercedes commented.

"The day may yet come when some pro independence *criollos* will threaten the proslavery *criollos* to burn their properties if they betray them and fight on the side of the Spaniards," Tula said. "One way or another, nothing pleasant will happen in Cuba for a while. Independence without slaves will eventually come, but it will leave the island in ruins, burned by ourselves, by the Spaniards or by both. And at that point we will be an easy prey for the British or the Americans from the north. The money makers of New York and Philadelphia will be our most vehement suitors, not the cotton growers of the south."

"It will be an unholy alliance. Cuban magnates joining forces with Spanish liberals. Slavery would continue. The sugar, coffee and trade interests in Cuba, all benefiting from slavery, would not support independence. The bighearted and broad-minded Spanish liberals, now firmly in control of Cuba, would offer all sorts of concessions to make the British happy and keep the Americans in line. They would probably be satisfied if Spain bans the slave trade and proclaims humanistic rules that punish the abuse of slaves. Everyone would be happy except the poor blacks and the patriots," asserted María de las Mercedes. "Spain would not hesitate to stoop to whatever level it has to in order to safeguard its last possession in the Americas."

"Yes," they all agreed, as they began to sip their tea. Josefina had either agreed with everything or did not feel she could interrupt the dialogue among these cultured and assertive women. Her opinions were never asked and her silence was never questioned.

With a motion of her hand the countess had one of her aides take care of the expenses. She then offered Josefina a ride home.

Once María de las Mercedes and Gertrudis left Josefina at her home, they resumed their conversation on the way back to the *rue Jacob*, where they would have dinner that night. For a brief moment they continued their dialogue on the future of Cuba and the mixed blessings that slavery was bringing to what Gertrudis called "their island-nation."

"Is it not it too early to call it an island-nation?"

"Perhaps not," was the answer.

It was then that the Countess changed subjects as she tried to know Gertrudis better. "Have you ever thought of moving to Paris? There is much more room to grow here as a writer than you'd have in Madrid."

"I have thought of that. Tell me, how do you spend your time in Paris?"

"Well, aside from the seduction of writing and talking about Cuba and its future I am very committed to education, particularly the education of young women."

"Tell me what you know about the education of young women in France. The subject is also quite interesting to me."

"Aside from the big colleges the state of education is quite deficient. There are no doubts that the Royal Colleges have very high levels of scholarly excellence. But when you come down to the schools for children you realize why the big colleges are getting only the students from the upper classes. The situation at the lower level schools is dismal. The buildings are old and decrepit. Classrooms are dark and soggy. Parents have to furnish the armoires and desks for their children, as well as all the tools needed for education."

"Are there schools for all the children who need to attend?"

"No. There are very few public schools in Paris, and to make things worse, there is the problem of transportation. It takes a long time to travel across the city. The schools for children are not available at the neighborhoods but at very specific locations, mostly around the *montagne Sainte Geneviève*. Outside of the area of Luxembourg, for instance, the other only secondary schools in Paris are the Lycée Bourbon and the Charlemagne."

"Something similar happens in Madrid."

"Here, we also have private schools, but they are expensive and only the children of the aristocrats have the means to attend."

"Who sustains these schools, the Church?"

"No, it is mostly the work of women like the Duchesse de Berry, who founded the *Couvent des Oiseaux* at 84, *rue de Sèvres*, and the Duchesse d'Agoult, who sponsors the *Sacré Coeur*."

"Mostly in the left bank, near Montparnasse, aren't they?"

"Yes. That's where most private education takes place. By the way, have you heard the story of the *Couvent des Oiseau* before the Duchesse took it over?"

"No. Tell me."

"During the Terror the *Couvent des Oiseaux*, which had been turned into a prison, became an Eden of captivity. The only thing it lacked was the right to leave. Its name was due to the existence of a large cage with exotic birds in its inside patio, which the revolutionaries kept intact for unknown reasons. People were sent to this prison with a sort of insurance against the guillotine. During the initial period of the Terror only 2 out of 160 inmates were condemned to death. Of course you had to be rich and pay an exorbitant sum to be incarcerated there. The guards pampered their small herd of prisoners and discretely safeguarded their names."

"How long did this situation last?"

"It all ended when one fateful day the public accuser, Fouquier-Tinville, asked where one of the condemned, the Princess of Chimay, was serving her sentence. Upon being told of the *Couvent des Oiseaux* he visited the prison at *rue de Sèvres* and was dismayed at the luxurious accommodations. The very next day, 7 Thermidor, a *charrette* was sent to the *Couvent des Oiseau* and the Princess of Chimay the Countess of Plessis-Chatillon, her niece the Countess of Narbonne-Pelet, the Duke of Clermont-Tonnerre, the Marquis de Crussol d'Amboise, Monsieur de Saint-Simon, the Bishop of Agde, the Countess of Gramont, lady of company of Marie-Antoinette, Madame de Colbert-Maulevrier and Madame d'Armenthières, were all taken to the Conciergerie on the way to the scaffolds."

"That's a sad story, but not untypical of what Fouquier-Tinville used to do as the public accuser during the Terror. They say that it took him minutes to condemn people to the guillotine. He would simply ask: *What is your name, Madame*? After hearing the answer he would reply: *That is not your name; that was your name.* And he would dictate the horrible sentence right away. He ended up at the guillotine himself, of course. His last words were : *Je meurs pour ma patrie et sans reproche. Je suis satisfait: plus tard, on reconnoîtra mon innocence.* Years later Madame, la Duchesse de Berry bought the convent and all its facilities on April of 1824 and gave it to the *Congrégation de Notre-Dame* with the express agreement to found a school there."

"Finish what you were telling me about the schools for children."

"Oh, yes. What a sorry state of affairs when it comes to the education of young people! In all of France there are 39,000 towns of all sizes and 15,000 do not have any schools. Believe it or not there are only 2,000 children in public schools in Paris. Forty two percent of the population in France is illiterate. This is in contrast with the richness of the budget for libraries. The moneys spent in the Parisian libraries, which are mostly for the exclusive attendance by the faculties of the colleges and the institutes, is larger than the entire budget for the education of children in all of France."

"Call it the remnants of the privileges of the *ancien régime*, which have survived the revolution."

"Luckily, thanks mostly to Monsieur Guizot, Louis Philippe has opened 2,275 public primary schools since he came to power."

With that sentence the carriage arrived at the home of the Céspedes and both women were helped to the front gate. Watching them from a second door window next door was Didier Hervi, a man also consumed by a passion for learning. He had in his hands his personal copy of *Arliquiniana*, a 1694 collection of anecdotes relating to Giuseppe Domenico Biancolelli, the main star of *Commedia Dell'Arte*, an Italian drama group who had been the personal favorite of Louis XIV. A book he had promised María del Carmen he would lend her at dinner that night.

☙ ⌛ ❧

THE *CAFÉ TORTONI* IN 1840

The extraordinary popularity of **Café Tortoni** in Paris was that, contrary to the social rules prevalent in London and other places in Paris, women were allowed to visit *Tortoni's* and dine leisurely in company of other women. The preferred menus included coffee, chocolates, tea, ices, and all sorts of light appetizers, full *dejeuners* and a wide selection of wines. *Café Tortoni* in 1843 competed with *Café Pierront, Café Cardinal*, and *Café de la Banque*, which were all situated close to the *Grands Boulevards*.

9

"The true character of liberty is independence, maintained by force."
Voltaire

*"It is my living sentiment, and by the blessing of God it shall be my dying
sentiment, independence now and independence forever."*
Daniel Webster

*"Let those who desire a secure homeland conquer it. Let those who do not
conquer it live under the whip and in exile, watched over like wild animals,
cast from one country to another, concealing the death of their souls
with a beggar's smile from the scorn of free men."*
José Martí

Most evenings, the Céspedes and their guests would sit in their *salon* to share their visions as to what was happening in Cuba and what the future would bring. These were inspiring, absorbing and riveting sessions and many years later, in the mountains of Oriente province or the savannas of Camagüey, Céspedes would have given anything for having taken notes that would bring these thoughts faithfully to his mind. There they were, six very smart, educated minds trying to make sense of a very complex sociological reality that was running uncontrollably through history, with unpredictable consequences for both themselves and the land where they were hoping to live for the rest of their lives.

Céspedes and María del Carmen, having recently concluded their studies in Barcelona, were 24 and 22 years old. Domingo Del Monte, the senior person in the group and certainly the person with the longest and most distinguished track record as a freedom activist in Cuba, was 39. The Aldamas, Miguel and Rosa, heirs to one of the most illustrious and solid fortunes in Cuba and already protectors of artists and intellectual types, were 23 and 22; Gertrudis, already a recognized writer and acknowledged women of letters in Spain, was only 29.

These were very complex and difficult times in Cuba. The society that the Spaniards had constructed in Cuba on the foundations of slavery and colonial exploitation seemed to be coming apart. Slave revolts were everywhere. Cuba's *criollos* had developed a separatist sentiment because of Spain's reluctance to liberalize its tight grip on the political life of the island and its apparent inability to guarantee life and property. British abolitionists and American annexationists were tempting the young Cuban born citizen-leaders to revolt and shake off the Spanish yoke.

Rumors of conspiracies were everywhere. In Sabanilla del Encomendador, a placid agricultural enclave near the city of Matanzas, barely 60 miles east of Havana, troops under the leadership of Captain General Leopoldo O'Donnell had made a strong stand, apprehending, torturing, and executing the organizers of the conspiration. Two pre-eminent Cuban intellectuals had been implicated in the rebellions: José de la Luz y Caballero and Domingo Del Monte himself. David Turnbull, the former British consul in Havana, had been convicted *in absentia*. The Spanish army was on the trail of Gabriel de la Concepción Valdés, a mulatto and a free man, reputedly one of the best romantic and renowned poets in the literary circles of Havana. Thousands had been banished, persecuted, imprisoned, both blacks and whites, in what seemed to be either Spain's last stand in the defense of its most precious colony or Spain's overreaction to a novel assertion by the blacks of their right to be considered human beings.

Domingo Del Monte was the natural leader of these *tertulias a la francesa* or intellectual gatherings at the Céspedes household in Paris. They took place at the big drawing room that dominated the large and comfortable quarters of Carlos Manuel and María del Carmen. The drawing room was a large space with four full length windows facing *rue Jacob*. Gorgeous embroidered azure silk curtains framed the windows. The room seemed crowded because it was decorated in the best of French traditions with due reverence for the exotic. Lots of souvenirs from Cuba and Barcelona lined the floor space between the sitting furniture. It included some Cuban-African musical instruments, an antique tobacco stripping table crowned with primitive *Taino* pottery pieces, and a small stone baptismal fountain recovered from the ancient Conquistadores' settlement at Baracoa, which María del Carmen had purchased from a merchant in Barcelona.

On one corner of the room, under one of the windows opening to *rue Jacob*, a richly decorated Jewish Passover Haggadic prayer book sat on a small table, with 128 of its 322 pages richly ornamented with fanciful figures and pictorials depicting Jewish life in mediaeval Spain. It had also been bought by María del Carmen in the old Medieval area of Barcelona, at the point where the *rambla* meets the harbor. Eight tall *Sèvres* vases were on display in several areas around the room, some resting on the floor and others on small tables. Others, in glass, were full of antique jewelry and trinkets of predominantly trans-saharan ancestry, mainly from the Maghreb culture of both Africa and the Middle East, from such cities as Fes, Sale, Rabat and Tlemcen. They were purchased by Carlos and María del Carmen during some of their walks through Paris.

On the night of June 22, 1843, after receiving a *communiqué* from his friends in Havana through the private courier of the Havana Docks and Warehouses Company, one of his many holdings in Cuba, Domingo Del Monte began the conversation at the *tertulia* with an ominous announcement.

"What's happening in Cuba is a pre-emptive strike by the Spanish government, who wants to get rid of any and all attempts at liberating the slaves because they know that the political liberation of the island will come next. I have been falsely accused of providing aid to several conspiracies, just like José de la Luz y Caballero has been accused. The troubles are exaggerated by the government to justify their policy of colonial repression and obedience. The fear they are instilling in the white population is worth 100,000 men. Spain is behaving like a two headed hydra. One head supports and defends black slavery at all costs, with whatever arguments they can muster about economic imperatives and the disaster that will occur if our sugar mills and crops can not count on the free labor of the Negros. The other head takes care of the political slavery. It is inculcating on our minds the fear that only Spain can save us from a rebellion like the one that occurred in *Española* and that it is better to seek refuge in the protective arms of Spain than perish under the machetes of thousands of blacks revolting against us like they did in Haiti."

"Well, the Spaniards should not count on us to be their ever faithful servants," retorted Carlos Manuel. "Our hopes for political liberty are stronger with every year that passes. We have profited in Cuba from the prosperity that came about after the end of the Seven Years War and from the economic vacuum after the revolution in Haiti. But the Spanish government has inundated the island with slaves in the last 50 years, looking only after their own investments. It is one thing to rely on slave manpower to bring about prosperity and another to allow Cuba to be Africanized."

"But who is protesting?" asked Miguel.

"That's the point; we have become so used and comfortable with the presence of slaves in our economic life that few Cubans have ever asked themselves when this damaging phenomenon should be brought to an end. It has become a habit, a pernicious tradition, and no one sees anything wrong with it," Céspedes added.

"Our friend Arango y Parreño, who has all of his fortune invested in our economy, does not have a clear vision of what's wrong with this business of slaves and cheap labor on one hand and no political concessions on the other," interrupted Gertrudis. "He thinks that in Haiti the blacks overwhelmed a much smaller white population but he maintains that in Cuba the situation is not as critical. He feels that white Cubans have a superior advantage in numbers and we can safely continue to import slaves, as long as we carefully watch the census figures. Arango is a good man that laments the reality of slavery but justifies it on the basis of economic necessity. Now, however, we have seen the true intentions of the Spanish regime and we should not fall into that trap. The Spaniards will never give us political freedom; we will never be able to vote, or elect a government of our own. Slavery only benefits the colonists. Our rich Cubans can enjoy and profit from the advantages of cheap labor, as long as they do not harbor any expectations of deciding on their own destinies. Slavery is the sweet bait that makes us return day after day to our incarceration."

"Very well said," asserted María del Carmen. "Arango y Parreño never thought that blacks would ever exceed the white population, but he is deadly wrong. As José Antonio Saco recently wrote, «the prosperity of the moment is blinding them of the perils of the future.» Arango is also dead wrong when he justifies his beliefs by saying that slavery has always existed and would always exist in the minds of humans. He is also wrong when he feels that slavery can be taken as a temporary diversion on the road to prosperity and that times eventually will come when white free labor will be plentiful and societies will do away with slavery. I love our dear friend but I always felt he did not like black people, or at least he did not think they had the same rights as everyone else, including us."

"Well," said Carlos Manuel, "the independence of the American republics to the south presented Arango with very difficult choices. These republics, to say the least, very soon began to face almost intractable problems of governance. They got social disorder and economic ruin side by side with their freedom. Do we wish the same for Cuba? Arango used to say, very pointedly I believe, that our people do not have the education or the virtues to appreciate freedom and liberty, and that when people do not know how to be free, they do not deserve to be free. I tend to agree with him, even though it sounds very discouraging. Look at what has happened among us after the restoration of the Bourbons in Spain. I know of at least two dozen of our friends who have gotten noble titles since *Fernando VII* came back from France. We are now surrounded with Counts and Marquises. How vain can we be? Even Arango got an appointment as Intendant. Beware of felons bringing gifts, as the saying goes."

"It is true. An identity crisis is upon us," Gertrudis said. "It has not been easy to harmonize our bourgeois cravings with the realities of slavery and our repugnance for colonialism. Arango, however, is right in his insistence of education as the only possible redemption in this quandary. A democracy develops men and women through secular education, and it thus facilitates their ability to fulfill their material needs and personal happiness while contributing to the general progress of society and the nation. It is very symptomatic that the schools in Cuba are always deprived of good teachers and instructional materials. The restored Bourbons, generous in blessing our native sugar planters with titles and honors, have reduced the funds for public education after they found that many of our teachers suffer from incurable liberalism. They fear the *criollos*, just like the *criollos* fear the slaves. The Bourbons have always been like that. Remember the royal orders of 1828 and 1832 prohibiting young Cubans from getting an education in the United States."

"I should know this," Domingo interrupted. "I made a survey a few years ago of educational conditions in Cuba and presented the result at the *Sociedad Económica de Amigos del País*. Forty percent of the districts have neither schools nor teachers. Places like Alacranes, with some of the largest sugar plantations in Cuba, never had a school. The excuse for not having schools in places like Bauta or San Antonio, a few kilometers from Havana, is presumably that the population lives in deprived and miserable conditions, not worthy of the conveniences of a learning institution. I have concluded that less than 10% of eligible whites in Cuba have any sort of education. When I presented the results to the Spanish authorities they claimed that those not receiving opportunities were all enemies of the tranquility of the country. My report has never been printed and distributed in Cuba or in Spain."

"It is a pitiful situation," continued Del Monte. "Do you know that Cuba imports technicians and engineers to operate its sugar mills and the big trading companies have to import accountants from Spain because the scarcity of educated people in Cuba? I am quite disgusted with the situation. In the face of every slave without physical freedom I can see myself, deprived as I am from political, educational, artistic and every other kind of freedom. I am a slave of the spirit and my servility is as profound and onerous as that of the most humble of blacks. I know someone who talked to José Cienfuegos when he was *Capitan General* of Cuba in the late 1810's and asked him to provide, on behalf of the *Sociedad Económica*, some leisure and educational facilities for the free blacks. His answer was that the blacks could not read and did not need a place to dance."

"Well," said Céspedes, "if Cuban *criollos* can not find educational opportunities in the island, our families will send them to the United States, to Spain and to other places in Europe. The proportion of Cubans with money that send their children to study here in Paris should be shameful for the Spaniards. Almost every Cuban doctor in Medicine has been formed at the *Sorbonne*. The Spanish government prefers, of course, to have them educated in Spain, where they could acquire the habits of 'loyalty and grateful obedience' to the crown. But more and more, the preferred place for studies is in France or in the United States."

"What we need to understand," Gertrudis said, "is that there is a closed circle, like the *ourobus* serpent, that includes education and political freedom. We need the first to obtain the second, and vice versa. Where do we break this dilemma? We better figure that out fast! The wealth that we now enjoy due to the bountiful yields of the sugar crops may be temporary. We must convince the autocratic, dictatorial, despotic and tyrannical government of Spain to invest in the education of our youth, on a road parallel to the official Spanish educational system, or we will be forever condemned to be politically submissive to Spain. Of course, they won't do it."

"Spain has always been an autocratic, dictatorial, despotic and tyrannical society, as you well said," interrupted Del Monte. "This tradition took root in the Americas and unfortunately it has been preserved amongst us. The slave economy is but a manifestation of this trait of the Spanish character that makes every peninsular to believe that he or she has more rights and class that anyone else. This regrettable belief has been reinforced by their contempt for physical labor."

"Recently," he continued, "Francisco Dionisio Vives, justifying as Captain General of Cuba the shortage of labor and the need for continued reliance on slavery, proclaimed that 'physical work will always be done by colored people because only they could perform these functions without fear of further degrading themselves.' His successor Miguel Tacón, Marquis de la Unión de Cuba, in 1834, declared that the Spanish race disdains any but the most indispensable physical labor because it is not becoming of them, and they rightly rather prefer vagrancy or idleness. All of you know that there are few cities in Europe or the United States with more loafers and do-nothings than Havana."

"Oh, yes, I agree," stated Aldama. "The higher classes are more prone to work than the general populace of Spaniards. Nevertheless, it is not uncommon; our maids tell us from other houses where they have served, that many educated and prosperous men sit in their *salons* all morning and half of the postmeridian, doing nothing, with their night caps and night robes on, until they are ready to move to their clubs at 3 in the afternoon. An even worst disinclination to work or exert themselves is prevalent among the Spanish men of lower socio-economic classes."

"Not very different from the women," interrupted María del Carmen. "If you looked to lower class women in general, perhaps half are employed as farmers, seamstresses, washerwomen, maids and day laborers. The other half sits idle at home and join their men to form lines in front of the houses of the rich, practically every Friday, to receive their charity. Cuba has become a society where the slaves work and the white lower class sits idle and counts on handouts from the wealthy. Unless we do away with slavery, the ethical fiber of our citizens will forever be compromised. It is more than an issue of social justice and humanity. It has to do with national character and the quality of the Cuban persona..."

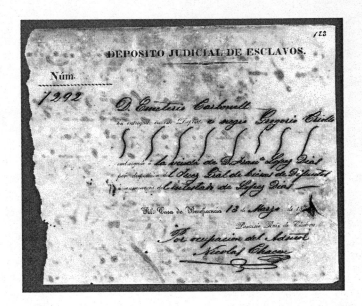

SLAVES DEPOSITED AS MERCHANDISE IN HAVANA

The document reads: "**JUDICIAL DEPOSIT OF SLAVES**. Number 1292.
Don Emeterio Carbonell has given to this deposit a black man named Gregorio Criollo,
taken from the widow of Don Francisco López Díaz, by order of the Inspector General
of Goods of the Deceased, as a consequence of Mr. López Díaz having died
without a will. Given at the House of Charity on March 13, 1852.
Signed, in lieu of Pascasio Ruiz de Córdoba, by his assistant Nicolás Chacón."
Original document in the collection of the author.

10

*"O Man! Thou feeble tenant of an hour / Debased by slavery,
or corrupt by power / Who knows thee well must quit thee with disgust /
Degraded mass of animated dust!"*
Lord Byron

"Slavery they can have anywhere. It is a weed that grows in every soil."
Edmund Burke

*"If you put a chain around the neck of a slave,
the other end fastens itself around your own."*
Ralph Waldo Emerson

The conversation which started at *Tortoni's* between the Countess of Merlin and Gertrudis Gómez, was continued on the following day at the home of the Countess, this time in the absence of Josefina Cipresti, who was not really on the same league or of a mind with these two formidable women.

The private mansion or *hôtel particulier* of the Countess was located on the *Marais*, the low laying but very fertile and superbly located area that in the XVII Century, during the reign of Henry IV, had become the hometown of the French aristocracy. The house had been built in 1637 by Jacques Androuet du Cerceau, the architect to Robert Gallimard Mesme de Gallet. M. de Gallet at the time lived in the *hôtel* at *62, rue de Saint Antoine* that was purchased in 1624 by Maximilien de Béthune, the Duke of Sully. The home built with great care for M. de Gallet, who was a financier and a Minister of Henri IV, was ransacked by revolutionaries in 1792, at the time of the assaults and murders on the nearby prison of *La Force*. It then became first a warehouse and later a shopping arcade, until it completely degenerated and became a squatter's paradise. Antoine Christophe, the Count of Merlin, bought it for a few *sous* and had it restored for a small fortune after marrying María de las Mercedes and returning with her to Paris.

As with most rich residences built in the XVII Century for the French nobility, you entered the Countess' *hôtel particulier* through a formidable gate that led to a courtyard surrounded by several lavishly decorated buildings arranged on a square. The courtyard was paved with fine marble gravel encased by a perfectly trimmed thick, tall shrubbery. On the left side there were several carriage stalls, stables for six horses and washing and conditioning facilities. They were all hidden behind several beautifully appointed tall French doors that protected the looks of this functional and normally messy working area. The buildings facing the street, known as the court side, housed the servants, the kitchens and the *hôtel's* warehousing facilities in what used to be a generation earlier the quarters for the guards and the custodians of the mansion. On the area opposite the entrance was what was then called "the garden side." It consisted of the main body of the residence, on back of which were the terraces and gardens of the house. On the extensive peacefully quiet gardens, there were plants and flowers geometrically arranged in perfect squares and ovals. These were sprinkled here and there with parks and sitting areas with large and small fountains. The Merlins, like many of their contemporaries, also had an *orangerie* or greenhouse, where their gardeners cultivated homegrown fruits, exotic flowers and vegetables during the winter months.

In the main body of the house, there were private quarters for the Count and the Countess, as well as rooms and sitting areas for guests. They extended through two floors, far and away from the smells, the noise and the general ruckus of the *rue de Saint Antoine*, which at the time was one of the most elegant avenues of Paris. On the right hand side of the court there were a music room, a formal dining area, a library, a ballroom and several drawing rooms where guests would be received and feted. On the inside the house featured skillfully carved and painted ceilings and elegant and expensive hallways and stairways. On the outside, the home of the Merlins was a model of the baroque style so prevalent in the best houses in Paris during the XVII Century. The architecture was very symmetrical and all walls were decorated with intricate sculptures with classical motives. Windows on both floors were capped with semicircular and triangular pediments and flanked by patterns of scrolls sculpted on the stone. On the main body and on both side buildings flanking the courts, there were sixteen figures in high relief symbolizing the four seasons across the four cardinal points of the French geography.

Gertrudis arrived at eleven in the morning, in time for the mid morning repast that the Countess, usually awakened since seven in the morning, used to have before her late luncheon in mid afternoon.

The conversation immediately took off where it had ended the day before.

"Slavery is an institution of the past and Cuba cannot count on it for much longer, regardless of the need for farm hands in the middle of this sugar boom," started Gertrudis.

"I agree, Tula, as the good times will not last for long. Several of our friends in France are investing heavily in the sugar plantations of Louisiana, which continues to be French in culture in spite of being now part of the United States. Sooner or later a collapse of the sugar prices will ruin and weaken the growers in Cuba. God forbid if the blacks take advantage of this and revolt."

"There are enough rich blacks in Cuba to finance a revolt today if they wanted to do it. The only thing that restrains them is the cruelty and criminal hand of Madrid: it kills and maims any suspects, whether they are white or black. Even if they are of noble origin and only wish that this repulsive institution of slavery would end."

"Oh, it is clear. They will not hesitate to incarcerate Luz y Caballero, or Domingo or el Lugareño. Anything to preserve the sacred cow that sustains the life style of Madrid. Spain is a shadow of what it was and is condemned to be less and less important as time goes on. You only have to consider the powerless and cowardly manner with which they surrendered to Napoleon."

"What cannot be ignored are the voices claiming for reform in Cuba. The Spanish have drastically reduced the market and availability of slaves."

"Indeed, and that has ruined many sugar plantations. The Spanish will not invest one more cent in Cuba. They enriched themselves when they brought thousand of slaves into Cuba. Now they preach that slavery has to end. We all know that the slave owners have to be compensated or they will cease to plant. The logical thing to expect is that the restitution and compensation to buy and free the slaves will come from the same pockets that profited from their labor. But not a chance! Spain wants the *hacendados* to absorb these expenses. There is not enough money in Cuba to carry this burden. Even in good times… The threat of ruin is in the horizon."

"Spain abandoned Santo Domingo because it had become a burden and not a source of income. Perhaps they will do the same in Cuba. If they liberate the slaves without helping the owners to recover the capital they have invested in them, there will be bankruptcies and chaos in the countryside. The plantations in Louisiana will benefit, because they will continue to count on slavery. The capital will flee Cuba in search for better returns. No more richness from

Cuba. Perhaps that will make them lose interest and leave us like they did in Santo Domingo. That may not be all that bad!"

"What a quandary! The dilemma in Cuba is that, for those of us who abhor slavery, freeing the slaves will bring about ruin and misery. And we will be an easy prey for interests quite foreign to our culture and idiosyncrasy. Not freeing the slaves will ruin us morally. We should not impose that burden on our children. We should not raise one more generation of our people with that encumbrance on their shoulders."

"That's why Carlos Manuel and Domingo feel that we need to liberate the slaves gradually. They think that when we feel ready to bring about freedom for Cuba, our enemies will be those who advocate for an immediate abolition of slavery. These ideas will only bring about chaos and that's precisely what the Spaniards want. That's what they are threatening to do if they see the forces of independence taking root among the population."

"Do you feel that there are people in Spain who believe in freedom for the slaves in the humanitarian terms that we do?," asked the Countess.

"In Spain the Church has not taken the high moral ground with respect to slavery. Neither have the most radical of liberals, to say it plainly. They do not see it as a moral question. They do not see the issue of respect to human dignity. They do not see the indignities of slavery. The most they are ready to concede is to believe and work for a more decent treatment of the slaves. You wonder if this is prompted by a desired to keep them healthy or for a compassionate reason," pointed out Gertrudis.

"Yes, that's the prevalent Spanish reaction to slavery. What distresses people in Madrid and all over Spain is the cruel treatment that slaves are receiving. The newspapers, the societies and much more the Church, feel that such cruel treatment has to stop. There are no voices claiming that what has to end is slavery in itself. The Spanish people will always be content to maintain slavery, as long as the owners are nice to their blacks. The moral issue is blocked completely. Luckily, that insensitivity has not taken hold among the *criollos* in Cuba, except among a few bastards who only look at their pockets. The vast majority of Cubans would like to see the end of slavery because they see human beings where the Spaniards only see property."

"Well, we can not ignore the profound impact of losing the slaves after they have become the backbone of our economic life. That's why Carlos Manuel and Domingo make so much sense."

"Look at someone who advocates immediate liberation of the slaves and you will see someone with bad designs over Cuba. I was surprised at Josefina's radical ideas that freedom for the slaves had to be granted at once. I thing she either does not have a good grasp of the dilemma in Cuba or she is advocating for economic and social ruin in Cuba."

"Do not take too seriously what Josefina has to say. Remember she is the mother in law of a wealthy Spaniard who would like nothing better than to see thousands of free slaves so grateful to the mother country that they will fight the *criollos* and prevent Cuba from being politically free."

"Yes, I agree. I am convinced that in the future, Spain will coerce the Cubans that seek independence or autonomy with a threat of liberating all slaves and opposing the Cuban fighters with a coalition of grateful blacks and recalcitrant Spaniards. To the Spanish government, the blacks are another commodity in their arsenal and they will use them to perpetuate their hold on Cuba. We are the last enclave of their decaying and corrupt empire and they will hang on to us at all costs."

"What you are saying is that, when it comes to issues in Cuba, there has never being such a thing as a Spanish abolitionist. I share that opinion."

"Even if you take into consideration Isidoro de Antillón, who brought to the courts the proposal to liberate slaves above a certain age and those born after a certain date. He never got anywhere. He never found support in the Spanish courts. Even after the British forced the 1815 resolution of the Congress of Vienna forcing Spain to discontinue the shipment of slaves to the Americas..."

"Well, the British did that because they wanted to weaken the Cuban competition in sugar production, which depended on continued importation of slaves..."

"I agree, but look at this: in 1837 the Spanish courts decreed that slavery was out of the law in the Spanish peninsula and in all the African possessions... but not in Cuba. Why was that? There were several reasons: it was the only way to protect the capital invested in Cuba, which depended on slaves to be productive; it was not politically desirable because hundreds of Spaniards with interests in the colony would detect a weakness in the Spanish government resolve; finally it would have preempted the weapon that the Spaniards had to dissuade the Cubans from insisting on independence: we will liberate the slaves and they will fight you at our side."

"Wholly Machiavellian, eh!" said the Countess. "Whatever the Spaniards did was simply under pressure from the British, who had no high motives of their own."

"Yes. As early as last year the government of Spain was dancing between not annoying the British to the point where they would take action against Spain and continuing profiting from the slave trade. The 1835 treaty with Great Britain forbade shipments from Africa to the Americas but not between two Spanish ports. Guess what? Almost immediately the traders were shipping slaves to Cadiz –I am talking about last year– and from there to San Juan and then to Havana. Commerce between Spanish cities, they claimed, laughing in the face of the British."

"But it gets even more cynical: the Spanish are using the abolition of slaves as the means to drive a wedge between the economic interests of *criollos* in western Cuba, with rather small sugar plantations, from those of eastern Cuba, which are mostly gigantic farms requiring thousand of slaves. They also played both sides of the divide between the gradualists, those like Céspedes favoring gradual elimination of slavery with appropriate compensation, and the absolutists, who were radical in terms of immediate abolition for presumably humanitarian grounds."

"No, for sure: I am convinced that there is no such thing as a Spanish abolitionist."

"Of course not. It is all politics everywhere. Politics of desperation and greed in Spain and politics of opportunism and arrogance elsewhere. The Spaniards claim to wish the slaves free because, by being agents of their liberation they would strengthen the loyalties of blacks, if there is ever a struggle for independence in Cuba. The British want the slaves to be free to guarantee that Cuba becomes a slave free area and the United States does not grow south by absorbing the island. Southerners want to keep their slaves and will not add a slave-free territory in their back yard. They want the Cuban slaves to be free, however, because it will ruin the economy of the island and benefit the infant sugar plantations of Louisiana. The French wish our slaves to be free because it will create such turmoil that the British would renounce all designs to control Cuba. Besides, their French colonial interests in Martinique and Dominique would accelerate their growth as the most reliable sugar supplier to Europe. No one gives a darn about morals or the rights of men. It is all dirty politics."

"Our independence will depend on our skills to overcome the many sins that Spain and the Church have inflicted on us. And I say the Church because since the times of Las Casas there has hardly been any voices from the Church speaking on behalf of human rights in Cuba."

"Varela and Espada excluded, of course."

"Yes, I have always considered them as the first Cubans. Varela because it was his birthright. Bishop Espada because he was the first who generously understood and nurtured our right to be independent. I think of this as a remarkable feat. Someone who was the prime Church authority in Cuba at a time when the lines separating the Church and the Spanish crown were completely blurred. I have never included Varela and Espada among the Spaniards; not even after father Varela served as a member of the *Cortes Españolas*."

"We did not invent slavery in Cuba, but we will have to pay the price for it. And the price will include the effort we will have to make to cleanse several generations of Cubans from the miserable dysfunctional ethical standards that the Spaniards will leave behind."

SLAVES WORKING IN A SUGAR MILL IN CUBA, 1760

The drawing shows every phase of **sugar production** in a single view. Starting on the top left, sugar cane is harvested in the fields. Moving counterclockwise from there, the canes are transported to the sugar factory, where the leaves are removed and the stalks moved to the mills (at the center left). The juice is then taken to the evaporators along the right wall, where it is concentrated until the sugar crystallizes. It is then poured into molds (notice a *coolie* pouring the concentrated sugar syrup) and transported to ships (center background) for their export destination. Drawing in the collection of the author.

11

"Colonies do not necessarily cease to be colonies
when they become independent."
Benjamin Disraeli

"A colony is lost when one lacks the statesmanship to know
the right time and the manner of yielding what is impossible to keep."
Elizabeth II of England

"Let us in education dream of an aristocracy of achievement
arising out of a democracy of opportunity."
Thomas Jefferson

IN 1843 CUBA was not only the last remaining productive colony in the Americas and the pride of Spain but probably the richest and most promising territory possessed anywhere by any European colonial power. Over 150,000 metric tons of sugar were produced every year, almost five times the amount produced at the time when other Spanish colonies obtained their independence. Havana harbor was the busiest in the American continent, followed among the twenty busiest by Matanzas, Cárdenas and Trinidad. Hundreds of deep water inlets provided secure anchorage to commercial vessels and sugar was being exported from every port. Nature had been so generous with the Cuban geography that the Gulf of Mexico and the Caribbean Sea currents, as well as the trade winds, made it very easy to reach Cuba.

The wealth in Cuba made it an important market for both the Americans and the Europeans. Mining equipment first and railroad locomotives later, were imported from Germany. Chocolate came from Venezuela and Ecuador. Carriage parts, iron products and fashions were imported from France. Liqueurs, olive oil, vine, soap and porcelain were brought from Spain. Foodstuffs of all kinds, lumber and cod came in from the United States. The balance of payments was skewed in favor of imports but nobody cared because the ability of Cubans to pay their debts was beyond questioning.

On the countryside there was an unmitigated wave of prosperity. Woods were been cleared and fertile agricultural land had grown at a rate of almost 7 per cent per year since the outbreak of hostilities in South America. Fifty three percent of Cuban residents were black but of these almost one in ten was a free man and many of them had accumulated considerable wealth. Unlike Barbados, Jamaica and Santo Domingo, there was such an attraction for European capital and immigrants that no one had fears that Cuba would turn into a black country.

Havana of course was the jewel in the crown of Cuba. Its refinement was comparable to that of the largest cities in the United Sates or in Europe. There were *salons*, churches, lyceums, two prestigious universities –the San Carlos Seminary and the University of Havana– literary societies, scientific associations, concert halls, theaters, chambers of commerce, convents and private schools, art academies and social clubs, clinics and recreational societies, hunting grounds and hundreds of *cafés* and fine eateries that would serve á *la Russe*. In Havana, numerous people moved in *quitrines* and *calesas*, elegant carriages with outsized rimmed wheels to smooth out any roughness from the stone paved streets.

Havana had a wall to protect it from attacks from the landside and powerful forts with cannons pointing to the sea. But by the end of the XVII century the city had outgrown its walls and more than fifty percent of its residents lived *extramuros*. Its streets had the quaint flavor of the old world and all the conveniences of the new. The Tacón Theater was at the center of the city, almost on top of the city walls on *San José* Street and *Isabel la Católica* Avenue. From there you could get to the port through *Teniente Rey* Street or by *Obrapía* or *Lamparilla* streets, which offered quick access to the Main Post Office and the Customs House. *Calles Egido* and *Monserrrate* ran parallel to the old wall from the northern to the southern shores of the bay. *Calle del Conde de Riela* or *Muralla* had elegant and small shops that could satisfy any necessity. *Calle Obispo*, running from the Havana Zoo (later the Villanueva railroad station) to the Fort of *La Fuerza*, had a similar but cheaper and broader selection of goods. As in many European capitals, the names of the streets of Havana either described their physical appearance, or their main features, or were named after a Christian Saint. There were names like *Lamparilla, Empedrado, Amargura, Sol, Luz, Mercaderes, Tejadillo, Jesús María, Santa Clara, Merced, Paula,* and *Cuarteles*.

Socially the population was fairly segregated by class and color. At the lower rung there were blacks and mulattos whose roots were in the tribes in western Africa: Mandinga, Gangá, Carabalí, Lucumí, Congo and Macuá. The blacks and mulattos would be further classified into slave and free. Slightly above the blacks and mulattos were the rural poor whites or *monteros* that, like the people of color, lived in the shadows of the wealthy *hacendados* in the countryside. Right above was the urban poor white, which performed services of all kinds in the cities: grocers, gofers, cigar makers, carpenters, sanitation employees, couriers, etc. There was a stigma associated with manual labor, considered by Spaniards as evidence of inferior status, hence many poor whites, just like poor free blacks and mulattos, roamed the cities searching for an easy life or gave themselves completely to vagrancy. Then came the educated and the rich, both black and white, and that included such trades as public employees, army and police officers, merchants, property owners, small businessmen, medical and dental doctors, engineers, accountants, etc. Finally came the very rich, which were by and large whites with titles of nobility or those who had accumulated a considerable capital. In this category one could enter only through purchased titles, landed wealth, bloodlines and/or loyal service to the crown of Spain.

There were twenty six Marquises, seven Dukes and thirty Counts in Cuba in 1840, as well as dozens of *Caballeros de Isabel la Católica*, the Knights of the Catholic Queen Isabella. The rich were seldom at their land properties since they preferred the comforts of Havana and, better still, the elegant life of Madrid or Paris. Even among the beautiful rich there were strata to take into account. Claudio Martines de Pinillos, the Count of Villanueva, for instance, could never shed the burden of having been born to a wealthy shopkeeper who bought his noble title from the crown. The Marquis de las Delicias could never overcome the fact that he had started as a doorkeeper and was the beneficiary of the wave of titles that Ferdinand VII dispensed over rich Cubans. The Marquis, after all, was happy to be among those who were willing to forget that His Majesty had betrayed the crown of Spain by consenting to the protection of Napoleon.

Among the heirs of the wealthy Cubans who became new aristocrats with old money in those years were all those whose last names included Cárdenas, Aldama, Herrera, Peñalver, Davis, Calvo, Chacón, O'Farril, O'Reilly, Montalvo, Sardiñas, Schweyer, Nuñez del Castillo and Pedroso. Many of them were tenth or fifteenth generation Cubans and among these families you could count more than half the nobility titles in Cuba. They also controlled, by the way, over 50 percent of the sugar crops in Cuba in 1840 and two thirds of the coffee. They would later control close to seventy percent of Cuba's railroads. They were the backbone of a society that was slowly developing its own characteristics and decidedly severing their emotional and spiritual ties to Spain. They were eventually destined to call other Cubans to fight for their independence and their influence in Cuban political life was destined to be strong until the middle of the XX Century. The peninsulars could not stand them.

After dinner, at the home of the Céspedes in Paris, the conversation often turned to the Cuba they knew and missed and its tenuous and fragile relations with metropolitan Spain. In spite of his youth, Miguel de Aldama was always a good *raconteur* of stories and anecdotes about his family and those of other prominent *criollos* in Havana's powerful economic and social circles.

"In 1828," he once recalled, "my father had a business meeting with Francisco Dionisio Vives, who was the Captain General and Governor of Cuba between 1823 and 1832; he proved to be one of the best Governors that Spain ever sent to Cuba. The meeting did not go very well and at the end of it, with characteristic Spanish sarcasm, Mr. Vives told him: "the problem with you Cubans is that as young children you suckled the same milk as some of these blacks. Now you persist in mocking the government of Spain by defending them. By protecting and abetting their behavior you are increasing the audacity of their delinquency and supporting their impunity…"

"Strong words for someone addressing your father," declared Carlos Manuel, "even if it was the King's representative in Havana."

"My father laughed, turned his back and left Vives' office. He never feared Vives, or Tacón, who became Governor of Cuba between 1834 and 1838. He could be as arrogant as they were when his turn came. Afterwards, he decided never to invite any Spanish governors to his home. I don't think he has since or that he will ever do it in the future."

"How could the learned classes in Cuba render homage to Spaniards who came or immigrated to Cuba on official or permanent business if they were seen mostly as socially and educationally inferior or, in the best of cases, as *petty bureaucrats*," added Domingo.

"Indeed. What these *parvenus* did not want to recognize was that Cuba, in 1840, was far more advanced than Spain. What they found upon arrival must have aroused their envy, their greed and the most racist of sentiments. Cubans liked to flaunt their prosperity and the Spaniards could not stand it."

"I entirely agree," insisted Domingo. "Consider Havana's stone paved calzadas when Madrid was full of dirt roads that turned into mud and grime every rainy day. Water was plentiful in Havana thanks to the Royal Zanja and the Vento canal. There were fountains and statues, mansions and buildings as beautiful as those in Madrid but our avenues were wider and had concealed sewers or *cloacas* to hygienically dispose of the city's liquid wastes. The Havana to Bejucal railroad had been approved and financed and construction was proceeding before anyone dreamed of a railroad in Spain. The commodes in many houses in Havana could be flushed directly into the sanitary sewer. We had more service in middle class homes than our counterparts in Madrid."

"They could not stand the thought," reposted Miguel. "They simply could not stand the thought...."

⤳ ⚄ ⤲

CAMPO DE MARTE AND PALACIO ALDAMA, 1848

A view of **Campo de Marte** in Havana, known later as *Parque de la Fraternidad*. On the forefront, the statue of *La India*, sculpted in Carrara marble in 1837. On one arm it showed the city shield of Havana, with the three fortresses: *La Fuerza*, *La Cabaña* and *El Morro*. On the other arm it showed a cornucopia of Cuban fruits, particularly pineapples. Across from the *Campo the Marte*, on the center in the distance, is the **Palacio de Aldama**, built in 1840 by Don Domingo Aldama, Miguel's father, with the technical direction of his son-in-law, Domingo Del Monte. It remains to this day the most interesting example of neoclassical architecture in Havana.

12

"Slavery is so intolerable a condition that the slave
can hardly escape deluding himself into thinking that he is choosing
to obey his master's commands when, in fact, he is obliged to."
W.H. Auden

"The tyrant grinds down his slaves and they don't turn against him;
they crush those beneath them."
Emily Bronte

"None are more hopelessly enslaved than those who falsely believe they are free."
Johann Wolfgang von Goethe

SLAVERY WAS CONSTANTLY in the minds of Carlos Manuel, Miguel Aldama and Domingo Del Monte as they regularly strolled from the *rue Jacob* towards the Seine. One of their favorite places to sit and talk was at the small plaza in front of the *Institute de France*, across from the *Pont des Arts* and the magnificent structure of the Louvre. There they would share the letters and other messages received from Cuba and Madrid. The subject of their conversations was always open but they kept coming to the same issues time and time again. They knew that in Cuba, as in many other latitudes, the question of slavery was intimately connected with human rights, economic prosperity, and ultimately, political independence.

The Cuban society of the times was deeply fractured over the issue of slavery. The division was progressively more acute because of the increasing blindness of the Spanish colonial administration. The Haitian experience had clouded their best thinking as an albatross that impeded a clear analysis of the options opened to the Cubans. Free thinking Cubans felt that the bloody revolt in Haiti signaled that the only way to prevent a similar situation in Cuba was to agree to make reforms. Not many had any hopes that Spain would grant some liberties to Cuba but they felt that it was worth their time to continue insisting on a revised relationship with Spain. Others thought that only an annexation with a strong and law abiding country like the United States could prevent a blood bath in Cuba.

Francisco de Arango y Parreño, the wealthy, popular and influential economist and statesman who had been Humboldt's guide in Cuba, enjoyed easy access to the then Governor General of Cuba, Luis de las Casas, and had played an important role in seeking concessions from Spain. The French Revolution had been a powerful incentive for Spain to act in time and prevent an armed conflict in Cuba. The colonial government had established schools and several educational programs in Cuba under pressure from Arango and the powerful members of the *Sociedad Económica de Amigos del País*, always with the support of Las Casas. Some concessions on freedom of trade were obtained, but Spain remained blind on the issue of slavery. In fact, to be truthful, most *criollos* did not want to face the problems created by the institution of slavery and continued to push the subject to the background. Only the voice of Félix Varela, the Cuban born priest on exile in New York, had consistently focused on the issue of slavery. Varela had been forced into exile after having hammered on the need to end slavery while serving in the Spanish Cortes. He relentlessly continued to speak for the abolition of slavery and political reform through his newspaper *El Habanero*. He was a strong intellectual influence on Céspedes, Aldama and other alumni of the San Carlos Seminary, where he taught before his exile.

Spain did make some concessions in the early years of the XIX Century. The intention was to placate the voices of nonconformity in Cuba by yielding a little on the economic front. Trade restrictions were somewhat relaxed. The exportation of tobacco ceased to be a crown monopoly in 1817. Beginning in 1818 trade was opened with any and all nations. Private ownership of Cuban lands was legalized and a property registry was created to the effect. The value of Cuban exports began to increase in unprecedented terms. The Spanish crown began to collect never before seen revenues, which the crown invested in the lands towards the south, fighting the numerous movements to achieve independence throughout the continent.

Cuba continued to be thought of as the "ever loyal," particularly after 1824, when Spain was left with no territories in the Americas except Cuba and Puerto Rico. To make things worse, James Monroe, fifth President of the United States, pronounced the declaration that became known as the *Monroe Doctrine*. On one hand it precluded any future interventions by the Spaniards, the British or the French to recover or establish colonies in the Americas. On the other hand it gave a blessing to the *status quo*, and Cuba had been left dressed but uninvited to the great party of national independence.

The *criollos* in Cuba, fearful of losing their economic and social preeminence, but even more fearful of following the steps of the creoles in Haiti, began to see with dismay how the slaves began to secretly and openly conspire to gain their freedom. Poorly organized but unwavering slave uprisings began to occur in western Cuba. The Spanish government responded in kind, spreading violence and torture not only among the slaves but also against presumed sympathizers among free blacks and educated white Cubans. As the result of these savage and brutal reactions of the Spanish authorities, an antislavery sentiment began to develop among the *criollos*. For the first time some powerful and influential Cubans began to approach the government of the United States to seek support through annexation. They found understanding ears in the south, but not where it would count: New York, Washington and Philadelphia.

These great issues were repeatedly discussed and talked over by Céspedes and his guests during those leisurely strolls along the left banks of the Seine: how to get slaves to be free, how to replace slaves, how many slaves were really needed, would wage workers be more productive than the slaves, were would you employ newly freed slaves by the thousands, should children of slaves be automatically free, could the slaves, having been deprived of any sort of education, be able to handle the new technologies that were being introduced in the sugar mills, what rights did the mill owners have over their slaves if they were introduced illegally in Cuba to begin with.

"Slavery is a sword with two sharp edges," Domingo Del Monte used to say. "On one hand it allows the owners to enjoy a bounty of free labor. On the other hand they have paid a small fortune for a field hand and yet they will never feel secure that their families will not suffer from the wrath of their avenging hands."

"Very well said, Domingo," Carlos Manuel would reply. "If you think of it, the same thing happens at the level of society as a whole. Cheap manpower in the sugar fields but sleepless nights recounting the nightmare of Haiti."

"The conditions at the *bateyes* are dreadful and one wonders if this will be profitable at all in the end. A pregnant Negress will enrich her master with a free youngster but, in the view of many slave owners, her pregnancy will be an excuse for many months of idleness and laziness."

"Oh, many owners do not care about pregnancies. They treat pregnant women brutally, just like every other slave would be treated. Miscarriages due to beatings are the order of the day. Death of newly born babies due to the filth of the barracks is almost assured. Most black babies live only a few days after they leave the womb. No wonder many black women dread to fall pregnant. They will be brutalized and if they succeed to bring a new life into this world, the baby would be condemned to live the horrifying life of a slave."

"There are no hopes of sustaining slave levels in Cuba without continued importation. The blacks are not reproducing themselves in sufficient numbers."

"Never mind if they don't. The issue is that our economic system is shamefully and dishonorably inhuman. There has to be a way to put a stop to all this. This is not a good foundation on which to build a new republic."

"Hiring locals or foreign wage workers has to be the answer. Even if they are indentured servants, it would be ethically better that having slaves."

"Well, the up front cost would be cheaper than with slaves and they could be fired if they do not perform."

"Yes, but we have learned with the *coolies* that bringing somebody from abroad can also be cruel, heartless and inhumane. The death rates in those crowded ships have been close to twenty five percent. Once they get to Cuba, they are prohibited by law to leave the plantations. They are quasi-slaves for many years and the fact that their commitment is temporary usually means that they are more forcefully pressured to perform."

"On the other hand the indentured servants are usually more educated and can understand and adjust to new equipment and intelligent schemes of production, while the blacks do not."

"Never mind that. In the ultimate analysis they will be nothing but glorified slaves. The plantation supervisors have no incentive to treat them well. After all, they would be gone in seven or eight years. As long as they work hard, who cares if they become syphilitic or if they get the whooping cough? Their own future belongs to them, not the plantation owner's."

"If you begin to bring indentured workers into Cuba to replace the slaves, how are you going to prevent a new headache if the indentured begin to discriminate and look down on the slaves? The poor blacks will then get it from the white landowners and also from the contracted hands. They are now considered as no more than chattel by their masters. They will be worse off when they become the butt where the indentured will discharge their frustrations."

And so on and on. So were the quandaries of these young Cuban businessmen, landowners and intellectuals who were realistically assessing the difficulties of bringing into a safe port a new republic which only existed in their minds. There they were, along the beautiful sidewalks of Paris. Snubbing the enticing beauty of the most perfect city that had been created by human hands. Ignoring the unparalleled and unequaled venues that had presided over so much of Western history. There they were, concerned and preoccupied for the present and future of a small lump of land lost in the temperate waters of the Caribbean, just as beautiful as any other in the world but historically trivial and insignificant compared with Spain, England or France. On one of those fruitful days of conversation, Domingo Del Monte, more experienced and knowledgeable than his two younger companions, squinted his eyes and went into a long reflection.

"The Spanish," he said, "arrived in Cuba in 1492. Soon they discovered that its flat lavish lands, moist terrain and mild climate were ideal for growing sugar, the most bountiful and pricey of grasses. They soon sidelined their search for gold, which was easier to find in other American latitudes, and flooded Cuba with both slaves and sugar cane. It mostly happened over the XVI and XVII centuries. Having a fertile and generous soil, however, the Spaniards became incredibly inefficient and lax when it came to exploiting the new colony. It was not until they temporarily lost the island to the British, in 1762, during the Seven Year War, that sugar production, the slave trade and the merchant practices were taken seriously and modernized. The British were not the ones who introduced slavery in Cuba but they were certainly the most aggressive and effective slave traders. Over the XVIII Century the slave business grew more than 25%, and it doubled during the first half of the XIX Century. Most of the slave trade, however, was the result of deceiving and unethical activities by the Spaniards."

"The British, on the other hand," continued Del Monte, "needed to slow down the progress in Cuba to favor their own sugar producing colonies. According to the terms of the 1817 treaty that the British imposed on Spain, the slave trade into Cuba was forever abolished. The following year, however, twenty two expeditions smuggled four thousand blacks from Africa into Cuba. The British complained and the Madrid government proclaimed that any slave having proof that he or she had entered Cuba since 1817 would be declared free. There were of course few takers, fearing as they did that the Spaniards were not sincere and trustworthy. The British crown forced Spain to require captains of transatlantic vessels to turn their logbooks for inspection. Everybody knew it would not work. On May of 1824, for instance, a British war vessel followed the Spanish schooner *Minerva* to Havana, where six boatloads of slaves were seen disembarking. Captain General Francisco Dionisio Vives refused any calls for action by the British authorities. Cynically, at one point, the Spaniards even pretended that those slaves were actually refugees from the persecutions of the *Fulani Jihad*, recurrent enemies of the Yoruba people, who had invaded and conquered the Yoruba's Oyo Empire."

After a brief pause Del Monte continued: "Since very early and all through these shameful years, Havana was the center of slave trade in Cuba. The Spaniards lost no time bringing slaves into Cuba. The city became the capital of Cuba after its swampy original site on the southern coast was abandoned in favor of this fabulous port called *Carenas* in the northern coast. Soon Havana was selected as the only port authorized to send goods to Spain, and that required a lot of manpower. Under its bustling energy and progress the Havana trade in slaves began quietly and silently. Blacks were brought in to work as domestics or in the construction of ships and housing. Slavery soon turned into an addiction and became indispensable for the economy and well being of the residents of the city. There were already so many slaves in 1538 that a revolt was inevitable. Angry slaves joined forces with French pirates and burned parts of the city to the ground. The Spanish response was to build the *Castillo de la Fuerza* that now sits on a prominent place near the harbor. Its cannons could be pointed to sea, to protect the city from foreign intruders, or inland, to keep trouble makers in line. There you have it. Our entire history is totally enmeshed with the reprehensible and discreditable practice of slavery."

Another long pause followed, after which with a sorrowful voice Del Monte recalled: "Soon the slaves were found all throughout Cuba, working on the sugar, tobacco and coffee plantations. The slaves have continued to revolt and free themselves from their masters. Not finding much support in the cities, fugitive slaves have organized numeous settlements across Cuba. These are the well-known *palenques*, named after the Mayan lost city in Central America. Organized militias of Spanish soldiers have been eversince hunting down the *cimarrones* or escaped slaves in the countryside."

"The seeds of our independence are being planted as we speak, however," Del Monte said, ending the excruciatingly instructive address to his friends. "Some day these freed and escaped slaves will contribute with their blood to the freedom of both whites and blacks.

The Spanish government has fewer and fewer *criollos* on their side. The discontent among free blacks is unanimous. I know many of them: Manzano, Ble Rey, Plácido, Brindis, they are all ready to join any reasonable effort towards independence. So has in the past and will in the future every intelligent and patriotic white. The two of you know these people as well as I do: Luz y Caballero, Betancourt, Aguilera, Poey, Varela, Arango, Villaverde, the Countess, Tula, Masó, Heredia, Milanés, Martinez de Pinillos, Gener, Martinez Serrano. I can not even keep count anymore. The Spanish reprisals, if the past is an indication of the future, will be brutal and indiscriminate. The slave traders and a few recalcitrant *peninsulares* are the only people with whom they will be able to count."

"It may not be as easy as it sounds," replied Céspedes. "There are powerful interests. Too many people still hope for a liberal Spain that would treat us with the guarded respect with which the French treat their colonies. Too many *criollos* are afraid of radical elements among those who wish to see Cuba free."

"It will take sacrifice and a powerful example on our part," Miguel said. "Our family is being threatened with confiscation in Cuba. My father, who is the one with the most to lose, does not care. He will stay firm. We will recover our patrimony after we have thrown the scoundrels from Cuba. In the meantime, let them think they can sway our wills with threats. Spain will lose all its support and only despotically and with oppressive practices it would be able to slow down the clamor for independence."

"They can send thousands of men into Cuba to fight us," warned Domingo.

"They can and they will," Céspedes said as he pointed and aimed the trio in the direction of *rue des Saints-Pères*. "Let them…"

❧ ⌛ ❧

MANIFEST OF A SHIP BRINGING
INDENTURED SERVANTS INTO CUBA, 1867

The document reads: **"List of the workers** who came aboard the Portuguese frigate *Joven Thomas* with its captain P. Campos, who arrived at this port on the 13th of the current month, with a consignment for *Lombillo, Montalvo and Company*. This document also lists those workers who died during the trip and the causes of their deaths. (A list follows consisting of number, name, age, sex, occupation, causes of death and Christian name given to the workers. At the end it lists 44 out of 400 men who perished during the travesty and states that 356 arrived alive). Dated in Havana, March 14, 1867 and signed by an officer of *Lombillo, Montalvo and Company*."
Original document in the collection of the author.

13

"I believe that in a great city,
or even in a small city or a village, a great theater is the outward and visible
sign of an inward and probable culture."
Laurence Olivier

"Nurture your mind with great thoughts; to believe in the heroic makes heroes."
Benjamin Disraeli

"Fame is an illusive thing / here today, gone tomorrow.
The fickle, shallow mob raises its heroes to the pinnacle of approval today
and hurls them into oblivion tomorrow at the slightest whim;
cheers today, hisses tomorrow; utter forgetfulness in a few months."
Henry Miller

IT WAS ON a crisp and clear morning, with an unusual transparency in the air, when Carlos Manuel and Domingo finally decided to spend the day visiting Picpus, the cemetery where Lafayette was interred in Paris. Both were enthusiastic devotees of the French Marquis and admired his noble and selfless roles in the American and the French Revolutions. Lafayette had also valiantly opposed Napoleon at a time when most Frenchmen tolerated his ambition. That in itself was reason enough to undertake the long journey across Paris to pay their respects at his burial place. They had been planning such a trip for days, but the weather had been uncertain and heavy with clouds. On this day however, everything was propitious. The Aldamas, María del Carmen and Gertrudis had planned a visit to Mme. Sand, who was elated by Chopin's success in signing several important musical contracts in Vienna. They had a mission of their own: to arrange for a visit of the master to inaugurate the first concert season at the National Theater in Havana.

The National Theater, or *Teatro Tacón* as it came to be known, had been inaugurated in 1838 with a Carnival Ball which Don Miguel Tacón, the Captain General of the Island of Cuba, had attended. It was a magnificent building occupying the entire block limited by the streets *San Rafael, San José* and *Consulado*, with its front to the *Avenida Isabel la Católica*, which was a continuation of the *Paseo del Prado*. No expense had been spared in its decoration and the Aldamas had lent to Don Francisco Marty, the Theater owner, an enormous and heavy chandelier, best know in Spanish as an *araña*, made of fine crystal by the *Saint Louis* glassworks in Paris. A popular song of the times celebrated this generous loan: "...*tres cosas tiene la Habana que no las tiene Madrid... el Morro, la Cabaña y la araña de Tacón...* " (Havana has three things that Madrid does not have, the Morro, the Cabaña and the Tacón's chandelier).

The National Theater was the largest and most luxurious in the American Continent, New York included. It had been rated only behind La Scala and the Vienna Opera in terms of its acoustics. Don Francisco Marty was a prosperous Spanish merchant, whose family had roots in Dijon, France. He did not know how to read or write when he first arrived in Cuba and even after making colossal amounts of money he continued to live modestly. Now that the Tacón Theater had been finished, for instance, he had chosen to live on the premises, on a rather modest apartment he had built behind the stage. No technical advances were spared when the Tacón was built. A large system of jacks and pulleys permitted to clear the stage in record time. It even included an electrical operated intercom system, the first ever in recorded history, which allowed communications between the stage, the orchestra pit, the box office and Don Francisco's house.

Domingo and Carlos Manuel waited until the Aldamas, Gertrudis and María del Carmen had left the house on a large and comfortable carriage and climbed on their own curricle for their trip to Picpus. Carlos Manuel, always a history buff, had planned to follow the route of the guillotine, as they both wanted to revisit some of the historical places where, a few years earlier, the revolution and the Terror had been staged.

The trip would take about two hours each way, and would start by taking *rue Jacob* to the *Carrefour de Buci*, the location of one of the original gates of the Philippe August wall into Paris. From there they planned to go north on *rue Dauphine*, across the *Pont Neuf*, in front of the *Vert Galant* and above the pumps of *La Samaritaine* to *rue Rivoli*. A right on *rue Rivoli* would take them past the *Châtelet* and the *Hôtel de Ville* to *rue Saint Antoine*, once one of the most elegant streets in Paris and, during the revolution, the scene of many tragedies. After overtaking the *Place Royal* on their left they would arrive at the *Place de la Bastille*, from where they would continue on *rue du Faubourg Saint*

Antoine to the *Place de la Nation*. A short ride before exiting Paris through the recently finished *Colonnes du Trône* they would find the Cemetery of Picpus on a dirt road southeast of the *Place de L'Ile de la Reunion*.

It was the same path that hundreds of carriages had followed to *Place de la Nation* or *Place du Trône Renversée*, each bearing a dozen or more of presumed enemies of the revolution. There they were decapitated, sometimes 20 or 25 every hour, and their headless bodies, twenty at a time, were neatly arranged into lead-lined barrows with their heads between their legs. These macabre carriages, many of them leaving behind a trail of human blood, would discharge their ghastly cargo in three open pits at what was now Picpus Cemetery, where the bodies would purposely be randomly dumped and thereby deprived of their human identities.

As Domingo and Carlos Manuel started their pilgrimage their first topic of conversation was the *Marquis de Lafayette*. He was the hero of Yorktown, the spiritual son of George Washington; a man who at the tender age of twenty years, in spite of being an aristocrat, had rebelled against oppression and become a General in the American War of Independence.

"What a remarkable man," Domingo said. "A key character of the French and American revolutions, with a place in the history of the two emerging democracies in modern times."

"And also, many years later, a lone opponent of Napoleon, when every free man should have opposed him."

"He was also a man of vision, the voice of moderation and an advocate for the rule of law in a time of discord and lawlessness. Very misunderstood by the French, in my opinion. I have always believed he was too gutsy for their taste…"

"Yes, you have to look around and realize that, to this date, their own compatriots have never erected any great monuments in his memory. I believe he is best remembered in North America than here, where he tried so hard to liberate the people but also to temper their wrath."

At the end of *rue Jacob*, as they entered the *Carrefour de Buci*, Carlos Manuel, pointing to the streets around him, said: "This is the heart of the *Quartier Latin* (Latin Quarter). At this intersection the streets *de Buci, Saint André-des-Arts, Mazarine, l'Ancienne Comédie* and *Dauphine* meet, and at the river, you have the boundary between the *Quai de Conti* and the *Quai des Grand Augustines*. Until recent times the *rue de Buci* was called *rue de Thionville* and at number 34, there, you can see the only lasting remains of the wall of Philippe-Auguste."

"Amazing history that of this City," commented Domingo.

"Going back to Lafayette," Céspedes said again. "You have to wonder why France was so intent on helping Washington to bring about the independence of the United States when the French had fought him almost to the death during the French Indian Wars twenty years earlier."

"Oh yes. The situation in America was dismal. The British were not only raising new taxes to the colonists to recover from the Seven Year War but they were also handing out more and more territory to new settlers from England. The Americans' only hope were the French, but France at the time was a decaying monarchy entrenched and enmeshed in the quackmire of medieval feudalism."

"Granted. It had an oppressive legal system, an ossified social structure and asphyxiating traditions. But there was nothing else to choose from. Spain had wasted away its colonial wealth and its army was outmoded and lazy."

"And also there was in the French horizon an alliance of intellectuals, *petit bourgeois* and country folks who had been encouraged by the writings of Voltaire, Burke, Montesquieu and Rousseau. Lafayette was inspired by these readings. His resolve did not come on a vacuum. He was among the first French revolutionaries. Pristine in his thoughts and more resilient to contamination than Danton, Desmoulins and, of course, Robespierre and Marat."

"Many French writers argue today that there was not an American Revolution but simply an economic revolt against a greedy British crown," Céspedes commented.

"Well, the American war of independence was a great political landmark, not only there but also here. They invented the notions of Constitution, human rights, no taxation without representation, and equality of opportunity. They simply had to extrapolate ideas that were in infancy in the British tradition. They were the first ones to implement the separation of powers, which until then had been a mere theoretical construct of Locke and Montesquieu," added Del Monte.

"The American founders followed that with universal suffrage, one-man-one-vote, separation of Church and State, secular public education, and many other concepts that were revolutionary, even for the most recalcitrant of *sans-culottes*. The repercussions in Europe, including France, were enormous. Remember that even France did not have this concept of one-man-one-vote until recently."

"Now that they have the concept, perhaps they will try someday to implement it," commented Domingo with a touch of sarcasm.

As they passed through the *Hôtel de Ville*, Domingo could not help but be distracted by this magnificent building whose story he had read many times. Its roots could be traced to the 1357 building first erected by Etienne Marcel, the *Provost des Merchants*, considered the first ever mayor of Paris. With its present looks, it had been first built with funds that Francis I provided in 1533. Louis XIII expanded it in 1628. Ever since its first opening, it became the place to burn when things went bad in France.

"The first building burning happened in 1772," Domingo stated. "It was on the aftermath of the massacre of Saint Bartholomew, when thousands of Protestants were murdered by Catholics responding to the bells of the Church of Saint German l'Auxerrois. It burned on the Day of the Barricades, May 12, 1588, while Henry III was been driven out of Paris by the Catholic League. It was reduced to ashes by the civil war called *La Fronde* in 1650. In 1789 Louis XVI was forced to show at its balconies wearing the *cockade tricolor* after he had to leave Versailles under pressure from revolting ladies. From its halls the Paris Commune had controlled the National Convention by sickening thugs against them in 1792," added Del Monte. "It was there, on 9 Thermidor (July 27, 1794), that a fugitive Robespierre was captured by a mob and taken to the guillotine. Finally in 1830 the building was taken by the *Communards* as Paris, immobilized by barricades, enjoyed a new revolutionary wave."

Céspedes interrupted that train of thought. "It was in this building, in 1789, that Lafayette added the royal white to the blue and red traditional colors of all civic ornaments in Paris to create what is now the French flag."

"Interesting, not many people know that," answered Del Monte.

They continued their journey through *rue de Rivoli*, going east, and soon they arrived in front of the Church of Saint Louis, on the east side of the *Lycée Charlemagne*, an upper class school founded in the XVII Century. They paused in front of the steps leading to a small plaza in front of the Church and Domingo continued his story.

"Louis XIII provided the original funds to construct this Church in 1641, and from him it took its name. Bossuet and Bourdaloue, the famous Jesuit sermonizers, preached here in the 1750's to the attentive and devout ears of the *Marquise de Sevigné*, a resident of the nearby *Place Royal*. In 1791 the church of *Saint Louis* was ransacked and all its art works and furniture were burned in the middle of *rue Saint Antoine*. In 1792 the building was turned by Robespierre into a temple for the cult of the God of Reason. Its name would be changed to Saint Louis and Saint Paul after the nearby church of Saint Paul was burned to the ground by the revolutionaries in 1794."

"I know two interesting stories about this Church," Carlos Manuel told Domingo. "Do you want to hear them?"

"Absolutely!" answered his friend.

"In 1794 *rue Saint Antoine* was the path followed by the *charrettes* taking the condemned from the *Palais de Justice* to the *Place du Trône Renversée*, where Danton had ordered the guillotine to be placed. It is said that on one of these fateful trips a civilian and two soldiers that were guarding the convicts made a swift motion and took a ten year old girl from the *charrette*, covered her with a bedspread and ran into the patio of Saint Louis Church. There someone had placed a coffin where they hid the girl and proceeded to the church graveyard to bury her. They entombed the girl on a previously excavated shallow pit that someone had dug there, in a hurry and without ceremony except with a priest, or someone posing as a priest, to provide credibility to their deception. They had intended to come back to the site, excavate the coffin and set the girl free," added Carlos Manuel with a grave voice. "Unfortunately someone became suspicious and denounced the civilian, the soldiers and the presumed priest to the authorities. All four were condemned to death and taken to the guillotine two days later. No one was left to rescue the young girl and the incident was forgotten. Some thirty years later, in 1825, there was a project to reorganize the church cemetery after it had been returned to the Jesuits," continued Carlos Manuel. "A gravedigger exhumed a misplaced coffin, the one where the girl had been placed, removed the nails and opened it. Instead of a ten year old girl he found the remains of a young woman of 20, still dressed with clothes of a size belonging to a girl of 10. Someone had wrapped her with a bedspread as if to protect her from the cold. Her nails were well done and her hair arranged in a beautiful style. Her body was perfectly preserved and her face showed a peaceful and angelical smile. The gravedigger, satisfied that the girl was no longer alive, nailed the lid of the coffin back on. With a piece of chalk he marked the casket with a *fleur-de-lis* and reburied it on the eastern church wall, near the graves of other victims of the French Revolution."

Domingo was enthralled with that story and eagerly awaited Carlos Manuel to continue rather than pause at this point.

"The Archbishop of Paris," Céspedes continued, "has tried many times to exhume the coffin to find out if the body of the young girl is still undecomposed; to find out who she was, and to clarify by whom and when was she protected from the cold with the bed-spread," concluded Carlos Manuel. "But the cemetery now belongs to the state and its functionaries have refused permission to search for the coffin with the *fleur-de-lis* on the grounds that only her family is entitled to do so."

"There you have a classical example of French bureaucracy, added Del Monte. "No exhumation because the family has not asked for it, but we will never know who the family is because there can be no exhumation to identify the girl."

"You know what they say," added Céspedes. "It was the French who invented bureaucratic entanglements: they are still the best practitioners of the art."

❦ ⌛ ❧

WASHINGTON AND LAFAYETTE AT VALLEY FORGE, 1778

Marie Joseph Paul Yves Roche Gilbert du Motier, the **Marquis de Lafayette** first landed in the North American territory near Charleston, on June 13, 1777. Because he represented the highest rank of French nobility, the Congress soon recognized his patriotic motives and commissioned him a Major General on the 31st of July, 1777. In December he went with Commander in Chief **George Washington** and his Continental Army into winter quarters at Valley Forge. Early in the spring of 1778 he was involved in the action at Barren Hill and remained at Valley Forge until Washington departed to meet the enemy in New Jersey. This 1909 painting by John Ward Dunsmore shows him at a review of the troops with General Washington.

14

"If the Revolution has the right to destroy bridges and art monuments whenever necessary, it will stop still less from laying its hand on the life of men, no matter how great their achievements."
Leon Trotsky

"Great men are those who see that spiritual is stronger than material force, that thoughts rule the world."
Ralph Waldo Emerson

"To fear death, my friends, is only to think ourselves wise, without being wise: for it is to think that we know what we do not know. For anything that men can tell, death may be the greatest good that can happen to them rather than the greatest of evils. What a shameful ignorance to think that we know what we do not know."
Socrates

"THE SECOND STORY," Carlos Manuel continued, "also has to do with *charrettes* carrying the condemned along the *rue de Saint Antoine*. Danton had proclaimed that the Republic was in danger in April of 1793, giving absolute powers of life and death to the *Comité de Salut Public*, the Committee of Public Health, which launched a purge that was later called the Terror. Dark intrigues and desperate struggles followed and France was plunged into bloodshed. From the chaos a ruthless man consolidated his power, Maximilien Robespierre. Over 40,000 people died in a few months, until July 27, 1794, the so called *Coup de Thermidor*. The Conventioneers decided that the only way to stop the Terror was to pass Robespierre himself through the guillotine, and they did." Céspedes explained.

"All through the Terror the condemned were deprived the right to confess to a priest or receive the last rites of their Church. A secret practice was established of confessing to a lay person, which in turn restated the words of the penitent to a priest hidden somewhere in Paris. The penitent was told that the required absolution would be granted by a priest on the steps of the Church of Saint Louis on the day of execution. As the charrete passed in front of the church, the penitent would have to acknowledge his repentance by doing the sign of the cross on his chest. The priest, in civilian clothes, would be the person raising a forgiving hand on the steps of the church while watching the *charrette* go by."

"Imagine the rue de Saint Antoine on that fateful last day of the Terror," continued Céspedes. "The last *charrette* of the day was making its way towards the *Place de la Nation*. Just by a twist of fate it stopped in front of the Church of Saint Louis, and indeed the priest was there with his hand raised. Two soldiers on horse suddenly approached the cortege and told the custodians that the Terror had ended and the lives on those on the *charrette* were spared. The soldiers departed but the condemned remained motionless. People on the streets began to call on them to escape, yet they remained still, as if paralized."

Céspedes voice began to break down. "A few minutes later, a fresh detachment of soldiers showed up. Uninformed about Robespierre's defeat at the Convention they took over the task of escorting the prisoners to the guillotine. The gruesome parade continued its course towards the *Place de la Nation*. The guillotine, ordered to stay still, was busy one last time. These were the last men and women martyred, this time by mistake, during the Terror in Paris."

A profound silence ensued, as the coach taking Carlos Manuel and Domingo continued towards the *Place de la Bastille*. In an effort to break the grim stillness, Domingo spoke first. "There are some great paintings by Delacroix on this church, from his early periods, when through his art he deplored the revolution's attack on family values and paternal authority."

"Yes, I have seen these paintings," answered Carlos Manuel. "Delacroix, since his younger years, was an advocate for patrimony, history, lineage, order and authority. Even his *Liberty leading the People*, which many people feel is the definitive image of the French Revolution, is a romantic more than a revolutionary painting. It portraits a moment of anarchy in an otherwise eminently bourgeois revolt. It shows a poor and mischievous city boy sporting two pistols. Everyone who studies this painting comes to the conclusion that this poor boy will not outlive the day. Next to him you can see a seemingly irritated top-hat clad bourgeois, which is Delacroix himself. What you sense is that this man is reluctant to be in the picture since he never before had a weapon on his hand. *Liberty leading the People*, by the way, was painted in 1830 and refers to the cautious revolt that overthrew Charles X, not to the passionate revolution of 1789."

"I know. The restored Bourbons, one because he died and the other because he was deposed, were replaced by citizen-king Louis Philippe, a quasi constitutional president with very restricted powers."

"Delacroix, by the way," said Domingo, "was an avid reader and devoted student of Benjamin Franklin, and he was endlessly quoting his puritanical maxims. What more proof of his democratic inner core! Delacroix knew that revolutions never have happy endings and he enjoyed painting the 1830 revolution because it was not a revolution at all, only a burst of romantic energy after which the only thing left to do was to sing *La Marselleise*."

"Very well said. You know, Louis Philippe himself bought this painting for 3,000 Francs, framed. Amazing. He never hung it anywhere."

"I guess the day of anarchy portrayed by Delacroix also signaled the demise of Lafayette, since he was the man who persuaded the Duc d'Orleans to take the crown."

"Well, Lafayette was by then 73 and he always regretted having supported Louis Philippe D'Orleans. In the few years before he died in 1834 he supported the creation of a republic in France."

"Deep down Lafayette was a tragic figure. After his phenomenal success and popularity in the United States, with an offer of instant citizenship by George Washington, he returned to France and tried unsuccessfully to curb radicalism against the monarchy. When he joined the revolution the nobility, including many in his family, turned their backs on him. Then the King decided to escape and did not trust him with his plans. He had to order his troops to catch up with him and bring him back. That's the sad story of Varennes. Later on, the troops he tried to use to control the mobs in Paris disobeyed him. He was denounced as a traitor and had to leave France. As a former revolutionary, he was held prisoner by the Prussians first and later by the Austrians. His considerable fortune was confiscated by the revolutionaries. He was rescued by Napoleon but then his conscience made him vote against Bonaparte being crowned as Emperor. Needless to say, Napoleon did not like that. Returning to public life in 1800 he found no political support except to be elected with a bunch of incompetents to the Chamber of Deputies."

Carlos Manuel concluded: "This is the man of whom Thomas Jefferson said: *he was brave to rashness and never shrank from danger or responsibility. He always looked for a way to spare life and suffering, protect the defenseless, sustain the law and preserve order.*"

The coach by then was rapidly approaching la *Place de la Nation* and Domingo reclined his head on the folded canvas cover behind his back. Céspedes was trying to absorb every fraction of his surroundings, and continued reflecting on his conversation with Domingo.

"Great men, after all, have feet of clay," he mused. "To many Frenchmen Lafayette belonged to a past that they did not want to remember. In those prosperous but seemingly aimless days of the first half of the XIX Century the last thing most Frenchmen wanted to recall was the blood, the incivility and the cruelty that the Frenchmen had inflicted on each other."

Céspedes knew that his personal destiny was heavily focused in the independence of Cuba. And he wondered if his future would also be full of ungratefulness, jealousies, betrayals and the perfidy of his own countrymen.

He recalled having read that when Lafayette made his last visit to the States, he stayed at Monticello at the insistence of Jefferson. There was a glorious day in August of 1825 when his host invited James Madison and James Monroe as surprise guests. Jefferson had jokingly mentioned that young countries, like the United States, "were subject to the wrath of God unless they had a revolution at least every 20 years."

Domingo suddenly came alive and continued the conversation at the point where he felt it had been left.

"Lafayette was a very honorable man. His love for freedom has no parallel in modern history. He could have seized power in France in 1789 and become a dictator. He could have allied himself with Napoleon in his mature years. But he never betrayed his ideals or soiled his honor."

Céspedes added: "When Lafayette learned of the horrors and chaos of the Terror in France he wrote to Jefferson saying that he would have preferred to see the earth desolate and bare of life rather than betrayed by the enemies of freedom." To which Jefferson responded his famous sentence, "My friend, the tree of liberty has to be sprinkled from time to time with the blood of patriots and tyrants."

They were now rapidly approaching the humble cemetery of Picpus, far from the luxurious burial chamber and golden dome of Napoleon's Basilica in *les Invalides*. At Picpus, Lafayette was laid to rest next to his wife Adrienne de Noailles in a modest tomb that one day would also guard the final remains of his son George Washington Lafayette. Adrienne was the first to die; she had prompted Lafayette to ship some soil from the valley of Brandywine in Virginia, where Lafayette saw action for the first time in the cause of American freedom. Both Adrienne and the Marquis were thus buried on American soil.

"The first time I was here," Céspedes commented, "I had a very difficult time finding the place. Every time I asked anyone if they knew where to find the Picpus Cemetery, all I got from the neighbors was a resounding *"pas de tout"* (not at all). I walked in circles for two or three hours and even went into the garden of the hospital and saw the cemetery from the other side of the wall. But finding the entrance was something else. The only clue to its existence is a small sign on the side of a gate."

Carlos Manuel and Domingo descended from the curricle and approached the large wooden gate at *35, rue Picpus*, which had been the entrance to the *Couvent de Chanoinesses de Picpus*. They rang a bell by the small sign that Céspedes had mentioned and a few minutes later the gate opened slowly and a short man in working clothes appeared.

"Qu'est-ce que vous voulez, messieurs?"

"Nous aimerions visiter la tombe du Marquis de Lafayette," responded Carlos Manuel.

"Entrez s'il vous plait" was the answer.

The custodian of the Cemetery, visibly moved and without being asked, began to relate to the newcomers the story of Picpus.

"The guillotine had first been placed in front of the *Hôtel de Ville* and later across the street from the Louvre, where some of the initial victims of the revolution found their fate. It was Danton who first suggested a more visible place and had it moved to the *Place de la Revolution*. When Robespierre was planning his feast of the Supreme Being, and because of the unpleasant smell of dried blood in the summer time, the revolutionaries decided to move it first to the *Place de la Bastille* and finally to the *Place de la Nation*. At the first four venues it was easy to dispose of the bodies since the Cemetery of the Innocents was close by. Not so when the emplacement was at the *Place de la Nation*, which was barely on the inside of the wall of the *Fermiers Généraux* on southeast Paris. The solution was to confiscate the Convent of the *Chanoinesses de Picpus*. The convent, founded in the XVII Century, was at the center of a long track of land measuring fifteen hundred feet in the front and three thousand feet in depth. For many years it had functioned as a place of retirement and quiet worship by the pious religious order of the Canonesess. In 1792, three years into the revolution, it was declared a *"bien national"* by the Assembly and rented to a M. Riédain, who allowed the nuns to stay but began to use the chapel as a market for the produce grown by the nuns in the grounds. M. Riédain also turned part of the convent into a *"maison de santé,"* a simulated health sanatorium. He provided asylum to many noblemen, people of means and priests posing as patients but actually looking for a safe living place where they could escape the guillotine."

The custodian opened the locked gate leading to the area where the Lafayettes were buried and continued his story.

"On 25 Prairial (13 June 1794), the grounds were confiscated by the Paris Commune and M. Riédain, the fake doctors, the nuns and all their patients were thrown out. Sanson, the Parisian executioner who single-handedly had guillotined every victim of the revolution at every location where his infernal machine had been placed, had moved to *Place de la Nation,* and he needed a burial ground."

As Carlos Manuel and Domingo entered the property they first saw a small building on the right and a long row of small rooms on the left.

"This was the *accueil* or welcoming area, where the only nun allowed to break her silence vows would greet visitors," mentioned Carlos Manuel, pointing to his right. "and those were the rooms for the help."

"There on the right is what remains of the old convent, and the Chapel would have been in front of you," added the custodian.

"There is a feeling of desolation, sadness and unhappiness in this place," commented Domingo.

They continued to the back of the ruined structure of the Chapel and came into a large garden with a small gate on the left. The wall from the servants' quarters to the end of the property was made of solid stone, perhaps ten feet in height, with no entrances except a small gate at the end. Almost before the gate one could see a rectangular pit, fifteen feet by thirty, partially refilled with soil, which had been dug a few feet from the wall. Along the wall a row of ancient elms was only interrupted by a rotting wooden barrier that divided the area in two. At the end of the furthest half, on the right, there was an additional opening on a similar stone wall leading to a small courtyard. The area was also divided in half by a stone wall. On its right there was a gate leading to a small garden where you would find two additional pits refilled with soil. On both of these there were two stone grave markers inscribed with some writing. On the right of the gate leading to the small garden there was a large slab of marble with two inscriptions: Adrienne de Noailles, *Marquise de La-*

fayette on the left, Marie Joseph Gilbert du Mottier, *Marquis de Lafayette*, on the right.

"This is a sacred ground of immense historical significance," muted Domingo.

"A hallowed ground it is," added Carlos Manuel. "Thirteen thousand and three men, women and children were murdered nearby. They were transported here in wagons and stripped of their clothing, which became the spoils of the drivers. Their bodies were carelessly and hurriedly dumped in these two common shallow graves. Many of them were ordinary people of all ages and occupations. Some were from religious orders, like the sixteen *Carmélites de Compiège* who were guillotined on July 17, 1794. Very few were aristocrats. The third grave was never filled because, after months of impotence, indifference and shameless denial, Parisians could not stand any more bloodshed. It all happened between June 14 and July 27 in 1794, sometimes at the rate of two souls per minute."

"How has this place been preserved?" asked Domingo.

"Right after the end of the Terror the place was shut down and the property sold secretly to princess Amélie de Salm de Hohenzollern-Sigmaringen, the sister of one of the victims. Amélie got together with twelve of the families of other victims and formed a society who took title to the property and turned the former convent and its gardens into a cemetery. Only the immediate families of those originally buried here have the right and the honor to be interred here now."

"Lafayette, I presume, belonged to one of the twelve families."

"His wife Adrienne lost her parents to the guillotine on June 22, 1794. Lafayette is here because of her," replied the custodian.

"When did all that happen?" asked Domingo.

"Well, the princess Amélie de Salm bought the property in 1795," the custodian continued. "She formed the society in 1803. The society has successfully recovered the names of all those interred here and is raising funds to rebuild the Convent and the Chapel. They also began to look for a congregation of sisters to take over the convent since the original sisters of the canoness were dispersed and probably murdered. A few years ago they offered to the Sisters of the Sacred Heart, who have a Convent nearby, to come and reside here. The sisters have instituted a 24-hour vigil praying for the victims and the executioners. It has been now almost 38 years, and at least one nun is always praying for these poor souls, day and night."

Carlos Manuel and Domingo stood briefly in silence at the tomb of Lafayette and his wife before departing the cemetery. Here were two men seeking freedom for their country paying homage to a man who had given his entire life to a quest for the freedom of his two countries. In their minds, for some reason, Lafayette always evoked the presence of Jefferson, who once, at a Charlottesville dinner in Lafayette's honor in 1824 had urged Americans to honor the Frenchman as their "benefactor in peace as well as in war."

"Jefferson's persona comes to my mind every time I think of Lafayette," explained Domingo. "He once said, and Lafayette concurred, that *this ball of liberty is now so well in motion that it will roll round the globe, at least the enlightened part of it, for light & liberty go together. It is our glory that we first put it into motion.*"

"You know," responded Carlos Manuel, "after many years of absence Jefferson and Lafayette saw each other again when Jefferson was 81 and Lafayette 67. It has been said that when they saw each other they simply said "Ah, Jefferson!" to which there was a simple reply: "Ah, Lafayette!" before they ran to each other bursting in tears."

So there were then four honorable men instead of two: Lafayette, Jefferson, Domingo Del Monte and Carlos Manuel de Céspedes. One had fought on two continents for the rights of people to be free. The second had written the Declaration of Independence and the Declaration of the Rights of Man. The third was tirelessly shaping the character of a new Nation. The last one was called to be the Father of his Land. Their spirits were sharing an instant of undefinable closeness. It was hard to imagine a more wondrous scene in a revered but little known plot of blessed land called Picpus.

15

*"Simplicity is the final achievement. After one has played
a vast quantity of notes and more notes,
it is simplicity that emerges as the crowning reward of art."*
Frédéric Chopin

*"Once my heart was captured, reason was shown the door, deliberately
and with a sort of frantic joy. I accepted everything, I believed everything,
without struggle, without suffering, without regret,
without false shame. How can one blush for what one adores?"*
George Sand

*"The more a race is governed by its passions,
the less it has acquired the habit of cautious and reasoned argument,
the more intense will be its love of music."*
Stendhal

THE DAY HAD finally come when Miguel and Rosa Aldama, María del Carmen and Gertrudis visited Mme. Sand in an effort to secure the commitment of Frédérick Chopin to inaugurate the first concert season at the National Theater in Havana. As they prepared for their meeting with the eminent musician, they had reasons to be optimistic about the outcome of their request. Céspedes was already a legal advisor to Chopin and had successfully negotiated several publishing contracts on his behalf. María del Carmen, a beautiful and delicate young woman, had been Chopin's favorite piano student in the short time she had received lessons from the master. A common friend of the Céspedes and Chopin was Custine, in whose good business and common sense Chopin trusted blindly. Besides, they all cherished many common friends such as Wagner, Baudelaire, Delacroix and Balzac.

The visiting Cubans however, were mostly counting on an ultimate persuader, if it became difficult to convince Chopin to travel to the Caribbean, sick as he was with the *tisis*. It was Julian Fontana, an old family friend of the Céspedes and the Aldamas, whose father had been a partner to Domingo Aldama in the acquisition of lands in western Cuba.

Julian Fontana (1810-1870), aged 34 at the time, had been born to a family of Italian immigrants that made a sizable fortune with tobacco in western Cuba. When Don Julian Fontana Sr., his father, became alarmed by the reports in the press of the slave revolts in Haiti, and particularly the frightful burning of *Cap François* in 1793, he panicked. Mindful of the wave of fearful immigrants seeking refuge in Santiago de Cuba, Philadelphia, Charleston and New Orleans, he decided to move to where his brother had moved years before: Warsaw, Poland.

In Warsaw, Julian Jr. began studies at the *National Lyceum*, and after a distinguished career he received his diploma in 1828. Two of his classmates became friends for life: Frédérick Chopin and Dominik Magnuszewski. All three graduates had entered the University at the same time. Together they attended English classes three evenings per week from a teacher of Irish ancestry called Makartnej. They shared the same patriotic fervor and joined the uprising against Russia in November of 1830 and, after its failure, they immigrated together to Paris. Once there Fontana published arrangements of Polish National Melodies to make a living while Chopin published his Opus 1, 3, 5, 10 and 11, all under a subtitle "arranged by J. Fontana." A few years later Chopin would publish in London *Les Deux Polonaises*, Opus 40, "dedicated to my friend Jules Fontana."

Fontana became a multitalented darling of the social scene in Paris. He was a pianist, piano teacher, composer, journalist, trained notary, author and businessman. He spoke fluently half a dozen languages: Polish, French, Spanish, English, German and Russian. He became the number one critic, copier, editor, arranger and performer of Chopin's music, aside from being his manager, agent and promoter. Given the poor nature of Chopin's health he took care of his life necessities and, after his death, was his posthumous executor. He never charged Chopin or his family for all these efforts and spoke of them as "a labor of love of one friend for another..." Needless to say, Chopin never declined any petition by Fontana if it was in his power to grant it.

At the time of the visit of Miguel and Rosa Aldama and their friends, George Sand (1804-1876) was at the peak of her fame. She had been born Amandine Aurore Lucile Dupin in Paris and had inherited a substantial fortune after her grandmother died in 1821. The following year she married the Baron Casimir Dudevant, also solidly moneyed, whom she abandoned in 1831. After that event she became entangled in multiple love affairs in Paris with such prominent men of letters and arts as Prosper Merrimée and Alfred de Musset, both notable French romantic dramatists and poets. She met Frédérick Chopin in 1838 and instantly became her companion and perhaps her lover. Other occasional flings were allegedly with Eugène Delacroix, the Count of Saint Simon, Frank Listz and even the much older and by then inveterate recluse François-René Vicomte de Châteaubriand.

By 1832 she had published her first novel, *Indiana*, a disguised autobiography telling of a naïve, love starved woman abused by her much older husband and deceived by a much younger selfish seducer. Soon after she began to write for *Le Figaro* and the *Revue des Deux Mondes* and became an influential friend of poets, artists, politicians and philosophers, a thorough and veritable *who is who in Paris*. Her life, at age 36 when she received the Aldamas and their friends, was already quite controversial. The French Senate had opposed the purchase of her books by public libraries because of her questioning of sexual identities and the sanctity of marriage. She was herself accused of nymphomania and lesbianism, given her presumed indiscriminate affairs with well known celebrities. But she had found her own voice in literature and her memoirs and short stories were already playing an important role in the evolution of the novel as an artistic form.

Frédérick Chopin (1810-1849), on the other hand, was in many ways a much simpler person than George Sand. He was the son of a French language and literature teacher at the Warsaw Lyceum who also had a second job as a tutor in a boarding school for the sons of the gentry. As a child Chopin began to show musical talent and was inevitably compared to Mozart. He had written and published two Polonaises (in G minor and B flat major) by the time he was 7. Young Chopin, soon after, began to be featured in the Warsaw newspapers and became the attraction of the most lavish receptions at the elegant salons of Warsaw. At age 12 his piano teacher, a renowned professor of the Warsaw Conservatory, resigned after proclaiming that Chopin's skills had overcome his own.

At age 19 Chopin was anxious to travel through Europe and anchor his musical career in one of its great musical capitals. After a brief and bloody uprising, the Kingdom of Poland had been subjugated by the Russian Tsar and Italy and Austria were openly increasing their hostilities. That precluded Warsaw, Vienna, Milan or Rome. Chopin opted for Paris and moved there in the autumn of 1831. He became an instant success since his fame had preceded him and the musical milieu welcomed him with open arms. He became friends with Liszt, Mendelssohn, Berlioz and Schumann. The Parisian *salons* of the Polish and the French aristocracy became his favorite places to perform. His income was assured by the piano lessons he gave to a selected group of talented pupils. Always a patriot, he refused to follow the Tsarist's regulations and allowed his passport to expire rather than updating it at the Russian embassy. He never returned to Poland again, setting an example to other Polish nationals in Paris, many of them infiltrates or agents of the Russian invaders, who espoused dialogue and agreements with the oppressors.

At age 27 Chopin fell in love with one of his young pupils, whose family rejected his wedding proposals due to the poor state of his health and his irregular lifestyle. Dejected and desirous to enter a stable relationship, he met George Sand, six years his senior. She was a divorcee with two children, extraordinarily tender, warm and with a tinge of maternal instincts towards him, which he needed and longed for. Together they visited Spain and knew about Cuba when they met Domingo Del Monte in one of his frequent business trips to Majorca. The island had received many refugees from Catalonia during the Napoleonic invasion and had developed one of the best light shipbuilding industries in Europe. Del Monte was negotiating the construction of several ships for his sugar business. George Sand and Frédérick Chopin were honeymooning at the former monastery of Valdemosa, where he was convalescing after his first symptoms of tuberculosis.

George Sand and Frédérick Chopin received at their home at *16, rue Pigalle* the visit from Miguel and Rosa Aldama, María del Carmen and Gertrudis. Waiting for their guests with them was Julian Fontana, all excited at the prospect of convincing his life long friend, at the time the most acclaimed musician in the entire world, to visit Cuba, his country of origin, a place that he could not remember but through the many stories of his mother and father.

George Sand was a tall woman, with an interesting rather than pretty face. She was slightly overweight and had a rather bulky mane of pitch black hair, which made her look older than her years. In fact, Chopin had not liked her on first sight and had written to his father that *"something about her repels me..."* Her face was rather maternal, however, and her eyes were expressive and an evident assertion of her devotion to Chopin. She liked to dress in hulking but expensive clothes, mostly with dark and somber colors. There was never a scarf or any accessory in her wardrobe. Were it not for her cultured and educated spirit and her passionate beliefs and impassionate, thunderous and eloquent diatribes for worthy causes, one would not think of classifying her as an appropriate mistress for a man of great genius.

Chopin also looked older than his years in the 1840's. He was to his contemporaries "the tall man that never smiles..." His hair started at a receding line on his forefront and extended down to the base of his neck, thick and heavy. He had a protruding, somewhat curved nose and dark and heavy eyebrows to match. He was always dressed in the most formal of attires, with tie and vest under a long coat that he kept on, even indoors. He had thick lips over a square jaw and strong cheekbones. His eyes sank deeply on his face giving him an expression of permanent preoccupation. At the time of the Aldamas and their friends' visit, he was coughing quite frequently and had to excuse himself oftentimes to retire and regain his composture in the quiet of his room.

After the proper introductions, the conversation started by a reminiscence of Cuba. Chopin, who had seen Aldama in Paris a few days before, commented on the difficult political situation there.

"I believe your island is been invaded by slaves and most *criollos* are anxious because what happened in Haiti," he said.

"Yes, we are not going through very good times on that regard," responded Miguel. "On the other hand we are living the best of times. The island is very prosperous and Havana is growing in leaps and bounds. The city is expanding into its surroundings, much as Paris is, and dozens of ships crowd in the harbor everyday, discharging or reloading merchandise."

"I know a lot about Cuba thanks to Julian, who is obsessed with a return to the island," Chopin indicated. "I always tell him that since he left at age two he can not possibly remember anything and his memories are only fantasies inculcated by his father."

"Well, it is not easy to postpone visiting your land when you have been away for so long," Gertrudis said, almost applying the maxim to herself rather than Julian.

"I know. I love Paris but I long for Warsaw," responded Chopin. "I miss the cold chilly days when you had to walk fast to prevent your feet from freezing. I miss the smell of the Vistula on a summer night. I miss the *Rynek Starego Miasta* (Market Square) and the Town Hall built by *Tylman de Gameren* which they tore down a few years ago, when I was a child. I miss all my childhood friends. I have not heard from them in a long time."

Chopin's eyes sank even deeper on his face. "I do not know if I will ever return. Certainly not under occupation. I know that we have difficult times ahead; that the Russians have been trying for generations to destroy Poland and that now they have the upper hand."

The guests remained in silence for a few seconds, after which Chopin said: "But tell me about Cuba and about Havana. I understand you wish to bring some of my music to the new theater. Tell me about it."

Rosa Del Monte spent the next few minutes describing in her best words the *Teatro Tacón* and their plans to turn it into the best cultural institution of the Americas. At the end of her description Chopin began to reflect on her words.

"I have been thinking about the Tacón and your city for quite a while. The word in Europe is that Havana has become a world class city and that the *Sociedad Económica* and other literary societies are turning Havana into the prime European city in the New World, if it is not yet at that level. I am also impressed by what they say about the acoustic quality of this new theater. And I know that you have acquired a Pleyel piano."

"When the time came to make the decision for a piano we knew that Beethoven played the Broadwood and Liszt the Beckstein but that you played the Pleyel," María del Carmen quickly responded.

"The foundation of a good piano is the soundboard, which must have a sort of a "crown and tone," Chopin explained. "Then, of course, is a matter of matching the strings, the hammers, the tension on the bridges, the weight of the keys and the regulation of the tone. Broadwoods and Becksteins are very good pianos but nothing equals a full size Pleyel."

"I am glad we made such a smart choice. We are hoping that you will soon test it," added Gertrudis.

"*Quand je me sens en verve et assez fort pour trouver mon proper son, il me faut un piano Pleyel,*" responded Chopin. (When I feel witty and strong enough to find my proper rhythm, I need a Pleyel piano). He then reflected for a few seconds on his own words before he finally spoke with a quasi solemn voice.

"I will play in your Pleyel," Chopin said. "I will be much honored to help this young Nation develop a strong musical tradition. I know that Julian wants to establish himself there for a while and he has told me of some very salubrious mountains, east of Havana, that will be good for my health."

With a very timid motion Chopin stood up, bid his guests good by and retired to his room. The gentle George Sand, hoping that all would understand the shyness and physical weakness of the master, raised her shoulders and slowly inclined her head forward, as she began to pour some tea to her guests. The Cubans felt their hearts jumping on their chests. They had secured an opening season for their new National Theater with the most distinguished composer of the times. They sipped their teas with style and elegance but were eager to be by themselves to embrace and congratulate each other for the magnificent accomplishment they had scored.

With tears of joy gracefully contained, María del Carmen got hold of Gertrudis' hand and squeezed it hard, until it almost brought her to tears.

"Watch it, María del Carmen," Gertrudis whispered to her. "This is my writing hand…"

THE TEATRO TACON (LEFT), HAVANA

The **Teatro Tacón**, shown here on the left, next to Hotel Inglaterra in Havana's *Avenida Isabel la Católica*, boasted more than two thousand three hundred seats in 1846. The stage had room for six hundred and fifty musicians. It presented all types of performances: operas, symphonies, *zarzuelas*, ballets, dramas, choral works, popular orchestras, military bands and light concerts. It was purchased in 1905 by the corporation that built the *Centro Gallego* and was completely enclosed inside the building of this regional Spanish society. Its name was changed to *Teatro Nacional de Cuba* in 1917, a few months after Anna Pavlova premiered there her first role of *Giselle*.

16

"If you cry "Forward" you must be sure to make clear
the direction in which to go. Don't you see that if you fail to do that
and simply call out the word to a monk and a revolutionary,
they will go in precisely opposite directions?"
Anton Chekhov

"Clemency was also supposed to be a revolutionary measure."
Camile Desmoulins

"Men fear thought as they fear nothing else on earth -- more than ruin -- more
even than death... Thought is subversive and revolutionary,
destructive and terrible, thought is merciless to privilege,
established institutions, and comfortable habit."
Bertrand Russell

IT WAS NINE o'clock in the morning and the Aldamas, the
Céspedes and Gertrudis were anxiously waiting for Domingo to return from a quick early meeting he had with one of his representa-
tives in Paris. All six were hoping to have a trip to the *Manufacture
des Gobelins*, the acclaimed tapestry factory that Colbert had founded
in 1662. As a minister to Louis XIV Colbert had consolidated under
the direction of Charles le Brun, the King's favorite painter, all the
workshops first founded by Fouquet for his own palace.

The tapestries, as well as the carpets of the *Gobelins*, were weaved
using the cartoons of the great masters of the times, Ingres, Gros,
Gericault, David, Cabanel. They were mostly intended to be used as
decorations for the royal buildings and as diplomatic presents. There
was always room, however, for someone with the right contacts to
have access to a good *Gobelin*. The Aldamas had acquired seventeen
pieces for the new palace which the family was building on Amistad
Street in Havana. They had planned today to check on the progress
of their order and to show their choices to their friends.

At seven thirty in the morning, when Domingo had left the
house, the streets of Paris were deserted. Only butchers, bakers and
water carriers could be seen in the streets at that hour. No carriages

were yet in transit. It was only at nine that you would start to see movement on the streets. Young *garçons* taking coffee to many rich and poor households in every neighborhood; men followed by their servants riding their horses towards the Boulevards; bureaucrats converging towards the *Châtelet* and the *Palais*; pious women walking to the nine o'clock mass; shop owners sweeping the streets in front of their establishments; cleaning ladies washing glass windows on the businesses which were about to open.

Most of the people on the streets, however, were walking towards the public markets that authorities allowed on certain intersections of the city. The intersections were located where in years past there were gates to the walls that surrounded Paris. In spite of the five hundred years that had passed since the removal of the wall of Philippe August, for instance, there were markets in the early 1830's in the areas where gates had been before: at *la Bastille*, across from *Saint Eustache*, at the *Porte de Buci*, at the *rue Mouffetard*, among others.

A lot of activity could be seen around the markets. The French have always liked to purchase their food fresh, on the streets, at stalls that have been turned from father to son for many generations. These markets were originally on the outer edge of the walls of Paris, just as you would exit one of the gates. There the merchants, by simply not entering the city, avoided paying the *octroi*, the tax on supplies brought into Paris. Customers of these markets, where everything was a lot cheaper than inside the city walls, had to exit through the gates, purchase their supplies and reenter the city. The tax collectors would not bother to collect taxes from a housemaid with a small sack of tomatoes and thus they would enter Paris tax-free. But if a seller ever tried to go past the gate with his cart full of tomatoes, his merchandise would be imposed the detested *octroi* and his produce would no longer be competitively priced when compared with the offerings of those merchants who stayed outside the walls.

Domingo Del Monte finally arrived on his regular two-seater personal carriage and joined the group at the entrance of the house on 12, *rue Jacob*. They were all in good spirits and the day, although cloudy, was foretelling a good excursion. Their plans were to get to the *Quai des Grands Augustines* through *rue Guénégaud*, to look at the place where the Tower of Nesle had been placed, and then continue all along the Quai, going east, to the Church of *Saint Julian le Pauvre* in the *Quai de Montebello*. There they would cross into the Latin Quarter towards la *Place Maubert* and the *rue Descartes*. Heading south, within a few city blocks, the *rue Descartes* changed its name to *rue Mouffetard*, and that street would take them past the Church of Saint Medard to the *Manufacture des Gobelins*.

The *Quai des Grand Augustines* was thus named in the XIV Century, after the convent of the *Grand Augustines*, where Marie de Medicis had been proclaimed regent in 1610, after the assassination of Henri IV. The priests there were mostly of Italian origin and different from the monks of the *Petit Augustines*, which were further down the Seine in what later became the *École des Beaux-Arts*.

The Céspedes knew the area well because at number 51 was located one of their favorite restaurants, *Lapérouse*, first founded by Jean Françoise de Galaup, *Comte de La Pérouse*, a well known chef to the Kings of France. They dined quite often at *Lapérouse* in the company of Alexander Dumas père, whose *La Tour de Nesle* was already considered a great masterpiece of French melodrama. A frequent visitor with them, also a devotee of *Lapérouse*, was Victor Hugo, who had read for them at *Lapérouse* the first pages of his *Le Voyage aux Pyrénées*, a novel he never got to finish because of the drowning on the Seine river of his daughter Léopoldine.

Leyend had it that at *Lapérouse* many mistresses had scratched their names on the glass windows to verify the value of the diamonds they received from their lovers and to embarrass them if they ever had the audacity to take their wives there.

A brief detour to the place where *la Tour de Nesle* had been was always *de rigueur*. The tower had been located on the opposite side of the Louvre, and in fact it was the southern anchor of a huge chain that extended across the Seine at night, in the XIII Century, to prevent ships from going downstream and attacking the city from its rearguard.

"There is an act of the city fathers, dated 1210, that called this tower as *Tornella Philippi Hamelini suprà Sequanam*," said Céspedes. After a brief pause he continued: "the tower was at the end of the Mazarine Library, far from the building, and it was said that because of its remoteness it became a lover's nest. Even one Queen, the story goes, used to leave the Louvre, cross the *Pont Neuf* and run through an underground chamber to give herself there to debauchery, after which her servants would throw one or two of her lovers' throbbing corpses to the Seine."

"Which Queen was that?" inquired Gertrudis.

"The story is attributed to a well known poet and story teller, famous for his exaggerated tales, whose name I rather not mention.

The same goes for the name of the Queen. I do not wish to be remembered in the future as a gossip!," joked Carlos.

"Come on, Carlos," said Rosa. "Are you also going to translate that piece of Latin that you quoted from the 1210 act of the city fathers?"

"Not really. I will not disclose that either. Let it be a mystery to you," replied Carlos Manuel, giving a signal to the coach master to resume his journey.

They all laughed and within minutes they were in sight of *Saint Julian le Pauvre*.

As they pulled close to the church, in front of the oldest tree in the city, it was Domingo's turn to tell his story. "This church is older than the Sorbonne and even older than the tower of Clovis. Its walls reek of Chilperic and Fredigonda, Petrarch and Abelard. It was a well established church at the time of the Merovingians and there was a *Te Deum* here when Louis IX brought to Paris all the scrap and rubble he obtained in the Holy Land. This church is really old."

"There was a time," added María del Carmen, "when the Chief Director of the University of Paris was elected at *Saint Julian*. Let me remind you of those who taught or preached here. To begin with Petrarch, Rabelais and Thomas of Aquinas. To cap it all, guess who loved to come and participate in the sort of *tertulias* that were organized on Sundays, after the main mass? Dante Alighieri. Isn't it remarkable that we can contemplate the same walls that he probably did as he pondered some of the points he was about to present to others?"

"The Church is so conveniently placed across the river, on the side of the University, that it has been witness to hundreds of conversions and spiritual rebirths."

It was now Domingo again. "The surroundings are so beautiful and make you feel so insignificant in the big game of history that it has inspired many an epiphany among visitors. Many of those who returned here to the embrace of the Catholic Church may be disappointed when they learn that there is talk of turning this Church to the *Melkites Ortodoxes*, which are theologically but not liturgically similar to the practitioners of the Catholic faith."

"But then, is it not all the same?" commented Gertrudis. "Besides, there are many other Catholic choices nearby. Almost across the river there is *Saint Germain l'Auxerrois*, the Church where the bells sounded the *tocsin* of Saint Bartholomew, calling Catholics to murder and exterminate the Protestants."

"A very deplorable incident, to say the least," exclaimed Carlos Manuel. "And not the right place for a spiritual rebirth, if I may say so."

"Well, I like *Saint Julien* Church much better than *Notre Dame*," said María del Carmen. "It does not have the frightening monsters, elfs, griffins, huge pillars and forbidding nooks, the overstated capitals and arabesques, and the dark and dreadful dark corners of *Notre Dame*."

"I also like the human scale of *Saint Julian le Pauvre*," exclaimed Gertrudis. "I love the spring sunshine that makes the lilacs come alive in the little garden in front of *Saint Julian*. I love this huge mastodon of a tree that provides shade and shelters the nightingales from the noises and the filth of the city. I am content with the subdued light of this Church, which magically never turns into shadows. It fills my heart with love and happiness and whenever I am here I desired nothing, nothing at all."

The noises of the city had disappeared in the distance, and a profound silence, uncharacteristic of the *Quai de Montebello* surrounded the six excursionists. It was gently broken by Céspedes by saying "let's go on to la *Place Maubert*. I need to show you something."

A few minutes later they were at the *Place de Maubert*, in front of a building owned by the *Mutualité Sociale*, a society of French mutualists, who lent their facilities to cultural and political organizations for all sorts of social or educational events, as well as balls and banquets. The building, like the *Place de Maubert*, was named after Jean Aubert, second Abbot of Saint Genevieve in 1202.

"I want you to know," Domingo stated, "that if you have ever been impressed by the stories they tell about *Leonardo Da Vinci*, you have to be doubly impressed by the knowledge of a man who used to preach in a little plaza that was right on this spot. He was the famous Dominican priest *Albert le Grand*. On his teaching sessions he would lecture on such things as the physics of Aristotle, the principles of the wheel, the mechanics and design of beams and the workings of screws to move power in all directions. Unlike *Da Vinci*, who was a great painter and illustrator but not the great scientist some of his followers like to portrait, Albert really understood what he was presenting and truly advanced the knowledge of the physical world, all of that during the reign of Louis IX."

Not wanting to engage into a polemical discussion with Domingo, who had strong feelings about what he felt were undeserved attributions and unjustified accolades to *Da Vinci's* scientific genius, Carlos Manuel changed the subject. "We have permission to use the main meeting room at the *Mutualité* to gather many Cubans scattered all throughout France to discuss our political future," indicated Carlos Manuel. "I met in Madrid one of the Directors of the *Societé*, Alexandre of Sommerard, who also owns the *Hôtel de Cluny* nearby. He sympathizes with the Cuban cause and has been very supportive in letting us meet with small numbers of Cubans in the *salons* of the *Societé*. We are hoping to have a large meeting that will bring together everyone: those who own slaves, those who abhor the practice and those who are indifferent; those who favor independence as well as those who would like to see the United States take over our political destiny and those who are planning to stay in France forever; all Cubans will be welcome. We are hoping for a date early next year, as soon as the cold weather dissipates."

They stepped down from the coach and took a look at the reception and the rooms of the *Mutualité Sociale* and, finding that it was rapidly approaching mid morning, they returned to their vehicle on the way to *rue Descartes* and *rue Mouffetard*.

The conversation quickly turned to politics, the situation in Cuba and the French experience.

"Revolutions, however desirable or inevitable," said Domingo, "are rarely constructive. All across France Abbeys, Churches, convents, schools, palaces, businesses and residences came tumbling down, some on pure anti-religious or anti-clerical grounds. Many envious souls took advantage of the chaos to seek revenge for past grievances that had nothing to do with freedom or liberties."

"Here in Paris," he continued, "the bones of Kings, Queens and Saints were removed from their resting places and thrown to the garbage pails. Thousands of years of French history were left without its icons. People need to see, touch, smell their past to feel proud of it, and that was forever lost in France. Confusion went rampant. The *Place Louis XV* became the *Place de la Revolution*. *Place Royal* became *Place des Vosges*. *Notre Dame* became the Temple of Reason. The *Saint Chapelle* a grain warehouse. The *Conciergerie* a waiting room for the guillotine. What a disaster."

"Very destructive," Céspedes agreed. "The revolution lacked a strong hand. It needed, but never had, a leader which was popularly elected but forceful and decisive. Not even the collective strength of the *Jacobines* or the *sans-coulottes* could replace a strong man. That's why a man like Napoleon had to surface. Whatever the revolution accomplished was between 1799 and 1814, when Napoleon was its strong hand. He was the first "*caudillo*," and as most *caudillos* in history, he ended up being a tyrant. His accomplishments, however, were short lived. They were all gone within years, as fast as they came into being. The empire was wiped out. The *Grande Armée* decimated. The Egyptian expeditionaries stranded on a strange land. The revolution thrown away like the remains of Clovis. Plumpy little Louis XVIII could not turn everything back because he was too incompetent. Not much happened when his brother Charles X assumed the throne. We will see what happens with Louis Philippe. At least he is not as blue blooded as the Bourbons. During the revolution the *Marais* came apart. The great houses were split into small apartments and were taken over by thousands of ignorant bureaucrats or middle-class *functionaires* who in a few years had become convinced that they were born there and that they purchased their apartments. The stables were emptied. The *façades* crumbled. Empty lots were full of garbage that no one picked up. At hospitals like *Bicêtre* the sick lied in dirty beds with their feces on the ground. The water service was discontinued. The voluntary ladies were no longer visiting. The squalor was rampant. The nobles and thousands who knew how to do things left or joined the populace and dressed like the *sans-coulottes* or worse."

"One wonders. Was it all worthwhile?" reflected Rosa.

"The problem was," Domingo replied, "that the revolution fell in the hands of the criminal and the naïve. They somehow believed that it was just a matter of political reconstitution. They were simpleminded believing that once every man had been declared "free" and once the "nation" had been established and everyone proclaimed as "equal," the rest would follow and the task was completed."

"Yes," added Carlos Manuel, "but they also sinned by being excessively capricious and inconsistently selective in their beliefs. It was a time of ups and downs. For instance, they almost immediately granted citizenship to the Jews. Yet they were slow in emancipating the slaves. In spite of that, we must confess, they did it faster than in the United States. But then they voted a constitution that was patronizing and authoritarian, in spite of Jefferson's best advice. Lots of ups and downs and inconsistencies. The poor and the non-proprietors, after much deliberation, were excluded from voting. So were the women, except that they did not even take the matter under discussion. They did nothing for the freedom of the press, in spite of the many pamphlets that were being printed and that signified the people's desire to opine publicly. That was why on the eve of the Terror the ground had been seeded and was ready to suppress all opinions without major consequences."

"I believe that what froze the will of the leaders was the unexpected unmanageable, rambunctious and indocile behavior of the crowds," added María del Carmen. "The violence very soon became uncontrollable, like a leak in a dam that cannot be stopped."

"Not only that," replied Gertrudis, "but the response of the masses to the high ideals of Condorcet, Desmoullins and Mirabeau was to riot because of such a plebeian issue as the price of bread. The Parisian masses that needlessly destroyed the Bastille were divorced from any notions of political and economic freedoms. These important issues were the exclusive concern of those who ended up leaving the country or dropping their dreams at the foot of the guillotine. The desire for freedom and the rights of the common man were really never abandoned by any of the great leaders of the revolution, and that speaks highly of these men, rushed by the masses into incoherent and poorly thought decisions. The dynamics of a popular movement like this are impossible to anticipate. No one could any longer predict what would happen next. At some point it was not even clear who had the right to govern and who should make decisions. No wonder when they finally condemned Robespierre to the guillotine he exclaimed "*au nom de qui?*" (on whose authority?)"

"The worst thing about revolutions," concluded Céspedes, "is that one expects that the bitterness, the conflictive encounters and the animosity that impels people to fight, destroy and hate, would eventually lead to reconciliation, as the passionate opinions must sooner or later cross a threshold where peace becomes imperative. But what is likely to happen is precisely the opposite. It may take years before men and women act rationally after the bitter debate of an ongoing revolution. Aside from that, revolutions have a way of "sacralizing" their political leaders, much as the French culminated their revolution with the *sacré* de Napoleon. The cult of heroism is hidden within every revolution. The despair, hopelessness and the aimless advances and recoils of all these events, running by themselves as they are, finally end up with a clamor for charismatic leadership. This desperate cry is advanced by a majority of those who cannot conceive of any other way out of the mess in which revolutions have placed the people."

～ Ⅺ ～

17

*"The revolutionary spirit is mightily convenient in this:
that it frees one from all scruples as regards ideas."*
Joseph Conrad

"We must remember that Satan has his miracles, too."
John Calvin

*"I have always cultivated my hysteria with delight
and Terror. Now I have received a singular warning,
I have felt the wind of the wing of madness pass over me."*
Charles Baudelaire

AS THEY WERE debating the pros and cons of revolutions, the carriage crossed the *rue Thouin*, on the back of the *Lycée Henry IV*. A few meters later the *rue Descartes* turned into *rue Mouffetard*.

"This used to be one of the roads leading into the southeast, Lyon, Avignon, Geneve, etc.," stated Carlos Manuel. "But its real importance was the *Bièvre*, an important tributary of the Seine running along farms and country homes. There used to be Bishops, Lords, and all sorts of aristocrats with estates along this river which now has disappeared under *rue Mouffetard*. There are accounts of huge river shrimp and salmon running through the pristine waters of the *Bièvre* until the Manufacture of the Gobelins was established upstream." Céspedes then pointed left and right the old houses on both sides of the street.

"According to Rabelais in *Pantagruel*," interrupted Gertrudis, "the river became polluted by the wrath of two dogs that were drugged by a man who had been scorned by the woman he loved. The dogs were made to attack the lady's house and they urinated so much on the gate that a potent stream became a creek and ran into the Seine with quite a stench."

"Not the most romantic of stories," said Rosa.

"Whatever you want to believe, the *Bièvre* became the most pol-luted river of the region because of all the tanning and skinning of hides around the Gobelins, as well as all the spilled wool colorants and dyestuffs, and the discarded animal remains that were left to rot on the empty lots," added Céspedes. "It became such a smelly nui-sance that people began to call the river *le mouffette*, which in French means *skunk* or *awful smell.*

"There is another theory, however, far older, from Roman times, which tells of this hill as *mount Cetardus* or *mont Cétarius,* and from there evolved the *Mouffetard,*" riposted Domingo. "At one time or another, this street has been called *Montfétard, Maufetard, Mofetard, Moufetard, Mouflard, Moufetard, Moftard and even Mostard.* This is a truly Neolithic street if there was one. Originally the road led south, towards Italy."

"I do not know if it is my imagination but I can smell a foul odor right now, something akin a sewer," María del Carmen said.

Carlos Manuel pointed to the numerous drinking establishments and pointed out "The tanners, slaughterers, skinners and dyers of the shops around the *Gobelins* were mostly Flemish and they also brought a lot of beer into this neighborhood."

The coach, several blocks down rue Mouffetard, came to a pause to allow for a good view of the street, slowly descending into the low laying area where the steeple of the Church of Saint Medard could be seen in the distance. They were at a point where the street simply widens and allows for a brief rest if you were climbing the hill: *la Place de la Contrescarpe.*

"Here was one of the gates of the wall of Philippe Auguste," de-clared Carlos Manuel. "Outside the gate there was a moat with an earthen slope towards the wall. That was the *contrescarpe.* It is now a flat area full of lively activity."

As they looked around they could see shops in every direction. Wine merchants, small grocers, delicatessens, butchers, *cafés*, horse meat dealers, *pattisiers*, cheese merchants, fruit stands, as well as pot-tery shops, sewing establishments, shoe makers, hatmakers, laun-derers, millineries, barbers, *herboristeries*, midwiferies, dentists, hatters, coal merchants, eateries, rooming houses, flower shops, fruit wholesalers displaying their products on glistening pyramids, vege-table stands, creameries, *charcuteries*, … you name it.

"It seems that all vendors and shops of Paris are here," declared Rosa. "It would take years to familiarize yourself with all the mer-chants."

"Look," interrupted Carlos Manuel, "that house at number 69 was home during the revolution to one of the largest clubs of *sans-coulottes*. It is the house where this famous convict, Vidocq, used to live after he became inspector of the *Sûreté*."

"Carlos," asked María del Carmen, "who was this Vidocq? You are a real encyclopedia of Parisian anecdotes and trivialities."

"His full name was Eugène-François Vidocq. He was the son of a *boulanger* and while very young he joined the revolutionary army. He fought at *Valmy* against the Prussians in 1792, which is the battle that turned around the defeats of the French revolutionary armies on the field. He then became an adventurer, a thief and a swindler, sought by the police all across France. They say he eventually repented and went to the *Préfet* of Police and offered his services as an agent. In time he became the chief of the *Sûreté* and, when he resigned, he opened the first private detective agency in France, the *Bureau de Renseignements pour le Commerce*, which is still the largest organization of its class."

"Good story," said Domingo. "This street is very interesting. There are few new establishments. Most of the merchants have been here for a generation or two. I presume that after a while, if you are a neighbor, you get to know everybody."

They approached a stand where some tender and fragrant pears were arranged in straight rows and Rosa and Gertrudis began to talk with the vendor. Domingo stopped at a *fromager-affineur* and began to inquire about cheeses, while Carlos Manuel and Miguel continued the conversation and the musings about the myths and realities of revolutionary events. They were certain that the times were near in Cuba when a revolution of sorts or an insurrection would face them, and they had an urgency to understand what had happened in France and what lessons were there to be learned.

"We were talking about the inevitability of a hero in every uprising," started Carlos Manuel. The artists, who are always so sensitive to the feelings of the time, are the best witnesses for this inescapable need for investing a leader with the mantle of a hero. Take Beethoven's impulsive dedication of *l'Héroïque* to Bonaparte or David's coming of age as Napoleon's apologist. Some of their best work was done when they had the fervor of hero worshipers."

"Beethoven repented almost as soon as he realized his mistake. David never did," exclaimed Domingo.

"Some times I wonder what triggers a revolution and how its events differ from a simple uprising. Take *La Fronde*, when in 1653 the Parisians erected barricades against Mazarine in opposition to the royal authority. It shook the French nation but then it subsided. Why did not the same cooling off happened after *La Bastille*?" asked Carlos Manuel.

"That's very difficult to discern," Domingo said. "Do you need a complete break with the past to have a revolution? Do you need a bursting of the reservoirs of decency and outrage that have been quietly accumulating over many years or generations? Is a revolution a relapse into a past full of ideals that have been betrayed, sort of a return to a better world that actually only existed in the minds of the philosophers? Moreover, does a revolution increase the probabilities of a more moral society, fairer than what men had built out of greed, ambition and the thirst for power?"

"Another good question," Céspedes interrupted, "is this: was all the blood of the French Revolution worthwhile just to create a merchant class and leave everything else as it was, as it indeed has happened?"

"I have always believed that a revolution is simply the most visible and dramatic sector of a circle that always returns to the starting point," Domingo stated. "One has the illusion of giving birth to a fundamental and forward looking departure from an *ancien régime*, but what usually happens is that you go back to where you came from, like a pendulum swinging in free space."

"I do not have great doubts about the lasting effects of the French Revolution, but I can understand how many people do. They claim that it has not had an impact on the rest of Europe as it would if its example would have been contagious."

"Well, you can not ignore that the ideals of democratic participation and political access for everyone are now firmly entrenched everywhere. Rousseau opened that Pandora's box and mankind has never been the same. Ignoring this was Louis XVI gravest mistake. He thought that in post-Rousseauian times you could call an assembly of notables just to ask for help. When he faced the demands for participation and openness by the Third State he tried to back down but it was too late."

"Just like in Cuba we are not merely asking for a better structure to support the demands of one group against another. The Spanish crown believes that our struggle is simply a quest for the right to press our interests against those of the king or the *peninsulares*. They do not understand what we mean by *patria*, nation, self-government, our own flag, our own icons…"

"Well, look at France. After loosing all the wars in which it entered in the XVIII Century; after its evident technological and social inferiority when facing modern Prussia and England; after having exhausted the pockets of ordinary people with excessive taxation, the *ancien régime* could not restore the prestige of France unless it counted with the opinions and contributions of France's thinking citizens."

"The same goes for Cuba and Spain. After having miserably succumbed to Napoleon, after having squeezed every ounce of richness from our soil, and after having exploited the natural human rights of the *criollos* for the benefit of the metropolis, Spain will not be able to restore peace in Cuba and prestige to the kingdom unless it seeks the opinion and support of free thinking Cubans. It is as simple as that," declared Céspedes.

The group reassembled and moved on foot towards the Church of Saint Medard, with the coach following them through the narrow *rue de Mouffetard*. By now it was almost one in the afternoon and they sat on a café across the street from the church, next door to *Androuët*, the Parisian *maître fromager-affineur* of ancient fame.

Domingo opened an *Epoisse* cheese and a bottle of *Pouligny Montrachet* which he had bought up the street. A baguette of golden-brown crusty bread with a spongy white crumb, *pas trop cuit*, according to María del Carmen's instructions, was produced and the six had a great *repas française*. They ended their delicious but meager lunch with some cinnamon and orange flavored *ganaches* and chocolates from *Montbourgeau*, the best *chocolatier* on *rue Mouffetard*. They were now ready to immerse themselves into the fascinating stories of the long proscribed Jansenistic rituals of Saint Medard.

Carlos Manuel, as an accomplished history devotee, continued to delight his friends by exploring every corner of Paris where something interesting or transcendental had occurred. Saint Medard was a feast for his intellect, first because its traditions and specially the personality of *François Paris*, the charismatic priest that had caused so much discomfort to the Church and the Crown in the XVIII Century. Saint Medard was also important for the Jansenist tradition itself, which was championed in the early 1700's by its priests.

"There was a chapel on this spot, along the Roman road from *Lutèce* to Lyon, as early as the year 700, dedicated to Saint Medard, Bishop of Noyon and Tournai. This church, however, is much younger since it was started in 1163, when Pope Alexander III came to Paris to consecrate Notre Dame," declared Carlos Manuel with a smile on his face. "In the second half of the XV Century it was burned to the ground by the Protestants and the King had to fine the

Protestants and allocate his own funds to repair it and placate the belligerent Catholics."

The group entered the church and everyone was transfixed by the descriptions of Carlos Manuel.

"What you see here is a somewhat eclectic style, very prevalent in the XV Century. The nave and the façade are Gothic but the chapels, the windows and the choir are Renaissance in style. It is a five bay nave, flanked north and south by a series of chapels. The space is topped by a wooden diagonal rib that was probably installed after a roof collapse in the XVII Century. In fact, only the front side of the church is from the XII Century, the rest is a lot younger."

"How about the revolution?" asked Domingo.

"During the revolution it became the *Temple of Labor*, a citizens' meeting place. The sign that was hung outside the façade in 1791 is now hanging below the choir. The most interesting story is however that of the Jansenists and the novice *François Paris*. The Jansenists, of course, were heretical Catholics who sought to reestablish Augustinian thinking in the Church doctrine. They proclaimed that humans were born sinful and that only through divine help they could become good and be redeemed. They also maintained that only a portion of the human race was elected to be saved, much as the Calvinists thought. The Catholic Church repudiated these ideas and cried heresy," Céspedes explained.

"To make things worse, in came *François Paris*," María del Carmen added.

"Yes," Carlos Manuel continued to explain. "This young novice had a well earned reputation for humility and service to others, and became sick and died at age 36 at the height of the persecution and excommunication of the Jansenists. People from all over France came to pray by the side of his tomb and, to the consternation of the Church, pretty soon they began to speak of miracles."

"Young women, students, old ladies," added María del Carmen, "as well as other priests and hundreds of pilgrims became hysterical at the sight of the tomb, to the point where it became customary for pilgrims to eat some of the dirt from his grave. The parish priests placed a large black slab of marble on top of the grave to no avail. Pretty soon the devotions turned into convulsions, then neurosis, delirium, hallucinations and even atrocious self flagelations."

"Devotees began to implore to be beaten, stepped on and trampled until they fainted," Céspedes explained with a mysterious and grave voice.

"You must be exaggerating," said Miguel.

"No, every word of it is true," explained Céspedes.

"Please continue," asked Gertrudis.

"Well, some people did penance or wanted to stand out by piercing their tongues or their breasts. Others covered their bodies with tattoos, hung pendants from their eyebrows, or perforated the lobes of their ears with two or more rows of rings. Others left their abdomens exposed to show how their repentance was secured by permanently installing a bolt or a ring across their navels."

"They must have been quite a sight to behold," remarked Gertrudis.

"Indeed they were. In the midst of the collective psychoses, convulsions and mass hysteria, miracles were presumably occurring every day. Magic cures, the blind recovering their sight, paralytics walking and dancing on the streets, the deaf intoning perfectly pitched psalms of gratitude, the demented recovering their sanity, and all of them carpeting the ground with wild flowers from the nearby fields and offering lilies, daisies, roses, carnations, lilacs and gerberas in bundles to the shoppers looking for meats and vegetables along the *rue Mouffetard*. They called it *the new age of love*."

"How long did this last," asked again Gertrudis.

"The crowds kept coming for five years, until on January 27, 1732, full of despair, the Crown had the cemetery walled and locked. Two guards were placed there and a year later they were still being showered every day with flowers, petition notes and an occasional rock. Soon a hand written sign was posted by a sarcastic follower of *frére Paris*: "*De par le roi, defense à Dieu de faire miracle en ce lieu.*" (In the name of the King, it is forbidden to God to perform miracles in this place)."

"And finally the hysteria came to an end, except that over the next year or so the *ecstastiques* were followed by the *mélangistes*, who in turn were followed by the *secouristes*, and then by the *meowists*, and so on."

"Carlos, we do not really want to know who these people were."

"God forbid. No need to go there. Just think of nuns meowing hysterically in perfect pitch and coordination for one full hour every morning during Mass. And the National Guard threatening to invade the convent and give them a flogging unless they stopped," concluded Carlos Manuel.

"This must have been the love of God taking a wrong turn," added Gertrudis.

They continued in silence, baffled and mystified by the stories they had just heard, until they reached the *Manufacture des Gobelins*.

When they finally reached the compound of the *Gobelins*, Carlos Manuel spoke: "Miguel, you are a customer here and know this process and this factory very well. Why don't you explain it to us?"

"Well, tapestries and carpets can be weaved by laying them horizontally, which is called *en haute lisse,* or growing the fabric while the threads are vertically arranged or *en basse lisse.* They do both here but the trend is now to prefer *en haute lisse.*"

"Any advantages?" asked Domingo, and then interrupted himself saying "Oh, who cares…"

"We don't need to go into much detail, otherwise we will be here forever," replied Miguel. "There are 250 *tapissiers* here, all living with their families on the premises. In the past the designs were sort of incomplete and the *tapissiers* had a great deal of flexibility to add their own details. After Le Brun, in 1690, they have had precise and detailed information on how to weave and what was expected of them was to provide the craftsmanship and not any design elements."

"They went by cartoons or full size colored drawings, right?" asked María del Carmen.

"Yes they did. At that time there were 19 work stations for *haute lisse* and 34 for *basse lisse.* Now it is almost the reverse," answered Miguel. "When Le Brun died the *Manufacture* closed but it reopened again in 1748, under the direction of Jean Baptiste Oudry. He is the director that first introduced the notion that a tapestry has to look like an oil painting."

"Very demanding."

"Yes indeed. Before him Le Brun had asked for threads of 141 different colors. Oudry established the rule that the wool had to be dyed in 365 colors. Just imagine the complexity for the weavers. Oudry is the director that really made *les Gobelins* a unique shop in all of Europe, considerably better than the Flemish and the British. He also insisted in lighter and sweeter tones, to better imitate real life. His influence lasted until the years before the revolution, when a style called *d'alentours* became very popular: a main subject at the center of the tapestry surrounded by decorative elements, instead of a landscape or an interior scene. Right now they have eighty work stations, all weaving on the vertical, and that's the reason our tapestries and carpets are taking so long. Each piece can take as much as three months, with four men working all the time. Just to let you know how advanced this art has become with the dyes that are produced here, think of almost thirty thousand different tonalities that can be achieved from thirty six different colors. Nowadays the dyes can be mixed and that has been a blessing for the *Manufacture des Gobelins.* Just ten years ago, since many dyes were not compatible with each other, you needed 72 different colors to obtain fifteen thousand *nuances.*"

A mixture of confusion and tedium had invaded the faces of everyone except Domingo. They began to look around the room where they would be received by the director of the *Manufacture,* their eyes resting every now and then on some of the samples that were exhibited along the walls. The director finally came into the room and, after greeting everyone, started his presentation.

"I do not know how much you know about weaving at the *Gobelins,*" he said. "Tapestries and carpets can be weaved by laying them horizontally or *en haute lisse* or growing the fabric while the threads are vertically arranged or *en basse lisse...*"

A sign of dismay went across all faces as mouths opened and all eyes popped upwards.

"But I sense that this group is not interested in technicalities. Why don't we try to see the progress on the work orders for your father's palace?," the director said, nervously looking at Miguel.

"Good thinking," exclaimed Gertrudis. "Let's get go see Don Domingo's weavings."

✦ ⌛ ✦

DAVID'S DESIGN CARTOON FOR
HIS *JEU DE PAUME* TAPESTRY, 1791

French painter **Jacques-Louis David** (1748-1825) was one of the central figures of Neoclassicism in XIX century Europe. He actively sympathyzed with the 1789 Revolution, became a Deputy and voted for the execution of Louis XVI. After the fall of Robespierre in 1794 he was imprisoned. After 1802 he became an ardent supporter of Napoleon and painted many pictures glorifying the exploits of the Emperor. After the fall of Napoleon, he had to seek assylum in Brussels. His work had a resounding influence on European painting, and his many pupils included such luminaries as Gérard, Gros, and Ingres.

18

IT WAS NOW late afternoon and on the way back from the *Manufacture des Gobelins* the Céspedes and their guests stopped briefly at the *Lycée Louis le Grand*, the school founded in 1563 and named after Louis XIV, King of France. Several students from Cuba were at the school preparing for entrance at *l'Ecole Polytechnique*, at the *Sorbonne* or the *Collège de France*, which were all in the same neighborhood, within walking distance to the *Lycée*. Among them was Leonardo Aldama, nephew of Miguel, who had started his studies at the *Lycée* the year before.

Louis le Grande was the place to study for the French elites and those foreigners who could afford it. Its alumni had become statesmen, diplomats, marshals of France, prime ministers, and the most distinguished men of arts and letters of their times. Molière, Voltaire, Diderot and Hugo had studied here, as well as Baudelaire, Felipe Poey and Lafayette. Felipe Poey had been the first Cuban to study at *Louis le Grand*, at the time of the restoration of the Monarchy, after the second abdication of Bonaparte. He had reached the first place among the students enrolled in the university level *classes préparatoires* and his fame had opened the door for the children of many other affluent families in Cuba, such as the Aldamas, to be admitted to receive the best of an European education in Paris.

The conversation between young Leonardo and his uncle took place in front of the student's residence on *rue Saint Jacques*. It was brief but left a shade of curiosity and anxiety in Miguel, who was normally a self assured and confident person.

"One of my classmates is Adolphe Guizot, grandson of Françoise Guillaume Guizot, the former French ambassador to Queen Victoria and the mastermind of the current French government," Leonardo started to say.

"I know of Guizot," interrupted Miguel. "I have heard him in parliament several times. He is probably the best orator of the times, probably comparable to Mirabeau at his best."

"Adolphe got word from his grandfather that he knows you are in Paris and would like to see you."

"Do you know who Guizot is?" asked Miguel.

"Not really," was the reply from Leonardo.

"He began as a literary critic and became famous at age 22, for an essay on Châteaubriand's *Martyrs*, which won Châteaubriand's approbation and respect. He is a translator of Shakespeare's and Gibbons' works and on that account earned a chair at the Sorbonne when he was 25. He has been Secretary of Justice and Secretary of the Interior and opposed both Louis XVIII and Charles X. I don't want to bore you but his histories of Europe and France are regarded as classics of modern historical research. Why would he wish to see me? Did he give you any reasons?"

"No, Adolphe simply said it was important for you to see the old man before you leave Paris. He said twice that you would know how to get in touch. I took the message and I am delivering it."

"Very clever. You did not even inquire if they were going to deport me."

After that lighthearted remark Miguel returned to the coach and the group continued its journey to the nearby garden of Luxembourg.

The Luxembourg was the largest garden in the center of Paris and the city's most favored place for a quiet stroll or a discreet romantic encounter. The palace on its north edge was built by Marie de Medicis during her brief turn at the reins of France after the death of Henry IV. During the revolution it was turned into a prison where Josephine de Beauharnais, future wife of Bonaparte, bid good by to her first husband as he was taken to the guillotine. Napoleon himself moved there as First Consul of France and it was there that he made friends with the most cynic and rascal of French politicians: Charles Maurice de Talleyrand-Périgord, Prince de Benevente (1754-1838). It was while living at Luxembourg that cash-deprived Napoleon gave a pearl necklace belonging to Josephine to his sister Caroline as a present for his wedding to Joachin Murat, one of Bonaparte's generals. It is said that Josephine had a fit and instructed a guard to shave Caroline's head as a reprisal, with no objections from the future Emperor.

"Few places in Paris have been witness to so many important events and have seen so many important people as the area that surrounds the Luxembourg," Céspedes said. "Imagine Saint Francis de Sales walking the streets side by side with Saint Vincent de Paul giving alms to the poor, on the same stones where Balzac's possessions were discarded after being evicted from his printing business."

"Or Balzac being threatened with prison for his debts and daring only to go out at night, mostly here at Luxembourg, because no one could be arrested after dark," added Gertrudis.

The conversation turned to Balzac. "Balzac was a very successful author and made lots of money in his lifetime. He was a work addict and lived very sparingly," added Céspedes.

"How do you explain his debts?," asked Rosa.

"He was a fool with his money. He would come to a café and pay for everybody's bill. Somebody would cry on his shoulders and he would empty his pockets. Without inquiring or studying a situation he would invest money in all sorts of deceitful schemes and speculations just to avoid saying no to those he thought were his friends. Like the time he bought a two story house on the countryside that had no stairs to reach the second level."

"George Sand once told me she thought he was too soft spoken with his gentlemen friends and too blunt with all the women he knew," said Gertrudis. "She told me that after one of his crude remarks she had said to him: *you are a lewd fellow*. To which he replied: *and you are a beast*. Her retort was simply: *I am well aware of it.*"

"Very spirited conversation between two outspoken literary wizards," indicated María del Carmen, then adding, "George Sand does not have too many friends. She is too deliberate, too methodical. Even when she lights a cigarette she acts like if she is signing the Declaration of Independence. Don't take me wrong: I like her and she is a good-natured woman, but somewhat somber and drab for our Cuban blood."

They found the *Luxembourg* closed and therefore they asked their driver to take them to la *Taberne du Panthéon* for an aperitif before getting home for dinner. There they continued gossiping, like most

French people do in bars and cafés when they take time for the *collation*.

"Across this street Marat was living on the third floor of the house with the green door," pointed Carlos Manuel, "but he was evicted for the stench that always accompanied him. He moved nearby to *rue des Cordeliers*, where Charlotte Corday had no trouble finding him and stabbing him to death. That tells you that bathing every day and having a *concierge* downstairs can substantially increase your life expectancy."

They all smiled at Céspedes sense of humor and his extraordinary timing for an intelligent remark. They all loved this man, so generous, approachable and charismatic. On occasions like this, you could always read on María del Carmen's face the admiration and pride that she felt as his wife. You could not miss either his quick glances at her when he said something witty that merited her silent assent; he simply loved her praise.

"Was Marat an intelligent man?" asked Miguel. "After all, he was a physician with a Saint Andrews degree, a student of politics and a superb *pamphleteer*."

"Oh, there is no denying he had abandoned a profitable career to work for the revolution and that he was a passionate writer," exclaimed Gertrudis. "The trouble came when he indulged in indiscriminate executions."

"I do not think he would have supported the massacres of September of 1794 at *le Force*, *Saint Germain* and *des Carmes* if he had been alive," Miguel replied. "And if he had been alive perhaps Desmoulins, Danton and Robespierre would have survived."

"I fully agree with what you are saying," retorted Carlos Manuel. "I believe Marat, because of his repulsive physique, has been unduly condemned as a man of extreme cruelty. Robespierre, however, once said of him that no man had a stronger zeal for justice and had made a wiser contribution as a parliamentarian. Nevertheless, there was much hate in his heart and too many people perished because of his insidious diatribes."

Suddenly all realized that Alfred de Musset had made a ceremonious entrance at the *Taberne du Panthéon*.

"Speaking of George Sand, here is her alleged martyred lover. What a happenstance," Carmen María said.

"And speaking of Marat too, because here comes a man with something in common with him." They all looked surprised until Carlos Manuel explained. "Alfred was a medical student, just like

Marat, and the story goes that he abandoned the career for that of a writer after fainting on his first visit to a dissecting room."

"Yet it takes a stronger stomach to be a writer than a physician," pointed Gertrudis. "A medical doctor buries his mistakes when he fails, while a writer has to live with them until she dies."

"In the case of Alfred, he also fainted after the humiliating failure of his first play at the *Théâtre de l'Odeon, La Nuit Vénetienne,* if I remember correctly. He never again dissected anything nor would he allow his plays to be ever performed in his lifetime."

"Poor man," María del Carmen said, "he looks like a finicky and dandy cavalry officer out of his military uniform."

A loud smile came to everyone's face at the image suggested by María del Carmen.

"We all agree that he is a writer of great promise," María del Carmen added. "But he is a man weakened by his never-ending disappointments. When he became the lover of George Sand, one of the first things he did was to take her to Venice. There they both became terribly sick and had to call a doctor. She fell in love with the physician and talked Alfred into returning prematurely –and sick– to Paris. Talk about tough luck."

"Speaking of physicians and going back to Marat," Carlos Manuel said, "when Mirabeau died his funeral procession was more that three kilometers long, with more than a hundred thousand mourners. They stopped at *Saint Eustache* where the benches had been burned by the revolutionaries. There, on an empty church, they had Mirabeau's formal funeral. Over two thousand soldiers paid a last tribute and fired their rifles in the air, but of course they were inside the Church. That's why you do not see any stained glass windows on the higher levels at *Saint Eustache,* and the reason you see so many patched holes on the walls. Afterwards, the procession came to the Pantheon, were he was buried. Years later Mirabeau's cadaver was summarily expelled from the Pantheon because of his letters to Louis XVI urging him to flee Paris. His place was occupied by Marat, his mortal enemy. Marat was carried to the Pantheon in a funeral car designed by no other that David. Marat's lease on the crypt of the Pantheon, however, was even shorter than Mirabeau's. His remains were hastily moved to Montmartre, which prompted Balzac to say something like… *"Shorter rest had no man in those difficult times. He longed to enjoy all the vices but even there he failed…"* Marat, of course, went on to be immortalized at his most vulnerable time by David, who playing on both sides of the fence, gave as much importance to Charlotte's note as to Marat's face."

"Interesting observation," said Gertrudis. "Charlotte would have been a heroine of the French Revolution except that her note, unlike what David painted, was a call for help, and read more or less like this: *"I am being persecuted for the sake of liberty; I am unhappy, and that is enough to give me the right to your protection..."* In other words, she accomplished her murderous deed by appealing to Marat's kind-hearted sympathy. That did not play well among French feminists of the times. Madame Roland was a much better example of a woman who was ready to shape the future of France. She was the Joan of Arc of the revolution, and still remains its best heroine."

"I fully agree," added María del Carmen. "Madame Roland was condemned to the guillotine, among many other things, for having written to a friend after the September 1792 massacres: *"You know my enthusiasm for the Revolution. However, I am now ashamed of it! Its face has been tarnished by these villains. It has become repugnant!"* Within a week she was a prisoner at *la Conciergerie* as her husband escaped to Rouen."

"A few days later," replied Gertrudis, "as she saw a plaster statue of liberty on her way to the gallows, she proclaimed one of the most accusatory commentaries on the character of the French Revolution: *"O Liberté, que de crimes on commet en ton nom!"* (Oh, liberty, how many crimes are commited in your name!)

It was getting dark and they soon stood up and started to drift towards the carriage. It had been a day of solid reflection, humor and gossip. Nothing could have been more French during the *Monarchie de Juillet* in Paris.

~ Ⅻ ~

19

*"A politician needs the ability to foretell what is going to happen
tomorrow, next week, next month, and next year.
And to have the ability afterwards to explain why it didn't happen."*
Winston Churchill

*"You have all the characteristics of a popular politician: a horrible voice, bad
breeding, and a vulgar manner."*
Aristophanes

*"It has been the political career of this man to begin with hypocrisy,
proceed with arrogance, and finish with contempt."*
Thomas Paine

THE *MONARCHIE DE JUILLET* was proclaimed in France on
July 29, 1830, after the riots of July 27, 28 and 29, which became
known as the *Trois Glorieuses*. On those three memorable days, a
crowd of much better quality than the one that took the Bastille in
1789 rose in revolt and overthrew the monarchy of Charles X. To
celebrate the event which resulted in his accession to the throne,
Louis Philippe d'Orleans, King of the French but not King of France,
had a bronze column erected at the Place de la Bastille and commissioned Berlioz to write his *Symphonie Funèbre et Triomphale*. It was
premiered at the *Place de la Bastille* in 1840, in the open air, under the
direction of Berlioz himself. The Céspedes had been witnesses to
these celebrations and had recalled them to their friends a few days
before Miguel Aldama finalized the appointment to see *Monsieur
l'Ambassador de France à l'Anglaterre*, Françoise Guizot.

Françoise Pierre Guillaume Guizot (1787-1874) was a tall and
rather stern and solemn man, the child of French Huguenots. He received Miguel Aldama and Carlos Manuel de Céspedes at the *Palais
de Salm*, a magnificent late XVIII Century building designed by architect Pierre Rousseau for Frederick III de Salm-Kyrbourg, a German
prince. The building had been confiscated by the revolution and
turned into the home of the Legion of Honor in 1804. The foreign

ministry had offices in its second floor for private, unavowed gatherings. Present at the meeting, besides Céspedes, Aldama and Guizot was Jacques Laffitte, former Prime Minister (1830-1831) of France and a good friend of Céspedes. After the appropriate presentations a few pleasantries followed.

"Sorry I am not receiving you in our Foreign Ministry building but, as you probably saw, it is far from ready. The architect is Lacornée, the designer of the *Palais d'Orsay* and the *Caserne de Cavalerie* next to it, both of which we are dismantling to make room for a much larger and dignified structure," Guizot stated.

"When do you expect to finish it and move there?," asked Aldama, as he continued: "Constructions, particularly beautiful places like this *Palais de Salm*, take time and half the life of those entrusted to see them through. Materials do not arrive on time. Sculptors take other commissions. The accessories do not fit. Sloppy apprentices are left in charge of important work that has to be removed and repeated."

"Oh, you are very aware of the perils of embarking in these grandiose projects," replied Guizot, who swiftly put an end to the small talk and dived forward into the purpose of the meeting.

"Gentlemen: you are here because France needs your help and it is always ready to recognize those who contribute to the fulfillment and realization of its destiny," began Guizot. "I trust that you realize that we are talking outside the limits of our authority and on a very grave matter that needs to be guarded with the strictest of confidences."

"I need not to extol the virtues of my friends, dear Françoise. I simply vouch unconditionally to their discretion," expressed Laffitte.

"Very well, let's get to the point," replied Guizot as he stood up.

They were sitting at a large mahogany rectangular table with an intricate work of inlaid woods showing an elaborate map of the world. Guizot walked briskly to a cabinet by a large window opening to the Seine and removed a large roll, which he extended across the table facing Céspedes and Aldama. The map represented the western half of the United States, from the Mississippi to the Pacific Ocean and from the British possessions in the North to the waters of the Mexican Gulf. Some red lines had been drawn across the map forming a sort of skewed rectangle, which enclosed within it the delta of the Mississippi and the western part of the peninsula of Florida and opened into a much larger longitude as it came north from the gulf.

"This is the very map that Bonaparte relied on when he made the sale of the Louisiana to the United States. It is a mouthful of territory, all of which Spain had just transferred back to France in 1800 under the Treaty of Saint Ildefonso. The Crown of Spain was reverting to us what we had ceded to Spain in 1762. Little men we all were, playing with over two million square kilometers of land as if it were a large backyard," stated Guizot in an almost imperceptible voice.

"When Jefferson sent Robert Livingston and James Monroe here to negotiate this purchase in 1801 nobody showed any concerns since we were involved in the war with England and Leclerc was loosing his campaign against the rebels in Santo Domingo. In fact, the only strong opposition to selling *la Louisiana* came from Talleyrand, whom we all detest but had a clear vision at that time," added Laffitte.

"Santo Domingo was a brief stop on our way to the territories of the southern and western side of North America. Unfortunately what was a detour to resolve a required yet simple annoyance in Haiti became a major deterrent to our plans for the American continent. We ended up neither with Santo Domingo nor with the territories we already possessed in the central part of North America. The losses in *Española* depressed Bonaparte to the point where he decided to leave the game to others. One bad decision followed another. Jefferson only wanted to buy the port of New Orleans to secure the shipments from the Ohio valley. We threw in, for a mere pittance, almost as much land as Jefferson had to begin with. Had Leclerc prevailed in Santo Domingo we would be now the largest power in the new continent," explained Guizot.

"Napoleon's policies were a complete failure. In order to expand his presence in the American continent he needed to maintain peace with England, befriend the American colonists and mount a successful campaign in Santo Domingo. He failed in all three," added Guizot.

"He knew of course, that the American colonists sooner or later need to expand west of the Mississippi and would oppose any French designs over those territories. He was certain of Jefferson's determination to keep New Orleans opened to American traffic. He knew our navy was second class compared to the British and that any large moves towards the southern states' coveted main port would be thwarted by her majesty's ships. Finally he knew he needed lots of money and the only place to get it fast was in Santo Domingo, provided there was peace and quiet there. He committed his army to the Haiti revolt and that was no light hearted decision," stated Lafitte.

All through the presentation the Cubans had patiently listened with interest but without making any comments. They were wondering what was the point and why they were there. Finally, Céspedes decided to speak, if only to reiterate that they were good friends of France and were ready to play the diplomatic game should there be a need for it.

"Your losses in Haiti have changed our demography and our plans to bring peace, freedom and prosperity to Cuba," Céspedes started. "We now have an even more serious slavery problem in our hands: thousands of slave owners from Haiti have sought refuge in our island. They are replicating on our shores the conditions that were their pitfall in Haiti. Meantime, a greedy Spain will not yield an ounce of autonomy to us for fear that we could mount a similar revolt and seek the independence or autonomy of Cuba," continued Carlos Manuel. "Spain is sucking every ounce of our freedoms and has shown no mercy with anyone that resists the economic and political shackles that oppress us. But, gentlemen, what is the point you are trying to make with us?"

"We believe you will be far happier as Frenchmen than as Spaniards," replied Guizot. "If the French flag were to take to the air in Cuba, you will have full citizenship rights just as any French born citizen has in territorial France. Far better than the second class citizenship that you now have under a Spanish crown that will never grant you any freedoms or equality. Spain is a crumbling and disappearing political entity," he continued. "Its power and its culture are no longer what they were in the XVI Century. Napoleon's victories humiliated the Spaniards as nothing had before. We took a stroll through their territory, sequestered their King, emptied their coffers, drank their rather poor wine until we could not stomach it any more, made love to their best women and soiled their flag with hardly any effort on our part. We left because of problems elsewhere, not because the Spaniards forced us to leave. Do you really want to be part of this dilapidated and bedraggled culture that must be asfixiating your best people or would you like to share with us the traditions, the glory and the culture of France?"

"What the French government is proposing," Laffitte expanded, "is to take Cuba and make there an example of what Santo Domingo could have been. A French citizen in a French Cuba would have the same rights as any of our citizens in Toulouse, Lyon or Paris. We will incorporate Cuba as we are trying to incorporate Algeria. The French rights of men and citizens will be spread over five continents and across the seas."

"And why are you talking to us?" inquired Céspedes after a short silence.

"Because you could be the accelerators of this process. You represent the future political and economical leadership in Cuba. You are concerned about rumors of annexation to the United States and the immobility of the Spanish government when it comes to reforms," said Laffitte.

"You also know," added Guizot, "that things are bound to get worse in Cuba. You know very well that Spain will fight eye and tooth to keep the colonial situation as it is. Having lost all in the rest of the continent, they will hang on to Cuba with the hope of using it as a base to recover part or all of the lost territories in South America. Cuba is too small to defend itself against the new nation to the north, which craves your agriculture and would turn Cuba into a bulwark to protect their southern borders. You are a coveted possession for the British because they need to halt the expansion of the United States and need to continue trading with the southern States."

"For the Spaniards you represent survival. They will cease to exist in the Americas if they lose Cuba. Having so many avid suitors, your self determination will always be in peril. You need an ally. Better yet, you need to be an organic and constitutive part of an enlightened nation, rather than an appended ornament; and which better that France?" insisted Laffitte.

Françoise Guizot added "We hope to count with your power to influence the Cuban proprietors to the side of France. We hope you can talk to your friends who are wishing for a future as part of the nation to the north and convince them that their culture is too foreign to your roots. You know, as well as we do, that your dreams are closer to France's than to the illusions of the Anglo Saxons. If you help France to fulfill its destiny in the Americas by making Cuba part of our heritage you will be bringing prosperity to the island and to yourselves. His majesty Louis Philippe, but more than him the entire French nation, will be forever grateful and will not forget those who help from inside Cuba the cause that we would be ready to thrust from outside."

As Guizot made these last remarks, Laffitte brought from the cabinet by the window a large map of Cuba and extended it on top of the map of the Louisiana territory. It was Guizot, however, who continued his arguments.

"For the French people Cuba is the key to recover all the lands that Bonaparte gifted to the United States in a moment of weakness. Those lands rightfully belong to us, not to Spain and not to the North Americans, and we intend to recover them. They are mostly uninhabited and we know of many colonial families that still have their hearts with the French nation. This might look as a wild notion but we also have allies north of the United States that would welcome a French republic in the continent competing with the former British colonies."

"As you see, we are thinking in republican terms," added Laffitte. "Louis Philippe is a man of transition. He was the way to say good riddance to the Bourbons, but the future of France is a second republic, where all the principles of the revolutionary days of 1789 would come to a reality, now forged and refined by the wisdom of many years of sufferings and tribulations."

"Those are France's dreams." It was now Guizot speaking, his body facing the window from where you could hear the noisy *Quais* of the Seine, his arms extended as if embracing imaginary French citizens across two continents. "Think of a republic that extends from the cold plains and the rugged mountains south of Alaska, down to the rich lands of the western margins of the Mississippi and into the warm waters of the Caribbean. A French republic that shares the continent with the United States. A republic where the rights of men and citizens are identical as those in traditional and historical France. A colossal republic, the largest ever in history, with four political centers, Paris, Havana, New Orleans and a new city by the rocky mountains."

There was an extended silence after those words. Guizot felt that he had made his case conclusively. Laffitte was speechless and moved almost to tears. He had heard those grandiose dreams from the mouth of his friend many times in recent years, but they had never been so well recited and Guizot had never been so well timed in its delivery.

Aldama's mind seemed to be elsewhere, perhaps figuring out how his future would look if Cuba ever came to be part of a French republic. Céspedes was astounded by the unreality of those dreams of grandeur and at the same time amazed that a Prime Minister of France could be so flaky and bizarre.

"How can they keep in power a man of such outlandish and feeble minded ambitions," he thought for himself.

Their ruminations were interrupted by Guizot. "Let me introduce to both of you a person that could be of great help in achieving these goals and who enjoys the unconditional trust of the French government." He left the room briefly and came back holding hands with Willard Capacete.

As they were introduced and shook hands with Capacete, both Miguel and Carlos Manuel took and instant dislike to the newcomer. They discreetly looked to each other and wordlessly wondered who was this sapless and effeminate character that Guizot had brought into this apparently important meeting?

Willard Capacete, they learned, was born in Santiago de Cuba in 1806. His father was a high level official in the *Cuerpo de Voluntarios of Santiago*, the Spanish group of mercenaries who openly organized acts of repression against any Cubans who defied the authority of Spain in the cities. As the son of an important official supporting the Spanish government in Cuba he enjoyed the best education at one of Havana's most advanced and exclusive schools. His family moved from their modest home in *Barrio Del Monte* in San Luis, Oriente, to the elegant home of the Gabriel de Lombillo's family in Havana, whose fortune had been confiscated because its opposition to the Spanish regime. This made it possible for young Willard to be raised among some of the most favor-endowed children of the colonial capital.

In the summer of 1824 Capacete had met Marina Proutier, the daughter of a Parisian engineer that had gone to Cuba seeking employment in the soon to be opened railroad between Havana and Güines. Years later Marina became a secondary school teacher in Paris and brought young Willard to study at her school in the northeast side of Paris. Capacete was never comfortable with his past history as a recipient of many benefits reserved for pro Spanish Cubans. He knew but had chosen to ignore the fact that many Cuban patriots were struggling and dying for freedom. Once established in Paris, he decided to make his name in the world of literature and literary and musical criticism. For a time he succeeded in throwing a veil of silence over his pro-Spanish past.

He would have been a handsome and very personable young man, were it not for a reptilian aura about him. His looks were decidedly common, but his natural talent and skills could have made it possible for him to reach great literary heights had he had the patience, intellectual honesty and discipline to learn from others. But his cultural endowment was insufficient and his effortless life in Cuba had gotten him used to expect or demand everything from others. Not having enough talent to be published by professional book editors, for instance, he published his own rather insipid poetry and short stories in Paris and Madrid. In those two learned venues, in spite of grateful and generous payments for multiple positive accolades, his literary works never found a single serious follower.

He had to resort to writing prologues to the works of friends and would-be writers of his same condition, a task to which he devoted considerable energies. One of these would-be writers, with enough resources to have her works prologued and published by Capacete, was Georgina Cipresti de Boix, Countess of la Paniega, the daughter of Josefina Cipresti. She had produced in 1842 a rather forgettable collection of her poems. Grateful for having seen her mediocre literary production between book covers, she connected Capacete with a man who was much older than herself and of whom she was a former but rather forgettable lover: Françoise Pierre Guillaume Guizot. The now Prime Minister of the *Monarchie de Juillet* immediately recruited Capacete for his dream of a Cuban anchored French republic across the Americas.

"I understand you like France and share our dreams of a French republic in the Americas," Capacete said before sensing the mood of his compatriots. "I am very well connected in Cuba and also know everyone at the Spanish embassy and at the court of Louis Philippe. If you need me to write articles or essays that help the cause, let me know. I have been published in *Le Moniteur Universel*, here in Paris, as well as *El Correo Español*, in Cadiz and *The London Chronicle*, in England."

Céspedes and Miguel did not betray their dislike of Capacete as they looked discretely at each other, unconvinced. True, they had a long tradition of affection for France and its culture. But they could not see how changing a master for another or a Cuban flag for a foreign one could be an idea that would drive the hundred of followers needed to bring about this plan. They politely stood up and thanked their hosts for the enlightened conversation.

"When will we see you next?" asked Laffitte discretely. "We understand very well that these things take time to settle into our own personal plans but we would like to have the opportunity to further discuss these concepts in real depth."

At that point Céspedes brought the conversation to an end. "I can tell you that you have aroused our curiosity and that we will think this over very carefully. You must understand however that for many years our thoughts have been very focused on seeking the total independence of Cuba. Intelligent people, however, never reject a novel idea without giving it the consideration it deserves. You have our promise that we will not cast aside these notions lightly, as they are worthy of a great deal of reflection and thoughtful rumination, especially because they come from both of you," finished Céspedes.

"Thanks. We both understand that," replied Guizot.

Carlos Manuel and Miguel shook hands with the two Frenchmen and were about to do it with Capacete when he said "I will accompany you out."

The day was clear and transparent and, although they had a carriage waiting for them, they asked the driver to follow them at close range. The three walked through the left bank *quais* past *Solferino*, the *Pont Royal* and the *Pont du Carrousel* and turned into the city at the *rue des Saints-Pères*. All along Capacete dominated the conversation with a mixture of self promoting statements and what he thought was a well-hidden probe for information.

The Louvre was radiating back the sun rays of this glorious afternoon and they could not figure out what to do to shake Capacete off except remain in silence. Finally Capacete stopped a passing coach and bid them good bye, not before making an appointment to meet the following day. A reluctant Carlos Manuel saw it as a temporary but valid relief from the dense and soggy utterances of Capacete and agreed on a meeting.

Once by themselves Carlos Manuel asked Miguel: "Is this the way in which political alliances are forged or is it the way treason makes it way into the minds of men?"

Miguel, at that time at least, did not know how to respond.

◠ ▣ ◠

THE TERRITORIES OF THE LOUISIANA PURCHASE, 1803

On April 30, 1803 France sold to the United States 530 million acres of territory at about 3 cents an acre (about $ 0.51 per acre in 2006 dollars, according to the Consumer Price Index, or $ 0.91 per acre in 2006 dollars, using the Gross Domestic Product Index). The acquisition amounted to **22.3% of the current territory of the United States**. The transaction was made through the Barings Bank of London, which charged a 12.5% commision to Napoleon. The Federalist Party of John Adams, Alexander Hamilton and Daniel Webster opposed the purchase as unconstitutional. The transaction was strongly supported by Thomas Jefferson and James Madison.

20

"Some theories are crazy, but not crazy enough to be true."
Bertolt Brecht

*"It is strangely absurd to suppose that a million human beings,
collected together, are not under the same moral laws
which bind each of them separately."*
Thomas Jefferson

*Everything great that we know has come from neurotics.
The world will never be aware of how much it owes to them,
nor above all what they have suffered in order to bestow their gifts on it."*
Marcel Proust

THE DAY AFTER the meeting of Céspedes and Aldama at the *Palais de Salm* they were at the house on *rue Jacob* waiting for Willard Capacete. The sun was out and bright although the day was rainy, which happens in Paris quite often in the spring time. The stone pavers on the *rue Jacob* looked like a multitude of small marble tiles shinning in the sun, perfectly arranged in intersecting quarter circles. It was midmorning and Capacete had been asked to come at 11 am. Sitting in the studio the conversation drifted into subjects easy to halt if their guest would suddenly be announced.

"Carlos, why is this street called *Jacob* if there is no such name in the whole of French history?"

"It was a whim of Marguerite de Valois. She named the street after the biblical patriarch. Many times we wondered, when we first moved here, why the street preserved this name through the revolution. After all, many saints whose names were carved on the street corners had been deprived of their sainthood during the revolution by skillful stone masons. Marguerite, after all, had also been an inveterate and hopeless aristocrat, and nothing coming from her should have survived. Perhaps the *sans-culottes* were not up to speed on the Old Testament."

"Quite a character this Marguerite," added Miguel.

"Oh yes. Marguerite, or *chère Margot* as her father Henri II used to call her, was the only daughter that Catherine de Medicis had given to the King. Catherine was too busy building an empire and did not have the time to personally supervise the education of her children, which included two future Kings, Henri III and Charles IX. She did not know, for instance, that her young Marguerite *had known love at eleven* until a lady in waiting told her."

"Amazing neglect. Was this the Catherine de Medici, daughter of Lorenzo de Medici, the Italian Duke of Urbino?"

"Right. Nothing like that, however, alarmed the great Catherine since her son, the future Henri III, was said to roam around the royal quarters in the company of several *mignons* and her son in law, Henri IV was said to have entertained some 25 mistresses while married to *chère Margot* a few years later. Indeed, Catherine had her hands full. When Henry II died she had to take over because the future Charles IX was then only 10 years old. And when he became of age he became the puppet of Admiral Gaspar de Coligny, the greatest Huguenot that France ever had. There Catherine lost control of her children for the second time –remember Margot– and began to conspire secretly against Charles."

"Oh, she even tried to have Gaspar assassinated," interrupted María del Carmen as she entered the room for a few moments. "Catherine was no wall flower. Since Gaspar survived she schemed to bring about Saint Bartholomew and, as they say, *do Gaspar in* during a wholesale dispatch of all the Protestants."

"Three thousand Huguenots were killed in one night in Paris, Coligny included. About twenty thousand across France. Catherine justified all this as *legibus solutus*, the right to act for the public good," added Carlos Manuel. "She then invited Pope Gregory XIII and Philip II of Spain to say special masses of thanksgiving, which they did. The same Philip II who was so devout that for the sake of penance and to secure a permanent state of grace, had ordered that his mattress in *El Escorial* should have no more than two inches of padded filling."

"Two things have been said about Philip II," commented María del Carmen as she left the room. "First, he showed himself keener to the desk than to the saddle, and more addicted to the pen than to the sword. Second, he was extremely licentious and this self mortification with the thin mattresses made his knees permanently swollen."

"Good point, added Carlos Manuel, happy to continue the story where María del Carmen had left it. "Let me count those ladies that Philip II knew in the biblical sense. At least those who were recorded in history. As wives: Princes María Manuela of Portugal, Mary Tudor, Elisabeth of Valois and Anna of Austria. Known mistresses: Doña María de Osorio, Helen of Savoy and Catherine de Navarre. Known candidates that most probably field-tested his two inch mattress at *El Escorial*: every courtesan in Spain, the American possessions, his inheritances in Italy, Naples, Sicily and Burgundy, the Netherlands and Franche Comté, as well as in the Duchy of Milan."

"So much for the presumed severe, sedate and restrained King of Spain, otherwise known as *Philip the Prudent*," concluded Miguel.

"But going back to Saint Bartholomew, nine years after his coronation, Henry III banned the Protestant religion in France and escalated the Religious Wars into the Wars of the Three Henrys: Henry III, of the House of Valois, murdered in 1589; Henry de Guise, of the House of Lorraine, murdered in 1588; and Henry de Navarre, of the House of Bourbon, who finally prevailed and became Henry IV by marrying Catherine's daughter, María de Medici, but was nevertheless also murdered in 1610."

"The Henry IV who said *Paris is well worth a Mass?*"

"The very same. But let me get back to Marguerite," Carlos Manuel said to continue his scholarly story telling. "The wedding of catholic Margot and protestant Henri de Navarre took place in 1572 when they were both 19 years old. It was said that Henri de Navarre stayed most of the wedding outside the Church so as not to offend his friends the Huguenots. Little did he know they would be slaughtered by the thousands during Saint Bartholomew. Had he known of the coming massacre, he would have guessed that it would be orchestrated by his own mother in law, the same woman that was waiting with her future bride at the foot of the altar."

"I have read that the massacre rated a strong condemnation by no other than Russia's Ivan the Terrible."

"Yes indeed. Anyway, as a reprisal for Henry de Navarre not coming into the church, Marguerite did not respond in the positive during the ceremony when asked if she would take Henry for her husband. King Charles IX, her brother, had to move to her side, grabbed her head and shook it up and down, thus producing the ritual nod of consent. It was a clear omen of things to come in this marriage."

Céspedes continued. "Having been a royal bride did not quench Marguerite's thirst for amorous adventures and it became such a public scandal that her own brother, when his turn came as Henri III, denounced her debauchery in front of the French courts. This provoked a heated denunciation by Marguerite of Henri's own nightly saturnalias and drunken revelries with his gay friends throughout the entire second floor of the royal palace."

"Eventually the situation became out of control. Henry de Navarre, by now Henry IV, righteously having restrained himself from his mistresses after their wedding, had embarked upon very ambitious projects and matters of state. He could not ignore the entanglements of Marguerite with her lovers so he divorced her. He banished Marguerite to the *Château d'Usson* in the *Auvergne*, where *chère Margot* seduced several members of the royal guard before settling to write her *memoires*."

'The bacchanalia and promiscuity of the royal families at the time knew no limit," interrupted Miguel.

"Rather than that I would say that their lives were unhinged by a continuous struggle between love stories that never got to marriage and marriages that never got to be love stories."

Carlos Manuel knew all those chronicles well and he continued. "The aftermath of Marguerite's passions, after she returned to Paris at age 52 to live at the *Hôtel de Sens* on *rue de Seine*, is a sad ending to any life. By then she was bald and rattling fat and carried around her torso a chain with dozens of protective amulets. She nevertheless sported every month a new lover, none of them older that 18 to 20 years old; by then, she had become wholly demented."

"The sins of the young are paid with the currency of the old," Carlos continued. "By the time she was 61 she was seriously brain-sick and very disturbed. She had a convent built for the *Petit Augustines* on the *Quai de Malaquais*, where ten friars had to sing praises to Jacob around the clock, with music and words composed by *chère Margot* herself. Nobody knew why she baptized the street *rue Jacob* and not Methuselah, Abraham or Isaac. Permanently disabled by her madness and unable to conciliate her sleep, she would show up in the middle of the night to rehearse the friars of the *Petit Augustines* every time her inspiration produced a new psalm. She soon dilapidated her fortune and died in 1615, in near poverty, accosted by her creditors, who seized every single one of her jewels."

"Indeed a very sad ending to her life. How did you get to know her story so well?"

"Because Alexandre Dumas is writing a novel based on her story with the title *La Reine Margot*. He gave me the galley proofs for review before turning them in. It is set during the reign of Charles IX and the French Wars of Religion. The story centers on her fears during and after Saint Bartholomew, her love affair with a noble Protestant named La Mole and her marriage to Henry IV. I believe it is a fabulous novel, in the same category of *The Count of Montecristo* and *The Three Musketeers*."

No longer had he said that than the butler entered the room and announced that Monsieur Capacete had arrived.

"Send him in, please," requested Céspedes.

After a few seconds Capacete entered the studio. He was over-dressed for the hour, with shiny patent leader shoes, dark pants and a stripped shirt with a silk vest. He had his hair cut very short and it was closely profiling his well shaped skull. He carried a large bouquet of flowers on one hand and a box of small sweet confections on the other.

"Bonjour Messieurs Aldama and Céspedes," he said. "I hope the ladies like fragrant roses from *Malmaison* and the gentlemen enjoy *macaroons*." As he said this he laid the flowers on a nearby table and opened the box of candy. "I buy these from a friend, Louis Ernest Ladurée, who has a *pâtisserie* at *16, rue Royale*, near the *Madeleine. Cet endroit est une adresse unique à Paris, symbole de l'art de vivre à la Française*," said Capacete, not aware that he had turned to the French language to proclaim the virtues of his *macaroons*.

"I did not know your individual tastes, so I brought several flavors: pistachio, almond, raspberry, black currant, lime, chestnut and I believe these last two are lime basil."

"I have seen *macaroons* many times but never like these!" exclaimed Carlos Manuel.

"Oh you will love them. Under this paper-thin crust you will taste a moist cookie with a creamy interior. The best thing about *Ladurée's macaroons* is that as they get a little bit older they just get a bit crustier & chewier."

Carlos Manuel asked the butler to take the flowers to the ladies, who were meeting on a separate parlor, and to bring a dish to send them some of the *macaroons*. The conversation then turned to ways of getting more information about the redoubtable M. Capacete.

"I understand you came to Paris to study and then decided to stay here," started Miguel.

"Yes. I came to Paris to register at the *Sorbonne* and to finish my career here, after having studied five years at the University of Havana. I came here also because I abhorred the regime in Cuba, the lack of freedom and the excesses of those who dismiss the careers of others and look down on them. I have been always active in the defense of Cuban freedoms."

He then went into an uninterrupted diatribe. "I could have spent my life dancing in Paris or giving myself to an old rich man and living like a princess but I have chosen a different path. A path of dignity and serious work. My pen has always been ready for the cause of Cuban independence. Regardless of what my enemies are saying about my works, I have written two very good essays on the music of Cuba and one on the work of Plácido and other Cuban poets. I have published their works at the expense of not publishing my own and I have organized numerous exhibitions to introduce to the French the work of Cuban painters and sculptors."

Carlos Manuel was surprised by the extent to which Capacete could gratuitously inflict on them this self-aggrandizing harangue. He thought ill-timed that the young man had assumed such a surprisingly long and gratuitous defensive position, but he decided to be patient and defuse his aggressiveness. "We did not know any of this but, if it has been your contribution all these years, we congratulate you on your concerns and your achievements."

"I have two unpublished novellas and I can not find the time to get them in print. Yet I can show you copies of hundreds of letters to the authorities in France soliciting their support for Cuban independence."

"Why do you feel that there are Cubans or Frenchmen that look down on your career and your skills?" asked Miguel. "Are there other Cubans in Paris who compete with you and feel envious? After all, there is always room for more poetry, more essays and contending insights. Do you feel sidelined by other Cubans?"

"The rivalry of Cuban males for power and their indecent race for personal benefit and control over others, even at the expense of bloodshed and suffering in Cuba, is offensive. The long nightmare and the outrageous and absurd shipwreck which is Cuba today should be appalling to all. It makes me cringe," replied Capacete.

"But there are also good Cuban men everywhere," interrupted Miguel. "They are supporting the creation and synthesis of a new Nation. They are following a course of action and personal sacrifice painfully conceived by people like José Agustín Caballero, Félix Varela and Luz y Caballero. They are keeping alive the flame that they lit and that hopefully will not ever be extinguished."

Ignoring Miguel's words Capacete continued: "If all the Cubans were to act with the ethics, the integrity and the love for Cuba of women like Josefina Cipresti and Marina Proutier, our independence would have come a long time ago. We would be free overnight if all Cubans would have the humility, the strength, the cohesion and the sisterhood of these two. We would have prevailed over Spain a long time ago had we behaved like them, never with a disagreement and never with one voice prevailing over the other."

Carlos Manuel and Miguel looked at each other in disbelief but before they could mutter a single word Capacete continued his tirade.

"They are women who carry, at the same time, the face of mourning and the countenance of hope. It is women like these two who are showing the French and the Cubans that in spite of the twists and turns of history, a Cuban republic can be founded on the truest of symbols, the heart. It is because of women like them that on the streets of Paris and Havana, for both the oppressor and the oppressed, there will always be the whispering voice of a woman bespeaking for peace."

Carlos Manuel and Miguel looked at each other again as if asking: "Is this man advancing the idea that only a misogynic movement could liberate Cuba?" As they attempted to break the monotonic rant of Capacete they realized he was not yet finished.

"I remain powerless in front of this almighty army of women. I feel like a sort of an elusive pet seeking shelter in the warm pectus of valiant women. Particularly when my own strength is undermined by treason, meanness and the abandonment of my fellow Cuban men. Yes, on those occasions, I am inclined to feel and proudly clothe myself in the garb of women... "

Those last words left Carlos Manuel and Miguel stunned and speechless. "May Carlos and I talk briefly in private," Miguel interrupted. Carlos made a signal to the waiting butler on the other side of the entrance to the studio and addressed him: "Please Ahmed, offer some refreshments to M. Capacete while we check on something we need to confirm. We will be right back."

They both left the room and walked into the patio, where they stood on a small withdrawn area under one of the large elm trees on the inside court.

"This man has gone into a transsexual hysteria while talking to us!," Céspedes said.

"Do you think the French know about this? This man's speech of today... it does not agree with what I was expecting after the good words of Guizot and Laffitte yesterday. Either these two French are past the prime of their judgment skills or this man Capacete is a born prevaricator, the most hypocritical and overambitious liar I have ever met."

"There is something strange in all of this. Do you feel that the French are possibly testing our good judgment? They could not have linked us with a more distressful personality that M. Capacete's."

"Perhaps they know him very superficially. He causes a good first impression and he certainly could sport a good garb and presence. The detail of the flowers and the *macaroons* can mislead anyone. He also has a good command of the social necessities and apparently he writes well."

"But behind all this is a sick soul. Egotistic, self-conceited and narcissistic. Regardless of his good virtues, it throws the balance overwhelmingly to the wrong side."

"Not the type of person you could trust. Here in Paris or in Cuba or even on a desert island if he were be the only person to talk to," said Carlos Manuel.

"As a young boy, my mother would not have allowed me to bring him home as a friend," added Miguel in jest. They both smiled and got ready to get back to the studio. They found Capacete curiously inspecting the books in the library shelves. The drink that Ahmed had brought to him had not been touched. Instead Capacete was munching on some dried slice of fruit he had taken from his vest pocket. Among many other things he was a consummate and strict vegetarian, obsessed with keeping his slim figure in shape.

The conversation was resumed as the three men sat by the window in their comfortable leather chairs. Capacete kept silently nibbling on his dried fruit when Céspedes began to speak.

᠕ ▥ ᠏

21

"Though those that are betray'd Do feel the treason sharply,
yet the traitor Stands in worse case of woe."
William Shakespeare

"The person who cannot laugh is not only ready for treason
and deceptions; their whole life is already a treason and deception."
Thomas Carlyle

"He that has eyes to see and ears to hear will convince himself that
no mortal can keep a secret. If his lips are silent, he chatters with his fingertips;
betrayal oozes out of him at every pore."
Sigmund Freud

"TELL ME WILLARD, what do you think of these French plans to incorporate Cuba and make Havana one of the capitals of the French empire?" Céspedes asked to continue the conversation.

"I believe it is a great idea. I came to this country when I could not stand it anymore in Cuba and I now feel like a Frenchman. There is freedom here to do whatever you want. Nobody bothers you, regardless of who you are, how you dress or with whom you party. I think it would be a nice change in Cuba if we all start thinking French," responded Capacete.

"How do you think your friends in Cuba would react? Is there in Cuba among those your age a sense of hopelessness, or cynicism or rebellion?"

"What prevails in Cuba among those of my generation is a terrifying need to survive, which is more germane to the animal world than to humans. Survival at all costs, at any price, which is after all what has always driven humanity. I was born within a system in which survival means to have no concerns whatsoever with what happens to future generations. In fact, no sympathy for the rest of the present generation either."

"That's a heavy burden, to live on the margins of goodness and generosity, and what the French call *fraternité*," interrupted Miguel.

"Oh, these are beatitudes which will make you enter the kingdom of God but will make for a very unpleasant stay in this world," responded Capacete with a sarcastic laugh. "The system in Cuba does not allow for a look at your own past. You only have time to look around and find some weak soul to trample, step on and continue on your journey thinking always only of yourself."

"Can you build a nation with people who think and feel like that?," asked Miguel.

"Who really cares? Nation builders die young and alienated from the main stream. Their only purpose is to provide heroes for the national holidays," replied Capacete.

"But nations have to be build on solid ethical principles," answered Carlos Manuel.

"Who wants to take a chance?" interrupted Capacete. "Take the case of Bartolomé de las Casas. He was a scholar and a historian as well as an energetic advocate for the rights of native people. Montaigne even quoted him in several of his works. Las Casas wanted to build a nation, like you say. He was fed up with Spanish atrocities in Cuba and had a Utopian, anti-racist and equalitarian society in mind. He fought the use of Indians on slave labor gangs, the dreadful *encomiendas*. At the end the encomenderos prevailed and Las Casas is now buried under an insignificant slab at the Chapel of our Lady of Atocha in Madrid, which no one ever visits."

"This is all true, but patriots do not do what they do expecting favors or fame… or even a great mausoleum! They do it because of a moral imperative that they cannot or would not shake aside. Whether they are recognized or not, the human race progresses thanks to the dedication of some lives to the betterment of the lives of others," riposted Miguel.

"Miguel, in Cuba your ideals are more chimerical than anywhere else because of the natural condition of most Cubans as pleasure seekers."

"How did you get the idea that Cubans are first and foremost pleasure seekers?" interrupted Carlos Manuel.

"Well, you only have to see them in Paris, well dressed, ready to go dancing or on their way to a good eatery, or looking for men or women at the bordellos, the lupanars, or *les Maison Closes, ou les cocottes rest à leur fenêtre pour se mettre en vue des passants et les attirer par des signes, des gestes ou des interpellations, souvent par des mises indécentes, quelquefois même par des postures lubriques.*" Capacete argued so intensely that he did not realize he had once more switched to speaking in French.

"Your experiences in Havana and Paris seem to have shattered your moral compass," interrupted Carlos Manuel.

"Carlos is right, dear friend," Miguel assented.

"There have been many Cubans that silently, generously and patiently have been devoted to a virtual ontogenesis of our nationality," added forcefully Carlos Manuel. "After many years of racial commingling, transculturation and religious syncretism, it has not been easy to identify and bring together our uniqueness and what makes us different from the roots that Spain and Africa planted in Cuba. It has not been easy to define what a Cuban is in order to bring all of us together as the hearty trunk of a new blooming plant species."

"Particularly since we have borrowed many cultural and ideological contributions from many confines across the world: the Spaniards that conquered us, the British that paid us a brief visit, the Africans who were dragged there against their will, the Germans and Welsh who settled in Matanzas, the North Americans who became our commercial partners and finally the French, running away from Haiti and to whose culture and history we have become so attracted," interrupted Miguel.

"Unfortunately," added Carlos Manuel, "our historical roots brought forth a complex ethnical make up that inevitably developed into a social class structure. I guess it happened everywhere, with the natives in the Americas and the slaves in the Caribbean and southern North America. But over those shaking foundations we are intending to build a solid nation, and it has not been easy."

Aldama continued, "What better and more dignified effort than that of Arango y Parreño or José Agustín Caballero?"

Carlos Manuel interrupted. "Then there are Varela, Luz y Caballero, Saco and, very close to us, Domingo Del Monte. They are not only generous but superbly educated. Through their minds are filtered the best ideas of the enlightenment, the encyclopedists, the British utilitarians, the French philosophes, the American libertarianns, the scholastics and the eclectics, the economic and political liberals, the reformers and the abolitionists. What a magnificent synthesis they have been trying to hatch!"

"I have come to believe that all of these patriarchs are simply looking out for their own interests," riposted Capacete while Carlos Manuel and Miguel listened in disbelief.

"The defense of personal interests is not necessarily incompatible with acting for the good of others. There are Cubans that seek benefits for themselves and others which are perfectly legitimate. The right to trade with neighbors, the right not to be taxed excessively, the right to express yourself. There will always be personal advantages which are not divorced with the benefits of others," added Aldama. "You can not exclude from political participation and even political ambition any of the Cuban land owners, the *criollo* merchants, the clergy, the current civil authorities, even the Spanish army and the Spanish intellectuals, as long as the directions they propose would result in the benefit of all of those living in Cuba. After all, your country is the place were you were born or where you have chosen to live, and you are in your perfect right to seek there your share of happiness, wealth and affections."

In the eyes of Capacete you could sense his disgust for the lesson he was being taught by Carlos Manuel and Miguel. He was used to receive assent and admiration by most of the Cubans he frequented in Paris. His somewhat light varnish of literary and musical knowledge had delighted his French friends and had nurtured his self perceived aura of triumphal intellectual superiority. Having a debate on matters of the intellect and not *fête* on the homage that he thought he deserved was more than he could stand. In his mind he resolved to destroy and make life difficult for these two Cuban aristocrats who had just minutes ago received his generous offerings of flowers and *macaroons*.

It had been almost two hours since he rang the bell on *12, rue Jacob* and he briskly stood up, ready to retreat to the streets. He could contain himself and be polite even under these trying conditions, and he did.

"Monsieur Céspedes and Monsieur Aldama," he said extending his hand, "it has been a pleasure sharing with you this morning. I bid you good bye and Godspeed."

Céspedes addressed him. "Are you not going to have your *déjeuner* with us Monsieur Capacete?

"No, thank you. I have a very busy afternoon and I am still preparing a small novella for publication," he replied.

"Is it to be published in France or in Cuba?" asked Miguel.

"Neither, it is being published by an important house in Cadiz, Spain."

"Well, in that case I hope it will give you the success and good fortune that you deserve. Let us know when it is available in Paris and we will certainly read it. What is the subject matter, if we might know?"

"Let it be a surprise when you receive it, Messieurs. I will make sure you both get a copy."

"Thanks. We look forward to it." concluded Carlos Manuel as he began lo lead Capacete on his way to the front door.

"*Au revoir*, my friends."

"*Au revoir*, Monsieur."

Upon leaving the house of the Céspedes, M. Capacete got back on his waiting coach and instead of directing it to his home near the *Place de Clichy*, he instructed the driver: "*85, Avenue de Neuilly, s'il vous plaît.*"

Céspedes and Aldama, meantime, joined María del Carmen, Rosa and Gertrudis at the *salon*.

"Not a good conversation with this man," Céspedes said. "I think we will have problems with him because he felt humiliated while we were only trying to present our point of view. I feel it has been an unfortunate accident that we got to meet him through Guizot and Laffitte. I could sense the resentment of this self-promoting *dilettante* against us, probably because he despises what we are: two *criollo* blue bloods."

"I agree with you, Carlos. I do not think we have seen the last of him. How he could avail himself of the trust of the French is beyond my comprehension."

"How well connected do you think he is?," asked María del Carmen.

"I will let you know at the end of this week," responded Miguel.

Paris, in the years of the *Monarchie de Juillet* was seething with double agents, spies and unscrupulous would be merchants. Upon arriving at Hamburg on his trip from Cuba, Miguel had been warned by Albert Guichard, his *chargé d'Affairs* in France that two of his fellow passengers were probably secret French agents returning from their missions. When Miguel became curious and skeptical, Albert decided to be more precise, saying that actually there were three secret agents on board, one of which worked for the House of Aldama. He showed Miguel a small notebook where the Aldama's agent had kept track of his expenses. Several payments were annotated under the heading "secret intelligence services rendered." The man had been infiltrated in Cádiz and his duties consisted of reporting to him on any French subjects arriving from Havana or New Orleans.

"My father never mentioned that we had our own network of spies in Spain," Miguel commented.

"We have a special account in Paris just for that purpose," replied Albert. "We also have a number of private British banks in London with which we work. During the revolution your grandfather was up to date with everything that was happening in the Jacobin's clubs thanks to the help of no other than the Comte de Montgaillard, who was our agent in France. It is a necessity if you are engaged in international business today."

Within a day of the last meeting with Capacete, Miguel had contacted Albert at his home on 42, *rue Mazarine*, a walking distance from the Céspedes home. He asked him if he knew who M. Willard Capacete was and if he could find out everything that could be known about this man. Albert smiled and opened a small chest by the side of his bureau. He gave Miguel an envelope carefully tied with a blue silk ribbon which was marked "For M. Miguel Aldama or his father Don Domingo."

"Take this and study it carefully. It came to us from our agent in London. I was getting ready to transfer it to Havana but now I see that it is important for your well being and that of your friends. I am sure your father would not mind if you saw it before he does. No sense in having this document tied up here in Paris any longer. It does not directly concern our financial businesses but your father has to make a decision as to showing it to the *mystérieux* French *Secret Bureau 2, les espions de l'Empire*."

Miguel Aldama could not wait for his driver and his coach to show up at the home of M. Albert Guichard and briskly walked the few blocks to the house of the Céspedes. He immediately got into the studio with Carlos Manuel and they opened the envelope. Inside there was a light blue colored document in the size of the papers that were normally used for the protocols of notaries and by public functionaries in France. It had been folded in three along its width and its ends were tucked one inside the other. The edge of the folds had been stamped with a wax seal bearing the initials of M. Guichard in a way that the folded paper could not be opened without damaging the seal.

They undid the scrupulous safeguards of M. Guichard and Miguel began to read the document.

"M. Willard Capacete, whose real name is Antonio Capacete, is a valuable spy for the Spanish crown, although he is intent on extracting money from the French government by posing as a valuable intelligence resource. In Spain he reports to Don Pedro Téllez y Girona,

Prince of Anglona. In Paris he has earned the trust of Adolphe Thiers, Odilon Barrot and Mathieu Molé. He works out of Paris and in spite of his youth is up in the ways of the world. Count on his having seen everything, known everything and lied about everything." Miguel hesitated for a moment.

"Go on," pressed Carlos Manuel.

"He is in good terms with all political persuasions but would pretend to be a Cuban patriot. He is an ethical acrobat and a great mimic and would easily confuse you with whatever smile you are expecting: persuasive, satisfied, naïve, trusting. He can maneuver you to vice or virtue and will display more believable diplomacy than any ambassador. He is a juggler of truth and has a prodigious memory with which he will entangle you. He knows people, places and all higher ups by their names. He lives a life of perpetual festivity and likes to be feted by rich ladies who welcome, flatter and feed him whenever he pleases. He never touches them although he is drenched in the vices of Paris." A new pause was in order, followed by a new inducement to go on by Céspedes.

"Go on, don't stop."

"He can sell your soul for five or six thousand francs as long as he can continue to live the life of a sovereign. He is a favorite of *grisettes*, a man who would jump lightly to the fence of a stage-coach, give a hand to the timid lady who fears to step down and carry her down holding her by the waist. He can play a tune with his fingers on half filled champagne glasses without missing a beat and then would look at other men as if asking, can you do the same? With the same elegance he can follow a target on a dark street, pull his portable knife from his vest pocket and, in his own words, *check the color of any man's blood.*"

With a grave voice Miguel Aldama ended the reading of the document as an anxious Carlos Manuel once again requested him to finish.

"He can pass himself as a writer, a poet or musical critic, a banker, a magistrate, a teacher at the Sorbonne or a bourgeois. He is always what he needs to be. He has mastered the skills of persuasive eloquence, loosening of purses, and stirring jealousies in the hearts of husbands and wives. Capacete has a history of charming merchants and diplomats and disappearing when he has accomplished his goals. He will not hesitate to double cross his dying mother."

"We knew it. A vulgar and coward spy. He is probably right now scrutinizing his warped and sick mind on how to bring harm to us and our families."

"We need to outsmart him. He is a feeble man, a worthless and trashy brute in spite of his pretentions of class; he has been wounded and is thirsty for revenge. Men do not think rationally when they are obsessed with the desire for vengeance. We will outsmart him even if in the process we have to render an undeserved gift to Spain."

Miguel read and reread the document several times. For Céspedes a first reading was enough. He was now concentrating on how many ways he could bid good riddance to the traitor without jeopardizing the safety and the happiness that María del Carmen was enjoying by simply being in her cherished city of Paris.

"Time will tell," Carlos Manuel said. *"Nemo me impune lacessit.* No one hurts me with impunity."

NOTRE DAME AND THE SEINE IN 1840

The location where **Notre Dame** is today has always been the center for spirituality in Paris. The Celts had their sacred ground there. The Romans built on it a temple to Jupiter. By the 6th century a Christian basilica occupied the land. In the 12th century a Romanesque church was torn down to construct the present monumental structure. Its most dangerous times came during the French Revolution, when many of its sculptural features, including chapels and gargoyles, were demolished by the mobs. Napoleon Bonaparte declared it property of the State and, as with all church buildings in France, it is now merely assigned to the Catholic Church for its religious cult.

22

"Being a woman is a terribly difficult task,
since it consists principally in dealing with men."
Joseph Conrad

"Women's liberation is just a lot of foolishness.
It's men who are discriminated against. They can't bear children.
And no one is likely to do anything about that."
Golda Mier

"Hatred is a tonic, it makes one live, it inspires vengeance;
but pity kills, it makes our weaknesses weaker."
Honoré de Balzac

THE COUNTESS OF MERLIN and Gertrudis Gómez had not met since they had been at *Tortoni's*, a few days after Gertrudis arrived in Paris. It was María del Carmen who invited both for an afternoon tea at *Lapérouse* a week before Tula was planning to leave for Madrid.

Lapérouse had been founded in 1766 and was named after Jean François de Galaup, Comte de La Perouse. Its location was excellent, close to *Pont Saint Michel*, *Pont Neuf*, the old *rue de Seine* and the *Quai des Augustins*. You could sense the splendor of Paris in the Middle Ages by standing in front of the restaurant. As many other restaurants in Paris, *Lapérouse* was owned by a privileged family. Legend had it that it was one of the first eateries that opened a bar on a secluded spot near the family tables a where a sign was placed reading *"Venite ad me homes et ego restaurabo vos"* (come to me men, and I will restore you).

Unlike London, the Parisian restaurants, and *Lapérouse* particularly, were often frequented by groups of women that would come to dine by themselves in private rooms called *cabinets de societé*. They engaged in conversation topics that sarcastically became to be known by some men as *la rébellion des femmes*. The Countess was a frequent customer at *Lapérouse* and she was more than glad to share these sessions with Gertrudis and María del Carmen.

On the appointed day, the Countess was the first to arrive and almost immediately a coach pulled by the front of the restaurant with Tula and Mme. Céspedes. The butler in attendance promptly showed them to the cabinet where María de las Mercedes was waiting.

"Welcome to both of you," the Countess greeted her friends. "I had asked Aurore to be with us but unfortunately she did not want to leave Frederick by himself. He has had a relapse of his cough assaults and is not feeling very well."

"I am sorry about that, Mercedes," replied Gertrudis referring to the Countess by her first name. "I always enjoy talking to Aurore. She is a great novelist and a better activist for the rights of women."

"At a time when there is a common notion that women are simply servants to their husbands and decorations to show off at social functions, it is refreshing to find a woman like her," commented María del Carmen.

"SAhe has my undivided admiration too," added Mercedes. "I believe her work, as well as that of Flora Tristan, is breaking new ground on the needs for women's education and our right to divorce."

"Sometimes it seems that the only concerns of this society are aesthetics, desire, lust and money. Women are thought of as mindless beauties parading on the boulevards shading their faces with veils and umbrellas, leaning on the arms of men that have the right to act as their masters," María del Carmen said.

"Men will not yield their privileged position in society easily," added Gertrudis. "We just visited an exhibition at the *Louvre* last week and two of the paintings are quite telling: one of them by Edoudard de Beaumont called *Les Vesuviennes* shows women as warriors, having shed all their femininity and looking like street whores. The other, I can't remember the author, is called *Le Livre*. Although at first sight it seems to show a *liseuse moderne* (a modern woman) in a studious and docile female posture, the impression you get as you study her face is that she is aimlessly and mindlessly imbibing stupid notions from a novel rather than minding to her spousal and maternal obligations."

"That's why I like Aurore so much," added the Countess. "A cigar in her hand, wearing trousers and not having any qualms about saying what she thinks face to face to men. She has paid the price and has been accused many times as rude, coarse, unrefined and uncouth; they may charge her as vulgar and masculine. She does not care. The fact is that she always dresses well and she can put together a sentence like the best of writers. That's what counts for her."

"Of all the Frenchmen in my life of study," Gertrudis added, "my favorite is Condorcet. Years before it became fashionable, he wrote an essay entitled "*Sur l'Admission de Femmes aux Droits de Citoyen*" (On the Admission of Women to the Rights of Citizens). There, in well argued sentences, he expressed that there was no reason for keeping women from voting. At that time the arguments were that pregnancy and "*manque d'inclination temporaire*" (temporary indisposition), as well as a predisposition to suffer from gout every winter, were reasons to restrict women's rights to vote. Condorcet wrote the definitive sentence: "*If women can go to the guillotine for breaking the laws, they should be able to vote if they do not break them.*" It has always been a splendid argument; in fact, one of my favorite quotations of all time."

"Women were taken to the guillotine in these days and often their transgressions went into the records as "*négligé les vertus adéquat de son sexe*" (neglected the virtues befitting her sex)," added the Countess.

"Well, the story of women's rights is full of heroines," added María del Carmen. "Madame de Staël once wrote a fictional story which criticized France's reluctance to come to terms with divorce and the connotation of outcasts given to women who do not marry. Bonaparte exiled her. His code was entirely biased in favor of men. He outlawed divorce and almost *verbatim* declared that the normal function of women was to bear children. For women, marriage was more stringent than slavery in those days. Men could free their slaves but were prohibited to relinquish any of their rights over their wives."

"Yes, the famous Napoleonic Civil Code gave equal rights to all men but also plugged all the ambiguities of the law that women had used during the *ancien régime* to exercise some of their rights. It set the interests of women back one hundred years," said Gertrudis.

"I believe that there is hope in the horizon for our rights, however," declared the Countess. "I am very hopeful with the work of Niboyet, Pauline Roland, Suzanne Voilquin, Elisa Lemonnier and other women within *Saint-Simonisme*. They have been asserting the legitimacy of women's claims to social and political recognition through *La Femme libre*, *La Voix des femmes*, *La Politique des Femmes* and other papers. They have infiltrated the Ministry of Education, the Commission of the Luxembourg and the revolutionary press, as well as many banks and the railways administration. That's the way to do it. We are in total accord on this matter with the Enfantins, the Pereires, the Talabots, the Julliens and every other enlightened man of *Saint Simon*."

"I receive the *Tribune des Femmes* and the *Gazette des Femmes* regularly. Carlos Manuel and I both read them from cover to cover," interrupted María del Carmen. "Unfortunately the *Gazette* is registered as a woman's publication and it legally can not be issued more than once a month. That by itself should be cause for shaming every man in journalism."

"Quite aside from women's rights," interrupted Gertrudis, "the issue of marriage rights is under scrutiny now. For many years we have been fed this foolishness of *amour romantique* (romantic love). For young women the idea of marriage has been to enliven men's lives with happiness and adoring attention. That placed women in the impossible position of simultaneously being moral guardians and helpless parasites. But under *l'amour romantique* there were two pitfalls, the fear of enjoying your own body as a source of pleasure and the fear of revealing women's most intimate fantasies as sexual marauders, if you wish."

"Tula, the Church fathers will burn you if they are listening. Those are strong words," María del Carmen declared mockingly.

"We have been too concerned with the preservation of modesty," added Gertrudis. "There is no reason to classify the human race as males who desire to mate and women who are semi angels. Enough of this literature that pretends to scandalize by presenting men with unsatisfied instincts and women with expressionless smiles and half closed eyes, only capable of shameful glances. The end is always the same: the girl succumbs to shame as she consummates her sins by passively accepting the caresses of a young man."

The Countess added, "In France, more than in Cuba I might add, married women are frequent victims of men "correcting" their behaviors with sticks, canes, belts and brooms. They are beaten, terrorized, coerced and frightened with little if any penalties for the abuser. The ultimate cruelty has been to legally spurn and disdain a pregnant woman by admitting the word of a scoundrel of a man arguing that '*l'enfant qu'elle ont n'est pas a moi*' (the child she bears is not mine)."

The waiter at *Lapérouse* came to check that all was well at the *cabinet* occupied by the three ladies and he was reminded to bring some more hot tea. The conversation continued:

"Take the case of Bonaparte," Gertrudis said. "He married Josephine as a widow with two children when she was 33. When he became convinced that she would not give him the blood son he wanted to succeed him as emperor, he convinced her to agree to a divorce on the grounds of mutual consent. He then violated his own Napoleonic Code three times: first overriding the law against divorce within the imperial family; second divorcing her when she was 46, which was beyond the time where you could divorce by mutual consent; third by marrying Archduchess Marie-Louise three months thereafter instead of waiting for the legal three years. So much for Napoleonic law applied equally to men and women."

"And so much for the fairness of this pudgy and chunky egocentric and tyrannical bastard that the French are idolizing as their best ruler of all times, even though he was not even French," added the Countess.

"Even worse," continued the Countess. "The Napoleonic Code prescribed that the only grounds for divorce by a woman was proven adultery by the man. A man, however, only needed the testimony of adulterous behavior from a third party witness. The woman, but not the man, could be jailed for up to two years on that testimony."

"No wonder there were so many notable cases of women taking the law in their own hands," said María del Carmen.

"Oh, I am writing two short stories based on real cases along those lines," added Gertrudis.

"Tell us about it," both of her listeners replied in unison.

"The first case is that of Eloise Marie Fortunée Cappelle. She was born in Paris in 1816, the daughter of a military man. At age 12 she lost her father and at age 19 her mother. Her dowry amounted only to 90,000 francs and she knew she was a difficult match for a marriage. So did her aunt, the wife of the President of the *Banque de France*, whose husband became her tutor and custodian. Without telling her anything, the uncle contracted the services of a matrimonial agency that produced M. Charles Lafarge, a coarse underbred and detestable iron worker with less than 30,000 annual income. They soon married Eloise to M. Lafarge and the couple went to live with his parents next door to the business."

María del Carmen and María Mercedes were listening with anticipation as Gertrudis continued.

"Once married, Eloise found out that her in-laws were even more repulsive, hideous and plebeian than her new husband. She became terrified by his crude and vulgar sexual demands and ended up closeting herself in a small room in the house. One day he broke the door and wrecked the house screaming that he would never renounce to his marital privileges. After that, she was tortured and forced to comply with his sexual requests in front of his depraved and perverted in-laws."

"What ghastly luck!" the Countess commented.

"But wait," said Gertrudis. "The situation lasted for several months until Charles began to complain about intestinal discomforts. He began to suffer more and more frequently of stomach cramps, nausea and uncontrolled puking and retching attacks. Tests after his death revealed high concentrations of arsenic in his bloodstream. Eloise Marie professed with a cloistered order at a *Convento de Clausura*, changed her name to Sister Evangeline and never again spoke to another soul until she died at age 68. Only to her confessor she once suggested that her husband probably deserved his unfortunate fate because *he had it coming*. The aging priest never understood the full meaning of this sentence but attributed his bewilderment to his decaying sense of hearing. Speechless as she remained, other nuns in the congregation were always puzzled by a curious smile that never ceased to glow from her face."

"Bravo for that story!" both friends applauded enthusiastically. "Tell us the other one."

"The other story is also real and her main character is Euphemie Verges. She was born into a bourgeois provincial family of limited means, the daughter of a small landowner. Her uncle Henri Lacoste, 33 years her senior, took a liking to her and got her parents consent to marry her. He was already retired as shopkeeper and had inherited the lands and vineyards of his brother, who had died of tuberculosis. Euphemie's dowry amounted to a mere 20,000 francs, which was less than Henri used to make from one of his farms in the course of one year."

Gertrudis took a sip of his coffee, providing the proverbial pause that all genial story tellers need to bring their audience into full concentration.

"Go on," María del Carmen said anxiously.

"Her parents nevertheless agreed dutifully to turn to her new husband her meager possessions at wedding time and Henri accepted them. That negotiation was finished a few days before the wedding and Euphemie learned of it the day of her marriage. Realizing that her husband was well endowed with years and money but nothing else, Euphemie took the duties of shaving him, removing regularly his numerous and recurrent warts, washing his feet, and even cleaning his toenails."

"Within a matter of months they were both discontented with their marriage. Henri was very jealous and never allowed her to leave the house. He complained to everyone about her failure to get pregnant. Euphemie was sexually unsatisfied and her hands looked like those of a farm girl because her endless duties as his laundress, cook, housekeeper and personal valet."

Gertrudis made another pause and it was now the Countess who fretfully insisted that she go on.

"Five years after their marriage Henri became seriously ill. He had an inborn distrust of doctors and had her prepare progressively stronger household remedies. When his condition became hopeless, he had her call a doctor but it was too late. He died convulsing of abdominal pains and was diagnosed with arsenic poisoning. She never showed any outward signs of grief after Henri's death. Widows were expected to mourn their husbands for two years but it was hardly a month before she was sharing her bed with a young man that had been in charge of the stables."

"I think those two stories will be a hit," the Countess said. "You will have women all over the empire rooting for Eloise Marie and Euphemie."

"Come on, ladies, control your enthusiasm!" interrupted Gertrude sarcastically. "Nobody ever knew whether these two ladies had access to arsenic, much less that they had fed it to their husbands. One has to presume that they were both gratuitously misjudged by their contemporaries, as well as by the two of you right now."

With that remark all three burst out in laughter and began to exit the *Cabinet* and the restaurant towards the coach that was waiting for them.

~ ⌧ ~

INSTITUTE DE FRANCE AND PONT DES ARTS, 1838

The monumental buildings on the *Quai Conti* include, on the left the **Hôtel des Monnaies**, built in 1771 on a lot originally occupied by the *Hôtel de Conti*. In that building Benjamin Franklin met many times with Mirabeau to draft the French Constitution of 1791. On the right, the curved *façade* of the **Institute de France**, the former *Palace Mazarin* designed by Louis Le Vau, the architect of Louis XIV. It was there that Jefferson and Condorcet worked on the Declaration of the Rights of Man and Citizen in 1789. Across the Institute, the **Pont des Arts** that links the *Quai Conti* with the *Quai du Louvre*.

23

*"Rhetoric is a poor substitute for action, and we have trusted
only to rhetoric. If we are really to be a great nation,
we must not merely talk; we must act big."*
Theodore Roosevelt

*"Old wood best to burn, old wine to drink,
old friends to trust, and old authors to read."*
Francis Bacon

*"The difference between coarse and refined abuse is the difference
between being bruised by a club and wounded by a poisoned arrow."*
Samuel Johnson

CESPEDES, ALDAMA AND DEL MONTE met at the studio on
12, rue Jacob so that the first two could appraise Del Monte of what
they had learned about M. Capacete. They also needed to discuss the
events that occurred in that room a few days before, when they received Capacete at the suggestion of Guizot and Laffitte. After listening to their story Del Monte spoke. "This is the reaction and the
behavior of a man whose character has been forged in captivity. A
man who has never enjoyed freedom and is victimized by his own
selfishness," he commented. "That's what happens to the fiber and
character of a young man after years of an absolutism that seeds and
hammers mistrust, blind ambition and hopelessness. Not very different from what results from a cruel and brutal revolution like the
one France had to endure."

Those words took Carlos and Miguel by surprise. They had never
heard Domingo expressing such reproachful and hostile opinions
about the French Revolution. After all, at the height of the *Monarchie
de Juillet* everything they heard and listened in Paris were praises for
the events of 1789. It was considered a watershed in French history
and most learned men, except the die-hard monarchists, spoke of life
and country before and after the burst of the revolution.

"For many people the French Revolution brings to mind the Declaration of the Rights on Man. One has to wonder two things: first, did men have any rights before the Revolution? Second, did the Revolution overturn any rights already in place? I think the answer to both questions is an uncomfortable yes," explained Del Monte. He continued: "One of the least studied and most shameful acts of the French Revolution, for instance, is the *révolte Vendéenne* or the events of the Vendée. Together with *la Terreur*, the Terror, they illustrate the arguments for not having a revolution at all, under any conditions and without any qualifications or exceptions."

"You are unusually radical on that statement," Miguel said.

"I am not an extremist at all," replied Del Monte. "Many people think *la Vendée* was a revolt by peasants instigated by the clergy and the aristocrats. Nothing of the sort. The *Vendée* was a prosperous area that welcomed the revolution with open arms, priests included. But then a bunch of Parisians, not yet truly representing the will of the people, imposed on them the Constitution of the Clergy, which forced the priests to swear alliance to the revolutionary government and not to the Church. To top it off, they also imposed conscription into the army for all citizens of age, again without consultation with anyone. The peasants did not like it and after trying to argue their point to no avail decided to arm themselves and revolt. They felt that a new tyranny had substituted the old one. It turns out they were right."

"The repression they got was worst than anything Louis XVI could have orchestrated," Céspedes interrupted.

"Yes," added Del Monte. "You could read in the minutes of the National Convention phrases like this: The *Vendée* needs to be destroyed. The land of liberty must be purged forever of that damnable race. The *Vendée* must be turned into a national cemetery."

"In fact," added Del Monte, "out of 800,000 residents of *la Vendée* more that 120,000 were decimated by the revolutionary armies, roughly one for every seven persons, women and children included."

"That was an ideological rather than a strategic slaughter," explained Del Monte. "What a contradiction with the official line! If the Revolution was the exaltation of liberty and human rights, why did it stomp on the liberty and human rights of the *vendéens*?"

"Because when it comes to revolutions it is impossible to separate their initial idealistic dreams from the horror that inevitably follows," added Carlos Manuel.

Del Monte interrupted to say: "At the core of this is the second great myth of the French Revolution. The first myth is that it was started by the bourgeoisie. The second myth is that the Terror was imposed as an urgent defense from internal and external threats. These two falsehoods are written in the revolutionary catechism and everyone seems to accept them."

"Many other myths are found in the minds of the public," added Carlos Manuel. "The *Jacobins* are praised as a positive driving force for change when in reality they were the pioneers in the art of establishing a tyrannical one-party system."

"Another myth is that a revolutionary process begets *un homme nouveau*," Del Monte said. "Every time people hope for that promethean creation, what they see is the birth of a cutthroat and bloodsucking regime."

"One wonders what was the real cost to France for its 1789 Revolution, in practical and concrete terms," asked Carlos Manuel.

"I will tell you what the price has been," responded Del Monte. "Two million French dead in twenty years, out of a population of twenty one million across France. Forty percent of France's wealth dilapidated and lost either by mismanagement, by emigration or by repatriation by foreigners. France, until then hand to hand with Britain, missed thirty irrecoverable years of Industrial Revolution and its production output could not recover the pre-revolutionary levels until after Napoleon was proclaimed Emperor. Popular education underwent a fifteen year relapse with the closing of church schools. The national patrimony was cut by one third, as irreplaceable treasures were lost forever because of the vandalism of the masses."

"And," added Carlos Manuel, " probably the worst of it, poverty and instability caused first the loss of Haiti and later the sale by Bonaparte to the United States, for fifteen meager millions of dollars, of one half of what is now the United States. After Napoleonic times France was left in the Americas with only a couple of islands in the trade winds with less surface and richness than their uninhabited territories of the Guyana."

"You wonder why the French still celebrate the 14th of July! Someday the victims of the *Vendée* will receive more homage as French patriots than the anarchic delinquents who took *la Bastille*," concluded Del Monte. "I believe you will find this a very prophetic statement. Write it down, Carlos, so that you could rightly attribute it to me after I pass away."

They half smiled and remained in silence, pensive, until Aldama spoke.

"But let's get to the purpose of our meeting. We have a request from Laffitte and Guizot and an obstacle in our hands which is this man Capacete, which we all agree is bad news. What are we going to do about it?"

"I tend to believe that the best thing to do is to politely refuse the French and ignore the Cuban," stated Del Monte. "We do not have the blood of traitors or mercenaries. To think of Cuba as a part of France is absurd and unrealistic from many perspectives: historical, political, demographic, and every other criteria you can think of. To pay much attention to this double-crossing slimy ragamuffin Capacete would be debasing."

It was then Céspedes turn to speak. "I do not think it will be easy on either count. The French have entrusted us with some very delicate information and it is not the type of thing that you disclose and take no for an answer. As for Capacete, it was very easy to obtain information about him, which is good from the standpoint of knowing what we are up against but is bad because it shows that he is well known and has been around many times."

While Céspedes, Aldama and Del Monte were pondering what to do and how to react to the expectations of the French and the perfidy of the Cuban, a meeting of equal importance was taking place at the home of Josefina Cipresti at *85, Avenue de Neuilly*, or rather the home of her daughter Georgina and her husband, the Count of la Paniega.

The residence shared by the two Cipresti women with old Count Ignacio was a large comfortable apartment near the Place de l'Etoile, one of the most exclusive neighborhoods of Paris. A triple window balcony offered a spectacular view of the Arch de Triumph that Napoleon started in 1806 in honor to his "big army" victory at Austerlitz and Louis Philippe had finished in 1836. Under the arch the remains of Napoleon had recently passed when they were brought back from Sainte Helene as a courtesy of the British.

The arch defined the neighborhood. It stood on a large plaza, isolated, massive and impressive. Around it, 12 radial avenues converged, one of which was *Avenue de Neuilly*. On the inside walls of the arch one could read the names of no less then 558 Napoleonic generals, with those who died in battle conspicuously underlined. On the outside, the names of successful battles, *sans* Waterloo of course, and four huge relief sculptures on the bases of the four pillars: *The Triumph of 1810* by Cortot; *Resistance* and *Peace* by Etex; and *The Departure of the Volunteers* and *La Marseillaise* by Rude.

In spite of Georgina being the woman of the house, her mother Josefina was its undisputed mistress. She was an authoritarian figure who pretended to be accustomed to royal treatment in spite of her well-hidden humble origins and her dearth to any claims to fame. It was because of these pretensions that she was always surrounded by people ready to take advantage of her money and her favors. Frequently she invited quite a retinue of followers to expensive *soirées* that the Count was more than glad to include among his household expenses. It was not unusual on those occasions for her to repeatedly request hundred pound bills from the Count to distribute to those making gracious remarks or pleasant compliments to her qualities. The Count gratefully distributed the requested currency and charged it on his mind to well-deserved spousal favors received from Josefina's daughter.

The old woman read voraciously but did not have the intellectual framework to assimilate what she read. She could not sustain an intelligent conversation with those contemporaries which she so much longed to call her equals. She was of slight build, always dressed on earth tones, particularly mottled leopard motives, and always sported a hat to obviate the need for hair dressing. Her apartment was full of memorabilia from real and imaginary trips to the furthest confines of the earth. Richly decorated ivory fans from the orient, exotic fabrics from Italy, ceremonial icons from Arabia and the Ottoman Empire, exquisitely printed books from Spain and London and all sorts of contraptions and widgets printed with or having the appearance or fragrance of roses.

Alita, the Philippine maid attending Josefina, came to the studio where she was reading and announced: "Monsieur Capacete is here, Madam. Shall I show him to the *salon*?"

"Yes Alita," replied Josefina. "Show him to the *salon*, offer him some refreshments and let him know that I will soon be with him."

Josefina continued reading for ten to fifteen minutes although she could not concentrate on her book. She knew that Willard had become an unconditional and loyal follower. She could never tell, however, if he had legitimately become a friend or if his irrational enthusiasm for her was the result of those weekly expensive dinners. For three years now she had dined him at *Les Ambassadeurs*, in the midst of its 25 foot ceilings, Baccarat chandeliers and seven colored marbles. Every now and then he had proposed and she assented to go to *Le Meurice*, to dine among its precious woods and Italian marbles and overindulge in its comfortable chairs and lounges decorated with dozens of precious fabrics and rare silks. The altered state of urgency and anxiety of the note that Capacete had brought personally to her house a few days before, was very distressing for Josefina.

They had agreed to meet for dinner on Thursday, like every week, yet it was now Tuesday and he had requested to be received today.

"What could possibly be so urgent that he cannot wait until our agreed meeting?," she asked herself. She finally made her way to the *salon* carrying a book on her hands to signify her dissatisfaction for having had her readings interrupted and to assert her resolve to return to her book at the earliest. When she entered the *salon* she saw Capacete pacing nervously back and forth.

"Bonjour, Willard," she said.

"Bonjour, Josefina," he responded. "Sorry to interrupt you, but we have a problem on our hands that needs to be resolved at once."

"What could possibly be a reason strong enough to annoy me during my reading time?," she asked.

He went into a fast paced and uninterrupted tirade, ostensibly to to not give her an opportunity to leave the *salon* during any pauses. Obligingly, she listened to him without interjecting any comments, as he related the conversation with Céspedes and Aldama a few days before.

"I do not see any reasons for alarm in what you are saying," commented Josefina once Willard had finished. "These are powerful people. They know their way in Europe and have almost unlimited resources and contacts. I am sure they already know you are here today and that all your complaints over the last two days have been fully reported to them. I suggest you stop your *delirium persecutio* and come to your senses. You need to choose your battles and this one is not yours to win."

Capacete became more and more furious as Josefina spoke. His head began to wobble diagonally as bulls do when they see the matador pulling out his sword.

"I cannot forget this affront," he said. "They made fun of me, my background, my writings, and my ego. They dismissed my value and ignored my worthiness. They have to pay for this. I will destroy their reputations, their fortunes and even their lives and those of their families."

Josefina was beginning to get alarmed at the obsessive fixation of Capacete and tried to calm him down and reassure him of his merits.

"My dear Willard," she started. "I have learned by experience to disengage and retreat before a superior force. These men have superior minds than the two of us. You and I have compromised our lives for undeserved glories many times, and we carry a burden of unspoken shame that we rather not make public. I advise you not to continue this wild burst of anger and wrath and come back to your senses. If you are determined to continue, leave me out of this battle."

Capacete was about to interrupt her when she continued.

"There is nothing I desire more that humiliate those who look down on me as a vulgar courtesan. But what is important to me at this point in my life is this home, these possessions and a future of comfortable and almost unlimited wealth. I have sacrificed my daughter and married her to the most boring and foul smelling of Spanish nobles. I have to calm her down every day and trust she will remain calm and accept her fate. She lives a lackluster life resigned to never show herself in the arms of a fine looking man. She has to degrade herself and have furtive trysts with lovers that she knows are after her money, the way you have always been after mine. This is the price we both pay for the Cannes vacations, the visits to the *Hotel Gritti* to share the rooms where the Doge of Venice used to sleep, and the dinners you have enjoyed with my francs."

Once more Capacete tried to interrupt. She raised her open hand with her palm facing towards him and continued.

"If you think for a moment that I will risk all of this to revenge an honor that you never possessed you are mistaken. I do not care about Cuba, the slaves or the freedoms of anyone but myself. Last year I went to Cuba with a mission from Ignacio. To find out where he could invest and purchase land to open a sugar plantation. I never talked to any Cubans but to the Spanish authorities in the island. I carried two letters. One for Francisco Javier de Ulloa, who was at the time the Capitan General of Cuba. He sold us, on his own, hundreds of acres belonging to the crown of Spain and for which, of course, he will be pocketing the money. My second letter was for Leopoldo O'Donnell, the Count of Lucena, and a friend of Ignacio's, who will be the next Capitan General and who will do likewise when his turn comes. Will I risk the success of these operations by fighting your wars in Paris against Cubans who are as well connected or better than my own Ignacio?"

By now Capacete knew he was wasting his time trying to form an alliance with Josefina. She had also humiliated him, reducing him to a beggar for favors. His eyes were protruding on their sockets and his brow was sweating profusely. His mouth was dry and he could not contain the tremor in his voice or the trembling of his hands. He slowly slouched his tired body on a chair and laid his head on its velvety back rest.

"All this for nothing," he thought. "Josefina is nothing but a bastard, a vile concubine, an ignorant phony that can no longer open her legs to receive favors and makes her child do it for her. She is like them and deserves the same fate."

With these thoughts Capacete stood up and walked towards Josefina. He raised his left arm over his right shoulder and discharged the back of his hand over Josefina's face, throwing her aging and defenseless body against an armoire; her head hit the armoire hard, at an unfortunate angle. She landed face up with her arms extended in a defensive position that she was not able to fully assume. Her eyes, deeply sunken into her face, looked upward once as if trying to see her forefront. They remained there, frozen, for a few seconds and then they closed.

Alita entered the room as Capacete was making a fast retreat into the hallway. She kneeled besides her mistress and began to scream unconsolably, while she raised Josefina's slacking head over her lap, repeatedly calling her name and gently hitting her right cheek with her hand.

Alita did not know enough French to call for help. All she could do was to scream in Tagalog: "...*tulong, pagdamay, abuloy. Isa manggagamot. Babae pasakitan. Saktan pasakitan, panginoong babae nobya...*" (Help, bring help. A doctor please. A wowan is hurt. My mistress is dying).

Ignacio Boix de la Revilla Donoso, fourth Count de la Pasiega did not lack money, good fortune or a sensuous bed. But now the life of her mother in law depended on someone understanding Tagalog in the affluent confines of Chaillot Hill in northwestern Paris.

꙾ Ⅱ ꙾

24

AS ALITA NANCIAGA was frantically trying to get somebody's attention to help her dying mistress in the apartment at *85, Avenue de Neuilly*, only one person could hear her. A lady sharing the same floor on a contiguous apartment: Madame Elisabeth de Lamoignon, the only surviving daughter of Guillaume-Chrétien de Lamoignon, Count de Blancmesnil (1721-1794).

Madame Lamoignon or Lisette, as her friends called her, was a mature and lonely spinster in her forties, who lived quietly and seldom had visitors. She attended mass regularly and spent her nights in prayer, in front of a wall completely covered with pictures and drawings of her once wealthy and powerful ancestors. Her father had been the scion of the *Lamoignons*, one the most exclusive families of the *noblesse de robe Parisienne*. He had married Mademoiselle Grimod de la Reynière and Lisette was their only child.

In 1741 Guillaume became *Procureur General* (District Attorney) for the parliament of Paris, and in 1744 first president of its *Cour des Aides* (Appeals Court). He was a graduate of *l'Académie des Sciences* and became director of its Library in 1750. As such, he was responsible for official censure, a position which he carried out with dignity and a liberal mind. The year 1775 was a pivotal for his career. Early that year he informally authorized the publication of *l'Encyclopédie*, a decision that eventually cost him his job. Later on the King appointed him as *Secrétaire d'État à la Maison du Roi,* but he resigned within 30 days as he was admitted to *l'Académie Française,* an appointment much more attuned to his scholarly interests.

In 1792 Guillaume emigrated to England, but came back to France with his family because he believed in the revolutionary ideals and wanted to participate in the defense of Louis XVI. It was he who gave the King the unfortunate news of his sentence on January 19, 1793. Once the King was decapitated, Guillaume was immediately arrested for conspiracy among the *émigrés.* His entire family, included his wife, mother in law, two cousins and his secretary were condemned on the same day. He saved his daughter by claiming it was not family but a slave girl he had purchased in Marroc as a child. He was punished with 25 lashes and a public proclamation of dishonor posted at the *Place de Grève* for having kept a slave girl at his service. But Elisabeth was saved and eventually she recovered some of the family fortune. She was able to pay for special education classes and lived a useful life afterwards.

Elizabeth was blind. She had lost her eyesight during an unfortunate explosion of fireworks on July 14th 1790, the first year celebration of the fall of *la Bastille.* On that day the family had sat in the chairs reserved for the deputies to the Constituent Assembly, right next to the *Marquis de Lafayette* and his family, as well as other trusted friends of the Royal family. The Assembly had voted the Civil Constitution of the Clergy the day before, and everyone sitting around the chairs that the Lamoignons were occupying was against it, including the Lafayettes. Nevertheless a quarter million Parisians were parading, together with hundreds of National Guards and a considerable number of noble and bourgeoisie families.

At the center of the vast esplanade of the *Champ de Mars,* Talleyrand, the infamous Bishop of Autun co-celebrated mass (his fourth ever) with over 300 priests on *l'autel de la patrie,* the fatherland's altar. After mass Lafayette took the oath of loyalty to the nation, and then the King himself took it, while Marie Antoinette raised the Dauphin in her arms to express similar sentiments. It began to rain and the person in charge of the fireworks let a first salvo out, fearful that they all might get wet and useless. In his haste he became careless and a rocket exploded very close to Lisette's face, leaving her blind.

Life for Lisette afterwards was a continuous struggle to get back to normalcy. She developed other senses to an extraordinary degree, thanks to her own efforts and those of her dedicated teacher, the wife of an Italian highway engineer called Madame Fissolo. It was known that after a few years Lisette could tell the *terroir* (origin) and the *milessime* (harvest year) of over two thousand wines. She could identify people by their perfume, or lack thereof, as well as by the gait of their steps and the sound of their shoes. She could hear and memorize conversations at long distances and could tell the quality and dryness of gunpowder by simply rubbing it between her fingers. Her skills became so celebrated that the Napoleonic army would not pack its explosives for long range incursions unless she physically gave her approval to every batch.

These skills became very handy as Alita Nanciaga was running out of energy while she screamed for help on behalf of her fallen mistress. Madame Lamoignon came from the apartment next door when she heard the screams. She found the body of Madame Cipresti on the floor and tried to get her to wake up by repeatedly running her hands over her face. Josefina was not responding to her efforts and Madame Lamoignon gave up and decided to seek help.

The police showed up within an hour after she came downstairs to appeal to a passerby. Unfortunately Josefina did not make it. She received a sharp jolt on her neck upon her fall. It fractured her spine at the cervical level, according to an attending physician. Direct cause of her death: the blow that had sent her to the floor. Two hours later, when the police left, they had to take Alita with them because she had been so distressed and hysterical that she was in no position to describe what had happened. Watching them a few meters down *Avenue de Neuilly* was no other than Willard Capacete, the man who had sent Josefina away without her last rites.

The policemen that came to 85 *Avenue de Neuilly* were based on the barracks at the intersection of *rue Neuve de Luxenbourg* and *rue du Mont Thabor*, between the Church of the Assumption and the *Ministère de Finances*, right around the corner from the *Hotel de Talleyrand*, at the westermost end of the *Jardin des Tuileries*. Alita had not been there more than an hour when Willard Capacete showed up, claiming he was proficient in Tagalog, the language of the Philippines. He was shown in and there was initially a sigh of relief from Alita after she found a familiar figure by her side. They were left alone in a sergeant's office after Capacete had asked for some fresh water for Alita before he began to interpret for her.

"Listen, Alita," he started. "I know you speak French very well and I will not pretend to be on your side. We do not have too much time. I also hope you will not betray me by mentioning my name as a visitor to Josefina's house this morning. Just tell these policemen that the man who rushed out of the house this morning was Carlos

Manuel de Céspedes, who was upset because he had not received a contribution for the war in Cuba. They will believe you because he is a foreigner and you have no reason to accuse him in vain."

"But master Capacete…" she was about to say.

"Shut up and do as you are told. I know you have been stealing from Josefina and if I tell the police that Josefina had found out, they will have good reason to believe you killed her. Your best bet is to tell them it was Monsieur Céspedes, who had been accosting her, asking for money ever since he got to Paris."

Having said that Capacete turned around and left the room; he then left the *caserne* casually, by the front door.

"A bunch of *salopards*," he thought as he went pass the inattentive guards. "I hope they protect the City better than they protect themselves." He walked briskly down the *rue Saint Honoré* towards the *Palais-Royal* and turned north at *rue Richelieu*. He felt lucky that no one had questioned him as he left the building.

Minutes later, on the sergeant's office, Alita was suddenly speaking fluent French and was testifying Capacete's version of the events word by word. "I saw it with my own eyes," she repeated over and over. "It was Monsieur Céspedes who struck Madame Cipresti, my mistress."

"It probably was a fight between Cubans," the sergeant thought. "Marroquians, Cubans, Spaniards, Martinicans, *c'est la même merde…*"

He addressed his sergeant and issued an order of detention. "Send two gendarmes to bring here this Monsieur Céspedes. Tie him up if he resists."

Walking north on *rue Richelieu*, Capacete's thoughts were not on Josefina or Alita but on himself and his future standard of living in Paris.

"I have to find another source of income and another sponsor," he thought. "The old woman was rather demanding on my time and loyalty. She always felt superior because she would pick up the bill at the *cafés* and rent the coaches when we went out, but deep down she was a bitch. From nothing but an overpaid courtesan she thought she had become a beautiful social butterfly. She remained a worm forever, a dragonfly that never came out of her cocoon. I have to find a new way to live comfortably now, but thank goodness I am rid of her."

He went on musing to himself, as he reached the National Library. Across the street he could see *Le Grand Colbert*, the restaurant attached to the *Gallerie Colbert* where he had had many a luxurious dinner with Ignacio, Josefina's son in law, picking the tab. Some irrelevant thoughts invaded his mind.

"*La Gallerie Colbert* will never compete with *la Gallerie Vivienne*," he thought. "Not even after they built at *Colbert* the glass covered rotunda and installed that magnificent bronze candelabrum with the seven glass globes. *Colbert* will always be number two." He became distressed with these idle thoughts. "How could I be so vain to entertain such banal ideas at such an important time in my life?" he thought.

Soon after he reached the building where Simon Bolivar, the liberator of most of South America, had lived the few years he spent in Paris. "Smart man, Simon Bolivar," he thought, "but not smart enough. He cleared out of Paris just in time. Became famous, took a mistress and in his spare time became the leader of millions of uneducated natives in America. But in the end, what did he get for all his troubles? A statue here and there and a horse to go out and die in a godforsaken shanty house. I've got to do better. Nothing of this patriotic hubris is for me."

He was getting closer and closer to the rented room where he lived in the lower part of Montmartre when he realized he did not have his white gloves on. "Damnation!" he thought, "I left my only pair of gloves at the *caserne*."

He was about to turn around and retrace his steps when a flash image hit him as a bolt of fire. "My God, I did not have my gloves on at the *caserne*. I must have left them at Josefina's house. Darn it, darn it and darn it! How could I be so careless?"

His face went into a premature *rictus mortis*, his eyes popped out and his mouth made the type of gesture that a child makes when he does not like his pabulum.

"There were no men living on Josefina's house other than the Count. The police will begin to search for the man that owned the gloves. If they come to me, and the gloves fit, they will convict. I've got to retrieve the darn gloves before the police get back there."

He turned around and started to walk briskly towards the *Place de l'Etoile*. This time his stride revealed the urgency of his purpose. He was bumping against people and pushing them away, right and left. He was dispensing with the polite *"pardon"* that seemed to be compulsory for any Frenchman colliding with any person, animal or object, whether it was his mistake or not.

"Bloody hell!" he kept saying to himself, "how can I be so stupid? This mentally retarded Philippine girl is likely to tell the police that those gloves are mine and they will want to talk to me. Why did they ever admit her in this country? She must have come to Paris through Spain, were women love these girls for their submission and men for their forbearance. Bloody hell!"

When he finally got to the house on *85, Avenue de Neuilly*, he saw two policemen standing casually on the front entrance of the building. "Damnation! They are already there asking questions," he thought. He discretely stayed on the corner where the *Avenue de Châteaubriand* met the *Avenue de Neuilly*, trying to pull his thoughts together.

Inside the former home of Josefina Cipresti there was an ebb and flow of activity. Several uniformed policemen were searching for clues everywhere, with the thoroughness but not the enthusiasm that had made famous their founder and former boss Jean Luc Vidocq. On the studio two men from the *Renseignement Française*, dressed in civilian clothes, were interviewing Madame Lamoignon.

"I can give you some clues as to who did this," Lisette was telling the detectives. "I had my front door opened because it was a very hot day and the staircase is always a good source of fresh and cooler air. I could not quite tell you about the contents of the conversation between Josefina and the young man who was there but I can almost describe him to the hilt."

"How do you know he was a young man," asked inspector Bourdaloue, the senior man from the *Renseignement*.

"His walk on the stairs and through the hallway was that of a man in his mid thirties. Older men never walk this fast and assertively, or at least they do not walk this fast consistently. They hesitate every now and then. This man did not. He is thin, about 5 feet 10 inches tall and he wears tall shoes, good ones, expensive."

"How do you know all that?" asked this time the other inspector, M. Bousset, with half admiration and half mistrust.

"Monsieur, the hallway is not carpeted and the sound of the steps clearly indicate he had strong shoes, with at least one inch heels. These heels generate a faint echo that normal heels do not. Also the sound was sharp and firm, which is only produced by leather covered heels firmly attached to the shoe sole. These are expensive shoes, barely worn. By the strength of the sounds I deduct the man could not have been more than 55 Kilos in weight. A young man of that weight must be 5 feet ten inches tall, give or take an inch. That's the man you should look for."

After two hours of searching and inspecting, inspector Bourdaloue and the policemen left the apartment. Monsieur Bourdaloue gave them instructions for filing their individual reports and requested that they be available to meet at the *caserne* the next day, in order to compare notes and produce a comprehensive report. He also asked inspector Bousset to stay behind and take a full declaration from Madame Lamoignon. They both went back to her apartment and, once more, she left her front door open, trying to get some fresh air from the hallway into her dwelling.

From his position on the corner of the *Avenue de Neuilly* and *Avenue de Châteaubriand,* Willard Capacete could see the policemen and Inspector Bourdaloue leaving the building. As soon as they were out of sight he rushed to the front door and quietly entered the lobby, making sure no one was around. He climbed the steps to the second floor. His heart was pounding fast. He could almost hear its beat and he felt every expansion and contraction of his ventricles on his head and on his chest.

He tried to concentrate on quieting his heart, in case Georgina or the Count would suddenly appear. He imagined himself on a lake, leisurely strolling around its shores on a beautiful spring day. Slowly he skillfully succeeded in pretending that he was on a normal and routine visit to Madame Cipresti. He saw the door to Madame Lamoignon opened and tried not to look inside, as he usually did. He finally reached Josefina's apartment, turned the key into the lock and went inside. A sight of relief came hastily to his face. He was safe so far. Moreover, the gloves were on a side table by the front entrance, exactly where he had left them a few minutes before striking Madame Cipresti.

"I will be able to pull this hoax," he thought, as a smile of achievement came to his face. Since the room was empty, he went in front of one of the windows that faced the *Arch de Triumph* and looked as far as his eyes could see, into the countryside beyond the *Place de l'Étoile.*

"I only need now to find another sponsor," he began to tell himself now that he felt out of peril. "Someone to whom I could read my sonnets and who would understand and applaud them. Someone willing to pay my friends in Cadiz to publish those brilliant but ignored novels of mine that Josefina had promised to pay but never did. Perhaps the time has come to find a rich old man who would take me for his bride and be my protector."

He went back to the table at the front door of the apartment. He took a quick look at the *salon* he had just left and thought: "I think I will miss this place. I will miss the Sunday afternoons when Josefina brought together her friends and made me the center of attention. I will miss the many times I came here to pick her up on the way to an expensive restaurant. I will miss the satisfaction it gave me to distance her from her former friends, like that cerebral Danilo Méndes against whom I had promised myself never to lose another intellectual combat. I will miss the times when she asked Ignacio, her dimwitted son in law, to give me a hundred pounds for a poem I had written but that she wanted to attribute to herself."

He then took the gloves and put them on, ready to depart forever from that apartment. All of a sudden the door was jolted open. Inspector Bousset and Madame Lamoignon were there, both standing up, defiant but serene. Bousset had in his hands the little book where he had been taking notes after the others had left the apartment. Lisette was holding the white cane that she felt she did not need but that she so skillfully used to move about.

"Arrest this man, Monsieur Bousset," she calmly said. "He murdered Madame Cipresti. I first smelled his perfume the day our dear lady was assassinated. It is unmistakably the same perfume he is using now. I know his stride; I would recognize the sound of his steps even if he were marching with a thousand soldiers. Does he fit the description I gave you and inspector Bourdaloue early today?"

"As if you had painted it on a canvas, Madame."

"Is he wearing a ring with a small square stone on his left hand?"

"You are right again, Madame," responded Monsieur Bousset.

"Arrest this man, Monsieur Bousset." "You do not have to look anywhere else. There are three pieces of indisputable evidence that accuse him. First, I have recognized his smell, his gait and his steps as the man who was here at the time of the crime. Second, this house is seldom visited by men. Alita and I will testify to that. The gloves found here are his; they fit him perfectly. In fact, he just put them on as he was leaving the scene of the crime. Third, you will find on Madame's left side of the face an indentation on her skin that will perfectly match his ring. My sense of smell and the fit of the gloves could be overlooked, Monsieur, but as the indentation will well attest, you should arrest."

With those words Madame Lamoignon secured her rightful place in the history of Parisian crime investigation.

∽ Ⅲ ∾

25

A FEW DAYS after the meeting of Céspedes, Aldama and Del Monte at Céspedes' library on *12, rue Jacob*, Del Monte and Céspedes were waiting at the reception room of the *Palais de Salm* for an additional meeting with Guizot and Laffitte. Del Monte had taken the place of Aldama when Miguel was called to London at the last minute for an important business decision. Monsieur Guizot had no objection to receive Carlos Manuel with Domingo, whom he had already met at the home of Monsieur Laffitte.

Even though they had agreed to ignore their disagreements with Willard Capacete, when they sent him a message about the meeting they did not get a reply, thus they attended by themselves. After several hours of conversation at home and while they strolled across half of Paris in a marathon of reflexion and study, they had agreed to say no. They were ready to refuse any part in the French plan to bring Cuba into the constitutional monarchy being forged in Paris by Guizot, Perrier, Thiers, Molé, de Broglie, Montalivet and others.

After a few minutes waiting in the antechamber of Guizot's office they were shown inside, where they were received very enthusiastically by the French minister. Guizot and Laffitte were in an excellent mood and were already savoring the success of this meeting with the three Cubans. They were both men of transition between the *ancien régime* and the *France nouvelle*. They were counted in many ways among the creators of the *classe moyenne* in France, which they understood to be nothing but a new definition for an old entity: the *bourgeoisie*. By 1840 the triumph of this *classe moyenne* had been sound, definitive and irrevocable. It had accumulated all the power and all the prerogatives of the entire government, and it had absolute control over the economic, social and political life in France. Guizot and Laffitte felt invincible and were looking forward to provide an adequate international dimension to their successes inside the French territory.

It was Céspedes who initiated the conversation.

"We have a rather serious concern, *Monsieur le Ministre*. You will agree with us that a society should not impose upon a citizen any obligations, duties and much less taxes without having given that citizen a substantial share of sovereignty. We can not reconcile the great post-revolutionary ideas of liberated France with an imposition of French citizenship to Cubans, even if it could be possible to do so bloodlessly through negotiations or pressure."

Del Monte added "France enjoys today the results of a struggle for popular sovereignty that took fifty years to culminate. Even if it is governed by a few privileged chosen from the many, its political leaders reflect the will of the people, distilled after many years of ups and downs, advances and retreats in the track of history. Do you not think that the Cuban people have the same right to choose, struggle, make mistakes and reverse courses, throw out some rascals and keep others, but fundamentally do whatever fits the national will as a voluntary association of free individuals?"

The assertiveness and early confrontation posed by the Cubans startled both Guizot and Laffitte. Guizot was an experienced chess player and his approach to politics was similar to the ways a tiger traps its prey. He had expected a round about way of bringing objections to the table but never a frontal approach in which the first salvo had mortal intentions.

"Listen," riposted Guizot, "in today's Cuba the people are neither properly nor improperly represented. If they rise to demand their rights, the Spanish *les jette dans les cachots* (will thrown them in jail). If they join together to demand a better salary or to protest their miserable lives, *ils les jette dans les cachots. Si ils ecrit sur son étendard «nous souhaitons représentation dans le parlement», ill les mitraille*. (If they ask for representation in the Courts, they will be blasted away). Spain," he continued, "only offers a dishonorable system, corrupted, perverted, depraved and vitiated beyond repair. You either change it soon or it will eventually lead to a bloody and violent massacre. Never mind doing it by yourselves. You will have to secure the help of the United States, the British or us."

After a brief pause Guizot continued. "No help will ever come from your presumed sister republics on the Southern continent. They prosper with your misfortune. We offer a radical solution. We will make electors of all Cubans and the men of virtue that you will elect will have the same influence on the destinies of France than the citizens from Lyon, Auxerre or Marseille. *Egalité et liberté pour tous.*"

"Excuse me Monsieur Guizot," interrupted Del Monte. "We will be joining a political system that does not have universal suffrage. Your women do not vote and we are counting on ours to do. You gave the vote only to those whose capital surpasses a certain level, 200 francs I believe, and we wish *all* of our people to vote. There seem to be profound differences between us that typically tend to be resolved by the stronger party in a negotiation."

"Gentlemen," interrupted Laffitte, "within less than a generation all Cubans would be fluent in French and will enjoy all the rights of free Frenchmen. You will be an integral part of *la France*; you will be entering *la France profonde,* and will revel into the life that befits to all members of this magnificent civilization, without having paid for it in blood and sacrifices. What's there to complain?"

"Monsieur Laffitte," Céspedes interrupted. "Not having paid in blood and sacrifices for what France is today is of no consequence. We have serious concerns about the very core of revolutionary France. As many of your current thinkers, we are not sure the balance of the revolutionary ideas and actions in France is at all positive. Perhaps is too early to tell but the revolution of 1789 has not given France an unchallenged reputation as the most advanced society from the human rights standpoint."

"Many years of Spanish domination," added Del Monte, "have made us very skeptical towards political power and have reinforced in our minds the concept that individual rights and personal freedoms need to be protected from the encroachment of the state in the lives of citizens. We are not sure France is moving in that direction."

"Even the most liberal tradition in France has an emphasis on state power and the order it can bring to society," added Céspedes. "To you the state is not a neutral entity that allows citizens to pursue their own ideals of what the good life is. In France the project of reconciling liberty and order is far from completed."

Céspedes and Del Monte were now getting into thorny and challenging grounds. François Guizot, together with Pierre Royer-

Collard and Victor de Broglie were, after all, the founders of the *doctrinaires*, a small but influential group of French political theoreticians that, following in the footsteps of Montesquieu, were proposing that social order had to precede both the political institutions and the individual freedoms and not the other way around. Guizot's sociological approach in his 1828 *History of Civilization in Europe*, for instance, had spoken for the first time of class struggles. It proposed that the essence of liberty lied in the simultaneous action of all interests, rights, powers, and social elements under an environment of social order.

Del Monte continued: "In spite of your Declaration of the Rights of Men, you subordinate individual rights to what you believe are the far more important rights of the state. In very nuanced and subtle ways you criticize individualism and advocate a strong role for the state, particularly the executive powers."

But Monsieur," interrupted Guizot, "only by subordinating contract theory and *laissez-faire* to the limits imposed by social order can you restore dignity and credibility to government. Peace only comes when government has mastery in the social sphere. I believe you are idolizing individual rights."

"State and society are involved in a mutual empowerment process, Monsieur," added Céspedes. "Society, which is the summation of all individuals, needs to feel free to graciously grant powers to the state. The state needs to feel empowered but dependent and grateful. Only then it will respect the rights of individuals from which the acquired power emanated."

"It is more than a matter of small versus big government," interrupted Laffitte.

"Of course it is," declared Céspedes. "Achieving this balance between power and society requires education on the part of individuals and statesmanship on the part of the political leadership. In Cuba we lack both. I feel you need to know the emotional soul of society in order to bring about this balance. You have a culture that we respect and honor precisely because it is so foreign and different from our daily experience. I cannot see how it could overcome its foreignness and gain the trust of many Cubans, who so far only understand that we lack freedoms and individual respect."

"We believe," added Del Monte, "that you could easily get to know such practical things as how our property is divided, how does our economy looks, who owns our land and our businesses, etc. But we do not think you can understand, on short notice, our social condition, our mores, our life style and customs, the relations between our social classes, our family traditions and our character."

Deliberately not paying much attention to what Del Monte had just said, Guizot continued his arguments. "It is more important to build strong institutions than to place limits on power."

"The political institutions have to be liberalized first and then strengthened," added Del Monte, setting aside for the moment Guizot's *non sequitor*. "Once you develop a government that respects people, a government within the rule of law, so to speak, you might be able to fortify and reinforce it so that it can lead the people towards progress and stronger social institutions. But the underlying political environment needs to be one of respect for individual rights and personal choices."

"Absolutely," proclaimed Guizot. "The development of a strong representative government will inevitably lead to a consensual strengthening of state powers. As long as freedom prevails the people themselves will welcome the strengthening of state powers."

"Possibly," interrupted Céspedes, "in ways in which they would have been considered authoritarian if they had not been undertaken by a deliberate decision of the citizens."

"Exactly," answered Guizot. "There need not be an *a priori* conflict between human rights and governmental authority, if it is properly exercised. Or between responsible individual freedoms and state power."

"Your thinking is quite a departure from Rousseau's political theories, Monsieur," exclaimed Céspedes. "In fact, you are parting company with every French thinker of the XVIII Century."

"Perhaps, Monsieur Céspedes," added Guizot. "I do not agree with their postulate that the only legitimate law for every individual is his own free will. It is utopian; societies can not be constructed that way. Rousseau's was a futile theoretical postulate since the rights of the individual and those of society cannot be considered separately."

"In other words," Céspedes said, "liberty can not be defined as man's sovereignty over himself."

"Absolutely," concluded Guizot, "but the deliberate and consented self restriction of individual rights provides legitimacy to the power of the state, as long as all individuals have been asked to consent."

"We agree wholeheartedly," added Del Monte. "The Spanish politicians that we have endured are married to the concept that sovereignty can emanate from divine right or from a narrowly elected group of individuals. We believe that legitimate sovereignty must be continuously subject to wholesome societal scrutiny and can only perpetuate itself if it continues to conform to fundamental principles of justice, rights and respect for others. The people have the right to disavow a power that does not comply with these principles, even if it is through rebellion and war."

Céspedes spoke again. "We also believe, Monsieur, that the only legitimate power is that which arises from the natural phenomenon of leadership. Baring external impositions, power will always be placed over the shoulders of those with the highest capacity to wield it and at the same time satisfy the common interest. The ones with the most skills in times of peace, or the bravest in times of war. Do you agree?"

"I do, Monsieur Céspedes. Superior force is almost always divorced with capacity and virtue."

"Then you must agree," added Céspedes, "that state power and government should not be the result of a political or survival pact through which many or few individuals seek to place their destinies under the guaranteed protection of a powerful but foreign sovereign."

An uncomfortable silence invaded the room where the two Cubans were meeting with Monsieurs Guizot and Laffitte. It lasted a few minutes but is solemnity made it look like an eternity. François Guizot stood up from his chair and walked towards the window. He looked first at the Seine and then at the Tuileries. There it was, the see of French power and the silent witness of so many events of vital importance in the history of France. The history of his beloved country began to roll across his head like one of these panoramas that were so popular with the masses up in the *Grands Boulevards*.

He saw in a spectacular parade Henry II and his wife Catherine de Medicis. Louis XIV waiting for Versailles to be finished. Le Notre planting its parterres. Louis XVI trying to escape on the evening of June 20, 1791. The Swiss Guard being massacred in 1792. The National Assembly, the National Convention and the Assembly of 500 meeting there. Marie-Louise as a young bride decorating the place for Napoleon's eyes. The Bourbons returning after the July 1830 revolution. Louis Philippe moving in through the influence of an aging Lafayette.

He turned his face to look once more to the two Cubans in his office, particularly this Carlos Manuel de Céspedes. He felt he had been taken for a ride. A ride across all of his political writings and beliefs to come to a sudden stop on this issue of the illegitimacy of foreign sovereigns. He could only whisper to himself a resounding *"Touché."*

"Monsieur Céspedes," he finally spoke. "You have won this *mano a mano*. France has no right to interfere in the valiant fight of the Cuban people for its independence. Your destiny is to be the leader of your people and bring them to the secured shores of a well deserved republic. I salute you as the next president of a free Cuba."

Céspedes, Del Monte, Guizot and Laffitte intently looked at each other as they recognized they would not meet again until the end of hostilities in Cuba. The Frenchmen were heartbroken, knowing as they did that those two Cuban patriots they were bidding good bye were ready to shed their blood for the cause of Cuban independence. Guizot was also profoundly sad for what he knew were the last rites for a French empire of tricontinental dimensions.

"What a lost opportunity," he thought.

As he once more looked into the old but lively river that had always been at the center of French civilization he thought... "The minds of Montesquieu, Voltaire, Diderot and Condorcet will forever lead men of other latitudes into freedom, the pursue of their rights and the enjoyment of liberty. We have lost these great thinkers as Frenchmen. They now belong to every citizen of the world, every decent man and woman seeking their own bliss. God bless France but also, may He bless that little island lost in the American continent that has produced men of such fine human qualities and intellect... like these two."

∽ Ⅺ ∾

FRANKLIN AND FRIENDS, 1782 DRAWING

A remarkable drawing by Jean-Michel Moreau le Jeune (1741-1814), showing the finest minds that inspired the revolutionary ideals of 1789 in France. From left to right: François de Salignac de la Mothe, aka **Fénelon**, Archbishop of Cambrai, Charles-Luis de Secondat, *Baron de* **Montesquieu**, François-Marie Arouet, aka **Voltaire**, Benjamin **Franklin** and Honoré Gabriel Riqueti, *Comte de* **Mirabeau**. Sitting on the left is Denis **Diderot**.

26

*"A man who sees another man on the street corner
with only a stump for an arm will be so shocked the first time he'll give him
sixpence. But the second time it'll only be a three penny bit. And if he sees him
a third time, he'll have him cold-bloodedly handed over to the police."*
Bertolt Brecht

*"At one time my only wish was to be a police official. I had the idea
that there, among criminals, were people to fight: clever, vigorous,
crafty fellows. Later I realized that most police cases
involve misery and wretchedness -- not crimes and scandals."*
Søren Kierkegaard

*"There is nothing more notable in Socrates than that he found time, when he
was an old man, to learn music and dancing, and thought it time well spent."*
Montaigne

ON THE WAY back to *rue Jacob* Céspedes and Del Monte were silent for a good part of the trip, as if reluctant to share their thoughts within earshot of Guizot and Laffitte. As they left the *Palais de Salm* they could see the magnificent construction work of the *Palais du Quai D'Orsay*. The building had been started in October of 1834 and the finishing touches were still underway. It was the first important building in Paris with a roof made of large sheets of zinc, a novel construction material who had brought to the site many engineers and architects for observation. Over the *façade* facing the river there was a large terrace with a beautiful and intricate balustrade from where you could see an admirable panorama of the Seine and the gardens of *les Tuileries*. More than a million francs had been approved the year before for the last construction details, bringing the total to close to 10 million francs. The building had been loosely destined to house the minister of the interior and other governmental dependencies such as the department of public works. But the last word was now that other offices would occupy the building and there was even talk of remodeling it on the inside to use it for meetings of the *Chambre des Députés*.

After going in front of the western side of the *Palais du Quai D'Orsay* their carriage took *rue Bellechasse* south, and then *rue de l'Université,* which changed its name to *rue Jacob* after crossing *rue des Saints Pères.* It was then that they felt free to comment on their visit with Guizot and Laffitte.

"Domingo," Céspedes started, "we just had a remarkable encounter with the best brains of what the French call *les temps héroïques.* I believe we have measured up to their expectations and we have possibly averted a crisis of huge proportions when it comes to the future of Cuba."

"Their dreams were without foundations and overly optimistic," Del Monte added. "There is no turning back to the growth of the United States. Once Napoleon sold *la Lousianne* to pay the enormous French debts there were no possibilities to recover those lands. I believe they knew that, but the elusive fantasy was so appealing that they could not rule it out of their minds. If anything, we have given them an opportunity to plant their feet on the ground and cast aside any dreams of American territories under a French flag."

"This is a period of French history when all sorts of realities have caught up with those grandiose anticipations of worldly influence which the French always had," added Céspedes.

"Those dreams had a basis in the past, from the times of Henri IV to perhaps Louis XV, but not anymore. A dozen years ago a feeble Charles X feared that the *monarchie* was under siege by what he called the 'men from the left'. His miscalculations led him to declare *nule* the Chart of 1814 which limited the powers of the King. The people's response was to produce the three glorious days of July 1830, celebrated in the column at la Bastille. They deposed him. Then came Louis Philippe d'Orleans. He is probably the last attempt of the French to unify the nation under one king, hoping that the glories of the past can be continued. But here is a King willing to accept the Chart of 1814 and who is crowned by a group of parliamentarians. He received his mandate by showing up at a balcony of the *Hôtel de Ville* on the side of old General Lafayette, who proclaimed 'Louis Philippe 1er, roi des François (pas de France) par la grace de Dieu et la volonté nationale',* with the emphasis, of course, on *volonté nationale.*"

They smiled as Céspedes raised his head as in a military salute upon pronouncing *volonté nationale.*

"There is no doubt," added Del Monte, "that Louis Philippe is one of the brightest and shrewdest monarchs the French have had in two hundred years. He has surrounded himself with good men like Perrier, Guizot, Laffitte, de Broglie, etc., and has successfully put a stop to the ebb and flow of power in France. His first measures were to clean the government and so far he has fired 79 out of 86 *préfets de la France*, 244 out of 277 sous-préfets and 65 out of the 75 division generals of the army. This has been, by any measure, a good move."

"I was told by the Venezuelan ambassador, who was a good friend of Lafayette," added Carlos Manuel, "that, like Napoleon, Louis Philippe was adamant in not tolerating any barricades or marches by students or working men. According to Lafayette, he had thrown out more than 70,000 petitions for government positions that had accumulated on the *Palais-Royal* and is committed to bring peace, order and legality to the government of France."

"Who would have thought of that," interrupted Céspedes. "The son of *Philippe-Egalité*, who voted to send his King to the guillotine and who was executed himself a few months later. After the execution of his father he went into exile where he married a niece of Marie Antoinette, the princess de Bourbon-Sicile, with whom, so far, he has had eight children."

"Most of his twenty years of exile, by the way," added Del Monte, "were in the United States."

"The French have not made up their minds since the start of the Restoration," added Céspedes. "There are the Royalists, who long for a return of the *ancienne monarchie*. Then the Orleanists, now in power and supporting a constitutional monarch. Of course there are also Republicans and Bonapartistes."

"Louis Philippe has done it well so far," added Domingo. "He has turned Versailles into a museum of French history instead of using it for himself and that has catered well to the French passion for history and romanticism. What we are witnessing today is the triumph of the bourgeoisie and a remarkable devotion and intense desire for progress on the part of government. There is new technology everywhere. Railroads, steam engines, photography, the electrical telegraph. All of that with a few insurrections but no riots. French foreign policy is nowadays very accommodating and moderate."

"Well, remember the conquest of Algiers," interrupted Céspedes.

"That was compensated by the support to the Belgian independence from Holland and, most of all, by the sympathies for the uprising in Warsaw against the Tsar's troops," added Del Monte.

"It was Lafayette himself who proclaimed from a *Hôtel de Ville* balcony, full of the emotion that only a man of his stature and age could summon, that '*Toute la France est polonaise.*' Add to that the remarkable achievement of *l'Entente Cordiale*, or the reconciliation with England. Just imagine, Louis-Philippe, King of France and Victoria, Queen of England hosting on their palaces each other's visits. Several times and across the same channel, silent witness to so many aggressive actions and mutual threats of invasion."

"Carlos," interrupted Del Monte, "in spite of all that, the French have not yet learned to live with each other in peace. Can you ignore the mayhem at the Church of *Saint Germain l'Auxerrois* and how the Church was sacked just because the monarchists were celebrating a Mass? Or the riots and the 800 deaths during the internment of General Lamarque in 1832? Or the rampage and public violence when Louis Philippe had 150 militants of the Society for the Rights of Men arrested just a few years ago? Or the repression after the attempts against the King in 1835, or the murders of the assailants of the *Hôtel de Ville* in 1839? It has been a relatively peaceful time, compared to the last 50 years, but Paris continues to be a City sitting on a barrel of powder; the stability of the French government is much less taken for granted than that of the British or America's."

"The balance of this government of the July Monarchy is nevertheless positive," Céspedes said. "Even the poets are satisfied. Gertrudis is, and so are George Sand, Hugo and Delavigne. Literature, music and the arts have benefited immensely from this peace and prosperity period. Louis Philippe is a *grand amateur* of the arts and has sponsored the works of Musset, Lamartine, Balzac, Stendhal, Dumas, Delacroix, Berlioz... "

"In that sense we don't need to even talk of architecture," added Del Monte. "It was Louis Philippe who finished the Arch of Triumph started by Napoleon and who placed on the *Place de la Concorde* the *obelisque* of the temple de Ramses II from Thèbes, which, dates from the XIII Century B.C., and is by far the oldest thing in Paris. All on top of his many restorations of *chateaux* all over France."

"Before we get too far," added Céspedes, "I will agree that there are also regrettable things by Louis Philippe. The crushing of the revolt of 40,000 silk workers in Lyon, or the bloody suppression of the rebellion by the Duchess of Berry at the *Vendée*, or his blind hatred for Louis Napoleon after his uprising at Strasbourg, or his unpreparedness for the cholera epidemic of 1832, which caused 18,000 deaths across France."

As Céspedes was getting into his own observations and private list of negative aspects of the *Monarchie de Julliet*, the coach arrived at its destiny on *rue Jacob*. They noticed the presence of two *gendarmes* on the street side of the gate as they prepared to descend from the vehicle. The coach master was asked to inquire about their presence and returned with the following information.

"The two policemen have been staged here by M. Treilhard, the *Préfet de Police* of Paris. They do not know the reasons for their assignment and have not been asked to take any action except to take note of people entering and leaving the house," reported Richard, the coach master.

"Very well, let us get inside," Céspedes suggested.

Inside the house María del Carmen, Gertrudis and Rosa Aldama had already noticed the presence of the gendarmes and had sent a message to the Countess of Merlin, who had arrived a few minutes before.

"It can not be anything serious or they would have already taken some action," explained the Countess. "It must be something having to do with the neighborhood, perhaps a march or a street demonstration of some sort for which they have been issued orders to prevent any disorders."

"I do not think so," said María del Carmen nervously. "They would be walking the streets. Instead they are fixed here, at our gate. They have been there for over two hours and they do not look very friendly."

"Never mind the friendliness," added Gertrudis. "The police are never friendly. These men, however, have been very courteous and polite with the maid and the messenger you sent out. I do not feel there is anything to fear. God knows why they are here but I presume we will know very soon."

At that moment the serene voice of Domingo Del Monte tried to reassure Carlos Manuel and María del Carmen of their safety and the need to keep calm and not anticipate trouble.

"There is no reason to fear anything. Gertrudis is right. Don't be alarmed and try to ignore their presence. You have a big affair tonight and you should attend in the best of spirits and have a good time. For all we know these men could be keeping an eye on the house across the street."

"Absolutely," added Gertrudis. "Get dressed, the four of you and let Miguel and I enjoy how elegant and proper the Cuban *bourgeoisie* could be in competition with the best Europe has to offer. You have been looking forward to the Ball at the Royal Palace and today is the time to forget everything and have a romantic and unforgettable time."

They all assented and retired to their rooms, looking forward with great anticipation to the important affair to which they had been invited. As María del Carmen entered her room she took in her hands the invitation they had received from the Royal Palace, closed her eyes and held it close to her chest.

Their invitation to the Royal Ball at the *Tuileries* was lithographed on a stiff, gold edged ivory colored paper at *Fonrouge*, the best printing atelier in Paris. It was addressed to *Monsieur et Madame Céspedes et ses amis de Cuba* and it read:

"Palais des Tuileries. L'Aide de Camp de service près du Roi et Mme la Marquise Dolomieu, Dame d'Honneur de la Reine, ont l'Honneur de prévenir Monsieur et Madame Céspedes et ses amis de Cuba qu'ils sont invité au Bal Royale qui aura lieu au Palais des Tuileries le prochaine Lundi courant, à neuf heures. Les hommes seront en uniforme."

Carlos Manuel and María del Carmen were told that all high government functionaries, the members of the old nobility friends of the Orleans, the members of the diplomatic corps, the most important bankers, industrialists, musicians, artists and authors had all received a similar invitation and that they could not graciously decline. There was, of course, nothing further from their minds.

Some 3,000 invitations had been issued and all but 20, addressed to deceased aristocrats that had not been expunged from the palace lists, had been properly acknowledged. The ball was intended as a philanthropic affair, with all the proceeds going to the soup kitchen at the Church of *Saint Eustache*. Nevertheless it was announced as a *"veritable rendez-vous de la bourgeoisie, sur laquelle s'appuyait la dynastie nouvelle."* (a true meeting of the bourgeoisie which is the support of the new dynasty).

The sale of tickets as well as the accounting was handled by the *Banque de Paris*. The royal house had contributed 10,000 francs and the promise that the King and the Queen would be in attendance. In years past, at a similar affair during the reign of the Bourbons, Charles X had contributed 60,000 francs but failed to attend. The effect on public opinion had been disastrous.

For this *Bal Royale* the tickets were priced as 25 francs for the ladies and 30 francs for the gentlemen. Over a thousand tickets were sold outside Paris to people that would find it difficult to attend. The *gendarmes*, the *sapeurs-pompiers*, the royal guards and the catering personnel from *Menus Plaisirs*, the establishment at the avenue of the Opera, all volunteered their services. All together the ball would report a net profit of 67,000 francs after expenses, enough to get the soup kitchen going for one full winter.

According to the stories that María del Carmen wrote to her friends in Cuba, "Before the guests entered the grand *salon* of the *Palace des Tuileries* their names were announced loudly at the top of the stairs. Everybody who was somebody during the Monarchy of July was there. The Marquises de Massa, de Caux, de Montreuil, de Duvilliers, de Saint Léger and de Duperré; The Fitz James and the Poniatowskis, the Colonel de Fleury, Marshal Bosquet and his wife, the Walewskis, the Mérimées, the Barons and the Baronesses de Lambert, de Persigny, de Bernis, de Demidoff, Monsieur and Madame Hamilton, the Counts of Saint Valier... "

"Add to this," she continued, "the entire diplomatic corps, the members of the Orleans family and the intimate court personnel of *les Tuileries*. According to the mores of the times, politics *"était la soeur de la danse"* (politics and dance were sisters) and it was with elegant orchestras, beautiful dresses and plenty of men with good manners that the French are trying to forget the bloody disasters of their revolutionary past."

The palace had been completely transformed for the occasion. The vestibule, the stairs, the hallways and the grand *salon* itself were inundated with beautiful roses, flags and statues, and all mirrors were encircled with green garlands. All drapes were festooned with red silk, with golden fringes and twists made of velour. Between the columns and windows in the grand *salon* there were numerous adornments and decorations showing the royal arms of the House of Orleans. Thousands of candles shone in the mirrors; two huge buffet tables had been set on the foyer, and numerous servants moved back and forth with champagne and delicious *amuse bouches* for the guests.

"But again, the most splendid thing," María del Carmen wrote, "was the luminosity of the entire scene. Under each of the regular gas chandeliers the royal designers had suspended large circular metal hangers at different heights holding thousands of candles of all colors. Their flickering lights were particularly generous in enhancing the beauty of all the ladies present. The ladies were dressed mostly in white and in full regalia, many of them wearing diadems with diamonds and rubies. Most men wore a blue vest over a white shirt, with the collars adorned by subtle embroideries, and all of them had white casimir trousers with golden strips on the sides."

The ball started at nine pm sharp, as the King, accompanied by Marie Amélie, the Queen and followed by the princes, Henri Eugène, François Ferdinand, Louis Charles and Antoine Marie, and the princesses, Louise Marie, Marie Christine and Marie Clementine, made their entry into the *grand salon* from a door leading inside the palace. The King, after walking the length of the *salon* greeting guests set himself up at the contiguous dining room, where many of his cabinet members had been waiting for him. The Queen, the princes and the princesses stayed in the *salon*; the Queen sat with her friends on a chair at a dais on the garden side of the ballroom, the children each choosing separately their place among friends that had anxiously looked forward to the accolade of their company.

Dancing lasted from eleven pm to almost six in the morning. Only one quadrille and one waltz were danced by the royal couple, the King being the Queen's partner, with the princes and the princesses completing the set. The princes danced several *contredanses* with the ladies that had organized the ball, the Duchess of Guiche, the Princess of Bauffremont, Madame Bourdon de Vatry and Mademoiselle Muenster, the daughter of the most important diamond dealer in Paris.

The following day *Le National* reported that *"une foule très mêlée"* had been in attendance. In fact there were Peers of France mingling with crown bureaucrats, Parisian bourgeois, British diplomats, Russian royals, German businessmen, Dutch merchants, Italian artists, and every other kind of beautiful people; what at the time was called *"tout Paris."* According to the paper 2,635 individuals had attended, of which 1,078 were ladies, "everybody in their own place, with a great deal of familiarity but also of *urbanité.*"

Carlos Manuel felt particularly entranced by the beauty of María del Carmen as they sat themselves almost at the center of the *salon* by a window facing the gardens of the Tuileries. *"Comme tu es belle!"* (how beautiful you are!), he exclaimed as he kissed her lightly on her lips. The *salon*, turned for the occasion into a true *Galerie de Glaces*, was full of people and was blazing with light. Under the wreaths of flowers hanging from the ceiling, Carlos Manuel felt himself the luckiest man in the world as he invited his beautiful wife for a dance. While on the first dance he presented her, as the custom was on such festive occasions, with a beautiful gold bracelet set with rubies and diamonds containing, on a small hanging charm, a strand of her hair which he had cut during her sleep a few days before.

At midnight the Queen and the King's procession was formed, and headed to the theatre, where supper was served for the royal family and their most close friends. The whole theater stage was covered with roses alternating with garlands of exotic fruits and olive branches. About sixty people sat in six small tables in groups of ten, each presided over by a member of the royal family. At each table a huge chandelier surrounded by flowers made the scene breathlessly elegant. An invisible band concealed on the orchestra pit played during dinner a smooth and soothing waltz.

Every now and then one of the guests would return to the main *salon* and bring someone to meet Louis Philippe and Marie Amélie at the theater. They patiently devoted most of the dinner time greeting friends of their dinner guests. Laffitte, a good and solid partner of Domingo Del Monte and a self-appointed mentor of Carlos Manuel brought both couples to meet the royal duo and for a brief moment they had the undivided attention of the King of the French.

"You are a beautiful woman, Madame Céspedes," expressed the King after holding Carmen María's hand to forestall her curtsying.

"Your Majesty does me honor," replied María del Carmen in a hushed tone.

"And so are you, Madame Del Monte," added Louis Philippe. "I did not know Miguel had such an attractive sister. What do Cuban women do to be so pretty?"

"We follow the standards of beautiful French women we know," Rosa Aldama responded, "particularly that of Madame the Queen of the French."

This time it was Louis Philippe who was caught by surprise, not having expected any response except a timid smile.

"I see that Cuban women are not only beautiful but also self assured, bright and bold," riposted the King. "I should have visited Cuba while I was in America."

"Your Excellency may not have returned to the old continent if he had," added María del Carmen.

The King burst into a felicitous laughter as he agreed. "Yes, I probably would not have returned, not voluntarily anyway."

"That would have been America's fortune and France's loss," added Céspedes.

"Thank you my friend," replied Louis Philippe. "You are very gracious. I only regret you are not part of my *ensemble*. My very best to you," toasted the King of the French, slightly raising his glass.

～ ▨ ～

LA PLACE DE LA BASTILLE IN 1841

This rare drawing of the **Place de la Bastille** by T.G.Hoffbauer (1810-1867) shows the July Column erected by Louis-Philippe d'Orleans in 1840 to commemorate the *Three Glorious Days* (July 27, 28, 29, 1830) when Paris rose in revolt and overthrew the monarchy of Charles X. It also shows, on the left, the plaster model for the bronze monument in the shape of an elephant that Napoleon planned to erect at the *Place* in 1808. Victor Hugo immortalized the elephant in *Les Misérables*, where it was used as a shelter by Gavroche. The monumental elephant was to be cast from the bronze of cannons taken from the Spanish but it was demolished in 1846.

27

*"When I write a letter, I put that which is most material
in the postscript, as if it had been an afterthought or a by-matter."*
Francis Bacon

"Chance has something to say in everything, even how to write a good letter."
Baltasar Gracian

*"Courage - a perfect sensibility of the measure of danger,
and a mental willingness to endure it."*
William Tecumseh Sherman

THE DAY AFTER the *Bal Royale* at the *Palace des Tuileries* the
Céspedes and the Del Montes slept late in the morning and came out
of their rooms at noon time. Miguel had been up since 8 in the morning and had breakfast with Gertrudis at the terrace by the garden at
9 am. He had read the paper by 10 am and had been asked by the
Céspedes butler to sign a receipt for an important letter hand delivered by a messenger from *Madame la Princesse de Lieven* at 11 in the
morning. Domingo soon woke up and was shown the letter by Miguel. Del Monte was an old hand at French aristocracy and knew
Dorothée de Benckendorff, *la Princesse de Lieven*, very well. He knew
that a letter from her was actually coming from Françoise Guizot, the
man Céspedes had met twice at the *Palais de Salm*. To Céspedes and
Miguel, Guizot was a powerful French politician. To Domingo he
was a man of intense love for France and a personal dear friend who
had spent a lifetime trying to erase the memories of rioters, vandalism and wholesale executions during revolutionary France, and was
committed to the restoration of French grandeur and the rule of law.
　Françoise Guizot was 53 years old in 1840. He had been a journalist, a professor of history at the faculty of letters in Paris and a president of the Society of Christian Morals in 1830. In January of that
year he had been elected deputy from the district of Lisieux, and in
1832 became minister of Education. He was the man behind the 1832
law committing each department to opening a public school system

by 1834. By 1840 he was minister of foreign affairs and it was in that capacity that he had met Céspedes and his friends at the *Palais de Salm*.

He was twice a widow in 1840 when he met Dorothée de Lieven, a woman two years older than himself. She was the daughter of a Russian general and from early age was under the mentorship of María Feodorovna, the mother of Tsar Paul I of Russia. She developed a relationship with Françoise Guizot which started in 1837 and would last until her death in 1858. Dorothée lived at *l'Hôtel de Talleyrand* on *rue de Rivoli* and from there she had send the letter from Guizot to the Céspedes.

She was a woman of extraordinary connections, who counted Guizot, Molé, Thiers, Chateubriand and Metternich among her friends and occasional *amants*. Not every one of her lovers remained a devoted friend. She spoke of Metternich as "a hunchback without the hump," referring to his ungainly shoulders and spindly legs. To Chateubriand she was a "mediocre creature," with a "sharp, repulsively ugly face and an assertive, masculine spirit," far from the blend of beauty and sentiment, intuitive sympathy and unselfconscious sensual charm that he preferred. Nevertheless she was considered by her contemporaries as the one person who used her influence to maintain amicable relations between Britain and France.

Aside from that, her means of connecting to the powerful were ruthless and impious. She had lost two daughters to scarlatine fever in 1835 and, knowing that Guizot had lost a son under tragic circumstances at the age of 22, she wrote him to presumably share in their sorrows. He responded and was caught in her web of lies, sham sorrows and pretended sadness. Soon afterwards they became lovers.

During the *Monarchie de Juillet* it was the women who organized and sponsored the afternoon *salons* where nobles and government people would know each other, share their ambitions and their dreams and made deals to increase their personal power or their fortunes. Madame de Lieven offered Guizot a space in her *salon* to develop his political contacts. From his side he offered her the respectability of his presence and his support. Except for his sister in law, Madame de Meulan, Guizot had no other avenue to pursue his political ambitions but Dorothée de Benckendorff and her well attended *salons*.

Once Céspedes and María del Carmen had finished their breakfasts, Domingo brought to their attention the letter that had been hand delivered by a messenger from Madame de Lieven. Carlos Manuel read it out loud, seeking the benefit of the opinions of Domingo, Miguel and Gertrudis, as well as María del Carmen's and Rosa's opinions. The missive read:

"Mon ami Carlos Manuel. A friend of yours, Madame Josefina Cipresti, was murdered last week at her apartment on Avenue de Neuilly near the Place de l'Etoile. Her dame de chambre, Alita Nanciaga, has identified you as the last person who saw the murdered lady alive.

She has testified that while you were in her salon she could hear loud voices as if in a heated discussion and that you rushed out of the room soon afterwards. The time she indicated for this presumed encounter is precisely the time you were at the Palais de Salm with Messieurs Del Monte, Laffitte and I. I know you are innocent and a victim of a malicious accusation by this Philippine lady, who is also an illegal resident of Paris without the proper documentation that would allow her to lend her services to a bona fide resident.

Because of my involvement in the French government I am unable to assist you directly to clear your name at this point. Rest assured, however, that you are under my protection and that nothing harmful will come your way. As I look to possible alternatives to bring help to your side I suggest that you do not leave your house during daylight since I suspect that the provost of Paris has given instructions for bringing you into custody at the earliest. French law precludes your arrest after sun down. I have no way of securing your freedom if you are arrested because it would be a conflict with the local authorities.

Although there is a suspect in police custody my best advice, nonetheless, is to stay out of the arms of the local police. Police bureaucracies are as untrustworthy as any other bureaucracy! On the long run I advise you to leave Paris. Once your name is in the records of the *Préfet de Police* you will not have the peace of mind that you want and deserve. They will continue to harass you at every opportunity. I can help you leave France if you desire to do so. Our contact could be Laffitte, with whom I have discussed your case and who is amenable to helping you. Sorry this letter does not bring better news. I trust you will be able to come back to France and be a part of our society in the future. God bless you and your family. I remain, dear Carlos, your devoted servant.

Françoise Guizot."

The Céspedes were speechless. So were their guests Miguel and Rosa Aldama, Domingo Del Monte and Gertrudis. There were no possible choices or suggested escape possibilities in the letter. Carlos Manuel and María del Carmen had to leave France and had to decide what to do, and how, quickly. They spent the rest of the morning looking at alternatives and strategies. Domingo offered to see to it that the house was closed and vacated and that the furniture was sold or distributed among friends and charitable associations, with a few favorite pieces sent to Cuba. Gertrudis was sure to get them residence permits in Spain, even if they became fugitives of the justice in France. Del Monte suggested they return to Cuba, where the leadership of Carlos Manuel and the support of María del Carmen to their cause were precious.

Their precarious situation in Paris became asphyxiating as the conversation went along. There was no turning back. There was not even a chance to have an opportunity to defend themselves. France, and Paris in particular, was a pusillanimous society since the days of the Terror. Deep down, no one trusted the government to respect human rights. To do so would be to risk becoming a statistic of how the powers of the state were still in the hands of the unruly mobs.

Even though the Monarchy of July had shown to be populist and inclined to defend the rights of the private citizen, everyone knew that the lynching crowds were hiding under the surface, ready to revolt at the first excuse. Under the circumstances, what best opportunity than having a rich man of business who wanted to go free after the presumed merciless killing of a defenseless lady. No, the decision was made that the Céspedes had to leave Paris at the earliest and that Domingo and the surrogates of the House of Aldama would try to secure their belongings and send them to Havana.

"Listen," Domingo explained, "the abuses of the *ancien regime* in France, while bad enough, did not compare with the tyranny and the despotism that came during and after the revolution. Blood, death and misery has flowed through the veins of the French since 1789. The States General, the National Assembly, the Jacobins, the Revolutionary tribunals, Robespierre and Nicolas Fouquier-Tinville, the guillotine, are just symptoms and evidence. How could you assume that it will be now different and justice would prevail in the case of Carlos Manuel?"

"Oh, it really does not matter who wrote what anymore," interrupted Gertrudis. "Politicians have always served nothing but their ambitions for power."

"Nothing escapes the fury of the mobs," Del Monte added. "They have always prevailed over the politicians and have crucified the truth tellers, the reformists and the idealists. Who cares if Louis Philippe is well liked by the French and has brought prosperity? He has started to muzzle the newspapers and those harsh measures show his true colors. He has brought an illusion of liberty. A fictional monarchy, a fictional populism, a fictional justice. Beautiful words like *liberté, equalité* and *fraternité* are just a pantomime catering to the chronic ailment of the French soul. This secret malady feeds the pro-letarian rabble that undermines all efforts to bring back civilization to this country. Carlos Manuel has to leave France because, having been falsely accused, there are no guarantees in this country that his name could be made whole again. Guizot, and probably Laffitte, have spoken clearly: get the man out of the reach of French justice!"

A long silence followed Del Monte's long speech. María del Carmen lowered her head and closed her eyes. Céspedes looked impassively to a distant point outside the confines of the salon. Miguel and Rosa Aldama sat in silence, motionless. Gertrudis assented with her head; she had been rendered mute by the wisdom of Domingo's words.

Carlos Manuel stood up and went in front of the window. He started to rock slowly, left to right, as he always did in moments of personal scrutiny, indecision or tension.

"I love this country, mostly for its past, which is venerable, rather than for its present which, like most Frenchmen, I detest. I was not planning to leave this soon but, yes, I am afraid we must leave now. Your words, Domingo, are full of wisdom. A great mission awaits all of us in Cuba and we can not jeopardize it or delay it one more second than it is necessary. If my commitment to the freedom of Cuba means bidding good bye to our beloved Paris, I will do it. We must all get back to our roots. I feel we have learned in Europe everything that Europe has to offer. The time has come to build a great nation in our small island. We will simply be the first to leave Paris. I know that all of you will follow me and join forces to accomplish in Cuba what has been so difficult to instill in this tired and abused land. We must leave for Cuba and we must leave soon."

Once the decision had been made clear that Carlos Manuel and María del Carmen had to be extricated from the quackmire of French bureaucracy, if not justice, Domingo spoke again: "Miguel," he said, "you are the man with the powerful business contacts in Paris. Carlos and María can not just get a coach and be taken to Marseille, Le Havre or Brest. They will need someone to vouch for them, to insure reliable companions and trusted scouts that can steer them out of trouble. Who do you know that could godfather them into safety?"

"I can think of three people," replied Miguel, "that I would trust with this mission, aside from Guizot, which I would reserve to be the man within the government that could disentangle the strategies if they come to a dead end. One of them is James de Rothschild, possibly the richest man in France, the second is Claude Philibert Count of Rambuteau, the *Préfet de la Seine* and the third would be Lady Granville, the wife of the British ambassador."

"Why these three... ?" asked Gertrudis, happy but not surprised that Miguel had such powerful business connections in Paris. "You have all but brought Louis Philippe himself into our cabal," she said.

"I think it is an important decision and we all should know what we are dealing with," replied Miguel. "Let me try to think out loud about our potential allies. Up front, let me suggest that we can surely count on any or all of them. They are close friends of ours, partners at one time or another of the house of Aldama; they are all are used to fend off the many shortcomings of the French justice system. I am sure we could find a determined and loyal schemer in any of them."

"James de Rothschild is as rich as any King that France has ever been. He is in his late forties and is a banker's banker. He recently lent eleven million francs each to Seillière and Delessert to prevent their banks to go broke. For years he was rejected by French society until Metternich appointed him general consul from Austria. He is the top man at the *faubourg Saint Germain* and his revelries nowadays are organized by Juste the Countess of Noailles and Marie the Duchess of Berry. He married Marie's niece Betty in 1824, when she was 19. James is a *bona fide* Orleanist and, aside from his money, he knows everyone who is worth knowing in the French government. The Rothchilds live at the *Hôtel de Talleyrand* and it is on the rooms that they rent to the Princess de Lieven, Guizot's mistress, that she holds her famous weekly receptions. James and his brother Salomon have *chateaux* at Ferrières and at Suresnes. These are the only *chateaux* in France that have incorporated gas lights all across their gardens. It has been said that if the Rothchilds were to move one tenth of their fortunes from France there would be no stable government in this country for the next fifty years. James alone, and unfortunately not Salomon, has been partner of the House of Aldama for the last 12 years," he concluded.

After a brief pause Miguel went on.

"The second man I mentioned is Claude Philibert de Rambuteau. He has been *Préfet* de la Seine for the last 15 years. He is now in his early sixties. As a young man he was the chamberlain of Napoleon. He is very comfortable moving in influential circles. He is a patriarch of the *Monarchie de Juillet* and no one, public servant or privileged aristocrat, dares to deny him a favor. He was born in the Bourgogne from a peasant family and made his money building bridges and restoring monuments across France. He is an iconoclast and likes to scandalize French society by bringing all sorts of nouveau rich characters, hundreds at a time, to the most elegant official functions; it has been called the *Rambuteau crowd*. Some people call him a fake. In fact, it has been said that no lady ever makes a claim for lost necklaces at the celebrations organized by Rambuteau for fear to be discovered as a show off with fake jewels. It has also become popular to say that the definition of "chic" is someone who has never been at a Rambuteau party. But never mind that. We have been contributing to the celebrations of *Monsieur Rambuteau* ever since he became *Préfet de la Seine*. My father has been a personal friend and a partner of his since they were very young. They met when Claude stayed in our house in Havana during his visit as part of a commission appointed by Bonaparte to study the Haitian situation in 1803. He can be counted on for whatever is needed. I vouch for his loyalty."

Finally Miguel described the wife of the British ambassador.

"Harriett Elisabeth Granville, the youngest child of the Duke de Devonshire, has been the hostess at the British embassy over the last 16 years. She married Lord Granville, Marquis de Stafford, in 1809 and they have five grown children. They own *Chatsworth House* in England and Harriett's sister, the Duchesse de Sutherland, is a dame to Queen Victoria. The importance of Lady Granville in Paris is due to the slant of the Austrian and other foreign embassies favoring the *legitimists* in French politics, while the British embassy, from day one, has made common cause with Louis Philippe and the *Monarchie de Julliet*. Britain, in fact, was the first nation to recognize the new King of the French and Charles Stuart, a distant cousin of Lady Granville, was the first ambassador to present his credentials to the House of Orleans. Louis Philippe is especially in debt to Lady Granville because she was one of the friends who convinced Victoria of England to accept the French invitation to visit Paris a couple of years ago. Lord Granville has been a custodian of our banking interests in Paris and was my mentor in England when I first went to study at Cambridge. I am sure Lady Granville can also be counted on for whatever is needed."

As the Céspedes, Domingo and Gertrudis listened to the stories of personal friendship that Miguel was recounting they could not be but impressed –if not surprised– at the depth of his contacts in Europe and particularly in France.

"Had I know that you knew all these people I would have hesitated to offer you my modest dwelling," said Carlos Manuel, laughing. Then, continuing, he said "at least I would have asked you to help with the street repairs needed at the corner of *rue Jacob* and *rue des Saints-Pères!*"

"Never mind *rue Jacob* and its mislaid stones," added Gertrudis also laughing. "It is because of their heartfelt easiness, in spite of their enourmous power, that we love this man and his sister!" she concluded.

Having had an overview of the resources they could count on to deliver Carlos and María safely from Paris they felt a great sense of relief. Miguel's impressive backing had definitely allayed everyone's anxiety, if not their sadness at seeing the end of their Parisian adventure.

"Well, let's rest a bit before dinner. I shall order the Chef to prepare a feast... in celebration of our friendship," María del Carmen said. Their legendary Cuban sense of humor had saved them from very real worries once more. Amid comments and good humor in the face of the challenges ahead, they each went to their rooms to rest before dinner.

28

"Those who won our independence... valued liberty
as an end and as a means. They believed liberty to be
the secret of happiness and courage to be the secret of liberty."
Louis D. Brandeis

"There is no pain so great as the memory of joy in present grief."
Aeschylus

"Sweet is the memory of distant friends! Like the mellow rays
of the departing sun, it falls tenderly, yet sadly, on the heart."
Washington Irving

THE NIGHT BEFORE their departure from Paris Carlos Manuel insisted on going to the *Pont des Arts* with María del Carmen. He had left the house sparingly over the last 10 days while his friends made all arrangements to secure his safe passage from Paris to London. Miguel and Rosa Aldama were already on their long trip to Havana via Madrid, and no one had placed any obstacles on their departure. Miguel had made all arrangements to secure the full support of the employees and associates of the House of Aldama in Paris and Domingo Del Monte had been left behind, in charge of the operation. They had received an understanding ear and full agreement and co-operation with their decisions by James de Rothschild, Claude de Rambuteau and Harriett Granville, and all three were kept informed of every detail by Domingo. There were no reasons to expect that anything would go wrong.

Carlos Manuel would depart in the morning, on a *berline* that would pick him up exactly at 10 in the morning at the door of the house on *rue Jacob* and would take him to *l'embarcadère de Belgique,* a sort of departing point from Paris built by Léonce Reynaud, the renown French architect. *L'embarcadère* would become la *Gare du Nord* after the advent of railroad a few years later. There, a *carrosse* would be waiting for Carlos Manuel to take him to Le Havre, and from there Domingo had booked a channel crossing to London. María del

Carmen would be following the same route the following day, and once in London they would be free to return to Spain or to seek passage to Havana. On both trips the *écuyers*, the *pages*, the *valets de pied*, the *palefreniers* and the *cochers* were all employees or paid helpers of the House of Aldama. Being used to thoroughness on his business deals, Miguel had spared no expense to insure that Carlos Manuel and María del Carmen would have a safe passage out of Paris.

It was only a short stroll from the house of the Céspedes to the banks of the Seine river. They both loved this body of water that had been witness to so much of western civilization. The Seine was running full, at a speed which would have cut very fast the life of anyone venturing in its waters, particularly at that time of the night. As they entered the *Pont des Arts* from the left bank, at the point where it is close to the Institute, they could not but reminisce their many discoveries in Paris a few short months before. The *Pont des Arts* had been one of the beautiful and romantic places they had come to love. This *passerelle* was the first iron bridge across the Seine and had been built as a toll bridge some forty years before they arrived in Paris. Even the name of its architect evoked romanticism: Louis-Alexander de Cessar. He included trees and flower pots along its wooden surface because he thought of and designed the bridge as a suspended garden.

Once they overcame the few stone steps leading to the surface of the *passerelle*, Carlos Manuel remembered that he and María del Carmen had met there, through Victor Hugo, one of the disciples of what Hugo called his *Cénacle*, Charles Auguste Sainte-Beuve. He became a good friend and had gifted María del Carmen a painting of the *Pont des Arts* with an inscription that read: *"Par un Ciel étoilé, sur ce beau Pont des Arts, j'ai mille fois rêve que l'Eden en ce monde... est ici."* (Under a sky full of stars, on this beautiful bridge, I have dreamed thousands of times that Eden in this world... is here).

Carlos Manuel, more than María del Carmen, could not contain his feelings as they walked the 1,500 feet length of the *Pont des Arts*. He thought he would certainly miss the *passage du Commerce Saint André*, with its old streets, and the souls of the great figures of the French Revolution still lingering at every corner: Marat, Desmoulins and Danton, but also, before them, Rousseau and Diderot. He thought of all the *petit restaurants* and the places they had been able to share with the great *philosophs* of the past, particularly *Le Procope*, the *mecca* of the seafood amateurs. There they had sat many times at the table where Voltaire had sat, or at the place at the bar where Benjamin Franklin liked to slowly sip his whiskey.

All of a sudden, as if from a great distance, he could hear the roar of the river at the foot of the cliff where he found himself. He had no more room to escape. This was an important tributary of the mightiest Cauto River in Cuba. He had descended to the margins of the Contramaestre many times, almost daily to bathe during the last few months. And he had no illusions that he could lower himself to the riverbed while running. He stood by the side of the ravine and knew he was all but lost. There was no way he could escape this determined young Spanish soldier that had been trained to hunt him. How could he explain to this youngster that all his life he had longed for a fair political system where all men, free by their own rights, could stretch themselves to reach their full personal potential? He felt very dejected by what this young soldier was about to do fulfilling his duties, and thought that his life had been a continuous sequence of failures and defeats. Yet, knowing that his end was near, he attempted to remember the glorious and happy moments. He thought of Jesús María and Francisca de Borja, his parents. Of Pedro, Francisco, Javier and Borjita, his brothers and sister. He wondered about Manuel, the brother that no one dare to mention in his home as he was growing up. Was it beyond the capacity for suffering of his parents to keep his memory alive? His mind wondered to the Convent in Bayamo where he had first been a student. He felt the presence of the nuns that had taught him logics and ethics and who had made easy for him to enter the Seminary of San Carlos and San Ambrosio and later the Real Pontifical University of Havana.

The streets of *l'Ancienne Comédie*, the *Carrefour de Buci*, the *rues Mazarine, de Seine, Dauphine* and *Saint Andrés de Arts* came in full view in his mind. How could he ever forget himself and María del Carmen walking thorough these old Parisian streets, holding hands and marveling at the opportunity to walk on the same stones where so many important people had made so much history? Even trivial scenes like visiting the *boucheries*, the *fromageries* and *boulangeries* of the neighborhood brought back unforgettable memories. How could he live without all that? he asked himself. How could he erase from his memory the *Quai des Grands Augustines*, at his time the greatest public meeting place in all of Paris? How could he forget the *Carrefour de Buci*, which his friend Balzac had characterized as "*un des plus horribles coins de Paris*" (one of the most horrible corners of Paris) but which both he and Balzac enjoyed visiting and where he had made the nearby *Alcazar* one of his favorite restaurants in Paris.

He saw himself as a gymnast and fencing enthusiast as well as a master at chess, enjoying a life that had been made possible by the extensive fortunes accumulated by several generations of hard working criollos that left their best years in Cuba. He remembered the stories about Juan Antonio de

Céspedes, a Spanish noble who in the early 1600's came to settle in Cuba and became major of Bayamo. He had a soft spot and immense tenderness in his heart for María del Carmen, whom he married very young and who gave him his first son, a Cuban, Carlos Manuel, shortly after they came back from Paris. He smiled as he recalled his days as an insurrect against General Juan Prim, who was the direct cause of his first exile out of Spain. And through his mind he saw himself writing his never published translation of The Aeneid from the Greek, as well as his comedy Las Dos Dianas, which was published in Spain but of which he never held a copy in his hands.

Holding hands with María del Carmen they both looked at *Le Pont Neuf*, across the river on the east side of the *Pont des Arts*. One last time he saw in the distance the statue of Henri IV, his all time favorite French King. The bridge reminded him also that its first builder had been Henri III, the son of Catherine de Medicis, who assassinated the Duque of Guise. How perverted the human race could be, he thought. As if the throne of France, any throne, merited an assassination. Henri IV, the man who finished the bridge, was also to perish under the knife of Ravillac. In his mind many images were now competing. He thought that public life, vulnerable as it was from jealousies and ambitions, was a dangerous profession, yet he was eager to make it a part of his life anyway. But more than any political considerations his mind was recalling the many times he had rented a boat at the *vert gallant*, the western most corner of the *île de la cité*, to take his bride on a tour of Paris as viewed from the Seine. He trivially remembered his troublesome decision, every time he found himself on a boat with María del Carmen, about whether to start upstream, towards la Bastille and the canal de Saint Martin, which meant a leisurely ride back downstream, or to start letting the boat go downstream first, towards the *Louvre* and the *Champ de Mars*, which meant having to row upstream to get back to the *Pont Neuf*.

He saw a parade of friends and enemies going through his mind. There was the gentle Francisco Vicente Aguilera, a rich man, owner of three prosperous sugar mills near Bayamo, educated in the United States, who never wanted an important position in the revolutionary army. He had died poor and heartbroken, certain that the internal struggles within the army of independence would be a serious obstacle for the independence of Cuba. And there was Perucho Figueredo. He was also a lawyer, a graduate of Barcelona, like Céspedes himself, a lover of the arts and literature and also a large property owner; the co-author of the Cuban National Anthem, for which Céspedes had improvised the music. Céspedes could see him participating in the assault on Bayamo and, later on, in its destruction by fire when the Spaniards were ready to retake the village. He mourned Perucho, taken prisoner and shot by the Spaniards without a proper trial. He saw his second son, Oscar, born in 1847 and his daughter María del Carmen, born in 1849, who died as an infant. What a lovely family they were when they were five, with beautiful María del Carmen presiding over every dinner and the young ones, Carlos Manuel, Oscar and María del Carmen sitting by their side on the family table.

He had sat at the table where Mirabeau had met with Benjamin Franklin to compose what the National Constituent Assembly later on approved as the French Constitution in September of 1791. He had spent many hours studying it and ended up considering it as a failed attempt to establish a liberal bourgeois constitutional monarchy. That, he was sure, did not work because republican ideals proved it to be out of tune with the times. He also recalled having had access to the old *Collège des Quatre Nations*, to the rooms where Condorcet and Jefferson had worked out an adaptation of the American Declaration of Independence as the French Declaration of the Rights of Man and Citizen. He remembered how he became an ardent defender of the government system in the United States. He never had any notions of incorporating Cuba to the United States, but he believed that a democracy organized along the lines of the American Republic was the best system for the yet inexistent Republic of Cuba.

The image of Lucas del Castillo, his uncle, and José Fornaris, his intimate friend, sharing a jail cell in Bayamo in 1852, during the governorship of Gutierrez de la Concha as Captain General of Cuba, crossed his mind. Concha was a friend of his family but had sent word that if Céspedes insisted on his independence ideals he should not rely on his friendship with the family. Céspedes remembered a letter he sent to Concha thanking him for his temporary friendship and hoping the Conchas would eventually enjoy being sent back to Spain by a successful Cuban army. A deep sadness embraced his soul as he recalled the days when María del Carmen died after a painful sickness. "I never thought I could go on living without her," he thought. His eyes betrayed him and he cried and knew not how to contain his sorrow. "How different would my life had been if she had remained at my side, as we both had planned and dreamed so many times." His strong body yielded to the burden of this repressed grief and he fell on both knees. "Oh God, why did you deprive me of her presence so early? I would have gladly spent the rest of my days in agony if only I could have had her presence, her laughter and her enthusiasm for a few more years. Having thought of María del Carmen for a few seconds, Céspedes lost track of the Spanish soldier that so impersonally but ruthlessly was hunting him.

As he looked into the *Institute de France*, on the left bank of the river, he thought of the many times he had visited the *Bibliothèque Mazarine* thanks to the efforts of George Sand. "I will miss this institution," he told María del Carmen, which until then had been silent. "We have had very good friends here. I will miss them forever. I will miss the *Institute's* fabulous *salle de lecture* (reading room), as well as the annual meetings of the academicians under the *grand coupole*." Through his mind crossed the notion that Balzac had once told him, after leaving one of these meetings, that both the Institute and the Pont des Arts were an *endroit maléfique*, a duet of malevolent places. He smiled slightly upon this image, particularly since, for such an important and dignified occasion, Balzac had failed to dress properly and was almost denied entrance by one of the door keepers of the Institute.

María del Carmen and Carlos Manuel embraced silently for a few minutes. They held each other as if mutually protecting themselves from the pain that would come upon leaving Paris. They would surely miss those beautiful places where they had learned so much and had been so happy and relaxed. "Too bad we have to leave this town, Carlos," María del Carmen strained herself to say. "I know," replied Carlos Manuel. "I would have stayed for much longer. But perhaps it is better like this. We have work to do in Cuba. The time has come to do it."

29

THE SADNESS CAUSED by a remembrance of María del Carmen was broken when he saw himself at the mercy of Salvador Cisneros Betancourt, who had delayed the uprising in Camagüey simply to make the point that he had to be counted on. Céspedes was sure this had caused the loss of Bayamo after they had taken the city and had felt jubilant with their first victory. The Marquis, as he used to call Cisneros, was his albatross during the entire war and was never a welcome sight in his mind. He was nevertheless glad that out of that episode he had emerged as President and Cisneros as head of the Legislative body, with Manuel de Quesada as Military Chief. An intense sadness squeezed his soul again as he relieved the days in the fighting fields. Oscar, his son, had been captured and killed with no trial, after he had declined to surrender to save his son's life. How could a father live with this burden on his soul, he asked himself? What feelings Oscar had about his father as he was facing the firing squad? Did he pardon or did he curse him? These were questions that had recurred in his dreams many times. These thoughts were like ghosts that had visited him every night for the last years of his life. He thought he could only cast them aside by ending his own life, and he had thought of doing it many times, and particularly now when everything in his life had turned against him.

In the distance he could see *Notre Dame*, the *Place Dauphin* and the *Sainte Chapelle*, one of his favorite places as well as María del Carmen's. On this final night he marveled once more at its delicate beauty. As Louis IX with his faith in his time, he was a profound believer in the right of Cuba to be free.

A recurrent and inescapable nightmare of Carlos Manuel during his days on the margins of Rio Contramaestre was the image of Ana, his second wife. After his son had been shot he had married Ana de Quesada, sister to Manuel de Quesada, the Military Chief of the Republic at Arms, who was eventually deposed. Ana's very faint image flashed across his eyes once more. At first when she was pregnant and alone in New York, then when she was very thin, ill dressed, hungry and looking as a pauper, as she suffered an exile that would never allowed her to see Carlos Manuel again. These terrible years went thorough his mind like a furious tempest. Aldama, his companion in Paris, and Manuel de Quesada, his brother in law, were immersed into painful struggles to unite the exile groups in New York and did what they could to save Ana from her misery and wretchedness. He nevertheless loved both men, always loyal companions. Aldama had been essential for his escape from Paris in the 1840's. Manuel, a veteran of the Mexican army who had fought under Benito Juárez, had generously given everything he owned to the cause of Cuban independence. Thinking of them and of Ana and his son, he could never understand why those who were safe and away from the action could so easily forget those that were living in penury and misery. How could they live with the emotional burden of having forgotten those who were on the trenches, risking their lives and dying everyday?

His mind drifted as his eyes encountered the right bank end of the *Pont-au-Change* with its magnificent architecture. "One of the few rare conquests of the spirit above the necessity of destruction," he thought as he remembered the many works of art that Paris had lost *renversée pendant la revolution*. He could understand the many losses of *la vieille France* due to accidents or important archeological studies, but he thought that the senseless destruction that had taken place over the last fifty years in Paris had been both stupid and brutal.

Unexpectedly, the image of young Ignacio Agramonte came to his mind. "What a brave soldier, and what a gentle and heroic man." He saw General Ignacio offering to command the army of independence on its planned invasion towards western Cuba. He had made a name for himself by rescuing Julio Sanguily when he was captured by the Spaniards. Ignacio had 35 men under his command and the captors were over three hundred strong and were carrying enough artillery to take a large town. But Ignacio felt that Sanguily had to be rescued the very same day he had been captured or he

would be a dead man. At full gallop his improvised group pierced the Span-
ish column that was marching fast with Sanguily under custody.
Agramonte knew that he could only make one pass across the Spanish forces
and only one pass was necessary. A corpulent Negro called Valdivia pointed
his horse at full speed towards Sanguily and in one masterful stroke he
grabbed him by the waist with one arm and sped up across the rest of the
column, while Agramonte and the rest of his men were brandishing their
machetes and screaming "Viva Cuba libre!" The vision that Céspedes had
in his mind was that of Agramonte, 32 years old, acting as the older brother
of Sanguily, who was barely 27. These images blended with that of Oscar,
his son, who was even younger at 26. It was a time when other Generals
were competing for the honor of taking the war into heavily guarded Span-
ish territory and he wanted to save Ignacio for a future leadership position
in the Republic. "We need many Agramontes in charge of our new Repub-
lic," he had told Ignacio when he broke the news that Máximo Gómez was
the man for the invasion. As he recalled the plans he had for Agramonte, his
face turned into that of Amalia, Agramonte's wife, whom he had met in
Camagüey, receiving from a teary-eyed Gabriel García, an aide de camp of
Céspedes, the news that Ignacio had been shot and died in combat, at a far
away savannah called Jimaguayú. A profound sadness invaded Carlos
Manuel, who could not contain his own tearful eyes.

The view of the Pantheon in the distance brought many treasured
memories to his mind. Céspedes lamented, as he saw his hours in
Paris coming to an end, that he had not completely mastered everything that there was to know about French political history. It had
been his passion even before coming to Paris. He had read every
book of French history that came across his hands. As Jefferson had
done during his stay in Paris, he had formed a serious collection of
history and science books, at quite a personal expense, which he
planned someday to gift to a future Cuban national library. As the
awe-inspiring dome of the Pantheon contrasted with the reddish tint
of the Parisian sky, he remembered Mirabeau and Tronchet. They
were his two most admired political figures in France. Honoré
Gabriel, Comte de Mirabeau, had been the great public speaker who
with Emmanuel Sieyès transformed the General States into a National Constituent Assembly in 1789. François Denis Tronchet, had
been the only man who, without hesitation, dared to defend Louis
XVI during the trial at the Revolutionary Convention. Mirabeau
made it possible to continue the meetings of the National Assembly
after Louis XVI had ordered in 1789 to vacate the room where the
Assembly was meeting. Céspedes knew his speech by heart: "*Allez
dire à votre maître que nous sommes ici par la volonté du peuple et qu'on ne*

nous arrachera que par la puissance des baïonnettes." (Tell your master that we are here by the will of the people and that we will not be thrown out except by the power of the bayonets). Tronchet had pronounced the only noble words pronounced in front of a Convention that had already decided to end the life of its King. *"Louis donna sur le trône l'exemple des moeurs. Il n'y porta aucune faiblese coupable ni aucune passion corruptrice. Je m'arrête devant l'histoire. Songez qu'elle jugera votre jugement et que le sien sera celui des siècles. Vous pouvez le trouver coupable mais l'histoire l'absoudra."* (From the throne Louis has given an example of good morals. He did not show any weaknesses; he is not guilty of any corrupting passions. I stand here before the judgment of history. It is history that will judge your discernment and it will stand for centuries. You might find him guilty but history will absolve him). Interestingly enough, Céspedes thought, Tronchet was the first French senator interned at the Pantheon after fifteen years earlier, as President of the Constituent Assembly, he had accompanied inside the Pantheon the remains of Mirabeau.

His mind then turned to Ana, and how he knew he would never again see her or his children, little Carlos Manuel and Gloria Dolores. He had never been able to hold them in his arms. By a strike of fate his worst political enemy, Salvador Cisneros Betancourt, the Marquis de Santa Lucia, had brought him some pictures of them from New York. Not related to the joy this brought to him, he had given the Marquis his best shirt, after knowing that he had lost all his fortune and did not have any. He pictured the miserable hut where he had been living for weeks after being deposed as President. He had hoped for a visa to leave Cuba, which had to be granted by the revolutionary assembly, but he knew it would never come. He had just lost Pedro, his brother, recently arrived from New York, on a battle of no apparent importance.

Céspedes embraced María del Carmen very tightly, and they both kissed as they reached the *Institute* on their way back from the *Pont des Arts.* She was pale and cold, shaking from emotion, and could barely stand up or contain her tears. He was her strength and held her tightly by her waist. "We are not leaving Paris forever," she said, trying to make the farewell to this City of their dreams a bit less painful. "I do not think we will ever be back," replied Carlos Manuel. "The world has become an inescapable battleground where some men try ceaselessly to control others and force them to live and believe what they wish. Good men and women are forced to either surrender to lifestyles which are contrary to their deepest beliefs or to join in this worthless and inhuman pantomime. As the years go by from now on, we will be more and more immersed in a battle that we did not call upon ourselves but which we cannot ignore or escape. I believe we will have no rest because the cause of freedom and political liberty is endless and vanity, self-importance and selfish ambition will never be fully eradicated from the face of the earth." They walked slowly towards the house at *12, rue Jacob*. The guards were still there, silent, circumspect and prudently keeping an eye on Carlos Manuel. A *carrosse* would be waiting for him at sundown the following day. The timeline for their departure from Paris had started. Inside the house everything had been packed or discretely given away to charity. Their fate now depended on the skills and cloak-and-dagger capabilities of the loyal employees of the House of Aldama.

In the few seconds that he had left Céspedes reviewed his situation. He had no escort to make a valid and worthwhile last stand. The troops of the Spanish battalion of Saint Quintin were by now probably surrounding the entire area. He had a weapon in his hand, and many times he had told his followers that it contained six bullets, five for the Spaniards and the last one for himself. His last nights had been full of nightmares as he "fought the demons that accosted him and the ones he loved." Many times he had warned himself that he would be betrayed and left to fend for himself. At this obscure and remote corner of the Sierra Maestra he could only trust his son, Carlos, and Pedro Maceo, a friend of his son, with whom he played chess every day. He had difficulty seeing clearly, having had a serious bout of conjunctivitis a few years ago. He had trouble controlling his hands and had recurrent pains in the legs and headaches. He was no longer the handsome man he had been in Paris or Barcelona in the 1840's. He had aged badly, weighted 125 pounds and had more wrinkles in his face than in his pants, which he had been able to wash at the river but which had not seen an ironing board since he left Bayamo seeking the refuge of the Oriente mountains. As if through a veil of celestial clouds he saw a young Spanish soldier approaching him. "He must be no older than 19 or 20," he thought. "We will need disciplined youngsters like this to rebuild Cuba."

The young man addressed him loudly: "Give yourself up. You are surrounded." He saw Oscar in the face of this young man. Or perhaps Ignacio Agramonte, or Julio Sanguily. He knew he could do no harm to this young soldier. Suddenly he remembered Carlos Manuel. Where was he? Had he been captured or killed? Had he been able to elude the tight noose the Spanish had forged around him? "Give yourself up," the soldier repeated, pointing his rifle towards Carlos Manuel. He could only think of Carlos and Oscar, his sons; one dead the other perhaps at great peril. He wanted to hold them and kiss them, as he had done when they were little but had not done for many years now. It was more and more difficult for him to see but he now realized the young man in front of him was Oscar, reassuring him he had stood at the firing squad as a brave man and had died with dignity, shouting, as his father had asked, "Viva Cuba libre."

He raised his hands to caress Oscar's face. He immediately felt a sharp burning sensation over his heart. His legs gave way and he regretted not having reached the face of the son he loved so much. As he now reached for the ground he found emptiness. His body unwillingly fell into the void and silently started to tumble towards the river. He felt another lightening bolt on his right leg. His arms were painfully battering against the shrubs by the side of the Contramaestre river. He felt the pain and knew he was in trouble. But all of a sudden the pain ended. He could only see the sky, bright and blue. And he thought he could see the stars. "There are more stars in the Cuban sky than in any other place on earth," he thought. Then the sky began to turn dark. He tried to fix his eyes in the stars he had just seen but he could not see them anymore. Slowly he closed his eyes and went to sleep.

A GATHERING OF FRIENDS, 1843

Joseph-Benoit Guichard's (1806-1880) "*A Gathering of Friends*," Oil on Canvas. 180x180 cm, 1843. Above, a charcoal study for Guichard's painting. Top row, from left to right: María del Carmen de Céspedes, Domingo Del Monte and Carlos Manuel de Céspedes. Sitting: Gertrudis Gómez de Avellaneda and Rosa Aldama. On the right, playing the cello, Miguel Aldama. After the hurried departure of the Céspedes from Paris, the finished Guichard painting remained in the artist's studio until his death in 1880. The painting is now lost, probably part of an unknown private collection in Paris. The charcoal study is in the collection of the author.

Aftermaths

Anti-Americanism. After the Céspedes left Paris a period of apparent good will to America seemed well established by the popularity of the best-seller *De la Démocratie en America* by Alexis de Tocqueville. Soon after its publication, however, the intellectual press in Paris was calling it *L'Amérique en Sucre* and numerous plays, essays, newspaper articles and scholarly books were issued, trying to compensate and demolish the positive image of America presented by de Tocqueville.

During the War Between the States, France openly supported the South, hoping that the US would be split into two or three countries and not become a powerful rival for world hegemony. The war was presented in the *salons* of Paris as a struggle between the Anglo-Saxon north and the Latin Mediterranean south. When the time came to celebrate the centennial of the US in 1876, all efforts to subscribe the cost of the statue of liberty in France came short of the necessary funds. The US Congress did not approve funding of the statue's base on New York. A wave of anti-American emotions soon developed in France and there were proposals to place the statue at the entrance of the Suez Canal or any other suitable and much friendlier venues according to French intellectuals.

An even stronger wave of anti-American sentiment invaded France after the start of the Cuban War of Independence in 1895, which soon became the Spanish-American War. The word in Paris was that the American Navy had bombed Havana to start the war and the circumstances of the Maine explosion in Havana harbor were never clarified. This negative sentiment lasted until after WWI, when French intellectuals took the participation of the US in the European war as motivated by greed and arrogance. They called the American soldiers *"ouvriers de la dernière heure"* (workers of the last hour) and, ignoring that the war had been fought in French territory to save France from disgrace, severely criticized the fact that France had 1,350,000 deaths to America's 56,000.

The French were particularly insulting to President Wilson during his term of office because of his religious outlook on life. He was severely attacked on the French press with phrases like *"America: le pays où chaque paranoïaque peut devenir president."* (America, the country where any paranoid could become president). These attacks, by the way, were enthusiastically endorsed by Sigmund Freud, who provided the European press with a highly biased and self serving psychological profile of the American president at the conclusion of the war.

Between the World Wars America was characterized as *"l'Ogre Réaliste,"* and the land of *"Oncle Shylock."* A similar situation occurred after WWII. The French communist party became so strong and influential after the war that by 1952, only one third of the French population believed that the Marshall plan had helped France to recover after the ravages of the war. Only in the north of France the intervention of the Americans in the war found a grateful acknowledgement. The anti-Americanism in the minds and actions of French politicians, intellectuals, artists and journalists has continued unabated into the XXI century. Historians cannot explain these facts given that America has never opposed France in a war, unlike it has England, Spain, Italy and Germany.

On the other hand, France seems unable to shake once and for all the presence and influence of America in its economic, social and cultural life. In spite of numerous efforts over two centuries, French leaders and opinion makers can not control the powerful attraction of the French masses for American values, lifestyle and popular culture.

There are no mentions of the term *"Anti-Americanism"* before WWII. It was first used in July 1948 at an article in the French magazine *Espirit (issue No. 7)* by C. Marker, followed in January 1950 by an article by M. Etienne Gilson in *La Nouvelle Critique (issue No. 12)*, a monthly magazine published by the French Communist Party.

Aurore Dudevant (George Sand) never got to accompany Chopin on his planned trip to Cuba. Shortly before his death she separated from him and continued her successful writing career. In 1848 she moved to *57, rue de Provence* with Franz Liszt. After having played an active role in the revolution of 1848 she exerted her influence to save many of her co-conspirators from sentences of prison and execution. Disappointed with politics, she began to spend most of her time writing at her home in Nohant, where she had arranged for the installation of a small private theater. She died there, on June 8, 1876 at the age of 72 and was buried in her property. It has been said that hundreds of people came from all over France to pay their respects at her funeral. In recent times there have been several proposals to move her remains to the Panthéon in Paris.

Astolphe Louis, Marquis de Custine. Custine was the son and grandson of noblemen that were guillotined by the revolution, and the son of a woman that reputedly was the lover of François-René de Châteaubriand. He served as an aide to Talleyrand but was forever banished from the right circles in Paris because of his homosexuality.

He became an expert on Russia, much to the disappointment of Tsar Nicolas I. His *Lettres de Russie* was a spectacular best seller in Paris in 1843. The Tsar had the book banned in his empire. Custine died in 1857.

Berlioz. At the time Carlos Manuel and María del Carmen met Hector Berlioz he had already composed his *Symphonie Fantastique Op. 14.* Over the next few years he became more popular outside France than in his own county, traveling extensively through Germany, England, Hungary and Russia. In 1856 he composed his *Opus Magnus, Les Troyens,* inspired by Virgilio's *l'Eneide.* He could not recover after the deaths of his wife Marie and his son Louis and after a triumphal *tournée* in Russia, invited by his pupils Rimsky-Korsakoff and Borodine, he died in 1869. He is buried at the Cemetery of Montparnasse in Paris.

Bibliothèque du Roi. It still functions as a library but with limited access to scholars. Its functions as a public library have been assumed by the Mitterrand Library, on the margins of the Seine river, across from Bercy in eastern Paris.

Buffon's Needle Problem. This question in probability theory, which is simply: what are the probabilities of a needle lying exactly on one of several equally spaced parallel lines on a plane where it is dropped? was originally proposed by George Louis LeClerc de Buffon in 1738 and was not solved until computerized Monte Carlo simulation methods were developed in the 1950's.

Café Tortoni. This most famous of French cafes situated at 22, *Boulevard des Italiens* continued to be the meeting place for fashionable Parisians for many years. It has been replicated in several other capitals around the world, starting a few years after the Céspedes left Paris. A list of its patrons over the last century would have to include Manet, Baudelaire, Oscar Wilde, Hugo, Verlaine, Maupassant, Casimir Perrier, Guizot, and many others, down to Borges and Gardel in its Buenos Aires replica, opened in 1858. It is said that Karl Marx wrote *The Class Struggles in France* at *Tortoni's* in Paris. There he noted with contempt that "*Tortoni* functions as a small stock exchange. Transactions are carried there once the Paris Bourse closes in the afternoons." José Martí mentions *Tortoni* in his book *Nuestra América,* when he scorns those *criollos* that pretend to be better than others: "*Si son parisienses o madrileños, vayan al Prado, de faroles; o vayan a Tortoni, de sorbetes.*"

Carlos Manuel de Céspedes. By the time he returned to Cuba in 1844 Carlos Manuel de Céspedes was fluent in English, German, French and Italian and he was translating the classics from Latin and Greek. After years of dedication to his writings and several periods of imprisonment due to advocating Cuban independence, he bought the Sugar Mill *La Demajagua*, near Manzanillo in 1867. Bartolomé Masó, manager of the estate of Francisco Vicente Aguilera, the *Propios de Manzanillo*, helped him staff his new property with slaves and Pedro (Perucho) Figueredo invited him to join the franc masons at the *Logia Tinima* in Puerto Príncipe, where Perucho and Céspedes improvised at the piano what would later become the Cuban National Anthem.

Early in 1868 María del Carmen died of tisis. Late in 1868 Carlos Manuel freed his slaves and led a group of 147 Cubans who declared independence from Spain and took Bayamo, their own town. A few months later, on a nearby farm owned by the Céspedes family, the *Hacienda El Dátil*, an unknown farm hand called Máximo Gómez joined the rebels, which by then had increased their numbers to 17,000. Not everything went well for the young rebels and rather than surrendering their conquests, their town and their properties, they decided to torch them. Responding to such a symbolic gesture the Spanish government confiscated everything in sight that belonged to the rebels. The headquarters of the insurrection were moved to Guáimaro where the Spaniards presented Carlos Manuel an ultimatum: surrender if you wish to save the life of your son Oscar. Carlos Manuel refused the bargain and his son was executed at a firing squad.

The rebel headquarters began to flow in a constant defensive motion, through the towns of Berrocal, Sabanilla and Magaramba. In the meantime numerous disputes fractured the unity of the Cuban patriots both in the island, where Salvador Cisneros Betancourt, Marquis of Santa Lucia presided the Chamber of Deputies in Arms, and in New York, where Carlos Manuel had sent a group of patriots under the successive leaderships of Miguel Aldama, Manuel de Quesada and Vicente Aguilera, in search for support and war materials. The disputes also involved Máximo Gómez, who by now was a General in the Cuban Army. Finally, on October 28, 1873, Carlos Manuel was deposed as President of the Republic and replaced by his now mortal enemy the Marquis of Santa Lucia, a very prestigious Cuban whose life long aims were the annexation of Cuba to the US rather than its independence.

Days later, probably as the result of a spy infiltrated by the Spanish army, the ship *Virginius*, finally arriving in Cuba with the war materials and ammunition so many times requested by Céspedes, was seized by the Spaniards. The *Virginius* was an ex-Confederate blockade runner that was used by Cuban rebels and their American collaborators during the first half of the Ten Years War (1868-1878). It was registered as property of General Manuel Quesada, acting on behalf of the Cuban Junta of New York. On 23 October 1873, the *Virginius* sailed from Kingston, Jamaica with the largest ever of its shipments of supplies for the Cuban War. 300 Remingtons, 300,000 cartridges, 800 daggers, 800 machetes, a dozen barrels of powder and several hundred shoes. About six miles from the Cuban coast, with the hills of Guantánamo in sight, the ship was intercepted by the Spanish warship *Tornado*. An 8 hour chase ensued, with the *Virginius* attempting to get back to Jamaica. Guns and equipment were dumped overboard to lighten ship, but the ship had to stop and surrender, even though it was 6 miles inside British territorial waters. The ship was towed by the *Tornado* to Santiago de Cuba harbor and arrived on 1 November 1873. On board were a total of 165 persons, the ship's crew and an expeditionary force consisting of six officers and 96 soldiers, all intending to aid the Cuban revolutionary cause. Fifty three of them, both crew and expeditionaries, were summarily executed. Pedro Céspedes del Castillo, brother of Carlos Manuel, was one of the first, once his identity was revealed by a traitor. The Consuls of Great Britain and the United States formulated complaints over the incident and the proceedings. Both were ignored.

The failure of the *Virginius* was the last straw of bad luck for the Cuban rebels. Carlos Manuel was made prisoner in the woods of Santiago province and released by mistake in December 1873. He immediately took back to the mountains and made camp at a site called San Lorenzo, on the banks of the Contramaestre river. It was the same river that joined the river Cauto at a place called Dos Rios, where almost 20 years later, during the second Cuban War of Independence, a new leader, José Martí, would fall during a charge against the Spanish troops.

The Carlos Manuel that took refuge at San Lorenzo was a different man from the brilliant lawyer that had called for a war of independence a few years before. Gone were the gracefulness and the robust constitution. The man that had so much enjoyed dancing and gymnastics, who had practiced fencing and had rowed at the Athletic Club in Barcelona, had now turned into a depressed and pessimistic soul. There was very little imagination or *joy de vivre* left in his demeanor, and only his will and his sense of duty remained. He was living life one day at a time, hoping that destiny would carry him to safe ground and give him the time to gather the strength to survive his many ordeals. Initially, he still had dressed with a touch of elegance. Dark cashmere trousers, a white well starched shirt, a small white silk scarf loosely wrapped around his neck, a black velvet vest with dainty grey square patterns and a dark blue velvet jacket. Eventually, life as an outcast in such remote places took its toll. He found himself without decent clothes, and worst of all, without a respectable pair of shoes to wear. His face betrayed a profound sadness and melancholy. He was now alone, without followers or political power, the trounced adversary of his envious rivals within the yet to be born Cuban political body and yet the indisputably vanquished general of an army in retreat.

At San Lorenzo he showered, shaved and dressed fully every morning and then spent the day reading and writing with difficulty, for he was going blind. There was a recurrent day dream that a courier that would bring him the documents he needed to be back in New York with his wife and children. After a meager breakfast he would sit for several hours at a table facing the mountains and would reflect on his, and Cuba's once promising past and his certainly hopeless future. Oftentimes he thought of his immolated son, and wondered what Oscar had thought the moment he realized that his father had decided to sacrifice him rather than surrender. It filled his soul with infinite sorrow. Had it been worthwhile? Did Oscar die with his chest full of pride for the sacrifice that his father was making or did he die cursing his fate? Would he ever have a sign that Oscar had accepted his destiny without any bitterness or rancor against his father?

He had no escort, for none had been provided by those who were now in charge of the Army of Independence. The only person he could really trust in this god-forsaken encampment at San Lorenzo was his eldest son Carlos Manuel, who was always tenderly trying to anticipate his every need. He felt he was at the end of a very dark tunnel, each meaningless day ending with the hope that something better would happen the next day. He was simply hoping that somehow he would be rescued and restored to a life where every day was normal, different and worth living.

Unbeknownst to Carlos Manuel, on February 26, 1874, two small gunships from the Spanish armada landed at *Playa Sevilla*, south of the *Sierra Maestra*, and within two days they were on their way to San Lorenzo, under the command of Don José López, Commander in Chief of the *Batallón de Cazadores de San Quintín*. Its mission was to find the ex President of the Cuban Army of Independence, dead or alive. The column under López included a former member of the Cuban Rebel Army identified as either Ramón Bradford, who had fought with Salvador Cisneros Betancourt, or Ramón Jacas, a former soldier under General José Lacret. Be the betrayer one or the other, or perhaps both if they were one and the same person, there is no doubt that he was very knowledgeable with San Lorenzo and its district, and that he was essential in the search for Céspedes.

Half of the men under the López command, guided by the traitor, approached the San Lorenzo encampment on February 27. After escaping detection by two listening posts they set up an ambush on one side of the camp where Carlos Manuel was, and waited for the arrival of the rest of the force. After waiting for one and a half hour and fearing discovery by the unsuspecting Cuban troops, they decided to attack the encampment. The shooting lasted for half and hour. Céspedes, his gun on his hand, ran for cover towards the nearby embankment of the Contramaestre River, where he could hide or offer resistance under the protection of some fallen trees and dense bushes. Just as he was approaching the steep slope of the river bank he turned around and fired three shots against a captain and three soldiers that were following him. He failed to hit anyone. A sergeant called Brígido Verdecía, attached to the Aserradero troops that reinforced the Spanish soldiers brought by Coronel López, fired his rifle in the direction of Carlos Manuel. He was hit but did not fall at that point. Gathering all his strength he threw himself towards the river embankment and fell some 40 feet towards the river. Tumbling against the bushes on his way down his clothes were torn and he lost the jacket, the vest and the scarf. A former slave of Francisco Aguilera, at this point a soldier under the command of Coronel López, identified the cadaver. Throughout this ordeal, Carlos Manuel de Céspedes y Figueredo was with his father at San Lorenzo but had left the camp searching for news and writing supplies. He heard the shots from a distance and rushed to the scene, but, by the time he arrived, the Spanish had left in a hurry, taking with them the body of his father, three wounded men and four prisoners. Carlos gathered up several of his fathers' possessions, which lay around, and buried them in the place where he had died. Days later the place was marked with a cross. Everything was eventually retrieved by troops under the command of General José Lacret.

It has never been elucidated if Céspedes was shot by the enemy or if facing capture he took his own life. Years earlier, at a meeting of Cuban patriots attended by Antonio Zambrana, Cisneros Betancourt and others in Camagüey, Céspedes had declared… "I intend to die with the dignity that every Cuban should have. My revolver will always have six bullets. Five for the enemy and one for myself. They will retrieve my corpse but will never take me prisoner…"

His corpse was taken to Santiago de Cuba on March 1. He only had one shot, of small caliber, under his right breast. Experts have claimed that such small wound could be only produced by a revolver, such as the caliber 44 weapon that Céspedes had on his waist, in which case he would have committed suicide before falling in the hands of the enemy. His head showed multiple lacerations. Some felt it was due to his fall in the embankment. Others have claimed that they were done by numerous hits with the butt of a rifle. His vest and coat showed evidence of a close range shot to his chest. They were retrieved by Simón Despaigne, a sergeant in the forces of Lacret, who turned them over to Carlos Manuel's son.

It is interesting to know that Brígido Verdecía, the man who chased Céspedes towards the embankment and perhaps shot him to death, as well as almost all of the guerrilleros of *El Aserradero*, who helped the Spaniards in the San Lorenzo ambush, fought with the Cubans against the Spaniards during the Cuban War of Independence of 1895. The initial reports of the Spanish troops after San Lorenzo indicated that an important archive of rebel documents had been occupied. Fernando Figueredo Socarrás, at the time secretary of the Cuban Assembly in Arms, testified a few years later that the only documents seized by the Spaniards were personal letters and documents belonging to Carlos Manuel.

Cathedral of Notre Dame. This church, the dean of the cathedrals in France since the XII Century, is widely considered one of the finest examples of Gothic architecture. Its predecessor was a Church built by Childebert I, the king of the Franks in 528. It stood on the site of Paris' first Christian church, Saint-Étienne Basilica, which was built on the site of a Gallo-Roman temple to Jupiter. The current building was started in 1164 by Louis VII and finished in 1345. In 1793 during the French Revolution, the cathedral was turned into a "*Temple to Reason*" and many of its treasures were destroyed or stolen. During several years *Lady Liberty* replaced the Virgin Mary on several altars. During the time of the Céspedes residence in Paris the Cathedral had uneven floors and was dirty and unpleasantly smelly. A restoration program was initiated under the supervision of Viollet-le-Duc. The restoration lasted 23 years and the Céspedes never got to see the results. In 1871, just as the renovation had concluded, a civil uprising leading to the establishment of the short-lived *Paris Commune* set fire to a mound of chairs within the cathedral and the entire cathedral almost went up in flames.

Céspedes Book Collection. An important library in five languages, it became dispersed throughout the eastern provinces of Cuba and irretrievably lost during the first Cuban war of independence in 1868.

Châteaubriand. At the time when François-René, Vicomte de Châteaubriand met the Céspedes, he had already retired from public life (minister of State and Foreign Affairs, Ambassador to Rome, Peer of France) and was concentrating on his writings. He moved to the *Abbaye-aux-Boix* with Jeanne-Françoise Julie Adélaïde [Madame]

Récamier (1777-1849) and until his death in 1848, held there one of the most successful literary *salons* of France. His last wish was to be buried in Saint-Malo, his birthplace.

Church of Saint Eustache. It continues to serve the Catholic community in Paris. Its musical tradition has a weekly climax every Sunday after the 11 am mass, when its organist improvises a superb organ concerto. A physical renovation of the interior has been going on for the last 30 years with no signs of ever concluding. It offers an opportunity to appreciate how artworks are preserved and restored throughout the times. Its soup kitchen continues to feed the poor and the homeless every winter to this day.

Claude Philibert de Rambuteau. He was *Conseiller d'État, Pair de France* and *Préfet de la Seine* from 1833 until 1848. He started many renovation projects that Haussmann continued during the Second Empire. He finished the construction of the *Arc de Triomphe de l'Étoile* and the *Avenue des Champs-Élysées*, which were started by Napoleon. He is also credited with the modernization of the sewer systems, the installation of many public fountains and thousands of gas lights throughout Paris as well as setting up hundreds of *vespasiennes* or public urinals for men. He died in 1869.

Domingo Del Monte arrived in Paris to visit the Céspedes after having established his name as one of the most influential intellectuals in Cuba in the first half of the XIX Century. Invitations to his *Tertulias*, the informal gatherings where all themes were welcomed, from poetry to politics to literature or science, had become the most rewarding gift for thinking heads in Havana. Del Monte was not just a theoretician but also a man of action. After divulging in one of his *Tertulias* the work of Juan Francisco Manzano, the first slave in the Americas to publish while still in servitude, he purchased Manzano's freedom for five hundred pesos. He could not do the same for Gabriel de la Concepción Valdés (Plácido), another one of his black protégées, who was summarily judged and executed because of his participation in an uprising called *Conspiración de la Escalera*. Domingo fell also in the same criminal cause and was sent into exile. He obtained Céspedes help in publishing several articles against slavery and the annexation of Cuba in *Le Globe* while in Paris. He wrote fluently in French and had been elected to the French Academy of History in 1838. He tried repeatedly but could never return to Cuba to restart his *Tertulias* after his last visit to Paris in 1848. He died in Madrid in 1853, at the age of 49. The Aldamas succeeded in repatriating his remains to be buried in Havana.

Eugene Delacroix had been born in 1798, the son of a royal furniture maker that had served Louis XV and Louis XVI. His early life was surrounded by rumors that his real father had been the Prince de Talleyrand, who had been Prime Minister at the time of his birth and who was his most ardent mentor during his young years. At the time he befriended the Céspedes he was already famous and had just returned from a successful trip to Morocco. The Céspedes, and particularly María del Carmen, visited him often in the company of George Sand, as he finished commissions for the *Palais Bourbon*, the *Palais de Luxembourg* and the *Chapelle des Saint Angels* at the Church of Saint Sulpice. The Céspedes commented many times that there were secret torments in Delacroix life about which he never talked. He died of a throat infection in 1863. He did not keep in touch with the Céspedes after they left Paris.

Françoise Guizot. Françoise Pierre Guillaume Guizot became the center of the longest administration, 26 years, under the constitutional monarchy of France. He is credited with the visits of Queen Victoria to Paris and Louis Philippe to London and with the development of a policy which united the two great and free nations of the West in what was termed the *entente cordiale*. After the fall of the *Monarchie de Juillet*, he passed abruptly from the condition of one of the most powerful and active statesmen in Europe to the condition of a philosophical and patriotic spectator of human affairs. His last of a long series of scholarly books was the *Histoire de France Racontée à Mes Petits Enfants*. Down to the summer of 1874, Guizot's mental vigour and activity were unimpaired. He died peacefully, and is said to have recited verses of Corneille and texts from Scripture on his death-bed.

Frédéric Chopin never got to play at the Tacón Theater in Havana. His health continued to deteriorate after the meeting with the Aldamas, Gertrudis Gómez and María del Carmen Céspedes and he became increasingly sick with tuberculosis. He offered his last public concert in London on November 16, 1848. Upon returning to Paris he never left his sick bed. He died on October 17, 1849 while living by himself in an apartment at *12, Place Vendôme* and was buried at the *Père Lachaise* cemetery in Paris. He requested that his heart be taken from his body and sent to Warsaw, where it rests at the Church of the Holy Cross.

French Cocarde. Originally a green leave from a chestnut tree, it was later changed to a red, white and blue rosette. It signified your adherence to the Revolution and it is still widely used in official France.

Gertrudis Gómez de Avellaneda had been born in Puerto Príncipe, Cuba and was almost thirty years old when she spent a few weeks in Paris with the Céspedes. There she shared with her friends the colossal successes of *Munio Alfonso*, her fist drama, and *Sab*, the first anti-slavery novel in the Spanish language, both of which she had just published in Madrid before going to Paris. Soon after leaving Paris she married Pedro Sabater, an important political figure in Madrid, who made her a widow in 1846 while they were living in Bordeaux. She spent a few months recovering at a convent in that city, where she wrote *Guatimozín, Ultimo Emperador de México* (1846). Later on she moved to Madrid and married Diego Verdugo a powerful Spanish military man and politician. In Madrid she wrote *Baltasar* (1858), considered the best of her works, and *El Cacique de Turmequé* (1860). She and Diego traveled extensively throughout Cuba, North America and France but he died in 1863. She returned to Madrid where she became a candidate for membership in the Spanish Academy. She was rejected, like was Emilia, Countess of Pardo Bazán, another notable talented writer and feminist. Gertrudis died in Sevilla in 1873, where she was buried at the San Fernando Cemetery.

Harriett Elisabeth Granville. Lady Harriet Granville became one of England's most famous ambassadresses. Her letters were compiled into a book, *Lady Harriet Granville's Letters, 1810-1845*, which even today provides an entertaining view of the life of a diplomatic couple assigned to a foreign embassy in mid XIX century Paris. The book has been in print continuously since 1894. Her services were not needed to rescue the Céspedes from Paris but she remained very actively involved in the entire process until she heard from Aldama that the couple was safe in Havana.

Honoré de Balzac went on to become the most prolific and read of French authors of all times. He never went out of debt and after selling his country house he moved to *12, rue des Batailles* in Paris. There he had a concealed back door to flee the house when creditors came knocking. He never opened the front door unless he heard such passwords as, *La saison des prunes est arrivé* (It is time to pick up the plums), or *J'apporte des dentelles de Belgique* (I brought with me the Belgian lace), or *Madame Bertrand était en bonne santé* (Mrs. Bertrand was in good health). After his death he was honored with a formidable and controversial sculpture by Rodin who now stands at the corner of Boulevards Raspail and Montparnasse in Paris. A copy of this sculpture greets visitors to the Museum of Modern Art of New York.

James de Rothschild was the founder of the French branch of the Rothschild family. He single-handedly financed the establishment of the Belgian State and the independence of Greece, among many other daring projects. His bank went on to be the foremost financial source for the governments of Italy, Spain, Austria and even the United States. He invested heavily and was a pioneer of railroad construction in Europe through the *Compagnie des Chemins de fer du Nord* and was the main backer of the *Parisian Exposition Universelle de 1855*. Balzac immortalized him as the *Baron de Nucingen* in some of his writings. He died in 1868, the same day that Céspedes brought about the uprising that proclaimed the *República de Cuba en Armas*.

Jacques Laffitte was already insolvent but could still wield considerable political influence when he began mentoring Céspedes in 1841. He had been born in poverty and was the wealthiest man in France in 1818, when through his bank he single-handedly saved the French government from ruin. He entered politics and was made premier by King Louis Philippe d'Orleans in 1830 but his sympathies for the causes of Polish and Italian independence estranged him from the King. By 1831 he had resigned and was bankrupt. In 1832 he created a credit bank which prospered during his lifetime but failed soon after his death in 1844. Carlos Manuel and María del Carmen never knew he died a few weeks after they left Paris for Cuba.

Jacques Offenbach was a year older than Carlos Manuel when they met in Paris while Jacques was studying violoncello at the Paris Conservatory and was performing at the *Café des Variétés*. They seldom saw each other after their frequent but brief encounters in 1842. Starting in 1849 Offenbach played at the orchestra of the *Opéra Comique* and in 1850 became musical director of the *Comédie Française*. In 1855 he opened his own theater, les *Bouffes Parisiens*, where he formalized the concept of *Opéra Bouffe*, a sort of ambitious *opérette*, with all dialogues sung rather than spoken. He composed dozens of works that have been performed continuously since the times of Napoleon III. His most famous, *The Tales of Hoffman*, was premiered after his death in 1861.

Julian Fontana became Chopin's musical executor after his death in 1849. He did get to visit Cuba in 1844 and offered several concerts and played the Pleyel piano at the Teatro Tacón, at the Havana Society and at the Philharmonic, thus introducing Chopin to the Cubans. He later married Camilla Cattley in Havana and took Nicolás Ruiz Espadero as a piano student. During the 1850's he lived, taught and played in Cuba and composed *Souvenirs de l'Ile de Cuba, op. 12* and *La*

Havanne , op 10, two works that became very popular in Paris. In 1855 Camilla died of pneumonia and Fontana moved the family to New Orleans first and then back to Paris. Having never recovered from the loss of Camilla, deaf and ill, he took his own life in 1869. He was interred at the cemetery of Montmartre in Paris.

Ladurée. This most famous of Parisian tea-rooms continued to prosper until 1871, when Baron Haussman began to change the face of Paris. A 1871 fire in the bakery made its transformation into a pastry shop possible. For its renovation the family used the services of Jules Cheret, who drew his inspiration from the pictorial techniques used in the Sixtine Chapel ceiling and the Garnier Opera house. As cafés developed during the Second Empire, the family owners combined the café with a pastry shop, giving birth to one of the first tea-rooms in Paris, and one which would welcome ladies without causing a stir. Its macaroons continue to delight the sweet teeth of Parisians to this day, now at *75, avenue des Champs-Elysées* and at the corners of *rues Jacob* and *Bonaparte,* a long block from the house where the Céspedes lived when they were in Paris.

La Jeune France. Under this title numerous societies, political groups, literary magazines, stores, songs, singing groups, etc., have been organized over the last two centuries. Perhaps its older use is on a 1830 caricature by Machereau entitled *Un Representant de la Jeune France sortant de Prononcer son Quinzieme Serment which* shows Talleyrand exiting the Royal Palace with King Louis Philippe. In 1862, the literary review *La Jeune France* was founded. Over its lifetime it included writers such as Anatole France, Leconte de Lisle and Sully Prudhomme. During the Congress of Tours in 1920, the junior chapter of the Communist Party made popular a hymn which started *"Nous sommes la jeune France..."*

Lapérouse. Opened in 1766 as a popular literary café, *Lapérouse* was scandalously famous for its private *salons particuliers* where couples could dine undisturbed. It is still situated at *51, Quai des Grands Augustins,* on the 6th Arrondisement. In the XIX century it became at the same time the place not to be seen, if you were with a lady other than your spouse, or the place to be seen in the company of Émile Zola, George Sand, and Victor Hugo, which were regulars. To this day the restaurant's mirrors, part of its luxurious *Belle Epoque* interiors overlooking the Seine, still bear diamond scratches from the days when mistresses didn't take jewels at face value.

Le Grand Colbert, at *4 Rue Vivienne,* is still open for business, with the same décor but without the *élan* it had during the last half of the

XIX century. Its location near the *Palais-Royal*, the French Comedy, and the Parisian financial district continues to make it a favorite for politicians, artists, financiers, people of fashion and Americans.

Les Halles disappeared as the *ventre de Paris* (the Paris belly) in the 1970's, when it was moved to Rungis, south of Paris. There, unfortunately, you can only shop for food if you are a restaurateur or a food wholesaler. When the decision to move was made, the authorities had to face the issue of how to prevent its thousands of rats (which were seldom seen but were there) from invading the entire city. A temporary wall was built around the grounds and tons of raticide were dumped around the buildings. Thanks to many dedicated artistic entrepreneurs, you can still find mummified rats dressed and posed as dentists, barristers, policemen, priests, etc. in many shops in the Marais. The formidable glass and iron structures of Les Halles were all destroyed except for one purchased by a Japanese industrialist and which today stands at Yokohama in Japan.

Louis Philippe de Orleans, King of the French people but not of France, seemed to be an exemplary monarch during his first years in the throne, living modestly and governing without arrogance or pomp. In spite of these appearances he was deep down a *grand bourgeoisie* who did not see the need to take care of the popular classes in France. During his reign there were seven unsuccessful attempts against his life. After several economic failures he had to abdicate his throne in favor of his son Louis Philippe II in 1848. The French people decided, however, to establish a second republic and did away with the monarchy. Curiously Jacques Laffitte was his first Prime Minister (1830) and François Guizot his last (1848). Fearing a destiny similar to that of Louis XVI, he obtained a passport under the name of Mr. Smith and left for England, where he lived under his title of *Count de Neuilly*. He had eight children, one of whom, the Count of Paris, considered himself the rightful current successor to the throne of France. Louis Philippe died in England at age 77, in 1850.

María del Carmen Céspedes returned with Carlos Manuel to Cuba in 1844. The young couple had three children: María del Carmen, who died as an infant, Carlos Céspedes y Céspedes, who was in his father detachment when he died in San Lorenzo in 1874 and Oscar Céspedes y Céspedes, who was made prisoner and shot by the Spaniards in 1869. María del Carmen died of tuberculosis in January of 1868.

Miguel de Aldama y Alfonso visited the Céspedes in Paris with Domingo Del Monte and his wife (Miguel's sister) Rosa, while in

Havana the architects were giving the final touches to his father's Palacio Aldama. The Palacio was located in the city block bound by Calzada de San Luis Gonzaga (later Calzada de Reina) and Amistad and Estrella Streets, across from the *Campo de Marte*. All through his twenties and thirties Miguel was known for his resourcefulness and his dedication to work. In 1847 he founded the *Club de la Habana,* a center for conspiracy in which he held a leadership position together with the Count of Pozos Dulces. His Cuban properties were confiscated and he immigrated to New York, where he prospered financially and also became an agent of the Cuban Republic in Arms. In exile he continued to forge important alliances with interesting people; Heinrich Schliemann, the discoverer of Troy and Mycenae, and Alexander von Humboldt, among many others. He returned to Cuba after 1868 when the *Pact of Zanjón* was signed with the Spaniards and recovered his vast sugar plantations in Union de Reyes, Bolondrón and Sierra Morena, in Matanzas province. He never again reoccupied his Havana mansion, which remained closed for many years. He died in 1888. His magnificent Havana home was auctioned in 1889 and sold for a pittance to the owners of a cigar factory (La Corona).

Monarchie de Juillet. In 1846 everything went sour for the *Monarchie de Juillet*. Wheat prices skyrocketed; purchasing powers diminished all across society; there was an industrial overproduction and prices fell; savings evaporated; workers were dismissed in large numbers; bankruptcies became common; the stock market fell; public works were stopped; the working classes took to the streets, all followed by scandals and corruption. François Guizot was replaced by Adolphe Thiers and Louis Philippe abdicated. The second republic was proclaimed on February 27, 1848 at the *Place de la Bastille.*

Palais-Royal. The pavilions of the Royal Palace, built by Philippe of Orleans around the gardens, are still open for business but the charm and luxury has long been lost. Most shops are barely viable but are kept by old French families by inertia or for sentimental reasons. The apartments, although dark, tiny and unkempt, are very sought after by the bohemian set, artists and even some famous designers. The palace itself now houses the French Department of Interior and is closed to the public.

Passage des Panoramas. The two gigantic panoramas are gone but the passage is still a workable market with small shops and boutiques at the same address on *Boulevard de Montmartre*. The glass roof is still in place and some of the original businesses are still functioning, notably Stern, reputedly the best engraver and stationer in Paris.

It is no longer the place to go shopping for fashion conscious Parisians.

Patisserie Madeleine. The Madeleines are small pancakes which were first baked in Commercy, Lorraine, by a young lady called Madeleine. She used for a mold a shell of the type carried by the pilgrims to Compostela to gather water from streams along their trip. Stanislas Leczinski, King of Poland, first tasted this sweet in Commercy in 1755. His daughter Marie, Louis XV's wife, took the recipe to Versailles and Paris where it became quite popular. *Madeleines* became even more famous after one day in 1909, when Marcel Proust dipped his *Madeleine* in tea and tumbled into the childhood memories that triggered his seven-volume, fourteen-year, *A la Recherche du Temp Perdue* (Remembrance of Things Past or In Search of Lost Time), one of the masterpieces of modern French literature.

Pont Neuf. It continues to be restored frequently and it has kept its majesty and significance. Charles Dickens in *Dictionary of Paris* (1882) wrote that, "during the 17th and the 18th centuries the *Pont Neuf* was the scene of much gaiety and merriment. It was there that mountebanks (charlatans) loved best to exercise their calling; there swindler surgeon-dentists established themselves; and there quack doctors of all sorts found patients innocent enough to entrust themselves to their care.

Salle de Manège, the building where the Legislative Assembly, the Conventional Assembly and the National Assembly met, was torn down by Napoleon III during the construction of *rue de Rivoli.* A plaque identifying its location is on the garden side of the street, across from the *Hôtel Meurice* at number *228, rue de Rivoli.*

Slavery. By the time the Céspedes were hosts to their friends in Paris, Cuba had received slaves from Africa for more than 60 years. This in spite of the British having forced Spain to accept a treaty in 1817 that abolished slave trade. From 1835-40, 165,000 additional slaves arrived. British cruisers began to patrol the waters of Cuba for slave traders with little results. The Cuban coast, with so many bays and coves, made it easy for the clandestine slavers to unload their cargoes without being seen. Only 5% of shipments were intercepted between 1840 and 1860. By and large, the population of the island was supportive of slavery. By 1850, prices for slaves in Cuba were 10 times higher than the amount paid in Africa. The beginning of the end of the Cuban Slave Trade came after the American-Anglo treaty of 1862, which made the business too risky for Americans. This was followed by Lincoln's Emancipation proclamation in 1863. With

American slave traders out of the game, slavery in Cuba began to wane. The last slave ship arrived in Cuba in 1866. When he started the first Cuban War of Independence in 1868, one of the first public decrees or announcements issued by Carlos Manuel de Céspedes was to liberate his own slaves and proclaim the end of slavery in the island. Twenty years later, slavery was abolished completely on the island. At the time, there were over 370,000 slaves in Cuba – 218,000 males and 152,000 females. Eighty percent were working on the sugar plantations. They were mostly *Lucumís*, of Yoruba origin, from Southwestern Nigeria, the originators of the *Santería* religion; *Carabalís* and *Abakuás*, from Southeastern Nigeria; *Congos*, the largest ethnic group, from the *Bantu* cultures of Angola; and *Mandingas*, from Sierra Leone.

Tacón Theater. The Tacón Theater never received Chopin for its inauguration. From day one, however, its proven acoustic value became known world wide and famous artists from all over the world began to include it in their tours. After several alterations over the years, its exterior walls were modified and made part of the façade of the *Centro Gallego*, one of the most splendid exponents of the German *neobaroque* in the new world. The *Centro* was planned and its budget approved in 1905. It was inaugurated in 1915 with an opera season offered by important lyrical figures of the time. It has since seen performances by Anna Pávlova, Antonia Mercé, Ruth Saint Denis, Ted Shawn, Vicente Escudero, Maya Plisétskaya, Carla Fracci, the American Ballet Theatre, the Royal Winnipeg Ensemble, Antonio Gades' Ballet, the Ballet of the Colón Theater of Buenos Aires, the Ballet Folklórico of Mexico and the Ballet de L'Etoile de Paris, among others.

Talleyrand. Charles Maurice de Talleyrand-Périgord, Prince de Benevente (1754-1838) died a few years before the Céspedes arrived in Paris. His memory outlived him, however, and his name was in everybody's mind during the *Monarchie de Juillet*. Some historians exalted him as the savior of Europe in 1815 (final fall of Napoleon Bonaparte) or as a witty statesman of great resources and skills, the most versatile and influential diplomat in European history. Others considered him a cynical and opportunistic scoundrel, and even a traitor, who deserved "infamy in this world and damnation in the next." His corruption and venality were undeniable, and his pliability enabled him to serve under Louis XVI during the *ancien régime*, with the Assembly during the French Revolution, for Napoleon I during Bonaparte's entire career, at Louis XVIII side during the Restoration, and close to Louis-Philippe in the times of the July Monarchy. He reputedly solicited payments shamelessly from France's friends and foes and during most of his service accepted bribes, particularly from Austria and Russia, to enrich himself, even if it meant betraying France. In 1798, for instance, he requested a bribe of $250,000 from the United States to stop French attacks on American merchant ships, precipitating a diplomatic disaster, the infamous "XYZ Affair," which worsened relations between the United States and France and led to the undeclared Quasi War of 1798. At the time when the Céspedes and their friends were in Paris he was considered the archetype of a diplomatic weather vane, and politicians referred to him as *le diable boiteux* (the limping devil, in reference to the handicap that barred his military career when he was very young). The phrase *"he is a Talleyrand"* has always denoted a statesman of great resource and skill but no morals. He shared the diplomatic stage in Europe with Klemens Wenzel von Metternich. It has been said that Talleyrand could fool anyone without ever telling a lie, as opposed to Metternich, of whom the exact opposite was said: that he always lied but never managed to fool anyone.

The Countess of Merlin. The Countess was already a public figure and a literary success when she met the Céspedes in 1842. She had already published "*Mis Doce Primeros Años*" (Paris, 1833); "*Memoires d'une Creole*" (1835); "*Ocios de una Mujer de Gran Mundo*" (1837); "*L'Esclavage aux Colonies Espagnoles*" (1840); "*La Havanne*" (3 vols., 1842), which included a biography written by Gertrudis Gómez de Avellaneda. She was preparing "*Les Lionnes de Paris*" (1845); and "*Le Duc d'Athenes*" (1848). She counted among her friends George Sand, Balzac, Châteaubriand, Berlioz, Chopin, the Baron of Rothschild and Madame Récamier, all of them also in the circle of friends of the Céspedes. Louis Philippe d'Orleans had given her the Legion of Honor and prince Jerónimo Bonaparte, Napoleon's nephew, had proposed to marry her. In the midst of all these triumphs she courted disaster when she fell in love with the wrong man. Her generosity and naiveté resulted in the loss of her fortune due to shady financial manipulations of her pretender. A trip to Spain and a plea for help to her friend Isabel II (1830-1904), daughter of Fernando VII, and to her Spanish publishers failed to return her to financial security. She moved with her daughter and son-in-law to the Castle of Dissais near Poitiers. From there she followed in silence the successes of her friends, particularly María Francisca, Duchess of Alba, in Spain, Hortensia de Beauharnais, Queen of Holand and Charles Luis Napoleon Bonaparte and Eugenia de Montijo, by then in the throne of France. She died there in 1852, alone and without literary, political or society friends, at the age of 63. She wanted to be buried at the *Cementerio Espada*, in Havana, next to her father, Joaquín de Santa Cruz y Cárdenas Vélez de Guevara (1769-1807), the first count of *Santa*

Cruz de Mopox and third count of *San Juan de Jaruco*, but her wishes were never fulfilled.

The Grande Chaumière of Montparnasse went out of business soon after the Céspedes left Paris. On its grounds the city opened the Cemetery of Montparnasse. The round cylindrical tall building where the milling equipment had been can still be seen in the western part of the Cemetery.

Vercingetorix. The last Gaul leader, defeated by the army of Julius Cesar during the conquest of the French province, had a magnificent monument built at a hill on *Alise la Reine*, in eastern France, at the very hill where his army was overwhelmed.

Victor Hugo. Carlos Manuel de Céspedes always considered Victor Hugo the brightest man he ever knew. He met Hugo when he was in his early forties and Carlos in his late twenties. Hugo was totally fluent in Spanish and their brief friendship took off instantly. Hugo had already written *Hernani* (at 27) and *Notre Dame de Paris* (at 29) and had just been elected to the *Académie Française (at 39)*. After opposing the *Coup d'Etat* of Napoleon III in 1851, he wrote two letters to Carlos in Cuba from his exile in Belgium. By the time Hugo had moved his exile to Guernesey, Céspedes was already fighting for the independence of Cuba in the *sabanas* of Camagüey. It was probably because of Hugo's friendship with Carlos Manuel that he wrote a powerful letter addressed to the women of Cuba in 1870, where he expressed: "*Aucune nation n'a le droit de poser son ongle sur l'autre. Un peuple ne possède pas plus un autre peuple qu'un homme ne possède un autre homme. Le crime est plus odieux encore sur une nation que sur un individu; voilà tout. Agrandir le format de l'esclavage, c'est en accroître l'indignité.*" (No nation has the right to possess another. One people should not own other people just like one man should not own other men. The crime is more odious among nations that among individuals. That is all. To acquiesce with slavery only increases its indignity). Hugo died in 1885. More than 2 million people accompanied the cortege to the Pantheon, where he was placed to rest among the great of France.

Willard Capacete was taken into custody when he returned to the scene of his crime searching for his missing white gloves. The Spanish government wanted to set him up with a lawyer but the French magistrate opposed the idea and assigned a court lawyer for his defense. He was found guilty on the testimonies of Alita Nanciaga, the maid who witnessed his crime and Madame Lamoignon, the resourceful blind neighbor. Capacete was condemned to 25 years in jail, to be served at the *Bicêtre* prison, south of Paris. There he tried many times to contact his publishing friends in Cadiz but received no responses. He soon was at odds with other inmates, took to eating food he would purchase from the guards and lived a solitary life for many years. His girth expanded considerably because of his lack of exercise, which caused him to be the subject of scorn from those who saw him daily. By the time he was 40 he could barely raise himself out of bed. On his 41st birthday he was stabbed to death by a fellow inmate during a robbery attempt. No one claimed his body and he was buried on an unmarked grave outside the prison walls.

Index

This book was printed in the United States by **ECPrinting**, 415 Galloway
Street, Eau Claire, Wisconsin 54703, in **December of 2006**.

The font used throughout the text has been **Palatino Linotype**, one of the classic old
style serif typefaces inspired by designs of the 16th century Italian calligrapher
Giambattista Palatino. The font was reissued in 1948 by **Hermann Zapf** for the
Linotype Foundy, the company created by Ottmar Mergenthaler, a German
immigrant to the U.S. who invented the revolutionary line typesetting machine first
used in 1890 by the **New York Tribune**.

The font used in the covers, title pages, headings and ornaments is **P22 Franklin
Caslon**, a faithful interpretation of the type used by Benjamin Franklin in the 1750's in
his printing shop and particularly in his **Poor Richard's Almanac**. This font was developed in 2006 by the International House of Fonts for the Philadelphia Museum of
Art to commemorate the 300th birthday of our most remarkable Founding Father.

Raúl Eduardo Chao received his PhD from Johns Hopkins University and after a brief stint in industry spent 18 years in academe. He has written four other books and numerous articles in newspapers and reviewed journals. This is his first historical novel. He and his wife live in Coral Gables and Paris.

DUPONT CIRCLE EDITIONS

www.DupontCircleEditions.com

Cover Design by Luciano Franchi-Alfaro.

COVER ILLUSTRATION: **La Ligne des Grands Boulevards**.
XIX Century Ink drawing by St. Elme Gauthier.
Reproduced in the book
450 Dessigns Inédits d'Apreés Nature,
by August Vitu. Paris, 1889, page 319.
Original drawing in the collection of the author.